FOREST OF SPIRITS

S.J. SANDERS

Forest of Spirits
A Dark Spirits Romance

S.J. Sanders

This book is a work of fiction intended for adult audiences only.

Editor: LY Publishing

Cover Artist: Sam Griffin

Many thanks to all the people who made this book possible!

PROLOGUE

Turan smiled as she strolled her beloved gardens. Cyprus was as eternal and constant as she was. All year round, it bloomed with the sweetest of flowers. Not the mortal island—though she bestowed considerable favors upon that sacred land—but her own divine domain that rose from the great cosmic ocean. This Cyprus, her birthplace, had been sung of and praised by poets from Hellas, Etruria, and Rome.

Plucking a flower, she brushed it fondly against her cheek. She loved each of the names she had been honored by. Each one was as unique and precious as the bloom she held in her hand. It mattered little to her if she was called Ouranian Aphrodite, the seaborn, Turan, the action which gives, or Venus, the very spirit of love and beauty. She cherished each of them even as she cherished the multitude of children she bore. Nothing gave her more pleasure than being a mother. The Etruscans had recognized this when they called her Ati: mother and queen.

A mother of Erotes, Cupids, many nymphs and spirits, even a mother of mortals, she loved all her children. For that reason, she interfered more than she probably should. She personally considered her interferences to be a good thing. There were a few incidents… Troy was not to be spoken of, though it had a far nobler purpose than what the common understanding of myths gave creed, and Eros still held a grudge over her *guidance* with Psyche, but overall things worked out well.

That was also why she had been unable to still her hand when the gates between Aites, the underworld, and the human world flung open wide. She had placed the woman, the key to ending the plague of infernal spirits, in the path of the gatekeeper. She had then sent her beloved son to assist them when their situation was most dire. She meddled only slightly, but it had been enough to save the world for the time being.

Unfortunately, her meddling couldn't stop the dangers that would come. There was a new hope, a promise of a new time to unfold, but such changes did not come without a cost. The matching of a human soul to an infernal spirit had been the first of many changes that would impact the cosmos. There would not be a single realm that would remain untouched. It had been bound to happen. All things were cyclic. Nothing remained the same forever. One era was preparing to slip into another, and the tremors could already be felt.

Her mind drifted to her son. The silvani lucomo had served her well, though he had been reluctant to get involved. He disliked her tendency to meddle more than most of her children did. She wondered what he would think of her latest involvement. Her lips quirked as she recalled the image that he had made as she had looked upon him—the arrogance and hardness of him.

When she put things into motion to draw his mate to him, she hadn't seen the darkness rising in the Eternal Forest. He was going to need his mate more than he ever would have realized. The dove would do its part, but Turan needed to move their meeting along.

Crushing the flower in her hand, she plucked a sphere from the air around her and called up the image of a huntress who lived alone at the edge of the woods. Lifting the crushed petals to her lips, Turan breathed them over the sphere. The woman stilled, her head turning, and Turan smiled.

"Hurry, my dear. He's waiting for you," she whispered as a soft humming vibrated in her throat, spinning the first songs of desire. That small encouragement was all that would be needed.

A touch was all it took.

CHAPTER 1

The woods themselves were alive in a way that was beyond all modern reckoning. They had been that way ever since the wulkwos ravaged the world, throwing the worlds of men and spirits back together. Things still lurked in the world. Ancient creatures that had been half-forgotten as human civilization grew. Since the mist came, the things of nightmares and legends returned, and people began recounting the old lore of spirits and monsters, but not as happy bedtime stories for children. The old tales were darker and far more complex, of the other worlds that men did not dare pass into. It was whispered about among those who knew, that the wild places were full of predatory eyes and teeth.

Don't go into the woods. People disappear in the woods.

That didn't stop hunters. Many of the young men saw it as a challenge to court the dangers of the woods and bring back food. It was a matter of survival. Though the community joined in their effort to toil on the farms, it never seemed to be enough. So, the hunters chanced the forests, whether out of bravado or need. People had to eat.

A lone huntress stood on a hill with her bow just outside the forest that bordered her town. Diana was wise enough to never trust the forest. When the mists came, enveloping the world in its impenetrable cloud, it let monsters loose upon the world. The people huddled in their houses, trembling at the sound of every terrible cry that came from within the unknown void of the white barrier, waiting for the day that it would leave. When it withdrew, it left behind an expansive, dark forest in its wake.

There had always been a small forested area that provided modest game, but nothing like what had come with the mist. During that time, it stretched out over the landscape, swallowing miles of highway and grass fields until it crept within a short distance of the town and finally stopped. She didn't know why it didn't just swallow the entire town and get it over with. The town was only a shadow of what it had once been as people clung desperately to what was familiar. They shunned the unnatural forest that stretched for miles in every direction.

The forest meant death for the towns bordering it.

All had the same rumors of disappearances. The rumors were what made "sensible people" stay well away from the woods and the game trails cut through the woods by some unknown force. Even most hunters spent as little time in the forest as possible, driving into the woods via that same mysterious path to fetch any game that they could find. Even the most reckless thrill-seeker among them was afraid of what had come with the forest. Fewer went by foot along smaller paths. It was a form of suicide to trust a forest where people went missing, no bodies recovered, no cries ever heard. It was as if they had disappeared off the face of the Earth. In response, all those who went to into the woods banded together to hunt in groups…

All except the huntress, who watched as a vehicle rushed from the town.

The jeep peeled up the dirt road and swung a sharp left, skidding and spraying dirt. The men inside let out excited shouts, their spirits high as they foolishly expended fuel. Diana huffed in amusement as she watched the vehicle disappear into the tree line. They were stupid for driving into the forest, but she still felt a little of their exuberance. She didn't even mind that they excluded her from their hunting parties. She didn't like relying on anything that she couldn't control by her own hand. Technology hadn't survived since the mist came. All that was left were flawed, dangerous remnants—gas-powered vehicles when there was fuel to spare, and guns, both with the habit of malfunctioning. She trusted neither with her safety.

Laying her bow across her shoulders, she hooked her arms over the ends of it and stretched as she took in the vision of the woods. It watched her, so she watched it back. It was only fair.

Despite the dangers, she could not hate the forest, nor did she fear it enough to stay away. Every breath brought with it the musky perfume of the wood, familiar and comforting. The secluded cabin at the lake that she inherited from her grandparents had been her sanctuary when madness struck the populace. She recalled childhood summers playing there, and then later, when she lived beside it after her parents died and her grandparents took her in.

Her grandfather had taught her to hunt and be self-sufficient in the woods near their home. To respect the woods. He often told tales of the fae folk, entertaining her during their treks. She had those memories to cling to when the world went dark, and the woods had encroached to gather at the edge of the lake like a protective sentinel watching over her.

She wasn't a fool, however. She didn't trust the forest—or rather, she didn't trust the beings that had crossed over to inhabit its dark depths. Still, those beings had been more reliable in behavior than most people she knew. When the mists receded, Diana had been equipped to take care of herself.

She went into the woods without fanfare and offered a small

gift to the denizens near her home to leave her at peace. It was common sense, really. A gift for a gift. Wasn't that what all the old stories recommend? In turn, she stayed only long enough to check her traps or bring down game if she was so fortunate. She never ventured deep into the forests and never forgot to leave a small portion of the bloody meat behind as payment. Diana could feel the eyes of strange beings touching her, cold and alien… and always hungry.

She never forgot to feed them.

Perhaps that was why she was left alone when others reported disturbances that plagued them. The sort of idiots who wanted to drive deep into the woods to hunt for game, intruding empty-handed. Let them. They were always chased out for their efforts, even when they managed to bring down game to carry with them in their escape.

Diana had no such problems.

Dropping her bow to grip it in one hand, she strode into the trees, taking the same route she always took along the smaller game trails, hazel eyes focused on the path. The breeze ruffled her bangs and toyed with the long end of her braid. The lower three quarters was platinum blonde from her last dye job that faded into her natural brown hair. She felt it swing behind her, safely out of the reach of treacherous branches.

It didn't take her long to arrive at the fallen trunk where she left her offerings. As always, the immediate area was absolutely silent. Though ragged from where it split, the rest of the length buried in the grasses and brush to the left of it, the tree trunk was like a short pillar that came up to her hip when she stood in front of it. The papery gray bark of the birch tree peeled in numerous places. On the altar, dipped at a slight angle in the only smooth part of the trunk, a small bowl and cup sat in the same place as always, never moved. Not once in the four years she had been coming into the forest had it been disturbed. Yet every time she entered the woods, the dishes were clean and waiting for her. A movement in the distance drew her attention, and she squinted through the trees.

Nothing.

A puzzled frown marred her brow, but she bent to leave her usual offerings. In the bowl, she placed a small chunk of bread and several strawberries from her garden. She removed the flask from the inner pocket of her leather vest and poured the mixture she had made earlier that morning of honey and milk into the cup. Returning the lid to the flask, she tucked it back into her vest pocket and stepped back from the makeshift altar. Her eyes scanned the trees surrounding her as she spoke.

"Whoever you may be, accept this small gift for safe passage in my hunt. A gift for a gift."

She waited for the usual sign of acceptance, not daring to move so much as a step away from the altar, not daring even a breath. The branches rustled as a wind blew through from deeper in the woods, the limbs bowing to her. Her breath left her in a loud exhalation. She never took it for granted that whatever lurked nearby in this part of the wood would comply and was always relieved when permission came. On the same token, she never breached the creek some few miles away that bisected the woods. Although it was possibly not a territory boundary, she chose not to take the chance with anything unknown on the other side.

Whispering her thanks, Diana strode deeper among the trees, heading toward where she knew the first of her traps awaited. The change in atmosphere was immediate. The moment she cleared the area and lost sight of the altar, birdsong burst around her, and the hum of insects filled the air. She relaxed somewhat, as much as she could with the awareness of being watched skating over her skin. She had grown used to it, and so it had become background noise over those few years.

The bushes to her side rustled, and Diana stopped and frowned at the spot. That was unusual. She waited to see if any animal would dart out, but all movement stopped. Her skin crawled. She didn't feel threatened, but the feeling of being watched weighed far heavier on her than it had before.

Minutes ticked by, and nothing happened.

Diana chuckled under her breath to ease her nerves. She could be getting worked up about nothing. It was likely just an animal that caught sight of her and hid. It didn't ring true, but she clung to the idea as she walked further into the forest and approached her trap.

The box trap was simple in design, ideal for catching small game. She knew that some hunters preferred to use snares, but Diana avoided the use of them. She wasn't always successful with her traps, but she fell into a comfortable rhythm with the forest near her house.

Spying the box lying flush against the ground, her nerves were forgotten, and elation filled her at the sight. Very slowly, she lifted the trap, revealing a fat rabbit hunkered in place. Whispering her thanks, she dispatched the animal quickly, dropping it into the small leather bag that hung from her belt while she reset and baited the trap. She didn't linger even a minute longer than necessary, striding off through the brush.

Diana didn't want to test the conditional benevolence of whatever watched her.

Instead, she visited her other traps, only two of which held animals. Another rabbit was added to her catch, providing a spare to be added to the growing stores of meat in her freezer. The weasel, however, she released and watched as it darted away.

Pushing back up to her feet from where she was crouched, Diana brushed her hands off on her pants. In the distance, she could hear the jeep in another part of the woods, the sound of the loud engine carrying. She had hoped to come across a buck, but that wasn't going to be possible with those fools in the woods frightening away all the game. She scowled in its direction, kicking a small stone out of her path as she turned and began her trek home.

The jeep roared in her direction, screams of terror separating and merging again with the mechanical rumble of the engine. Her blood chilled, and she stumbled over the thick root of a tree, startled at the sound. Regaining her balance, she glanced around warily for but a moment. Her breath rushed in and out with increasing distress, and she choked when the roar of some unearthly beast broke through the woods, nearly eclipsing the noise of the fleeing hunting party.

Whatever it was, the idiots were bringing it her way!

Jerking forward into a run, Diana darted through the trees at full speed. She hissed with displeasure, knowing without a doubt that her actions were stupid. She wouldn't be able to outrun the jeep, never mind whatever was chasing it. All the same, she wasn't going to stand about and wait for them to catch up either. The muscles in her thighs burned and protested as the trees whipped around her, half blinding her in a mad rush.

Why the fuck did they have to come this way? And where the fuck was the tree line? Diana turned her head this way and that, looking for anything familiar. This wasn't right. She couldn't just flee through the woods. She pulled to a stop, hissing between her teeth as she attempted to reorient herself. She had been so close to the altar near the edge of the woods, she should have run right into it. Shaking her head, she squinted at the sun and cut to the left.

The altar should have been right there!

As she delved further among the trees, her a frown knitted her brow. Where was it? Diana panted as she broke through unfamiliar brush. Had she somehow become turned around?

She could hardly think as she attempted to mentally backtrack the route she had taken. The sound of the jeep roared closer as she gasped for breath. Every branch on the trees quivered and trembled as if something monstrous was moving through them. Clutching her bow to her, her head whipped around as if trying to make sense of what she was seeing. The leaves quaked and shimmered, and tiny living lights bounced all around the woods in a dizzying swarm. A bulge in the brush raced in a line toward her, filling the air with savage, vicious snorts as it came closer. Diana shook her head in denial as she stumbled away.

This wasn't her forest!

CHAPTER 2

Something shuffled near her. Diana winced, bringing a hand up to her head. What had happened? She attempted to grasp at any memory. She had stumbled back, looking around the forest. Not her forest!

Diana's eyes snapped open as she jerked upright. Whatever had been beside her scurried into the bushes rattling to her right. She stared at them, her pulse pounding in her ears.

"Hello? Is anyone there?" As she rose to her feet, her eyes never left the cluster of brush. She craned her neck, widening her field of vision. "I am lost. I don't mean any harm."

"Carries a weapon but doesn't mean any harm she says," a soft voice whispered with a wicked chuckle.

The brush snapped as if something raced suddenly around her. Diana froze in place. Swallowing thickly, she shook her head. She was tempted to drop her bow, but she knew that was a terrible idea.

"I… I'm sorry. My bow is all I have to protect myself," she called out.

"Protect yourself? Ha!" the voice muttered with a sharp snarl as if speaking to itself. "Deceitful, lying humans." She jumped as a gray face burst out from the bushes beside her, the grooved, horned brow wrinkling as the face snarled, baring wickedly sharp teeth. Long pointed ears popped up from the curling dark locks of hair at either side of its head. "Go away! We don't want you here!" the thing snarled in a piercing shriek.

Diana stumbled away from the bush as the face disappeared once again.

The bush rustled and, faster than her eyes could track, bounded through the brush with the shrill sound of a raptor to settle in more brush behind her. She froze, slowly turning fully toward it.

"Please," she whispered. "I don't know how I got here. I never go into the inner woods. I just go into the outer forest and always with appropriate gifts for passage. This shouldn't have happened."

The thing hummed speculatively. Ever so slowly, it slipped out of the brush. It was short and lithe with the narrow chest and belly that reminded her of an adolescent, save for a heavy brow and bearded face. Hands were tipped with dark claws, and the body terminated into the hindquarters of a goat all the way down to his rough hooves. Horns twisted from his brow as he cocked its head and eyed her doubtfully.

"What gifts do you have?" he inquired in a soft, snarling voice.

Swallowing, Diana's fingers fumbled nervously with her backpack. She still had the portion of food she had reserved for her own lunch. Pulling out the bread and cheese, she thrust it toward the creature. Delight crossed his face and he quickly snatched it away. Settling on a rock, he bit off a large mouthful of bread with frightfully sharp fangs before glancing up at her.

"Drink?" he queried.

With a mute nod, she removed the flask and handed it over. There wasn't much honeyed milk left, but the creature sniffed the contents and tipped the flask back, swallowing the remaining few mouthfuls with a happy sigh.

"What are you?" she whispered, unable to tear her eyes away from the unusual-looking being seated on the rock in front of her.

He snickered, his eyes sparkling impishly as he bared his teeth in a cruel smile. "Do you not recognize what I am? So blind to not recognize a faun before you."

"A faun…?"

He scowled, his brow pulling low and making his face look all the more horrible as his body tensed and coiled with aggression. "A faun, a spirit of the woodlands and meadows, guardian of herds so on and so on. A child of the god Faunus?" he tried again at her blank look.

"Oh," she mumbled, clenching her bow tighter in her hands. "You speak of mythology."

The faun growled irritably, making the tiny hairs on her arms stand on end. "Humans." He growled as he stalked toward her, eyes glowing in the low light. "Would you like me to demonstrate how real I am?" he demanded with an aggressive rumble. As she stumbled back, her eyes wide with panic, he barked out a terrible laugh and shook his head. "I thought not. Be thankful you have purchased my assurance of safe passage in my wood."

"And who are you to guarantee me such?" she dared to ask, though her voice trembled on every word, her desire to flee warring with her natural caution.

The faun chuckled, the sound menacing. "This part of the wood is *mine*. That is all that you need to concern yourself with—and how you will safely leave the great forest."

She paced back from him nervously as he continued to circle her like a predator seeking a vulnerable place to attack. "And how will you offer me safety?" she whispered as every muscle tensed.

He gave her an amused look, a rattling laughter bubbling up in his throat. "By allowing you to pass through it without any harm coming from me or those under my influence. The oath is observed by the gods. You have been gifted with an opportunity to flee, my prey. Run home. You have no further bribes to give to other beings you may encounter. I do wonder how long you will survive… Such an amusing game."

Diana paled. "It is not a game," she choked out. "I'm lost."

"I disagree," he murmured as he circled her, his eyes glowing brighter in the shadows.

Swallowing thickly, she gripped her bow nervously as she peered about. "Do you know which way to go to return home?"

A jagged smile stretched his lips. "I know not such information. I recommend that you leave and make haste before something decides that you make a good meal."

She stumbled back, her heart pounding in her ears a staccato beat, making the faun's lip curl with undisguised glee. His nostrils flared and he licked his lips as if relishing the flavor of her fear. She struggled against it, not wishing to bolt mindlessly once again. She was already lost in a nightmare. Everything familiar was gone, replaced by another world with creatures that would terrorize and *eat her*. Her legs shook with restraint, and her breath slammed out of her lungs in a frightened moan.

The faun's glowing eyes narrowed on her. He nodded, his gray face suddenly appearing darker as the sun moved, casting much of it into shadows. "As a *kindness*, I will tell you only this. Most beings will toy with you, give chase to sate their appetites for terror, and they may go as far as to take a bite of you to see how you taste before they let you escape. Some few might kill you and leave you dead to fertilize the ground if you truly offend them. But none dare to offend the will of Silvani Lucomo, King of the Eternal Forest who loathes senseless dances of blood and death. Beware the ancient being deep within the woods, beyond even the deep halls of the lucomo. In the darkest depths, in the caverns below the very heart of the woods, Cacus wakens."

"And this ancient being… eats people."

The faun's lips pulled back from his teeth in a horrible snarl. "He consumes *everything*. Humans who trespass into our world are easy prey. You are slow with no defenses. The wiles of your race will do you no good here. You are *weak*. If you stay, you will feed his appetite." A rattle echoed from his throat as he spun around to crash back into the brush, leaving Diana staring after him.

Drawing in a shaky breath, Diana glanced around once more. *Cacus*. Why did the name sound familiar? Damn, she should have paid better attention to the mythology unit in high school English. Never in a million years would she have guessed that her survival in a world gone to shit was going to depend on dredging up knowledge she had barely paid attention to. Her life depended on the random facts her teacher took pleasure in quizzing them on. The kind of information that was likely going to kill her. She could practically taste the irony.

A shiver of dread raced over her body as Diana picked a direction and plodded forward. One way was just as good as another when she couldn't recall how she entered this part of the forest. Everywhere she looked was nothing but the endless, threatening expanse of the deep woods. Nothing recognizable or inviting.

The Eternal Forest was thick with ancient trees, reaching to the skies with twisted limbs as leaves quaked and rustled, each sound setting her nerves on edge. The foliage was so thick that in some places it blotted out the sun, leaving shadows where anything could lurk and wait. Squinting ahead, she wondered about the fate of the men in the jeep. Recalling their screams made bile crawl up her throat.

Shivering, Diana tugged the hoodie under her vest tighter around her. Never had she been truly frightened to be alone in the forest, until now.

CHAPTER 3

Sunlight filtered into the room from the numerous small windows cut into the rock's upper walls. It fell upon the jewel-laden ropes of gold strung between the tall antlers of the massive male sitting on a throne created from living trees that had been twisted together as saplings. His bulk reclined on them as pearl-white eyes narrowed in his hard face. His lashes were thick and black so that his eyes appeared to be thickly outlined in kohl like some desert denizen, offsetting his glowing eyes against the marble hue of his face. He was the picture of menace as he shifted his weight onto the forearm braced on his throne and glared down at the male bowed before him. A nymph with long blue locks of hair spiraling down her back approached him hesitantly, but he waved her off as he focused on his supplicant.

"What is one of the aelven court doing in the depths of the Eternal Forest?" he growled. "Do you not have enough with which to keep yourself occupied in the northern woods of your kingdom, Prince Bilban?"

The prince stood warily, his shining armor almost painfully luminous. "It is not that we wish to disturb you, Silvas, but my sire thought it prudent to send word to you."

Silvas sank back into his throne and smirked, the adornment between his antlers clinking. Throwing up a graceful hand, his obsidian claws flashed as he gestured for the prince to continue. "What is it that King Emidoran thinks he knows of the Eternal Forest that *I* do not?" he asked silkily.

If the male shuddered beneath his stare, it was slight. How disappointing. So little reaction. The tightly controlled aelven people always failed to be entertaining. Silvas sighed and waited impatiently as the prince bowed again.

"I bring warning of disturbances in the northern wood."

"Disturbances?" Silvas interrupted, brow furrowing. "What do you mean by disturbances? I trust this is more serious than puckish fae… Surely you would not waste my time with such things."

"It is quite serious, lucomo. There are reported sightings of things unnatural within the woods. Things that have been long since buried in our world when they used our forests to enter the world of men. None of us considered that the expansion of the Eternal Forest might break old magics keeping them tethered, but we are afraid that this may be the case. They are venturing into the human world once more. There are… disappearances."

Silvas scowled. *Impossible!*

"Clarify."

Bilban took a breath and met his eye. "Humans, lucomo. Whatever is coming out of our forests is taking the humans from their world. We find remains, at times near our kingdoms. They are terrible. We fear it may only be a fraction of the losses suffered in the human world. They are awake and feeding."

"What of Freyr, the lord who holds dominion over your world? Can he do nothing to preserve the human life at your borders?"

"The gods are restricted by the Fates. You know this as much as we do. Perhaps more so, I would wager, as ancient as you are. He aids as he can, but ultimately this is in our hands."

A low growl rolled out from Silvas's chest as his long, leonine tail flicked in agitation beside the seat of his throne. It cracked in the sudden stillness of his throne room.

"So you come to me…"

The aelven prince nodded, paling ever so slightly. "You are the oldest among us, the ruler of the Eternal Woods themselves. Although you do not interfere in the various domains that inhabit this world, it was only natural that we would seek your counsel. You possess considerable power to even pass easily between worlds. Did you not assist against the infernal creatures when they broke through into the human realm?"

"My role in that was small, to say the least," Silvas growled. He cocked his head, curious. "Are you not afraid that I will bring my terror through your sunlight, wood aelf? Is that not what your polite courts think of all silvani, that we are brutes of the wild woods who bring destruction and mayhem to any civilization we encounter? And I, the silvani lucomo, the king of all the silvani, am the worst of them all… Am I not?" he purred.

The male stiffened and met Silvas's gaze. Finally, he was able to catch the slightest perfume of fear from the aelf. It delighted his senses, feeding his pleasures. He inhaled slowly, drinking it in. Such sweet elixir.

"The silvani are known to be… unpredictable… in behavior, but careful guardians when it comes to the forests themselves. As the threat comes from the depths of the Eternal Forest, we humble ourselves before you. As of yet, the creatures only prey on humans, but how long will that content such monsters? The aelven court beseeches your mercy." He dropped to his knees in full supplication, arms held out before him and palms upward in entreaty.

A shiver ran over Silvas's skin as he sat back once more and stared at the male, savoring the moment. He tapped one long claw on the arm of his throne thoughtfully. “So, the aelves come to me not out of concern for the human populations among their new forest borders, but to save their own lives from the jaws of the creatures once more roaming their woods. How typical,” he sneered.

Bilban’s head shot up, his jewel-colored eyes widening. Silvas snorted mirthfully and waved a hand. “Calm yourself, aelf. I merely point out the more accurate details of your request,” he said, allowing his voice to drop into a purr once more. He traced a pattern with his claw on the wood beneath his hand. “But since you speak of truth, let me be direct with you now: I do not tolerate evil in my woods. I will search it out, but I will not favor your kingdom for the human world. If I must chase my quarry over the boundaries and leave your hallowed courts to whatever fate that might receive, I shall do so without hesitation or regret. My only interest will be in my hunt. Is that understood?”

A quiver shot through the male, but he met Silvas’s gaze without flinching. “Perfectly, lucomo. With your permission, I shall return immediately to my father with your word.”

Silvas flicked his fingers dismissively. He was done with the aelf, his thoughts turning already to the foul taint that had risen in his woods and yet had managed to keep itself hidden from him. “Go,” he rasped, turning to stare out of one of the windows.

Several nymphs approached, setting food in front of him. One reclined against his throne as she removed her top. Her eyes sparkled at him with humor as his lust raged to the fore. It was all a game with the nymphs, to tease and torment him without any hope of relief. Their only interest was to feed off the sexual desires they stoked. His body pinched painfully, and he groaned as her delicate fingers slid toward the cloth draped around his hip. He caught her hand and pushed it away with a low snarl.

"I am not in the mood for your games. Remove yourself," he hissed.

The nymph's eyes widened before she giggled and pushed up to her feet once more. Tossing him a wicked grin over her shoulder, she strode away, her hips swaying enticingly. The others mercifully followed her, exchanging sly looks as they glanced back at him. Silvas reached into his pants and shifted his cock into a more comfortable position as the last of them cleared the room.

Fucking nymphs.

His eyes trailed back once more to the window at the sound of wings. A pale dove landed with a flurry of feathers, its head bobbing with interest as it adjusted its position on the edge of the window. It cooed delicately, and he bristled.

Wretched creature of Turan, Venus—or whatever name his mother, the goddess of love and desire was going by as of late. He wasn't going to be a victim of one of her amusements.

"That goes for you too, Mother," he snarled. "I am in no mood for any lustful trickery. If you are looking to tease me, then leave."

The goddess didn't materialize, but then again, he hadn't really expected her to. She rarely showed up in person unless she had a specific reason. He should only be so fortunate that it wasn't one of those times. Instead, he was left glowering at a bird as it fluttered down into his throne room. A low growl sounded in his throat.

Oh, she wanted something though.

Silvas clenched his fist. He didn't have time for guessing games. If she wasn't going to explain what she wanted, he wasn't going to humor her by chasing after her messenger!

Shoving off his throne, he stalked away, giving his back to the animal. He had other things to attend to—namely finding out what exactly was occurring in the Eternal Forest. Fauns and red-capped goblins scurried out of his way as pixies darted out of the bushes in surprise. The trees bent, reaching toward him in silent tribute as he left his cavernous palace beneath the great tree of the forest.

His bare feet made hardly a sound on the forest floor as if he was made of the shadows that followed and gathered around him. Now that he was aware of it, he sent a part of his being into the woods and was able to feel the dark pulse of some malignant power awakening… feeding. Feeding in *his* woods!

His lips downturned into a fierce snarl. He was the king of the silvani, highest king of the kings of the woods, lord of the Eternal Forest. Whatever this creature was, it would not succeed against him. Not in *his* forest where he was king!

With a guttural growl, he quickened his pace. The trees blurred by him. He could feel them as part of himself, extending into the world around him. The animals called to him. His breath came in eager pants, the smell of growing things and decay filling his body with every indrawn breath.

With it came something else. At first, he scented the disgusting smell of something undeniably from the human world. The smell was revolting—hot and metallic, mixing with the earthy scent of mud.

Intruders were in his forest!

An enraged snarl bubbled out of him. The presence of humans was expected in the outer woods, but not in the Eternal Forest! None entered without his invitation. He would deal with them first. His nostrils flared, catching the scent as he altered his path to track it. It mixed with the scent of blood that made his body tremble with need. Fear, death, and sex were so intimately a part of his nature that his desire for the taste of it fueled his rage. That torment did not belong in his sanctuary! Just beneath the stench, he detected the sweetest perfume. It invaded and pulled at him, and he was lost to it. His cock pulsed, and his body quivered with need. With a snarl, he raced toward the strange mingling of scents, determined to find those who dared enter his domain and the feminine scent that lured him.

The very trees shook and moaned around him when he roared, broadcasting his pent-up desires. He was close enough that it took little time to close the distance between them. He caught a glimmer of gold hair, and a fresh wave of her scent that filled him like a sweet wine and made him drunk. With a triumphant bellow, he leaped out from the trees, arms outstretched to snag his prize into his embrace.

It was a human, and she was his!

For whatever reason, the human had enticed his instincts. Never before had such a thing happened, but he did not question it. She dared to lure him and now he was claiming her. No other would touch her or have any possession of the female until his passions for her were spent.

CHAPTER 4

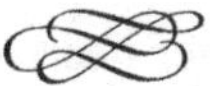

The smell of oil and gas was strong, as if someone had punctured and drained the fluids from a vehicle out in the woods. Diana wrinkled her nose and coughed. Still, she hurried toward it, trepidation filling the pit of her stomach. She knew what she would find before she even arrived.

Turned on its side, the yellow jeep dripped gas from the broken tank. It looked mauled, the metal twisted and torn as if enormous claws had ripped at the metal sides. There was no doubt any longer as to the fate of the men. She could smell the metallic tang of blood. Worse, she could see the vivid sprays of it upon the jeep's sides and pooling on the grass beneath where it dripped from the seats. There were no bodies, just the ruin of the jeep, and blood.

Stepping through the strewn metal, Diana made her way around the vehicle, curious to see if there were any footprints from someone who might have escaped. There were stray trails that made her hopeful that, just maybe, a couple of the men got out alive. Her stomach flipped, however, when she saw ragged chunks of torn flesh sticking to the seats, some coated with blood that slipped down to where a small collection of fatty tissue was gathering at the opposite side of the vehicle.

Diana gagged and turned away from the gruesome sight. Her muscles seized as she tried to resist the urge to vomit. Leaning over, she rested her palms on her thighs and took deep, shuddering breaths. She nearly had it under control when a roar ripped through the trees, making her heart surge with terror. She didn't know if it was the same creature she heard before, but she wasn't going to stick around to find out.

It was only with great effort that she managed not to scream as she tore away from the jeep. The trees moaned behind her, branches whipping as something came barreling at her. Terror clogged her throat, her breaths coming up in sharp gasps as tears tracked down her cheeks. She didn't want to die just yet.

She heard feet hit the earth behind her as if something had jumped to the ground, and another roar chasing on her heels. She wasn't going to be able to outrun it. She knew that with absolute certainty.

A small whimper squeezed out of her throat as she reached back and grabbed an arrow from her quiver. She was signing her death warrant attacking anything in the woods, but as far as she knew, she was a dead woman anyway. Trembling, she nocked the arrow into place, spun around, and raised her bow. The creature that charged toward her made her shake with horror. His face was contorted into a fierce snarl, long, horrible fangs bared. It was terrifying against his inhuman coloring, the bits of color flashing between massive antlers, unsettling her as they swung chaotically.

She did not think. Her arrow flew. The sick, wet sound of its impact was unnaturally loud as the arrow pierced the creature's shoulder. Its face wrinkled in fury as it pounced. Diana did not realize that she had notched another arrow until it lifted, but this time, there was no opportunity to fire as its body collided with hers, the feel of lethal muscle slamming into her as it brought her down to the ground. The arrow flew loose, and she heard it hit a tree some distance away, only an afterthought as she met the inhuman white eyes that stared down at her. The crimson ichor that seeped from its wound appeared similar to human blood, except the scent was wrong. It had a sweet floral smell as it dripped on her from above, its face leaning close to her, bringing its fangs nearer to her vulnerable skin.

Her breath left her in a reedy sound of despair. Whatever it was… it was going to kill her. Its tail, thick and tufted at the end like that of a lion, swished behind it as its silky ears turned toward her, its nostrils flaring. It pressed closer until she felt something familiar against her sex through their clothing, the hard length pushing at the juncture between her thighs. The monster holding her was an extremely aroused male.

Whimpering, Diana struggled to get free. His hold tightened, his blood splattering on her with every shift of the arrow in his attempt to keep her in his grasp as his pearl-colored eyes, bisected by a narrow, pale-gray pupil, shined down on her. He lowered his head until his mouth rested beside her ear, his tongue slipping out to caress the lobe of her ear before catching the flesh between his teeth and tugging with just the slightest pinch of pain. The touch zapped straight down to her clit, making her hips jerk against him as her pussy clenched.

Horror shot through her at the flood of arousal, her panties soaking as he continued to lick along her ear and neck, his hips grinding against her insistently as he growled into her ear.

"You shot me," a deep voice rasped, sending a new tremor through her.

"Please," she whispered faintly.

He nuzzled her lightly, a deep purr echoing from him as one hand slid up his chest to grip the bolt. With one hard yank and a fresh spurt of sweet-smelling blood, he pulled the arrow free and tossed it aside.

"Please?" he hissed. "For what do you beg?"

"Don't kill me," she choked out.

The creature stilled above her, nostrils flared, eyes half-closed in a look of pleasure. A thick black tongue stroked over his pale lips. "Your fear is exquisite, a liquor on my tongue. But never have I tasted anything like your desire, it burns within me. I am at an impasse as to which flavor I yearn for more," he murmured in her ear. "You are a rarity. The light desiring the dark. Life desiring the embrace of death. Nature fluxes now between the two of us." His lips dragged over her jaw, their touch petal soft.

Diana squeezed her eyes shut, her arousal swiftly dying at his words. She wasn't a fool—he was going to kill her. If he relished her fear, there was little doubt in her mind that he would enjoy her pain as well. He would terrorize her, torture her, possibly rape her, and eventually kill her. He was going to kill her just as he killed the hunters. She wondered if he had curled around them as well, tasting their terror before he finally tore them apart.

She felt his nose butt against her neck and heard a small growl of frustration as he shifted over her. If she could have done so, she would have curled herself into a ball at that moment to evade the touch.

"The scent is gone," he growled in frustration, and her eyes snapped open as he jerked away only by a few inches, a puzzled scowl knitting his brow. "Why?"

A weak laugh bubbled out of her. "I don't get my jollies from the threat of being terrorized and killed."

"Your jollies?" he breathed against her skin. "Hmm. No. There is no pleasure in death outside of the little deaths that we suffer at the culmination of our desires. Worry not, I have no interest in killing you. I shall find a much more interesting purpose for your intrusion into my woods."

"Did you kill them for intruding?" she whispered, glancing over at the remains of the jeep.

The monster on top of her froze and lifted his head, a scowl darkening his features as he seemed to notice the wreckage for the first time. With demonstratable reluctance, he lifted his body away from her as he stood once more, surveying the site. Scurrying back away from him, Diana pulled her feet under her and stood as well, watching his expression as it changed from confusion to rage.

She had assumed that he was responsible for the carnage. She was wrong. If anything, that made her more afraid. The monster in front of her was frightening enough. The fact that there was something else that was doing this terrified her. She wanted to inch toward him, but stayed herself. He was no source of comfort and protection either. He was death—he claimed the title for himself. He was dangerous.

Glancing around, she whispered nervously, "Was this Cacus?"

The male's head snapped around, his odd eyes fixing on her in a narrowed stare as he let out a thunderous growl. "*Where* did you hear that name?"

Backing up a step, Diana swallowed. "A…uh—" Fuck, what were they called? Oh, yes! "—a faun said something about Cacus rising from the depths and hunting."

His head tipped toward her as he rounded on her, his jaw hard. "A faun spoke to you?"

She nodded and attempted to backpedal as he crowded into her personal space until she was trapped between his strength and the tree behind her. "When I arrived here, I gave him what food I had, and that was the information he gave me, along with safe passage through his territory."

To her surprise, his lips quirked. He inclined his head, antlers dipping, making the jewels jingle softly with the movement. "Clever female, entering the wood with gifts of food for the fae." Turning his attention back to the jeep he let out a long hiss of breath. "Cacus," he hissed. "So the aelven were not exaggerating.

This may be far worse than even the aelven court feared if the Tainted Ones are awakening."

He spun around so abruptly that Diana flinched, but she was unable to draw back before he grabbed her hand, his long white fingers closing around her wrist. He didn't slow, yanking her with him as he strode by, nearly pulling her off her feet in the process. Stumbling along, she kept pace as he dragged her deeper into the forest.

"Where are you taking me?" she asked as he dragged her into the deep shadows of the woods, where numerous glowing eyes watched their passage. Small ghoulish-looking creatures with red caps bounded among the trees, their mouths parting in razor-sharp smiles and their broad noses scenting the air as they giggled. Their eyes glowed yellow in the dark, bisected only by an inky, diamond-shaped pupil. They licked their fangs and ran among the branches, leaping and ramming each other in their frolic as they attempted to keep up.

The male holding her arm did not glance back at her, but he answered her question at length, his deep rolling voice breaking the cacophony of the creatures following them. "To my home. I need to make inquiries. If it is indeed Cacus, I will need to prepare," he growled. "I am no son of Jove, but I fought in the divine wars against the Tainted Ones, the foul creatures of destruction. I am not without my own power."

"Tainted… You mean like the creatures that broke over our land, spreading sickness?" She didn't know much about the matter, but tales had spread about the ravagers, monsters from the underworld that destroyed their world.

He shook his head impatiently. "The miasma of the chthonic world intruding on the living world is different. It is more of a barrier between humanity and divine light that brings sickness in various forms. The Taint, however, is a true corruption that is against the gods and must be stopped. The Tainted Ones must be destroyed or returned to their prisons within the earth."

"Okay, great plan. But what are you going to do with me…?" she asked, praying that he might release her.

He shot her a hard look, his lips curving in a merciless smile as if it were carved into place. He stopped and turned to her, a large hand reaching up to delicately trace the line of her jaw with one claw. "Your fate is as yet undetermined," he murmured, his eyes glinting like moonstones in the dim light. "But whatever path it may take, your future now belongs to me." The promise came out as a purr, his smile widening into a feral grin. "If that comforts you any."

"Not even a little," she whispered under her breath as he snatched her wrist again and yanked her after him, his dark laughter rolling around her. The titter of the red-capped creatures made her shiver as she stumbled after him.

"Do not fear, little one," he rasped. "I am the most threatening king in these woods. I will not let you go, but you can be assured that only I shall devour you." His eyes turned on her, liquid white heat. "And when I do, you shall find a far greater release in your surrender."

She went rigid at his pronouncement, offended despite the hot coal that burst to life within her. Yanking her arm back, she struggled against his grip, but it didn't weaken or break, and the laughter of the little ghouls followed her as the male in front of her swung around and enclosed her firmly in his arms, lifting her easily off her feet.

"You bastard," Diana hissed, renewing her struggles foolishly against the supernatural being. She was all too aware that he could break her with minimal effort.

He purred and crushed her tighter to his chest. "Indeed I am. The son born of a passionate embrace of the lord of the wood and the goddess of love and desire. But you may call me lucomo—

your king." He said nothing more as he ran his nose down her cheek. She trembled at the touch and drew in a breath that turned into a gasp as he moved at a dizzying speed through the trees.

Resting her head back against his shoulder, Diana looked up and saw a pale dove lit from the branches above, its white body streaking through the trees.

CHAPTER 5

The beings of his court watched with open curiosity as he tugged the human huntress inside his abode. Though the palace was hidden from any who did not know its location, it was teeming with spirits whose eyes followed their movement from every corner. The human had mercifully ceased struggling before they arrived, so she did not attract undue attention or stir a feeding frenzy. It was all he could do to not imbibe of the fear that flowed off her. He was sated on the flavor, but did not wish to become drunk on it as some of his kind might. The wine of mortal essence stirred by their emotions was intoxicating and tempting to all of them.

Silvas preferred to remain in control.

All the same, he did not want the other denizens of the Eternal Forest to be feeding on the human. She was *his*… at least until the time that he finally tired of her. His hackles raised, and an aggressive shiver ran through him. No. Not even then. Perhaps then he would escort her back over the border of the Eternal Forest and into the human world. He could not tolerate the idea of another being touching her.

Bemused by his predicament, he shifted the weight of the

human, setting her a little higher and more comfortably over his shoulder. His possessiveness toward her defied reason. It was normal to feel attraction. Many beings enjoyed slaking their desires on humans, especially those that fed on human emotion. Lust was just as potent as fear to their palate. It was rare, however, for possessiveness or attachment to develop, and unthinkable for them to occur instantaneously.

It was also dangerous. He could not forget about that, no matter how much he was caught up in the female. He saw what it did. It made the powerful weak. Humans were even able to capture a gatekeeper of the underworld due to that weakness, and bound him in enchanted chains before he was able to break free. Silvas refused to allow that to happen to him, but he was also not in the habit of denying himself anything that he wanted.

One of the troll guards, his body as coarse as the rocky earth, rose to his feet at Silvas's approach, his dark green eyes filled with interest. "What delicacy do you have there, my king?"

The human in his arms stiffened and then began to squirm as she turned to get a look at the male speaking. Silvas knew the minute that she caught sight of the troll by her startled gasp. Her delicate human fingers gripped his hair, and her weak claws dug into his back.

Silvas snarled in the male's direction, his power flaring around him, an oppressive shroud crackling and billowing around him in an aggressive threat. Vines snapped free from the palace walls, whipping at the troll, and the room darkened as the trees bowed closer together, blocking out what little remained of the light. The guard stumbled back as he turned his head away.

"*Not yours*," Silvas hissed.

"Yes," the troll uttered with a raspy croak. "Apologies, lucomo."

Silvas strode through the throne room. The eyes of his court were on him, but he refused to acknowledge them as long as they stayed out of his way. He was the lucomo of the Eternal Woods. It was his domain, and the huntress was under his protection. He was well aware that the denizens of his kingdom were watching the human with expressions varying from lustful to suspicious to curious. If none of them attempted to touch or approach her in a manner that insulted him or harmed her, he did not care what they thought. Order was all that was important in the Eternal Forest, and even that order compelled a chaotic alliance between all the forces and beings dwelling within. It was never peaceful or agreeable. Such things did not belong to the wilds of the Eternal Forest, where even those of the fair courts did not tread.

Silvas's eyes narrowed on the hall, the stone walls that he had raised from the ground etched with roots and vines that had become imbedded over the ages. Glowing pods bulged out in many places, providing illumination. Flowers sagged from many of them, hidden among foliage, bearing a heady perfume meant to lure the senses. A shudder ran through his body, and he tried to ignore the seductive scents that made him ache with desire. Arx was a living thing as much as the trees of his woods, and set out snares to heighten passions that grew clustered around bedchambers. The palace was sustained by the inhabitants as much as they sustained themselves on other beings.

He respected the symbiotic relationship, but he had no time to indulge such things with his huntress. Not yet, anyway. First, he needed to visit the oracle of the cavern and speak to the ancient one who dwelled there. Silvas needed to know with absolute certainty that it was the most ancient and terrible children of the Earth that awoke. If Cacus indeed prowled the Eternal Forest and its outlying woods that breached the mortal world, Silvas would need to prepare.

Arm tightening around the human, he scowled as he ducked inside of his chamber. At his entrance, the glow pods lit up, and he glanced around speculatively. He would need to hide her somewhere that none would expect, and where none from his court could tamper with her until he returned.

At his hesitation, the huntress began to writhe, attempting to break from his hold. With one large hand, he swatted at her ass, catching her upper thigh, and she sucked in a breath between her teeth. He noted that the sound bore some semblance to an angry serpent stirred from the grass and wondered at what fighting spirit she might possess once she was released from his embrace. Tightening his hand around her thigh, he snarled a low reprimand until she stilled and fell silent. Fingers tightened their hold, but he cared little about that. The grip of a human was nothing but a pleasurable, amorous invitation to many beings of the forest. She would learn that eventually, when he had time to instruct her in such delights.

"Arx," he growled aloud to his abode in his ancient tongue. "Open a way, part and reform your living walls, and bring to life a chamber beside my own."

A low moan rippled through the hallway, making the female freeze in his arms, but his lips twisted in appreciation. The vines on the wall across from his bed writhed as the rock folded away with sharp cracking sounds. They reshaped themselves, and another doorway appeared. Still, he waited until the stone of the walls resettled before walking with his prize into the room provided for her. This room had more glow pods than his own, perhaps to compensate for her inferior vision, and a stone bed stood against one wall where it had sprung from the ground.

Setting the human on her feet with care, Silvas released her and stepped back to give her room as he watched expressions fly over her face. She gripped her bow in both hands, drawing it tightly against her chest as if for comfort as eyes the hue of summer's deep—lush green—darted around the room. He found himself fascinated with her eyes that seemed to appear varying dark hues of green, blue, gold, and brown. He wondered how they would appear when she was caught beneath him, her body straining with passion.

"This is your chamber," he rasped in a soft growl. "I will have basic comforts delivered to you so that you may rest while I am gone. You will stay here. You will not attempt to leave the chamber."

"And if I do?" she whispered, her eyes fastened apprehensively on him.

He shrugged. "It will do you no good. The door is bespelled, and you shall not be able to open it or exit." His gaze fixed on her, knowing that it unsettled her and using that to his advantage. "Know that I am not required to tell you these things, but I am telling you out of consideration for your comfort. I shall return shortly."

Her pink lips parted, but he did not allow her to respond, not wishing to listen to the pleas or objections that would fall from her tongue. Nothing she said would be able to sway him, so there was no reason to stay and listen, and in doing so give her false hope.

His little huntress would not escape him.

Pulling the heavy door shut behind him, Silvas strode from his room, returning to the hall. He peered at a particularly thick tree trunk that stretched along one wall before disappearing into the ceiling.

"Alseida," he called out.

The dryads of his court could hear him through the trees in every sector of his palace, and in some cases even out through his Eternal Forest when they chose to visit among their trees. He knew that Alseida would hear him and present herself at his summons.

The tree rustled, the lower leaves against the ceiling twitching as something pushed out from its bark, the cellulose growing thinner and splitting as a beautiful female stepped forward, pulling herself free from it. Her green hair was the last to appear before it dropped around her amber shoulders. She peered at him with brilliant green eyes, sharper and clearer in color than the warm green of the mortal. Her simple dress obscured much of her form, though as she bowed, she exposed her rounded thigh from the open side of her dress, and the upper swell of her breast.

"You summoned me, lucomo," she asked in a breathy voice, her eyes bright with interest.

"Not for anything which you might be imagining," he snarled.

Only for a short time had he been foolish enough to take the dryad to his bed and lost hundreds of years as she coupled with him and drained him. In the end, it had taken many silvani and several trolls to pull her away and free him. He had been so drained that he was a wraith in his own palace for the passage of centuries before he recovered. After that, he instated his guard, and Alseida was punished, bound to the service of Arx.

Green eyes narrowed on him with anger, but he smiled with satisfaction, reveling in it.

"What would you have of me?" she whispered venomously, all softness disappearing from her features as if they had never been present.

"I have returned with a very special guest…"

"A human," she spat disdainfully.

"A human," he agreed in a silky tone. The dryad was smart enough to pay heed now. "You will not enter her room. That is my order, which you will obey as my will compels you—but you will retrieve two of my guard and have them bring all manner of things to see to the female's comfort. A mattress, bedding, a table, fresh clothing, food, and drink. If I return and discover that she wants for anything, I will hold you completely responsible. Are my orders understood."

Anger flashed in the green eyes and her lip curled. "You plan to sully yourself with a mortal? They are prey to our kind, a passing amusement at best. Throw her to the trolls and allow them to debase themselves with their crude entertainments. You are lucomo. You deserve noble fare for your taste."

He darted forward, backing her into the wall, one hand gripping hard around her forearm. Slowly, he brought up his other hand and raised one finger in warning. An angry growl rumbled out of him as he barely leashed his temper.

"Do not utter such things again. As I recall, allowing you into my bed nearly felled the Eternal Forest. Or is your memory so short that you do not recall the barriers weakening to the point that men were able to pass indiscriminately? We nearly lost many beings to their appetites, all because *you* could not contain your feeding, nor surrender yourself to sustain me in turn," he stated flatly.

"I have changed," she said softly.

"You have not," Silvas growled in reply. "You have never shown that you improved on your selfish nature as you play your games in these halls. In any case, it does not matter—I have no use for you outside your current function in Arx. I find this mortal much more to my taste," he purred, relishing the way she paled at the truth he offered.

Dropping his hand, he stepped back, the jewels on his antlers jingling softly with his movement. He frowned down at her. "Do *not* disappoint me when it comes to the care of my huntress."

Mutely, Alseida nodded. She pinched her lips together for a moment before she dared to speak again. "She shall come by no harm from me, lucomo."

"Good," he snarled, turning away so that he did not have to look at her for even a moment longer. "See to my female promptly. I go now to the lower caverns. I expect everything to be done before I return."

With those parting words, Silvas strode down the corridor, and then another, walking the maze of hallways as he headed into the darkened heart—the hidden courtyard of Arx where once he seeded his home above the cavern of the oracle's spring.

When he finally arrived at the black staircase descending into the depths of the earth, he hesitated for only a moment. It had been a long time since he had last spoken to the oracle, and their last parting had not been a happy one. He only hoped that she did not still nurse her anger against him.

CHAPTER 6

Diana jumped to her feet from where she had been sitting on the stone bed, her heart hammering in her chest as the door to her room swung open. The strange protrusions from the walls kept the room comfortably lit so she was able to clearly see the pair of enormous gray males who entered. Stumbling back against the wall, she watched them as they dragged in a thick mattress between them. Though she stayed out of their way, she tracked their every movement, expecting some sort of violent behavior from them.

To her surprise, they didn't do more than glance briefly in her direction before setting to work, no doubt ordered by the lucomo. What were they? She couldn't even guess by looking at them, though they had a distinctly earthy appearance. Although one was only a few inches taller than the other, both were thick with muscle, and certain patches of their skin had a rough texture like broken rock. On the larger male there were also a few spots tinged with greens and blues, as if moss had attempted to cling to him at one point or another.

Despite their rough appearances, their heads were well-formed, and their ears were pointed like those she had seen on representations of elves. The biggest difference was that the long tips flopped over on the shorter male, made more prominent in appearance by the way they pulled their coarse hair behind into long ponytails hanging from the top of their heads. Those long, muscular bodies and strong arms and legs could almost be considered attractive, if not a bit rugged, with inhuman coloration and skin texture. But their faces were frightful! Eerie yellow eyes fastened on her in an unnerving stare, and though they possessed full lips, they smiled at her without any recognizable kindness, mouths full of sharp teeth, with long canines designed for tearing. As they turned, she stared in surprise at the cat-like tails that trailed behind them, whipping expressively as they worked.

They were followed by another pair of males and then another, each varying in shade, size, and features as she would have expected to find among people and less so among monsters. Each of them carried small necessities and comforts for the room as she had been promised. Her eyes trailed over them until arriving at the door where a tall woman of pale yellow complexion and vivid green hair stood still in the doorway. At five feet and nine inches tall, Diana wasn't little, and this lady had her beat.

Diana bit her lip and considered the woman in front of her. She obviously wasn't human, and she didn't look particularly happy at the moment. Perhaps there was some chance that she would help her get the fuck out of there. Swallowing nervously, Diana stepped forward a few paces to introduce herself, but changed her mind as cold, pale green eyes turned to peer disdainfully at her.

This wasn't the gaze of someone inconvenienced and irritable who could be swayed to her cause. Her eyes were unnerving with their complete lack of warmth. Sharp and cold, the hint of yellow to the pale green irises made Diana think of an alligator peering at her, though the pupil was diamond-shaped. Whoever she was, the hostility that came off her in waves had Diana flattening herself once more against the wall.

Definitely not any kind of friend or ally to be found there.

Although she never moved from the doorway, the woman conveyed a subtle menace as she stood there like a psychedelic green and yellow messenger of death, watching over the males. Her expression was so devoid of feeling that Diana found it frightening to witness. Despite her human-like appearance, this made her seem even more inhuman than the massive gray-skinned creatures who talked, growled, and laughed amongst themselves as they worked. She stood in complete silence and didn't so much as betray a flicker of emotion until the last hulking gray male left the room.

At that moment, her gaze once again focused on Diana, her face pinching with disgust. With one elegant hand, she grabbed the door and yanked it shut with enough force that the resulting bang sent an almost pained rattling through the walls. Although the vibration made her teeth chatter, Diana remained against the wall, her heart pounding too loudly in her ears as she stared at the door. At any moment, she expected someone else, another inhuman creature, to come inside to prowl through the room. She didn't dare to move even a foot from the wall until it became apparent than no one would return.

A short sob of relief burst out of her.

With her attention fixed on the door, she took one step and then another, easing herself away until she bumped against the hard frame of the bed. Upon contact she stilled, her muscles cramping slightly from the tension running through them, certain that someone would throw the door open and attack. As she stood there, Diana strained to listen for any movement on the other side of the door.

Complete and utter silence greeted her.

Licking her lips, she glanced down at the plush bed. With a

fine mattress thrown on the stone frame, numerous pillows, and thick bedding, it was an open invitation after the day she had had. She bent down and ran her fingertips over the bedding before placing her hand more firmly upon it. She waited to see if it got any reaction.

Nothing.

Sighing gratefully, Diana allowed herself to sink upon the bed, her weary muscles soaking in the comfort. Rolling onto her back, Diana stared at the ceiling. The monster that had brought her there said he would be back soon. Since no one had yet returned after delivering the items he promised, she surmised that no one would be back for some time yet. She could try the door…

Slipping once more to her feet before her nerve failed her, Diana crept across the floor, keeping her weight balanced on the balls of her feet until she arrived at the door. It didn't look like anything particularly special to her. It even had what appeared to be a perfectly normal—if somewhat old-fashioned—handle. Nothing looked especially dangerous or otherworldly about it.

Her stomach dropped, and instinct backpedaled in warning as she reached for the handle, but the part of her that insisted it was just a normal door was louder than the human instinct that had been tamed by modern civilization before everything fell apart. Her fingertips brushed through the air just above the handle when a blue light flared over the door. The power swelled and bulged out before releasing a boom that sent her reeling back several feet. A painful zap of energy licked through her.

Diana spun away and stalked back to the bed. She should have just stayed in the damned thing. With a few more shaky steps, she was able to sprawl haphazardly across the mattress. Her entire body ached from the blast of energy that came off the door. Maybe she would just lie there, rest while she could, and wait for her captor to return.

CHAPTER 7

Silvas descended the long stone steps leading deep beneath the floors of Arx. The damp air betrayed just how near he was coming to the spring that dwelt at the heart of the Eternal Forest. After a time, he was able to hear it bubbling over the rocks of the spring. It grew louder the closer as he approached, and along with it came the echoes of soft sighing sounds.

"Selvans," a voice whispered, emerging from the gurgles of the water before disappearing again.

He frowned as he descended the last few steps into the cavernous gallery, his eyes landing on the foam of the spring broken through the rock, feeding into a deep blue. "You know I have not gone by the name for a millennium. I am Silvas now, as I keep telling you."

The feminine voiced chuckled, disregarding him. "I knew you would come."

"Is that so?" he murmured, his eyes searching through the gloom. "Did you foresee it?"

Laughter echoed around him from all directions, and Silvas's jaw tightened with frustration.

"I did," the oracle hissed, drawing out the vowel in a long singing fashion. "I knew that eventually you would seek my council, golden lucomo of the wood."

"Then why do you hide yourself from me now?" he demanded.

"For what cause do I have to help you?" the voice sneered. "You who trapped me in the darkness."

"To protect your power."

"You lie," she breathed slowly as if savoring the accusation. The fountain surged, water spraying as the spout widened, allowing a sinewy body to slip through into the pool.

He saw little more than a flash of pale locks of hair, white arms, and pearly blue scales of a serpentine tail before she became a coiled black shadow within the heart of the water. The top of her head surfaced, revealing her crimson eyes. Gray locks of hair floated around her shoulders as she regarded him.

"Dorinda, come forth and speak with me," he growled impatiently as he prowled back and forth at the side of the pool.

Her raspy laugh filled the cave as she pulled herself up the rocky slope of her fountainhead, her long serpentine tail looping around it possessively. Her eyes narrowed on him as she sneered.

"You cannot command me, Selvans, lucomo of all silvani. Our power is equal, though I am the one trapped within a cavernous prison." A thoughtful look crossed her face before it was replaced by a hard smile. "I was tempted to ignore your summons, but I had to see for myself your desperation. You are desperate, are you not, brother?"

Silvas narrowed his eyes on the oracle and grit his teeth. Now she acknowledged their relationship? The water-born daughter of Turan did not fool him. Due to their shared mother, he was familiar with the cunning wiles she would employ. Dorinda had felt nothing but anger toward him since he seeded Arx over her cavern. Though it had not been intentional on his part, once he became aware of it, he built his palace up further to protect the entrance into his sister's abode from those who might stray into the Eternal Forest. He hid her well so that none would torment her. And this was how she thanked him!

"Ungrateful," he spat. "Your spring would have been subject to all without protections if not shielded by my abode. You are a vegoia, a sibylline nymph of the spring, and are as bound to it as I am the Eternal Forest. By my will, you are kept hidden and safe."

"To never feel a breath of air or warmth of the sun," she returned bitterly. She glared at him for several long, tense minutes before letting out an irritated sigh. "Stubborn, still. Very well, brother," she hissed, her eyes glowing as her lithe body began to sway.

"Your ruin comes to you," Dorinda continued in a gleeful whisper, "brought by your own wood. It shall change the expanse of the Eternal Forest forever, the very order of your domain… but the manner in which it changes is unfixed. It depends on you. Cacus, old Cacu, has awakened. Beware of him, brother. His sight is wide and his form monstrous, though he can appear to be quite fair. He hides himself away beneath the flesh of Earth Mother Cel, but he very much roams within these woods."

She tilted her head, listening. "I hear him at times, I think… or the echo of his passing."

Silvas closed his eyes as he attempted to gain control over his surge of annoyance, but he felt dread gathering in his gut. He had hoped that it was not true—that the human had been deceived or intentionally attempted to lead him astray. To have it confirmed sent a prickle of awareness through him as he instinctively reached for his forest.

Though he could not see through the trees, he sensed the pulse of life of all things within the woods at that moment. The trees quivered beneath the force of his power, but there he could not find Cacus outside of a stench of foul, greasy ash on the air that seemed to have invaded his woods, and lingered. That the creature was hiding and traveling within the cavern systems sent a blistering wave of fury through him.

Hissing through his teeth, he met the oracle's cool gaze and inclined his head in thanks. "My gratitude, sister, for this information. I appreciate that you did not deliver it in yet another terrible rhyme for me to discern as you did last time."

The vegoia's lip curved into a hard smile, and she raised one shoulder nonchalantly, her tail twisting along the rocks. "Times change," she observed callously. "Or rather, this instance requires a change. As entertaining as it has been to lead you about, there is too much at stake."

"What do you mean 'lead me about?'" he snarled.

Her smile widened, revealing her long fangs. "I freely admit that many of the rules my kind must obey pertains only to humans when utilizing a sybil, not to greater spirits that inhabit the cosmos. Your arrogance did not deserve such a gift. I admit that watching you struggle like a hapless mortal has been... satisfying."

Clarity swept over him. Every time he had come to see her, she toyed with him through her elusive riddles. A growl built in his chest as some his fury redirected toward the oracle. "Venomous creature, your intentional deviance has cost me much. Your warning about Alseida I unraveled only after succumbing to her. Do you have any idea of the damage you did?" he shouted.

Dorinda stiffened, loosing an angry hiss. "Do you expect me to feel sympathy? You locked me away! It is the only amusement I have had over centuries of isolation. You deserved every bit of your own personal suffering."

"And the others who were harmed?"

The vegoia frowned and turned her head away. "Your failures are your own," she muttered, a flick of her tail sending a spray of water to splash on the nearest wall of the cavern. "I may have been more enigmatic than necessary, but I could not foresee the exact consequences or provide you names then just as I cannot now. That knowledge is hidden even from me. The Fates only let me see a portion of what they devise. You must ask your questions wisely," she insisted earnestly, her red eyes glowing in the gloom of the cave.

Silvas was ready to spin on his heel and leave his viperous sister but paused at the note of desperation in her voice. "Why do you care?"

"I am concerned," she whispered, her narrow pupils expanding as she leaned forward over her rock. "I did not utter a falsehood when I said that these events will change the nature of the Eternal Forest. Though I want to be free, I do not wish any harm to my home, or even true harm to you, brother."

He barked out a hard, ugly laugh. "Seems unlikely as you allowed me to be preyed upon by that dryad for centuries."

"Believe as you like," she hissed, her tail striking at the water again. "I speak the truth when I say that as soon as I had a vision of what had befallen you, I alerted a silvanus traveling through the wood from the northern aelven kingdoms. He had a sorceress in his company as they headed for a portal that would take them to another part of the mortal world. I lured him through the cave systems until he arrived at my cavern, and told him what had befallen you. I wanted you to suffer humiliation, not harm," she snarled. "As I said, this is different."

He watched the oracle carefully. Her words answered questions that had gone unanswered for centuries as to his rescue from Alseida. He had been in no condition to be aware of much of anything. Cacus was a vicious creature that had taken the strength of Jove's son to subdue. If Dorinda was worried enough to actually help him and go against centuries of redirection and confusion by her various riddles to vex him, he could not ignore the danger that he was facing.

"The huntress I discovered in the woods—is she part of this?"

His sister's face became inscrutable, her pupils disappearing among the red irises as she began to sway once more. Water surged around her, her lips moving soundlessly as her scales took on a luminous cast. Her pupils expanded, engulfing her eyes in blackness as she stared at him, her body twining in an unending motion. The voice that came from her was raspy and multi-tonal as she connected to the weave of the Fates once more.

"She is, and she is not. She is caught in the web and has become a part of it. She can no longer be separated from the events that unfold."

"Is she dangerous to me?" he growled as he attempted to control his patience. She had warned him that he had to be wise with his questions… or more accurately, he had to be precise.

"She is a danger to who you have become. She will threaten the order you have established since breaking free of Alseida. You will be vulnerable and weakened, or you will be strengthened. Be wise in the decisions that you make, brother. The weave is tangled and does not show me a clear path in either direction."

Silvas's jaw tightened. That was not the information he wanted to hear. He wanted to enjoy the human and return her to her world. But if she were a possible threat, it was just as likely that he would end up being forced to destroy her. If there were any possibility at all of her being a threat, he couldn't risk letting her out of his sight.

"Is she a danger to Cacus?" he queried as he moved closer.

Dorinda cocked her head. "It is… uncertain. There are too many threads intersecting, too many possibilities. One thing is known: you will have to make whole your power to defeat him and retrieve that which you have cast aside."

He recognized the undeniable weight of dread as he posed his question. "Do I retrieve the sword Nocis?"

The blade was a terrible creation. A gift from Artume, the

lady of the night, it was created to be able to cut through anything and fragment light. He had wielded it during the battle of the gods and swore never to touch the blade again for the destruction that it brought to all things in its path in the effort to subdue a divine being. With each swipe, he had watched life wither and fall around him. The king of the forest, king of the eternal realm of light and life, even when thickened with shadow, was turned too easily to a king of death and sorrows.

The vegoia lasa looked at him knowingly, her red eyes staring through him. "There is no other to come to your aid," she hissed softly. "Hercules long ago ascended, and no heroes remain. The safety of the Eternal Forest and the human world in the face of Cacu rests on you. You will have to retrieve Nocis from the pit where you left her. Above all, keep the huntress at your side. She is the key."

Silvas growled, his hand rubbing at the base of his antler, the rattle of the ornaments hanging from it loud in the cavern. "Retrieving her from the ancient strix, Mora, is going to be difficult."

"It shall," Dorinda agreed solemnly.

That did not bode well.

CHAPTER 8

Diana lay in the bed, her mouth dry as she heard the heavy steps in the room beside her own. The strange sentience of the room had dimmed the lights to a faint glow as soon as she settled down into the bed. Unfortunately, she had been lying there unable to sleep for the last few hours, listening for any sign of the strange male returning.

If she concentrated, she was sure that she could hear his harsh breaths as he stalked back and forth. She was certain that it was him and not one of the others. His footsteps, while heavy, echoed in precise steps across the floor rather than the scuffing, rambling walk of the males who had brought in her furnishings. It sounded like he was prowling back and forth in front of her door, every pass making her skin tighten and shiver with awareness.

The tension that rolled over her was terrible. She wanted to shout out her frustration. Anything to end the twisting dance of uncertainty. The fire in her room had died down long ago, shrouding her in darkness. At the time, she hadn't minded, hoping that being sightless would settle her nerves instead of staring out at her strange surroundings.

At last, the door swung open, banging against the wall. In

the gloom of the room, she could only just barely make out the dark shadow filling the doorway, his antlers breaching her room. Diana saw little more than the brilliant white glow of his eyes.

Pulling her blanket tighter around her, she edged toward the head of her bed as he approached, his steps ending at the footboard. His eyes moved, and she had the sense that he was raking them over her. She stared right back at him, her body curling in on itself as she drew her knees up to her chest beneath the bedding. His eyes narrowed in response, and Diana had no doubt that he could clearly see her every movement. He wasn't impeded by the low light like she was.

"You are a puzzle to me," he whispered, his voice caressing her like velvet. Without being able to see him, the words seemed to surround her. His eyes slanted at an angle as if he cocked his head curiously at her. "Why would such a small, insignificant thing such as you be transported to the heart of the Eternal Forest? Your kind normally end up among the aelves or one of the courts that have closer connection to your world along the edges of the forest. I do not understand how this came to be, or this fascination I have," he purred.

The sound skated over her nerves, sending a tingling sensation shooting through her.

Nervously, she licked her lips. "Unlucky break? Look, I just want to go home… Please."

The jingle of small bells sounded in the room, and she knew that he shook his head. "Even if I could, I would not. Our destinies are entwined, it seems. The vegoia has seen it, and I feel it in my blood. Do you not?" he hissed the words seductively in her ear.

"I don't know," she choked out. "I feel so many different things that I cannot unwind one from the other. It's like I have this huge knot inside of me of many different feelings. What I feel is… confusing, to say the least. When it comes right down to it… I'm scared."

"It is instinct," he replied with a satisfied note in his voice. "You fight it and yourself, trying to dance out of the way from that which calls you. You try to escape. And now you are confused and lost. You fear this."

"Yes," she breathed. "I am lost."

"Then allow me to lend some clarity to the situation," he growled abruptly, and she felt the bed shake as his foot made contact audibly with the footboard as he climbed over the edge. "Together we will discover the purpose of your presence here, this strange connection between us and the events that shall come. We will unravel the mystery of you as the events unfold. When we are finished, and there is no purpose for you here any longer, I will personally drop you back into your simple human existence."

He prowled closer, dropping to hands and knees, his tail a dark blur of movement behind him as it swished through the air. Diana froze in place, her eyes fixed on the faint outline of his body and the white glow of his eyes as he came closer. Her heart jumped in her chest despite his odd assurance that sounded far from any real comfort.

In the space of minutes, the creature informed her that she would be used and then discarded, in who knew what sort of condition once she outlived her usefulness. At least it did not sound like he had any intention to kill her yet, but she didn't trust that not to change. In truth, even at that moment, Diana felt hunted as he drew closer.

"You could let me go now," she argued, uncomfortable with his approach. "I have no skills that would be useful to you, and you say yourself that I do not belong here."

A humming purr answered her. "I could," he agreed. "But I will not. Whether either of us likes this situation, our fates are entwined. Even if I wished it, I do not think the forest will allow you to leave so easily after snatching you into its embrace. The Eternal Forest brought you here, but its purpose is known only to the highest among the gods."

She felt the blunt end of his nose brush her cheek as he inhaled deeply. A shiver of awareness skated down her spine as she tensed. "Are you telling me that I would never have found my way out if you had not?"

"I was destined to find you," he purred. "But you would not have. Humans rarely find their way out of the border territories without a benevolent spirit taking pity on them. You do not comprehend just how far from your reality you are. The Eternal Forest is a dangerous place for humans, especially in the wild depths of my realm. Be grateful that the gods brought me to you instead of another."

"You mean like those creatures who were here earlier?" she whispered.

"*Creatures*?" he murmured, his tone scathing.

Diana cringed at the wealth of condemnation that came through in that one word. As the minutes dragged by, she further felt the critical weight of his scrutiny as he regarded her in silence. She was about to say never mind when his voice cut through the darkness.

"Those *creatures* as you call them are trolls. They are strong, reliable guards not only of my palace but also of the forest itself. They keep watch along the borders of the Eternal Forest against intruders who may come in from your world, guarding such bridges carefully."

"Trolls?" she whispered, an unmistakable shrill note entering her voice. They had been larger than most men and thicker of build, but trolls? "As in man-eating, pillaging monsters?"

"No species is perfect," he said. "They perhaps aren't seen in the best light when they are in the mortal world. Although I understand that they tend to keep to themselves now, in the past bands of them formed crude kingdoms. The thing about trolls is that they only respect strength. In your world, there is little to respect."

Diana blanched. "You are telling me that they're already in my world?"

He scoffed. "Of course. The barriers dropped, allowing crossings to many creatures, though few can find their way home, should they desire it, once they leave the Eternal Forest and other realms from which they might come. I know for certain that from the forest there are elves, orcs, trolls, centaurs, and all manner of creatures in your world once more."

"But they eat humans!"

"Seldom," he corrected as he shifted over her in the dark. "It is not an unknown occurrence, however. Most dead beings are considered meat in the mind of a troll."

Diana felt her jaw drop. "Are you saying that they would eat anyone dead—even one of their own?"

"That is difficult to say for sure," he admitted.

"And you trusted them in here with me?" Diana squeezed her eyes shut, fighting the grip of the panic. One of those monsters could have grabbed her, killed her, and dragged her off for a feast with her captor being no more the wiser.

The male above her snarled loudly in offense. The sound pierced right through her, pinning her place with the terror that surged through her. Eyes widening, she watched him the best she could through the thick gloom of the room.

He leaned in close, his hot breath fanning her face. Notes of a spicy scent, not unlike frankincense, clove, and apples, teased her nose. He dragged his lips against the sensitive skin at the corner of her mouth.

"They would not dare to offer any harm to you," he murmured in a husky tone. "All within the palace know that you are mine, and mine alone. They will protect you fiercely, even more so if you earn a place of honor among them. If you wish for such an outcome, I suggest that you refrain from calling them creatures or monsters."

"I am not yours," she protested, rebelling against the claim as she ignored his advice regarding the trolls. She had no intention of being there long enough to require such loyalty. Instead, she focused on the anxious way her body tightened at everything promised in his claim.

She couldn't be his. She wouldn't surrender herself into anyone's keeping. She refused to do so for any of the men who came to her door promising to take care of her, and she wouldn't allow this… being to make such a claim over her.

His laughter was full of dark promise. "You think not? From the moment I saw you and claimed you, my mark was placed upon you that any in the forest shall recognize. Make no mistake: you are most definitely mine." His fingers slid seductively around her ankles as he spoke. In one deft move, he pulled her legs out, stretching her out against the bed. Sliding forward, he flattened his pelvis against hers, and Diana was aware of the thick erection nestled against her belly.

"I don't want this," she hissed back. "You are fooling yourself if you think I am just going to spread my legs and surrender to you at your say. *I decide.*"

"Very well," he said, his lips brushing against hers as he drew the words out, the warm pressure of his body disappearing from her own. "You will find that silvani are patient hunters, and I am lucomo of all silvani, king of all the forest kings. I am even more patient than most." He nuzzled the sensitive place beneath her jaw. Seconds later, his tongue snaked out, caressing her pulse.

"I think your green-haired friend might have something to say about that," she gritted out, remembering the way the female had looked at her as if she were less than a bug to be squashed. If he was publicly claiming her, she wondered what that claim would stir up against her. "She did not look happy at my presence here."

"It is none of her concern," he replied sharply. The bright glow of his eyes was so close that Diana felt into his gaze, lost within the light. "Think no further of the dryad," he whispered as he pressed a soft kiss against her neck. "Are you sure you won't change your mind? Your body calls out to mine. I could show you such pleasures…"

Pressing her lips together, Diana flattened her hands against the solid, thick muscle of his chest—good gods, he had a wealth of hot muscle beneath her touch—and pushed against him. It did nothing to move him, but he did still after one last drag of his textured tongue against her skin.

"I'm sure," she replied with a soft gasp of pleasure. She shook her head, attempting to clear it.

"As long as you are sure," he chuckled.

He pulled away, his body lost to the shadows as he slipped off of her bed. His eyes glinted with what she imagined was a look of wicked promise. "Sleep then, human."

"Diana," she said. "If I am going to be here for some time, you might as well call me by my name."

She heard him draw in a sharp breath, followed by a whisper of a purr. "How interesting."

Frowning, Diana squinted into the gloom. "And what is your name?"

He did not answer. Instead, he spun around, his body completely submersed in darkness now that he had his back to her, and she could no longer see his eyes. She wasn't aware that he even moved until she heard receding footsteps as he stalked to the door.

"Rest well," he growled as he stepped through the door and closed it firmly behind him.

She stared after him for a long moment, uncertain of what to make of the exchange. She wanted to throw herself on the door and demand that he let her out, but the memory of what touching the door did before kept her in the bed. She could hear the silvanus moving in his room, and the rustling sound of his clothes hitting the floor as he prepared for his own rest.

The mental picture of his pale, honed body reclined in bed—his cock, thick and hard, pushing up from his pelvis—tormented her imagination and sent a surge of unwanted lust through her. Through the wall, she heard him still, and a low growl echo, stirring her blood and making her skin heat with desire. A lusty groan sounded moments later, followed by a slick sound of flesh slapping together.

Frozen in that spot, she listened, her eyes widening further even as her pussy dripped with her increasing arousal as he grunted with every slap of his fist against what sounded like the base of his shaft. It quickened, as did his heavy grunts and snarls until at last he shouted out with an abrupt bellow of pleasure.

It was only when everything silenced from the other room that she was able to hear her own harsh pants as her fingers (that she hadn't remembered laying against her clit) worked the nub of flesh harder until she, too, shattered, her breathing hissing out of her as she clenched her teeth against the orgasm sizzling through her blood. Her body spent, she collapsed against the bedding, all too aware of his dark, knowing laughter as it drifted through the wall.

CHAPTER 9

Diana woke with golden sunlight pouring through one window whose shutters had been thrown wide open. She groaned and threw an arm over her eyes. Who had done such a thing? She knew damn well that when the trolls left, those windows were closed. Rolling to her side, she squinted against the light. A startled gasp left her as she came face to face with the lucomo crouched at the foot of her bed. His strange white eyes she would have believed to be blind if she had seen eyes such as those on any human.

She had no doubt that this wasn't the case. She was aware of his eyes roving over her, watching her every movement down to the tiniest twitch. There was nothing that she could do that he wouldn't see and be fully aware of. His freaky gray pupils expanded. The speculative pinch to his brows and lips made her even more uncomfortable. She cleared her throat as she brushed the sleep-tangled mess of her hair fully out of her face.

"What did you say you are… a silvani?" she asked conversationally. Anything to get him to stop staring at her so disconcertingly.

"Silvanus," he corrected in a bland tone as he straightened and dropped silently to the floor. “That would be the singular term, although at times there are those who call me silvani because I am the first of all silvani, and others who merely call me Silvanus for similar reasons. It truly varies and, in the end, is inconsequential.”

“And they are all here?”

He arched a pale eyebrow and smirked. “Don’t be absurd. Why would they be? They all have their own territories, typically at the edges of the Eternal Forest where it intersects with your world. They concern themselves with keeping the forest healthy and the wildlife propagating. It would be ridiculous to keep them all here at my court. It gets bad enough with all the nymphs that like to make themselves at home here.”

Diana wondered just what it was about nymphs that he didn’t care for.

“We have much to do today,” he said brusquely. “Follow me. I will show you where you can attend to your needs.”

The lucomo strode out the door, leaving her with little choice other than to follow him so she wouldn’t be left behind. She was glad that she did within minutes of leaving, exiting through his room. Nothing looked familiar, although she had been observant the night before. The general layout seemed to be the same, but it was like someone had gone over it with a large brush, altering textures, colors, and the plant life that clung to the large stone walls. She was even certain that she saw a few new branches of hallways that she didn’t recall seeing before.

She came close to losing him twice when she became distracted staring at a wall that moved before her eyes, and only glanced up in time to catch a glimpse of his tail as he rounded a corner. Diana sure as hell didn’t want to get lost in a place that seemed to change on a whim, whose halls were prowled by impossible and dangerous creatures. The lucomo wasn’t exactly the epitome of safety, but she decided to stay with the monster she knew rather than take her chances with the monsters she did not.

Diana grunted in frustration and sprinted after him. To her surprise, he had gotten far ahead in the short amount of time, but he looked at her sidelong, one eyebrow going up in silent mockery that she was slightly out of breath. She was tempted to scowl at him but smoothed out her expression, determined not to appear ruffled by his rudeness.

She made sure to keep pace with him. Concentrating on her steps, she was surprised when he stopped without a word. It took her a moment to realize that the lucomo was no longer with her. Frowning, she turned back and glanced at him and discovered the silvanus standing beside a narrow entrance. His lips were ticking up at the corners, and Diana felt her cheeks heat with embarrassment. She hated the fact that she was caught trying too hard, and his smile was all the more knowing and condescending for it.

Gritting her teeth, she turned on her heel and slunk back to him, conscious of the fact that her face burned hotter the closer she got to him. She was certain that, by the time she stepped past him into the chamber, she was beet red right up to the roots of her hair.

"I will be waiting out here for you," he called in after her. "There are two running streams. The one on the right you cleanse yourself in, and the one on the left you relieve yourself in. Creatures that live at the depository consume and convert wastes into nutrients for the palace grounds. Be certain that you use the correct spring."

"Got it," she mumbled.

Although her tone was sour, she was rather impressed. Whatever the Eternal Forest was, it appeared to operate in a sustainable manner. It seemed that whatever magic and creatures existed in this world were far superior to human technology that had failed to be even a fraction as clean.

The springs were easy to differentiate from each other, outside of being on opposite walls. The spring for cleaning was the purest water she had ever seen, whereas the water for relieving herself had a greenish hue. She suspected it was recycled wastewater, but it was odorless. On closer inspection, she was certain that the color was due to a heavy concentration of plankton floating in the water tumbling down the side of the wall.

After relieving her bladder, she turned to the clear spring and eyed it. It wasn't big enough to submerge herself in. She wondered if there were a bathing pool elsewhere. At least she could sponge bathe. There was a small tower nearby with piles of clean towels. She imagined that it was a common room used by all those who dwelled within the palace, and was grateful that the lucomo was standing just outside. She felt certain that he wouldn't allow anyone to enter while she was occupying the room.

Or, at least, she hoped that was the case.

Grabbing a small towel, she stripped off her gear and the thick clothes she wore for hunting and ran the towel under the pleasantly warm water. If she wasn't mistaken, the water felt like it came up from a hot spring. It even had the slight sulfur smell she associated with them. Thank the gods it wasn't cold water. She didn't know what the limit was on conveniences in this world, but she was grateful that bathing in frigid water wasn't something that she was going to have to immediately face. At least not while she was in the palace. Though she bemoaned the lack of a tub, she made quick work of washing herself, and grimaced as the cloth turned gray from all the grime she washed away.

Humming a tune, she scrubbed herself clean. She hated to put the dirty clothes back on, but was conscious of the fact that the lucomo was waiting impatiently outside of door by the irate growls he let out every now and then. She wasn't sure if they were directed at her or someone attempting to access the cleaning room, but she rushed through dressing and hurried out all the same.

His eyes ran over her, and he stepped away from the wall he had been leaning against. His tail snapping behind him as he glowered at a peculiar male with a flat face and oversized pointed ears. The male offered a bow before darting into the room she had just departed.

Well, that explained the growling.

Shoving her hands in her pockets, she trailed at his side. "So, what now?"

"Now we visit the armory and get you some decent gear rather than the scrap you are wearing," he retorted with another critical glance her way.

Diana bristled. "What is wrong with what I have? I picked everything out to be durable and to camouflage as well as possible with the forest."

"They won't protect you in the Eternal Forest."

"You do realize that if you just return me home, you will be saving yourself a great deal of trouble," she advised softly.

The silvanus scowled at her so fiercely that she wished she could take back the observation. Eyes narrowed, he shook his head. "You know very well that isn't possible. I have already told you as much. Whether you like it or not, you are stuck here. You might as well make the best of it and tolerate receiving the gift of gear that few others among your kind would ever have access to. There are many who would covet armor and weapons crafted by the orc tribes and the aelven kingdoms."

"Are you suggesting I am being ungracious?" she sputtered in shock.

"I would say so, yes," he growled. "You know already that you won't be permitted to leave, and instead of inquiring about what you will receive, you protest and attempt to manipulate like a child. Perhaps it would be best to just allow you to go as you are and see how you fare and how well your current belongings protect you against the forest."

Diana flinched, aware that he had a point. "I had to try," she muttered.

"Perhaps," he said. "It is a flaw of your species, that you try to wager and bargain to keep whatever few miserable hours of life that you possess. You don't have the centuries to learn better or to suffer without the respite of death."

Her curiosity was piqued by the gruff words, but she didn't have the nerve to question him further. Instead, she shrugged and stared at the stone walls of the palace, watching the peculiar pod-like bulges light up at their approach.

"I guess I just don't understand why I am necessary. Why can't I just go home and forget all of this existed?"

He frowned at her. "Because this is a threat that spills into your world. Can you so easily dismiss it when you were allotted by fate to protect your world?"

"It is not something I wanted. I was happy with my quiet life," she said.

"Such things are never asked for," he said, a note of sadness to his voice as he seemed to be lost in his thoughts. He shook his head and looked over at her solemnly. "When they come, one must either rise to the occasion or be no better than that which would destroy our worlds. Refusing to act when you have the power to do so is just as evil. As I said before, the oracle did not foresee your purpose in the things to come, just that you have an important part to play. I prefer to hope that your presence is meant as a blessing rather than a curse."

Silence fell between them as she followed him through the labyrinth of the palace until they came to a pair of heavy wooden doors. Diana hated that his words struck a chord within her. She couldn't disagree with him. Human history had proved that point many times over. Although she hated that it took away her choices, she resolved to at least try to help. She didn't know why she had been dumped in the Eternal Forest, but the thought that it might have been to harm their worlds was too painful to consider.

She stepped back to give the lucomo room as he reached forward, gripped the ring handle on one door, and pulled. It was seemingly effortless, but Diana wasn't fooled. She could hear the groan of the hinges and walls as the massive door was pulled open. Revealed within were armor and weapons that seemed to almost glow on their own accord from the small amount of sunlight filtering into the room.

Aware that she was openly gawking, Diana followed the silvanus within. He didn't slow nor pause at any of the impressive displays as they made their way deeper into the room. At long last, he drew up short by a set of black-dyed leathers. With nimble fingers, he untied them from the mannequin base and draped them piece by piece over his shoulder.

Turning to her, he swept a critical gaze over her. "Strip," he commanded.

Diana balked. She wasn't exactly prudish, but she didn't make a habit out of stripping in front of men she didn't know. Not even men who were more spirit or fae.

His eyebrows raised. "Do you require assistance?"

She swallowed and shook her head. Obviously if she didn't get on the ball and do it, he was of the mind to do it for her. Which would be worse: undressing under her own power or being stripped by the silvanus looming in front of her?

A loud sigh filled the room as he looked up at the ceiling. "I forgot. Human modesty," he grunted. "I will keep my gaze on the ceiling until you finish."

Letting out a relieved breath, Diana hastily stripped off her gear and clothing. She hadn't even seen him pick up the soft leather pants and woven green tunic until he offered them to her. The pants were a little large on her frame, obviously designed for a male or a larger species on whom they would have been skintight. That said, it still managed to be snug at her hips. Diana folded up the ends and stuffed them into her boots.

The tunic, however, was surprisingly comfortable and flattering as it draped elegantly to her mid-thigh, but it did little to hide the fact that she lacked a bra. Diana tried not to think of the way her boobs jiggled and her nipples pebbled under the soft fabric.

Her last good bra bit the dust a few weeks ago, and she had not yet been able to find a suitable replacement in her size. Who knew that one of the more trying difficulties she would experience in a post-apocalyptic world was trying to find underwear that fit? Her big breasts made it even harder, and the pickings were even starting to get slim on panties.

"Okay, I am decent," she mumbled.

"Are you now?" he purred. There was a mischievous glint in his eye as he lowered his head and his eyes immediately fell upon her.

He didn't wait for a response. With a satisfied noise in the back of his throat, his eyes took her in. With a snap of his wrist, he opened and immediately wrapped a wide belt around her waist and the upper part of her hips. She really had no idea what the official names for every piece of armor were. Her time with the SCA had been some time ago and, even then, being able to identify armor by the correct names had never had been a priority since she hadn't bothered with most of it, but she did her best to be aware of everything he was strapping onto her so that she would be able to correctly put it back without assistance.

She recognized the leather vest that he laced around her chest, which was followed by a skirt-type piece that protected her thighs, and greaves fastened around her calves. Bracers protected her forearms, and another set that covered most of her upper arms followed them. They were heavy, studded with metal spikes in some places, such as on her upper arms. The larger pieces that protected her shoulders possessed some exceptional metalwork, but she found with a few stretches that she still possessed her full range of movement.

"Better," he said softly before continuing to a large locked case at the back of the armory.

The case was set aside from the rest of the armory, as if whatever it held had a distinguished and special place within the palace. The lucomo approached it, staring at it silently, then pressed his hand against an ornate disc at the front that appeared to serve as an occult lock. There was a flare of light before the mechanism that locked the case tumbled to the floor.

Diana's eyes widened as they fell upon the luminous silver armor that lay in numerous pieces inside. The breastplate and shoulder guard braces were enormous, made for a male of his build. In some ways, the pieces appeared nearly identical to her own. There was even some sort of silvery head piece, resembling a helmet, that appeared to be designed to hook around his antlers. He stroked the breastplate thoughtfully, and Diana wondered what brought the morose look to his face.

CHAPTER 10

Silvas could feel the eyes of the female, Diana, upon him. Even lost in memories of the darkness that had consumed him as he had killed with relish, mowing down all that stood before him as if he were the arm of destruction, he could feel her warmth beckoning him.

He could still hear the wild screams of the Tainted Ones. It had not been like the war of the gods that bound the titans to the new order of the cosmos. The monsters born into their midst, many sired by the monstrous Typhon—the bringer of calamities, lawless chaos, and the great weight of destruction—had ravaged the world until they threatened to very abodes of the gods by the lead of their sire.

He fought those vile creatures as he followed the lead of Apollo, whose venomous arrows spewed death everywhere they touched. There were few among the gods as revered as Apollo, the god whose face and limbs were black as night among the wealth of golden locks that fell along his brow, shoulders unrestrained as he destroyed the monstrous son of the Earth, the Python. By his hands, the blood of the first among monsters flowed wet over the earth. It had been before the time of Cacus, before Alcmene bore Hercules.

If the Tainted Ones were returning, uncoiling from the hidden places beneath the Earth, then the world wasn't ready for it.

He bit back an ugly chuckle as he thought of how Diana had called trolls monsters and wondered if she could fathom what true monsters were. They weren't people who bowed to order, even variations of it like those found among orcs and trolls and other beings who inhabited the worlds. They were true plagues, unholy nightmares possessing rapacious appetites.

He had come close to being lost in that madness in his quest to destroy them and root them out from the Eternal Forest. Those gods who loved his woodlands worked for centuries to root out the terrible stain wherever they found it and enrich the world and the fledgling humankind in the process.

Silvas dropped his hand away from the armor, his lip curling as he reflected on the history of the young race. Some days he considered them the gods' greatest mistake. Yet when he looked upon Diana, he had to admit that not everything of the species could be so bad to have produced her.

"What now?" she asked quietly as if loath to interrupt his introspection.

He supposed that he must appear to be some sort of brute to her if she was so uneasy to speak freely.

Letting out a long sigh, he gestured to weapons displayed on racks near his armor. "You bow serves you well, but arrows run out. You will need a good blade to keep you safe."

Diana looked at the offering skeptically. "I hate to tell you this, but I have never had to depend on a sword in my life. I was in fencing club for about five years and played around with a little bit of reenactment, but I don't know if I would trust it in a real fight. I can make arrows on the go—I've become pretty good at it recently since the world went to hell, actually. Are you sure it will be necessary?"

His lips tightened. She had no idea just how dangerous the first of the perils they were to face would be. Though he had been content to leave his sword with the strix when he received word that she had found it, confident that she would hoard the blade in her roost among her collection talismans and items of magic, he also knew she would not surrender it without a deadly-earnest fight. She would attack without remorse or any sense of loyalty. She would seek the weakest points to exploit. They would both need to be well protected and armed.

"It is good to have a backup that will serve you well," he stated as he began to strap on his armor.

"I take it that we are heading out somewhere?"

He nodded. "The Tainted Ones, true monsters of the world, cannot be killed by these weapons. They will slow them down given that, unlike the weapons of your world, they are crafted with magic. But the sword of Nocis was forged by the mighty god Vulcan himself in the furnaces of his metal-rich mountain. Few have such weapons. To possess such divine tools is a great weight, one that I could no longer bear the burden of after centuries of killing the creatures."

"You have a monster-killing sword made by a god?"

"Had would be the correct word," he said. "I flung it into the wild peaks of Hyperborean Mountains at the northwestern edge of the Eternal Forest."

"And that is a bad place?" she asked.

His lips turned up at the question. "In and of itself, no. The Hyperborean mountains are the border between this realm and the blessed isles that rest between the world of spirits and fae, and that of the dead. Like the Eternal Forest, the mountain range is far vaster than one can imagine. It connects with many sacred boundary mountains over the world. Because of its nature, it is inhabited by unpleasant beings who protect their territory ferociously."

"And you *threw it* there?" Diana gaped adorably at him. She swallowed back her nerves and gamely met his eye. "Is this like a sword in the stone situation? Are we going to have to pull it free from stone or mountainside it imbedded in?"

"Oh, if only it were that simple." He laughed, smile hardening as he crowded closer to the little human and his voice dropped low. "None but I know where it fell," he murmured so quietly that he knew that she was forced to strain herself to hear him. Yet even after so many ages had passed, he didn't trust anyone, not even his subjects, with the secret. "And one other."

Her breath rushed out in a hard gasp as she sighed one word. "Who?"

His gaze dropped to the line of her throat where her pulse raced. Her scent was rich, a complex barrage of conflicting notes that demonstrated the emotions that were rolling chaotically through her. Fear, anger, and the slightest flavor of… *yes*… excitement. He licked his lips, stroking his tongue to capture the flavors from the air and draw them over the more sensitive receptors in his mouth. He longed to stroke his tongue down her throat as well, but this was conversation, not seduction. Not yet, anyway.

Dropping his lips against her ear, he felt her shiver in reaction as he imparted the secret to her. The only one, due to the manipulation of the Fates, who was destined to witness the recovery of Nocis.

"Among the dwellings of the horse-devouring griffins, and great wyrms and dragons, along the lower elevations there lives a strix, one of many scattered throughout the worlds. She is a sorceress, a monstrous owl-like being who dines on the flesh of the mortal races—preferably the very young. In her caverns, she jealously keeps all her treasures, tokens of magic and power. I saw the sweep of her enormous feathered wings as she snatched the sword out of the air. At that very moment, I knew that it would be her greatest of possessions."

Diana jerked back as she met his eyes. "And you just let her have it?"

He shrugged and straightened. "Why not? Did I not just say that she guards her possessions? A strix is no easy conquest. They are not typically among the Tainted Ones, preferring solitude."

"Are you kidding me? You just said she eats children," Diana retorted. "How is that not bad enough?"

"She has stolen far more from the clans of trolls and orcs than from men. You are offended on their behalf? They would be touched to hear it," he commented with no little disbelief.

Her face flushed guiltily but she met his eye, lips pinching with disapproval. "I admit I was thinking more about humans at that moment, but that said, I don't approval of *any* child being eaten."

He lifted his eyebrows. "You certainly honor your namesake on this day. In any case, you do not need to fear. From what I understand, much of her diet is fawns and bear cubs and other creatures that she can easily snatch in her flight. Most figured out long ago how to ward against her. They know that, with the right protections over their home during the night, their little ones are safe from her hunt." He touched his first knuckle to his chin thoughtfully. "Well, it is well known among most species. With the human world being closed off for so long by the gods, it is hard to say how they will fair against any strix that have crossed over."

Diana paled. "Do you think they have?"

"Without a doubt. I imagine that, being a race of sorceresses themselves, they felt the magic of the barrier breaking far more intensely than many beings of this world. I have no doubt they were among the first to invade your world to glut themselves in the wake of destruction."

Silvas watched the human shudder, her eyes wide and lost in the suddenly sickly pallor of her complexion. At that moment, she looked painfully young to him, as her species tended to do even when aged and fading into the last days of their lifespans. Young, fragile, and short-lived. No wonder the gods loved the childlike races as much as they did. Even the many mortal races who possessed only slightly longer lifespans found favor above the immortal and long-lived races.

He scowled, uncertain of how he should be responding. Should he attempt to comfort her? He was not good at such things. Awkwardly, he stretched one arm around her back and gave her a few light pats before pulling away.

It seemed to have done some good because her coloring normalized and the expression on her face was one of confusion, though her lip quivered with amusement. "What was that?"

"An attempt to offer comfort?" he replied uncertainly. Should she have to ask? The gesture was an obvious one.

She chuckled, a small smile blooming on her lips. He was grateful that she spared him any commentary on his effort, though that smile not only failed to endear her to him but was also successful at rousing his ire at the same time. Diana looked at him as if he was the one seemingly helpless and awkward. He was a god in his own right, though not among the high gods. Still, his power and the eons he had witnessed were far beyond her imagination. There was no cause for a human to look at him with pitying amusement.

His scowl deepened as he began to strap belts of weapons to his frame.

"Are you offended?" Diana asked.

He scoffed. "What makes you think that you have the power to rouse so strong a feeling as offense from me?"

She fell silent, and for one blissful moment, he thought that just maybe she would cease speaking of it.

"Have you ever held a baby?"

"No," he muttered.

"A small child?"

"No," he growled with increasing impatience.

"Ever have anyone hug you?"

He attempted to think back. His furthest memories were dulled by time, far removed from him where he only caught echoes if he opened himself to them. He recalled his mother's fingers threading affectionately through his hair and caressing the nubs of his antlers. He was certain that she had hugged him to her breast when he had been young. He had been eager to please her then and ran among the woodlands, spreading lust and desire to renew life as if it were as effortless as breathing. The return of spring had become much more tiring over the ages. Even now, it sapped his strength. Yet in his memories, he didn't recall being embraced.

"Ah."

The wealth of sympathy conveyed in that one word sparked his curiosity. He glanced over at her and directed the full force of his displeasure in her direction as he straightened the last of his belts around him.

"What… do you mean by *ah*?" he bit out.

Diana bit her lip, and he could tell that she was weighing her words.

"I just meant that it is unlikely for someone who hasn't received physical affection to know how to give even simple expressions of comfort."

"I assure you I have known many physical expressions. I did

have a consort for centuries, and although it was ultimately a disaster, it was not lacking in *that* area."

She snorted and rolled her eyes. "We aren't talking about fucking. We're talking about touch without any sort of sexual intent behind it."

He paused, trying to come up with one instance to throw back in her face. To his dismay, he could think of not one. The nymphs touched him to arouse him to fulfill their mutual needs. Even Alseida, whom he had favored above all of them and eventually took as his consort, had not offered touch in such a fashion—and nor had he in return. The closest he got was in sparring with the other males of his kingdom, and even then, the good-natured tussles hadn't been anything he would consider affection.

Despite everything, he was set apart from everyone by who he was.

Silvas grunted and glared down at his belts as he inspected them. He was taken completely off guard when Diana stepped forward.

"This is going to be a bit awkward with all the leather," she said, wrapping her arms completely around him.

Laying her cheek against his chest, he felt his entire being flush against hers, the human warmth filling him at every point of contact. He could feel the steady beat of her heart thrum through him. He relaxed in her embrace until his chin dropped languidly against the top of her head. Distantly, he mused at how she had conquered him, but also found that he didn't care. Peace and contentment swept through him as he felt accepted and cherished in the simple gesture.

Just that easily, the eons seemed to melt away, and he cleaved to her until he finally forced himself away with a shake of his head. His antlers swung in his peripheral vision, and his tail whipped anxiously behind him. He didn't know what had gotten into him, but it wasn't something he could indulge in right now. There was too much at risk.

Diana blinked up at him in confusion, but he turned away from her. He couldn't bear to look at her right now.

"Come on," he snarled. "We have wasted enough time. We depart immediately."

CHAPTER 11

Diana stepped out of the lucomo's way as he stormed by her, her brow furrowed in confusion. For a moment there, something seemed to change between them, and she thought she saw something… Then it was gone, and he was like a stranger to her once more.

She welcomed the silence that fell as she followed him out of the palace into the gloom of the forest. Even over the courtyard gardens, the trees were so thick that they only let stray sunbeams pierce through to the gardens below. She was honestly surprised that everything wasn't dead, but apparently the blooms were shade-loving and, on several plants, their delicate tendrils were covered in dainty heart-shaped leaves. It was quite magical, made even more so by the pixies flitting among them.

Despite the glimpses of beauty, the forest appeared gloomy and dark, though she wondered how much was impeded by her vision. It wasn't quite menacing, but it was so alien from the woods near her home that it made the hairs on her arms prickle beneath the layers of clothing and armor. As they neared a cluster of trees nearest to the garden walls, a burst of pale lights floated around the trees as if released from the tall sentinels into the air.

The lucomo glanced back at her and noticed the source of her distraction as she stared in awe at the lights, trying to work out what exactly they were.

"It is the hamadryads, the souls of the trees. Those that live near the palace release small lights from their root bases as part of their symbiotic relationship with Arx itself, and as an expression of their ecstasy at being so close to it. Sometimes those near the villages of the Eternal Forest can be coaxed to do likewise."

"Arx?" she asked softly.

"The name of the palace. It is alive as much as the hamadryads are."

"They are beautiful," she said. "As is Arx. I have never seen anything like it."

"Nor will you," he agreed. "These things are of the Eternal Forest."

A tiny gasp left her as a luminous green woman seemed to step out of the heart of the tree and dance along the roots, playing in the light. There was something too sharp and inhuman about the structure of the spirit's face, and her hair seemed to wave around her head in a way that appeared unnatural. Even her movements seemed to bend and sway in a way that defied nature.

The green spirit stopped moving, and her head turned toward Diana. The movement was so slow that the eeriness made Diana's heart pound and her mouth go dry as the glowing white eyes seemed to stare right into her. The stillness of the spirit was so absolute that Diana half-believed that it would spring into action.

The hamadryad didn't move. She watched Diana with her unblinking gaze, her head turning marginally to follow Diana's movements. Another hamadryad stepped out and another. Soon the entire wood around the garden were filled with them, each one staring at Diana.

"Interesting," the lucomo muttered in passing but he gave

them no more attention than a curious lingering glance as he stalked forward at an even pace without breaking stride.

As the he neared the corner of the garden hedge that marked the border of the labyrinth of flower beds and ornamental bushes, a massive male, easiest the largest troll she had seen yet, stepped into view. The lucomo apparently expected to see him because his pace increased, leaving Diana to catch up.

"Where are we going?" she asked breathlessly as she struggled to keep up.

His eyes slid over to her and he let out an impatient sound. "We will need to journey far, so we will need mounts that my guard has readied for us." He tipped his head toward the troll waiting for them. "It would be quicker to fly, but you will require rest, and the forest doesn't allow easy access through the canopy. That would be too dangerous for a human. So, we will go for the next most convenient option. Few things in the Eternal Forest are as quick as the crocotta."

"Oh," she said, biting her lip. That he had to make allowances for fragility as a human made her feel like a burden.

He cast a curious glance her way, and his lips tilted in a small smile. "It will also save me the trouble of having to carry my armor, which would be required if I took another form, so it works out well enough."

She nodded absently. That made sense. She could imagine having to carry one's armor while in another form would be frustrating… Wait a minute. Her mouth dropped open as she tripped over a massive root and stumbled to a halt.

"Shapeshift?" she blurted out in disbelief.

The male cast an enigmatic grin over his shoulder but never broke his stride. He really wasn't going to elaborate any further. With a frustrated grunt, she chased after him at a steady jog before coming to a halt some feet away when she got a glimpse of the troll's companions.

Two enormous sandy-colored creatures stood together, yellow eyes staring balefully as they swung their heads in one direction and then another, nostrils flaring. To Diana, they resembled something almost like a hyena, except for the fact that their backs were more level than sloped. They also possessed long, tufted tail trailing behind their haunches. Sandy brown in color with chocolate stripes, they possessed beautiful pelts, the fur around their necks and down their backs particularly long and thick. Yet for all that beauty, they were monstrous. Their massive jaws parted every now and then to reveal teeth the size of her longest finger, the fangs double that.

Neither creature looked friendly. Even compared to the aggressive hyena, these creatures possessed sharper facial structures and a boxier head. It made them look both elegant and lethal. The only sign of domestication about them were the stitched harness saddles made of layered fabrics. Their eyes, striped in hues of yellow and gold, had the look of polished gemstones, gleaming with intelligence as they stared at her and let out low growls. Unnerved by the blatant challenge coming from the predators, Diana inched closer to the silvanus and troll standing close together in discussion.

"Are you certain of this?" the troll asked in a quiet voice, his eyes darting to her suspiciously. "No one knows how she got here."

Diana wanted to laugh. He said it like an accusation. What exactly did he think she was going to be able to do? Especially against the lucomo. She met the troll's stare and raised a polite eyebrow. She didn't want to be creamed by an angry troll, but she was starting to believe that none of those who dwelled at the palace would make an overt attempt to harm her—and if she didn't get too cocky, they likely wouldn't make a covert attempt either when the silvanus didn't have his eyes on them. At least, that was how she was determined to play her guards. She needed to win their respect to be safe among them.

The lucomo growled, a sneer pulling at his lips. "I am not a fool. I have consulted the oracle and trust my instincts on this matter. Physically, Diana is hardly a danger to me. Do not worry, Raskyuil. Even if she had a mind to harm me, I am difficult to kill, lest you forget."

"But not impossible to weaken," Raskyuil retorted. The flash of anger in the lucomo's eyes indicated that the troll had hit on a sore subject. "Without knowing how or why she came to be here, I feel that it would be wise if I went in your company to protect you, as your guard."

"And give the strix even more warning that we are coming?" he scoffed

"You may need the distraction. Your pet human may very well faint at the first sight of the creature rather than be of any true assistance. You can see for yourself that she is no warrior." Raskyuil flung a disdainful hand in her direction.

Diana bristled. She didn't have any supernatural powers, but she was far from helpless. She might not be a significant asset, but she was confident that she wouldn't be as much of a hinderance as he made out.

The troll was such as asshole that he didn't even acknowledge her offense as he continued making his case.

"If not for yourself, then maybe consider for the human. Though I do not trust her and care little for her wellbeing personally, I am sure that you desire her safety. You know how those creatures are," Raskyuil said. "The strix will use any distraction to aid in her attack, including targeting your little human here. If required, we could use it to our advantage. I could slit your pretty human's throat to distract her long enough for you to deliver the blow that will allow you access to her cavern."

A terrible sound burst from lucomo as he stalked toward the troll, the pale orbs of his eyes blazing as the trees shivered, plants rustling and twitching as if threatening to attack. A good head taller than the troll, the silvanus prowled around him, long claws extending from his fingertips. His lips pulled back from wicked teeth in clear warning. Even his hair seemed to float on a current of energy, his black antlers as a void that promised the utter absence of light and life in contrast to the blinding white luminescence he emitted.

Diana shrunk back as she watched the exchange.

"You will not threaten or entertain any idea of harming Diana," the lucomo growled, his voice echoing over itself as he spoke with crackling energy.

From the corner of her eye, Diana could see the vacant-eyed hamadryads approaching, their lips parted and mouths gaping in silent screams. They seemed to thin out, becoming even more wraithlike in appearance as they stepped further away from their trees. Long fingers became skeletal as they reached toward the troll. Diana whimpered low as Raskyuil dropped to one knee. A cold sweat broke out over him as he wilted in the face of the lucomo's displeasure.

"My apologies, lucomo. The suggestion was ill thought of, but only for your benefit. I swear I will not raise a hand toward your human."

The glowing white lucomo's eyes, so like that sightless glowing orbs of the hamadryads in that moment, narrowed. "Swear to me then, Raskyuil, son of Agranok, that you will protect this woman from harm. You will place yourself before her in danger rather than before me. You will treat her with care and consideration as you would bestow upon me."

"I swear it!" the male shouted, his head bowing low as the trees bent their branches toward him, insidious vines creeping forward from among the branches and rising from the ground.

Diana watched their progress in horror as they crept up the male's legs. The trees drew closer as if to swallow him whole.

"Please," she choked out. "Please do not hurt him. He didn't do me any harm, other than a foolish idea bid in a moment of desperation in hope that you would not leave without him."

The lucomo paused, his head tilting as he turned and fastened his eerie eyes on her. "You would stand for him?"

"He is your friend, and obviously loyal to you. This will not earn any trust toward me. He has pledged his vow… Now enough."

His faced darkened, and Diana felt her throat close in fear, certain that she made the matter even worse. The animals whined, their pacing loud over the forest floor. Finally, his eyes drifted close and he sighed.

With that gust of air that expelled from between his lips, the forest settled once more and the vines fell away, releasing Raskyuil. The troll fell to his hands and knees, his entire body shaking as he whispered fervently to himself. He looked at Diana, his expression guarded and wary, but it was perhaps an improvement on the thinly veiled hostility that had been there before. She only hoped that she had planted a seed of trust between them. Either that or she had been a fool to stop the lucomo. She hoped it was the former.

When the lucomo opened his eyes, Diana was relieved to see, as they settled on her, that they were normal again. A confused frown marred his brow. He prowled to her side to stop just in front of her. His stared at her for a time, taking her measure before finally reaching one hand out to trail his fingertips, the claws having retreated, over the delicate skin of her jaw.

"You are small and fragile," he murmured. "Raskyuil is correct about that, but there is no denying great strength in you. Perhaps this is what she saw."

There was no need to ask who "she" was. Diana presumed

that he had to be speaking of the oracle, the woman who convinced him that he needed to drag her along in his tasks—that she was important. Perhaps, even now, Diana was starting to believe it.

He glanced at the troll and grimaced. "You stopped me from doing something regrettable, caught as I was in my instincts. I do not know why they rise so fiercely for you, but you could have used it—could have used me—to your advantage and removed a formidable obstacle that the head of my guard presented. You did not." He took a long, deep introspective breath, his head cocking as his silky white stag ears tilted toward her.

Diana fidgeted under his scrutiny and felt a flush climbing her neck and flooding into her cheeks. She didn't consider it all that remarkable, just the right thing to do. She didn't know how to convey that without sounding weird about it, so instead she shrugged with a small smile.

To her relief, he turned away and approached the troll who had pushed himself to his feet.

"My apologies, friend," the lucomo muttered gruffly, his ears tilting back in expressed discomfort.

To her surprise, Raskyuil nodded, a wry smile curving his lips. "It is expected that one of the forest would follow their instinct. God or mortal, our kind, we denizens of the woods, are vulnerable to them. Perhaps the potential for it dwelled all this time in you most of all. I am honored to witness its first rise in you."

The lucomo smiled in return. "Go retrieve a crocotta while I introduce this pair to Diana."

A smile flashed over Raskyuil's face, and he hurried away as the lucomo pulled her toward the hyena-things.

The animals pricked their ears, their fur bristling at the sight of her. The moment that they saw that the lucomo approached at her side, they immediately settled, their ears relaxing as they whined for attention. He smiled and ran his fingers through the thick fur around their necks before plucking up one of her hands in his and directing her touch on the nearest animal. She was certain that she wouldn't have had the nerve to touch them under her own power if not for him leading the way, directing her every touch and stroke. Pretty soon, his hand left hers, and she had both of her hands buried in the white fur as the animal leaned into her touch.

"What are they?" she whispered in awe, her hand coming up to gently stroke and push away the huge muzzle that shoved into her face.

His smile remained as he watched their interaction. "They are a species called crocotta. In ancient times, lost explorers would enter the Eternal Forest and other worlds and come across some of the creatures who dwell in the various domains where they are not in danger of being hunted to the extreme that they would be in your world. While the crocotta dwell in many places, they are too intelligent to go beyond the borders of the human world unless it is asked of them."

"They are beautiful," she observed. "But obviously deadly predators."

He nodded. "Not only are they strong and intelligent, but their gaze, should their prey get caught in it, has the power to root their victim to the spot to await their death. They are not to be trifled with by any whom they don't accept into their clan. This is Keech," he said, nodding to the crocotta who was currently leaning his massive head into the lucomo's side. "And that is Keena. Keena is the matriarch of my clan, and Keech is her primary mate."

"Your clan?" she asked.

He nodded. "Like most silvani, I have the ability to shapeshift and take on the form of the creatures that inhabit my domain. They recognize me as an important male in their clan and for the most part follow my lead. You cannot shapeshift, but because I introduced you, it appears they have accepted you as well. Keena seems particularly taken with you," he observed. "I have no doubt that she will allow you to mount her. We will leave as soon as Raskyuil returns. I believe he went to retrieve Dagani, their eldest pup. He has favored him since the day he whelped."

Silence fell between them, and Diana hazarded a glance at him and smiled at the look of consternation on his face as he frowned down at the crocotta's fur he stroked beneath his fingers.

"Thank you," she said. He glanced up at her with a perplexed expression, and she laughed. "I mean it. You have done a lot more than you needed to, and I know I haven't been very grateful. You would have hurt him on the smallest suggestion that one loyal to you would kill me. I can't express how much that means, that my welfare has some meaning in a world where I doubt human lives have much value. Thank you, lucomo," she finished as she leaned down to bury her cheek against Keena's pelt.

There seemed to be a softness to his eyes that almost made them appear a pale, velvety gray rather than their usual pearl hue. "Names have power among my people, but I wish to give you mine. You may call me Silvas."

"Silvas," she murmured, and she hid her smile of pleasure within the crocotta's fur.

CHAPTER 12

Riding Keena was an experience. Diana had limited experience in her youth riding horses, but the crocotta's gait was more of a rolling lope. She actually found it comfortable to lean forward against the thick padding at the front of the saddle like Silvas and Raskyuil. Two handgrips on the harness allowed her to cling securely. At first, she worried about her ability to direct them without reins, but she soon discovered that a significant shift in her weight or the grip of her legs conveyed a wealth of commands in addition to the verbal commands that they understood.

Keena raced between the trees as green foliage whipped by them, her sharp pants loud in Diana's ear. The sound was comforting somehow, and Diana was certain that the closer she lay against the crocotta, she could also almost feel the large heart beating and the strong rush of blood through the powerful animal beneath her. Silvas had cautioned that even at the breakneck speed they were traveling at, it would take several days to make it to the Hyperborean Mountains. The hours they would ride would be long, but so far, she was enjoying every minute of it. She had the impression that her mount was enjoying the vigorous exercise too. Keena's mouth gaped wide like an enormous hyena grin. Every now and then, those large ears would turn back toward her as if assuring herself that all was well with her passenger.

Diana had no complaints, although there were times when she was startled by the sudden shifts that had her clinging to Keena's harness for dear life. The crocotta barely slowed to dip low and wiggle out from beneath obstacles, to climb up rocky hillsides, or leap over a fallen log. Though Diana could feel the pressure of her heart lodged in her throat, a dizzying rush of excitement flooded her, joy singing in her blood.

Just ahead of her, she saw Silvas's head turn, the long white lengths of his hair streaming behind him, mixing with the gold dripping from his horns, tangled over his face as he glanced back at her. His long tail was looped around the back of the saddle and curled through one of many small rings that were sewn into the saddle to carry supplies. The shift in his weight, however, made him release his tail. It arched behind him, the tufted end flipping in the air.

She couldn't hold back her grin as she met his gaze. His expression softened, his eyes shining with amusement. The tiny telltale smile tugging at his lips disappeared as Raskyuil made a derisive click in his throat from where Dagani loped at her left. Over the last several hours, she had concluded that the troll was a complete killjoy. Even though she had stuck up for him, he still strenuously disapproved of any unnecessary interaction between her and Silvas.

The moment he had discerned the fact that Silvas had granted her use of his name, he had been all scowls, irritated grunts, and grinding sounds beneath his breath. She wrinkled her nose as she glanced over at him. As far as she was concerned, he would fit in pretty well among the wretched ruins of some of the cities, scraping a living from the wreckage, with that sour personality he possessed.

Silvas turned fully in his saddle to call back to them. "We will be stopping just ahead at the next clearing."

Within minutes, they burst through the trees into a small mossy clearing. There was plenty of hard rock as well, but the moss was at least a small mercy. The crocottas slowed to a walk before drawing to a full halt. The waning evening light dappled everything in shadow. A small stream ran down a carved path in earth and stone, the wet banks providing fertile ground for several spring flowers.

"We could still get several more hours of travel before the dark becomes a nuisance. Why stop now?" Raskyuil asked as he dismounted. A scowl was plastered on his face as he glared at their surroundings.

The lucomo raised an eyebrow as he began to unstrap his armor. "This is a safe place to stop. While even that which is immortal desires rest on occasion, your bodies require it. Given that humans have poorer eyesight, it benefits us to stop now while she still can offer direction to Keena. I can take advantage of this time to scout ahead," he added as he shucked off the rest of his armor.

His clothes were thrown into the discarded pile, leaving the hard, muscular length of his body bare to her vision. Diana's tongue plastered itself to the roof of her mouth. Under all that alabaster skin, his muscles bulged as if here stood one of the ancient marble statues that depicted the perfection of gods. She remembered at least that much from high school.

What she didn't recall seeing was anything like the cock nestled between his muscular thighs. It was nothing like the dick of any man.

It was long and thick, with a pattern of knobs of various sizes that went up its length until it tapered at the head. Even the corona was different. It was fleshier at the top than a human phallus, and it was hard to miss that at the very tip it drew up into a small raised nub. That nub drew her attention until she realized, with considerable embarrassment, that she was staring. Still… What was its purpose? The texture along the shaft was certainly clear enough. It swelled beneath her scrutiny, and she tore her eyes away, heat flooding her cheeks.

Raskyuil frowned as he glanced over at her and back again to Silvas. "What if the lord or mistress of this territory approaches? We will be considered intruders."

"I intend to make my pass through their territory very obvious. If any dare to approach, they will have to contend with me upon my return. No doubt the spirit overseeing this part of the wood is already aware of our presence," he concluded as he tilted his face to the sky, nostrils flaring as if scenting the air.

"Very well," the troll mumbled as he unstrapped his ax from the harness on his back. "I will stay on guard until you return and then we will… *rest*." His lip curled on the last word, as if he were tasting something foul.

Diana was certain that he blamed her for this new inconvenience. She didn't particularly care at that moment since she was more interested in watching Silvas's body darken and reform into that of an ivory griffin. The twin crests of plumage over his ears lifted before flattening once more. He flexed his massive wings twice before leaping into the air, his wings beating furiously as they took him up into the sky. Transfixed, she watched as the lucomo flew higher, shrinking off into the distance. When she finally dropped her gaze, she discovered that Raskyuil was still watching her sourly.

Well, at least he wasn't suggesting murdering her anymore as an answer to a potential obstacle. Diana drew a heavy green cloak around her body as she unstrapped her bow from her harness and leaned it against a tree alongside her quiver. The belt that sheathed her shortsword followed next, along with the knives that were strapped around her thighs.

Once free of the weight from her weapons, Diana leaned against a large stone, half sitting on one sloped side, as she returned Raskyuil's stare. She cleared her throat, but flinched as a tiny dragon-like creature with gossamer wings, no bigger than her palm, zipped by. She opened her mouth to give voice to her awe when she saw the troll still staring at her, possibly looking less impressed and even grumpier than before.

"I appreciate you no longer suggesting my untimely demise," she offered in an attempt to break the ice.

"Are you mocking me?" he growled.

"No. Just expressing my genuine appreciation over the matter. I would like to survive all of this and return home in one piece, thanks."

His brow lowered, but his expression shifted to one of speculation. "You do not intend to remain with the lucomo?"

"Uh, I'm not sure where you got *that* idea. We're temporary travel companions because fate has a fucked-up sense of humor. As far as I understand, as soon as he finishes with me, Silvas is returning me back to my home."

His lips quirked in an unpleasant smirk, his dark eyes hard as they narrowed on her. "You are either foolish for believing that, or quite conniving to make a convincing show of it. I can assure you that your presence in the Eternal Forest will be for considerably longer than you believe."

Diana stiffened at his condescending tone. "The lucomo gave me his word that he would escort me himself once he no longer had need of me."

"That is an open-ended contract if I ever heard one," he said as he unfastened a canteen from his side and tipped back the contents. His thick neck worked as he swallowed. With a smack of his lips, he lowered the canteen and belched. "I wager that you will be remaining by the lucomo's side."

She wrinkled her nose, ignoring the comment as she stared with interest at his canteen. "That's not water in there, is it?"

A grin split his face. "There is a necessary percentage of water that was required during fermentation."

"Beer?" she asked. It had been a long time since she enjoyed a good Bud.

"Of course," he returned. "I brew it myself." He paused, no doubt seeing the longing that she felt twist through her. One thick, dark eyebrow rose. "I might be persuaded to share it with a fair bargain."

It could be hot and stale, and she would still drink it like it was ambrosia. She was so tired of water and the rare treat of fruit juice. Someone in town had started a cask of wine, but this crop of grain was considered too valuable to waste on brewing. Still, call her suspicious, it sounded a little too convenient.

Diana's eyes narrowed. "Like what?"

"That you will leave when we return to the palace. I will find you an escort back to your world. I can't guarantee where you will arrive, but at least you can find your way home."

Her brow fell. She should have known it would be something like that. "Fuck you. I gave my word to Silvas, and I will not go back on it."

She thought she saw something like grudging respect in his eyes, but Raskyuil shrugged and took another long swallow. "More for me," he retorted as he wiped his mouth on the back of his wrist.

"I hope you choke on it," she mumbled as she turned away, focusing on the sky. Maybe she would get lucky and whatever creature inhabited this section of the forest would come out and clobber him for being such a dick.

Probably the only circumstance she could think where she would actually be grateful to see another frightful spirit guardian. She might even have considered thanking it afterward.

An aggrieved sigh cut through the air.

"Take the beer," Raskyuil grumbled.

She glanced at him in surprise and licked her lips as she accepted the canteen that he thrust toward her. "I don't suppose that it's cold…"

He snorted, but the corner of his mouth lifted in an expression that looked something like a half-smile, amusement glittering in his dark eyes. "Of course it's cold. I'm no fool. Had this bespelled by a goblin witch to keep the contents always cooled. It was well worth the fee. It was only a minor inconvenience providing the head of her enemy in trade. Turned out to be a male from my gambling circle, but it is no great loss. The twerg was a cheating bastard, anyway."

"Twerg?" she asked as she took a huge swallow of cold, hoppy beer. She nearly purred in pleasure.

He pinched his chin thoughtfully. "Ah, yes. I believe you humans call them dwarves now."

"You killed a dwarf?" she asked.

She didn't know why, but she had expected something a bit less… humanoid. Like an annoying animal or something. Though she supposed in context it made better sense. It still disturbed her. Was it that easy for beings who inhabited the forest to indiscriminately kill each other? If that were the case, she was definitely better off getting out of the Eternal Forest as soon as possible. Her world wasn't a safe either, especially not if everything that Silvas said about creatures leaving the forest and other worlds to inhabit the human plane were true, but returning there seemed the smarter option.

The troll shrugged as she handed him back the canteen. "From what I understand, he had it coming for some time."

The laws and reasoning of those of the Eternal Forest were going to take some getting used to.

CHAPTER 13

Silvas flew high above the forest, his wings pumping around him as he peered at the landscape rolling beneath him. The forest stretched off into the distance until the trees finally gave way to mountains that jutted up against the sky. The Hyperborean Mountains were the purest white. A human would probably look at it and think that they were looking at snow, but it was really due to the blinding color of the quartz deposits in the mountain. Aquilo, the lord of the north wind, had his palace somewhere along those slopes.

Although he had passed by the outer limits of the impassable mountains once, he had never ventured upon the heights. He never had the desire. He hissed at the idea of having to breach unfamiliar terrain to hunt out Nocis. If possible, he would have left the sword in the company of the strix for all eternity. Unfortunately, it was that sort of thinking that had made his task now all the more difficult. Silvas couldn't ignore the fact that his reluctance to chase after Nocis had unnaturally extended the life of the strix guardian.

His stomach twisted with revulsion. The strix were long-lived, easily living a full century, but sustained by the sword, this strix, glutted on its power, would have lived eons. He couldn't even imagine how terrible she would be, how corrupt and twisted with the dark magic of the sword clutched in her nest.

Shaking his head with an irritated growl and a click of his beak, Silvas turned his attention back to the forest below. The trees were calm and undisturbed. He hadn't expected anything different. Most fauns and silvani would have recognized his movement through their territories. It would stop them from spying on him out of curiosity, but they wouldn't offer him or anyone in his company any harm. Once he entered the mountains, however, he would have to be on his guard. He was thankful that Raskyuil had insisted on accompanying them, even if the reason was misguided.

Tilting his wings, he turned through the air until he circled around. As he reoriented to head back to camp, a shimmer among the trees caught his attention. He cocked his head, his binocular vision zeroing in on the disturbance, when there was a ripple as if something large was in the branches, forcing them to bow under the weight. He considered circling around again to investigate when the ripple sped forward at alarming rate—heading to where he had left Diana with Raskyuil.

Thundering a cry in his wake, Silvas streaked through the air after whatever was plowing through the canopy below him. It was the only warning he would give. The deep, crashing sound of his battle scream was unlike the sharper, piercing shrieks of actual griffins. The pulsing energy within his voice never failed to alert those within the forest to his presence. Whatever it was, the creature moving through the trees was not reacting in the way it should. It did not slow or change direction in deference to his command for it to stay away. Nor did it behave in the normal ambling way of a wild animal within his forest. This was an intelligent creature, moving in a strike pattern from a distance now that he was separated from the female.

It was intentionally moving in closer to her, preparing to attack.

His temper, seldom roused, struck through him like a terrible viper. The faster he streaked through the sky, the greater his fury climbed as the brush below shook. Every shake of the tree limbs was followed by the darkening of the leaves, as if they'd been touched by something foul. Dropping down lower to the trees, Silvas drew back his head in disgust as a horrible smell battered his nose. The pungent scent of something rotting clung to area of the forest where the creature had passed. He wanted to gag at the putrid scent, but dropped lower into the trees.

Whatever it was that made that smell, it was not natural. It did not belong in *his* forest!

He searched for any sign of the guardian of this forest. There should have been some reaction. Something was not right. No silvanus would allow taint into his woods!

Folding his wings, Silvas dropped into the trees.

CHAPTER 14

Diana stepped over a log, her nose wrinkling as she picked her way through the brush looking for firewood. Raskyuil was just a few feet away, hefting a large log onto his shoulder. *Showoff.* At this rate, he would be done with his part of their shared task before she started. Of course, she was the one who agreed to grab the smaller sticks. Who knew that they would take twice as long to find?

Truthfully, it would be going much faster if she weren't distracted by a nagging discomfort that began after Silvas left and a putrid smell that seemed to get thicker. What the hell *was* that, anyway? She couldn't even put her finger on exactly what it was. It didn't quite smell like something had died, but it had the overpoweringly sweet scent of rotting flowers and vegetation with a hint of something foreign that made her stomach turn.

Gagging, she called over to Raskyuil. "Do you smell that?"

The troll cocked his head in confusion. Dumping his burden near the space that they had cleared of brush and lined with stones to serve as a firepit, he frowned and headed toward her. Within a few feet of her, she knew it hit him from the way his nostrils flared.

"By the gods, that is foul," he grunted as he curled his lip in disgust.

"What do you suppose it's coming from?"

"I don't know. Whatever it is, from what I can tell it is coming from just north of us… and it's getting stronger." He tensed as he drew a large blade.

That was not a good sign.

Diana froze, clutching the firewood to her chest with one arm as she allowed her hand to drift down to the shortsword at her hip. Several trees in the near distance shook violently, some bending and snapping as they crashed to the forest floor. Something approached at great speed. The dense foliage seemed to obscure whatever was traveling through the branches, but whatever it was… it was huge. With another large crack and an unearthly moan, everything went still.

The absolute silence made Diana's skin crawl. No bird calls, only the soft hum of a few insects.

"Raskyuil?" she whispered.

"Move away," he hissed as he began to slowly back up. "It may just be a silvanus or faun toying with us, but we will not take any chances. Be prepared for anything."

Nodding, she dropped the firewood as she stumbled to the side. Pulling her sword free, she ducked down into the bushes, her attention trained on the trees ahead. Her breath came out in short pants as she watched and waited. From the corner of her eye, she could see the way that the troll seemed disturbed. His head whipped from side to side as he shifted.

He didn't even glance at her as he whispered, "Diana, get to Keena and head west to the southern foothills of the mountains. We will catch up and reroute. Go now."

Diana wanted to protest, but his tone brooked no argument and sent her spinning around. With a leap, she cleared a fallen tree and sprinted back to the clearing. Her arms pumping, she pushed her muscles to their full exertion. Behind her, she could hear Raskyuil roar. She turned her head only slightly, just in time to see the brush near her snap in her direction.

Crying out in alarm, Diana flung herself to the side, barely dodging a long, thick whip of muddy-colored scales that would have slammed into her chest had it struck seconds earlier. In the distance, she heard Keena's peculiar warbling call. The sound of brush breaking as the crocottas charged forward was loud, but not as loud as the unholy shriek behind her.

Diana rolled over, her eyes widening in horror as a shadow loomed, dropping down through the canopy of the trees. What could only be described as a massive wingless dragon lowered its upper body as it descended to hang just above the ground. It had spines running down its body from the back of its head that seemed to terminate at some point before reaching the tip of its tail. Its fangs were nearly as tall as her as it opened its huge maw, saliva stretching between its jaws in a fashion that set it apart from reptiles as it loosed another horrifying shriek.

Raskyuil raised his sword, turning toward her with bleak eyes as he shouted only one word.

"*Wyrm!*"

Rising to her feet, she stared as its red eyes focused on them. The color nearly matched the finned webbing between the first dozen spines and the fanned spikes at the sides of its head like enormous ears.

"What the fuck is a wyrm?" she shouted back. Fear rose like an ugly specter in her mind as she took in its features. Its head bore no true resemblance to a natural serpent. It had the shape of some sort of dragon, though lacking refined beauty and possessing far more brutality. "Is it a kind of dragon?"

"No," he grunted as he dodged its massive head when it came crashing through the brush toward him. Diana's breath lodged in her throat, happy to note that he managed to escape its attack unscathed. He brought his sword down, but its head snapped back up, taking chunks of the earth and greenery back into the air before they gradually dropped away.

Withdrawing into the trees above, its eyes lit up with predatory hunger as it hung still in the canopy. Diana watched as Raskyuil slid further away in an obvious bid to draw its attention. He continued to speak, no doubt to keep the wyrm's attention focused on him. It seemed to work, because its head turned, following his movement.

"They only superficially appear similar to dragons," he retorted with what sounded like a hint of disdain. "They aren't creatures of magic, nor are they noble and wise as most mature dragons tend to be. A wyrm is intelligent, but only enough that it makes them formidable and destructive predators. Be on your guard and watch for the moment."

She choked, shaking her head as she stared at the creature. She couldn't leave him to face that thing alone now that she had seen it. In the blood red orbs of its eyes, there was no compassion or curiosity, only hunger—an insatiable need to destroy them.

The muscles in its neck tightened as it drew its head back in preparation to attack. At the last moment, however, it jerked higher in the trees with an angry scream as Keena leaped from the brush. Keech was right on her heels with Dagani close behind, and together they lunged toward the massive serpent, vicious teeth snapping and tearing at the enormous scaled body. Though the wyrm had retreated too far for the crocotta to get ahold of it, three muzzles were soon bloodied from the bites they managed before the creature concealed its enormous bulk in the trees once more.

Diana stepped to the side; her eyes fastened on the creature as she edged her way around. Her foot struck something, sending it tumbling to the side with a hollow clatter. Shooting a glance down, her throat tightened with a restrained scream as she saw the inhuman skull peering up at her from within the gap. It almost looked humanoid, except the bone structure was sharper and it still had a mouthful of sharp teeth. The bone looked almost crystalline. Even more telling was that there was no sign of rotting flesh like there should have been.

She probably would have felt better—though perhaps more revolted—if it had been a recognizable human skull decaying in the woods. This skull was almost worse in all its perfection just because it was so divorced from the familiar. Its presence sent an ominous awareness through her. If this being couldn't escape whatever had killed it… what chance did she have now? Had the wyrm laid it low, too?

She flinched as Raskyuil darted to her side, his thick gray fingers closing around her arm as he yanked her out of the way. The wyrm's massive head shattered the trees around them as it lunged, risking the crocotta to attack. Their warble was loud seconds before the wyrm screamed, its body jerking as blood sprayed everywhere. The troll hunched over her, protecting her despite the way he was currently glowering down at her.

"What are you doing?" he snarled. "You should have left while I had it distracted."

She shook her head and pointed down.

The troll stilled before an oath ripped out of him. He yanked her to her feet and pulled her further away from the reach of the wyrm, his eyes fixed upon it. The creature seemed to watch them back, and Diana felt a shudder run through the troll which did nothing to reassure her.

"That is why we did not encounter the silvanus of this territory," he stated hoarsely. "The wyrm killed him and took over. We are in very real danger. We must run while the crocotta protect our backs for as long as they can."

Diana shot him a panicked look. She had to shout to be heard over the chaotic warbling of the Keena, Keech, and

Dagani between their vicious snarls. "I thought silvani are immortal!"

Raskyuil growled as he ran, dragging her behind him. "They have long lives and don't age, but they can be destroyed. It takes considerable effort, but not as much as going against one of the greater spirits, or the lucomo himself. If this thing killed a silvanus, we are utterly without protection. We are fucked—do you get that, human?"

The tail of the wyrm smashed through the trees, ripping Diana's attention back to the monster, her scream at the unexpected action catching in a painful gurgle in her throat. Her fingers tightened around the hilt of her blade as she drew it and swiped defensively at the flesh as they ducked away from its reach.

The wyrm's shriek was closer as trees rattled and snapped overhead. Diana felt her heart surge within her breast and her stomach twist. The overpowering foul scent wafted from it as it broke through. Raskyuil growled and shoved her away as he raised his sword against the creature. He stabbed his blade shallowly into its neck as it plucked him from the ground in its powerful jaws. She could hear him bellow in pain, his blood falling upon her.

Tears of terror streaking down her face, she charged forward to slash through the skin of its thick neck with her blade. The blood that splattered her burned her skin, but she ignored it as she continued to drive her blade deep.

The wyrm let out a keening howl of pain as it dropped its prey, its body thrashing, ripping her sword from her grip as the wyrm tore away from her, wrenching her arm painfully. Diana cried out as Raskyuil hit the ground hard, his shattering moan of pain almost inaudible beneath the noise of the wyrm. Tears blinded her as she clutched her arm to her chest. When her vision cleared, she was relieved to see her blade was still buried within its flesh and that, despite all its flailing, the wyrm could not dislodge it.

With the creature weakened, the crocotta didn't hesitate to descend upon it, their massive, powerful jaws opening wide as they tore large chunks of flesh from the creature's body. Enraged with pain, it whipped its torso, shaking the crocotta loose and sending them flying into the trees, yelps ringing through the air. The wyrm swung its attention to her, its mouth opening wide in a screech as it slid its huge girth toward her.

An angry roar cut through the air, like that of lion with an overtone of an eagle's righteous cry. Jerking her head up, she saw a white griffin drop through the trees like a missile, claws digging into the wyrm's huge face in fierce assault.

Diana crawled over to Raskyuil. He was alive, though he was bleeding copiously from several places. He grimaced as she leaned over him.

"I'm okay," he grumbled. "Don't go looking all teary over me, female." He pushed himself to his feet. He stumbled before regaining his balance as he pulled a smaller sword free from his belt. "The one time I remove my ax is the time I end up missing it the most."

Diana unsheathed two long daggers. She definitely shared that sentiment as her mind strayed to her bow that was lying within feet of his ax in the small clearing of their camp, and her sword that was lost to the wyrm. All she had left were her smaller blades, but she would be damned if she would be an easy meal.

She would help Silvas in any way she could to defeat the creature.

CHAPTER 15

The shriek of an enormous wyrm shook Silvas. Many ages had passed since he last heard the ravenous sounds of a wyrm awoken from the depths of the earth, and even now he could not tolerate the presence of the creatures in the Eternal Forest. There were all manner of serpentine beings and spirits that inhabited the worlds, many of them blessed and powerful, some of them terrible, but the wyrm was the foulest of all.

And it was heading straight for the camp where he had left Diana and Raskyuil.

Silvas increased his speed. His wings beat through the air and he drew his limbs tight against his body to lessen the drag, but he knew it was not enough. Any attempt to overcome the wyrm was doomed. It simply had too much of a head start.

His wings shook and he nearly fell from the sky when a completely alien fear swelled within him. It was so strong that he could almost hear Diana's cry rip through him as the tang of her terror touched his tongue. Instead of desiring more of it, he recoiled as it soured in his senses. That had never happened before, but he didn't have the luxury to analyze it. Not yet, when his skin wished to split and peel away at the wave after wave of strong emotion sweeping over him.

In the chaos that flooded through him only one thing was certain—and he clung to it as an anchor. *I must get to Diana.*

Folding his white wings, he dropped from the sky, opening his feathers to control his descent as he plummeted through the trees. He stretched his talons out in front of him, preparing to strike as the branches dropped away and he got a clear shot at the scaled head of the beast. Snapping his wings open at last moment, he dug his talons into the wyrm's face, tearing through the hard-plated scales. As he clung to it, he was surprised at how disoriented the creature appeared to be as it thrashed with cries of rage rather than focusing its attacks on him.

The powerful creature appeared almost pitiful as it writhed. If it weren't for the obvious stench of taint to it, he might have some sympathy for it. There was something very wrong with this wyrm. Something that brought it into the Eternal Forest from the mountains. Everything about the creature ran contrary to its nature—even the way it rushed through the trees in a frenzy.

He would be merciful to give it a swift ending.

Dropping his beak, he ripped off the protective ridged scales from around the eyes to render them vulnerable to his assault.

Wings stretched open and flapping to aid his balance, Silvas dug his claws deep into the wyrm's hide. Once his seat was assured, he used his talons to pry out first the left red eye and then the right, each punctuated by a terrible scream.

Even blinded, the wyrm turned its head in an attempt to bite Silvas with its venomous fangs as he flapped away. It snapped as Raskyuil plunged his sword deep in the creature's belly. The wyrm rolled away, and as it did so, it turned its head and exposed the hilt of Diana's blade resting flush against the skin behind its jaw, piercing the back of its brain.

Pride filled him at the sight. No wonder the wyrm had been

disoriented. The aelven-crafted blade had located a vulnerable spot between the scales and sunk deep for its mistress. Glancing down at Diana as she danced around the creature armed with nothing more than two daggers, he wanted to smile, the mouth of a griffin not flexible enough to give much in the way of expression.

He believed that his huntress would want her sword returned to her.

Diving toward the silvery hilt, Silvas wrapped his talons around it and wrenched it free as he shot back into the air. Blood and slimy wet bits of what he assumed to be brain matter burst free from the wound with the removal of the blade. He didn't pay it any mind as he winged his way back to Diana. Circling above her, he allowed the sword to drop from his claws to the ground a short distance from her as he released a sharp bellow. As he predicted, it drew her attention and she scrabbled forward, yanking the blade from the dirt that it had sunken into on impact. The smile she rewarded him made his crest feathers fan with pleasure as he wheeled around and dropped to attack the wyrm again.

As he attacked the dripping wound at the back of the beast's head, his talons and beak cracking and breaking the hard planes of the skull, the wound widened. He was aware of Diana stabbing into its belly and the soft underside of its jaw whenever it dropped its head to defend itself. Every strike produced a new wound, releasing more of its essence, weakening it little by little.

Raskyuil, who had until that moment been targeting the belly with his blade, grinned with battle lust. Free to attack elsewhere, he darted along the side of the serpent, looking for his opening. When the creature dropped its head again, he took his opportunity. The troll jumped upon the horned snout of the wyrm as he pulled himself higher on the ridged brow. Lifting his sword high, he stabbed a weak spot between its orbital sockets at the center of the skull.

The crunch of breaking bone announced the death of the wyrm. With one last brittle sound, it pitched forward, crashing through the trees and brush. Its tail gave one last terrible whip through the air as death seized it.

Touching down once more on the ground, Silvas regained his natural form, his eyes trained on the wyrm as he studied it. On closer inspection, it showed signs of magical mutation. There were many more horns and ridges on its face, its snout almost grotesque in its unnatural transformation.

"What is this?" Diana asked.

He noticed that she was intentionally not looking in his direction as she posed her question and guessed that was due to his nudity. Instead, she jerked her chin to the ground, where her foot kicked the sludgy remains of one of its eyes to reveal the brilliant red gem that served as the lens of the creature's eye. Her breath caught in fascination.

"It almost looks like a ruby."

He cocked his head, studying her as she picked up first one and then the other, pocketing both lens stones. "It is valuable for its magical properties, but it is not a ruby, though it may be similar due to the nature of the wyrm."

With the frenzy of battle still burning in his blood, all he wanted was to sink deep into her body, to satisfy and burn out the flames roused within him in her arms and the tight fit of her cunt. He licked his lips. His cock was already swelling as he imagined spending his passion with her.

"I don't need to see that, Silvas," Raskyuil grunted in a weary voice as he limped toward them, his expression pained. "There is only one hard dick I am of a mind to look at, and that is my own."

Diana made a sound of distress as she stepped toward the troll and ducked under his arm to help shoulder his weight. "I knew you were hurt," she accused.

"Just a minor flesh wound," he grunted with a slight wheeze.

"Hold onto those wyrm stones. It's smart that you grabbed them. You never know when you might need something to barter. I am certain that a witch in your world will give you plenty for it. Been ages since there's been a wyrm there."

"I'll be sure to keep your sage advice in mind should I happen to locate a witch," she said as she shouldered more of his weight when the male groaned.

Silvas narrowed his eyes on Raskyuil with displeasure as he noticed the extent of the male's injuries. Deep gashes from the short spines on the wyrm's tail cut into his chest and abdomen, but they were not nearly as bad as the puncture wounds along his torso. The troll noted his scowl and chuckled weakly.

"Don't look too worried, Silvas. It got ahold of me and it hurts like a bitch, but thankfully it didn't have its fangs fully extended when it plucked me up. I'm not envenomated."

"That is fortunate," Silvas grunted. "Regardless, you need to a see a healer. Your crocotta will return you to Arx at once." He held up a hand as the troll's face hardened. "I will not yield on this. You *will* return." He held Raskyuil's gaze until the troll lowered his head in submission to his will. Good. He didn't have the time or patience for any foolishness. "I need you at your best, my friend," he said as he stepped away. Turning his head, he called for Dagani and followed the crocotta's name with a low vocalized warble.

There was no response.

Silvas frowned and repeated the call. He had seen the signs of the crocotta attacks all over the body of the wyrm. He had little doubt that it contributed to their successful slaying of the wyrm. His frowned deepened as Raskyuil joined him at his side.

"You should be resting," Silvas growled low in his throat.

The troll wrinkled his nose in response. "I'm not about to keel over any time in the near future. Besides, I've known Dagani since the day he was born. He's never failed since his whelping to answer to his name. I am coming to look for him even if I have to drag myself."

Silvas held back an exasperated sound and strode forward. "If you insist."

At his other side, he heard Diana's light steps as she joined them.

"They dropped after the wyrm threw them from its back. I know I heard Keena yelp," Diana said. "I think they were thrown somewhere over there."

She gestured to a shady area within a thick copse of trees. Nodding his thanks, he strode toward the trees as he repeated the call, first to Dagani and then to Keech and Keena. The mated pair answered him, though there was something subdued about their usual excited cry.

Silvas broke through the tight cluster of trees, sorrow filling him as his eyes landed on his crocottas. Keena and Keech appeared unharmed, their bodies pressed close around Dagani, who lay crumpled at the base of one tree. Dam and sire lifted their heads at his approach, and Keena dropped her head again to nudge her pup forlornly.

Kneeling beside them, ignoring the hard carpet of bramble beneath his knees, Silvas bowed his head, his dark antlers lowering as his white hair swept over his shoulders in respect. Reaching forward, he stroked one hand down the male's side, and then again. He continued to stroke him even as he willed the forest to reclaim what remained. He had done so thousands of times, easing suffering in his domain, seeding life with the remains of death. Centuries of witnessing the cycle though being separated from it. This loss was perhaps as close as he would get.

Just behind him, he could hear Raskyuil's choked, hard breath even as Diana freely wept. He latched onto their grief, allowing himself that outlet. He who had never truly understood or known grief, or any deep emotion, born as he was among the eternal ones, remained untouched by the living world and never truly knew the bonds of love. This was as close as he got to knowing love and showing it to another.

Despite that, through the spark of instinct that he had been trying to ignore, he felt and tasted the complexity of Diana's sorrow. It coiled through him, squeezing his heart and blocking his breath. His hands trembled, and beneath his palm the body slowly faded into the earth. That done, he stood and looked over at his companion and was startled when two wet drops slipped out of his eyes to trail down his cheeks.

Raskyuil, though battling his grief, looked at Silvas in shock as his eyes tracked the path of the tears.

Hardening his jaw, Silvas glanced once more toward the remaining crocottas, summoning them to his side with a low click, before giving his order. "Return to Arx with Keena and Keech so that they may be in the comfort of their clan, after which you will see the healer and see to your own recovery."

"Please reconsider," the troll replied gruffly. "This journey has barely begun, and already there has been loss to unexpected dangers. At least return the human with me so you can travel unimpeded."

"You know I cannot," Silvas said as he held the male's gaze. "These things must be done as fate wills."

Raskyuil let out a harsh sigh as he turned his head toward Diana. "You keep watch, girl, and return safely. Both of you."

Running his hand over his head, he grunted in resignation and approached Keech. Though the male crocotta's head hung with grief, his ears pricked forward once he was turned in the direction of the palace. The crocottas warbled softly to each other. Although they didn't have a language in the formal sense, Silvas understood the desire the communicated between them. Though they cried for their offspring, they were eager to return to their den, their young, and their clan.

At Raskyuil's command, they sprung forward, their tails whipping behind them as they broke into a fast lope. They soon disappeared into the gloom of forest as the sun sank behind the mountains.

A sound at his side drew Silvas's attention to the human who remained in his company. Her arms were laden with wood, and she gave him a small smile. As quickly as she seemed to have found the wood, he understood how the wyrm had come upon them so woefully unprepared and away from their most effective weapons.

"I'm sorry about Dagani," she said as she stepped closer to him.

"Thank you," he replied as he stepped away from her.

The words were sharp as they dropped from his lips, and predictably Diana recoiled, her lips tightening as a flush crawled up her cheeks. She didn't attempt to move any closer, and a strained silence settled between them, replacing the heat of intimacy that had burned in the air earlier.

Silvas felt the bite of regret, but it was necessary. What he experienced at the death of Dagani was still raw and unsettling. More so what it meant for him. Things had changed between him and Diana in a way he had not anticipated. He needed the space to think clearly. Searching for firewood to keep his human from getting chilled was a good distraction.

It didn't take him long to find the logs that Raskyuil had dropped when they were attacked. Their arms laden with their respective burdens, they made their way in the same direction the crocotta had gone as they returned to camp, a strange silence stretching out between them.

CHAPTER 16

Diana frowned at the silvanus lying on a mossy log at the opposite side of the fire. He had stripped off his armor and lay in nothing more than his pants, the sculpted muscles of his chest and abs bare as he stared up at the leaves above them. She knew that he had to be grieving, because somehow she felt a strange echo of it within her own heart. But there was no knowing by looking at him. Silvas's face was flat, expressionless, and beautiful in an otherworldly sort of way that was equally terrifying. He was inhuman, and yet in the flickering light of the fire he could have passed for a marble creation from the masters of old. He left no clue as to what he was thinking or feeling, and she didn't even know how to broach the subject as he had made it clear that he wasn't interested in receiving any comfort.

It was a change from the hungry stares as they stood beside the carcass of the wyrm. As he had stood there, naked and aroused, she had been tempted by the responding heat in her own blood. Diana had been aware of an echo of his presence moving beneath her skin as if he were already moving within her, exciting her need. But that was before.

Diana turned her gaze toward the flames, trying not to think of it as she burrowed deeper into the warmth of her cape.

This is so awkward.

At least the air no longer stank like the wyrm. After they had gathered the firewood, Silvas returned alone to take care of its corpse so it wouldn't attract any predators to feed on its diseased flesh. That it had so easily dispatched the silvanus who protected this part of the forest was going to give her nightmares. She couldn't stay awake forever, especially not with the distance they had to go tomorrow.

With a grimace, she settled into a bed of old leaves and soft grass and mosses and tried to get comfortable. Yet, as she looked up at the leaves, they appeared to be like moving shadows above that reminded her so much of the wyrm that anxiety rolled off her in waves and her thighs and arms tensed.

"Go to sleep," Silvas muttered, the interruption of his deep voice through the silence startling her.

He had to be kidding. There was no way she was going to be able to sleep when every stir in the forest made her think of the wyrm. Even closing her eyes, fear surged through her that another would come upon her while she was unaware and snap her up in its jaws before she even had a chance to wake.

The lucomo sighed. "I can taste how strong your fear is from here. As sweet as its flavor may be, you require rest."

Grateful for the distraction, she rolled her eyes. "Why do you keep saying that? You realize enjoying the flavor of my fear makes you sound just as bad as any of the tainted monsters you speak of."

He raised an eyebrow, his glowing eyes cutting to her. "How so? Does my enjoyment harm you in anyway?"

"No, but terrorizing people is cruel… What if someone had a heart condition? Besides, some of the species out here eat flesh. You admitted it. I really can't see the difference," she said.

"Can't you?" he asked as he rolled to his side, his eerie eyes staring through the flames at her. "Everything within the forest obeys the laws set forth within nature by the gods of the cosmic order, the highest of the gods whose very being make the succession of life possible. Even destruction and periodic dissolution of laws is part of that fundamental order necessary for growth. The Tainted Ones, however, thrive on chaos. It is not a matter of what is perceived to be right or wrong, nor what is pleasant or unwelcome to humans. Many spirits enjoy strong emotion and energy without causing harm, just as much as we enjoy the smoke of burnt offerings. Those that would harm you I suggest you stay clear of. In the end, however, it is about what threatens the very cosmos and violates the cosmic laws set forth in nature."

"I can't say that the cosmos or any god in particular gives a shit about the human race from what I've seen," she said. "Our world is completely destroyed."

His laughter broke through the dark, and for one shining moment, a smile lit up his face. "Ah, the human assumptions again." He clucked his tongue at her and shook his head with a playful pout, his ornaments swinging against his antlers. "Poor humans, your civilization has toppled like it has continuously over millennia, to make room through destruction for change so that something new can come forth. No doubt there was some god who fundamentally set the events into motion as their duty, but there have been gods and spirits that have intervened as it was their purpose. The rise of Tainted Ones, however…" He paused and frowned. "This is unprecedented and disturbs me. It can only mean that there are great changes to come that will be felt through the cosmos. Perhaps they have already begun, and I just didn't see it for what it was at the time."

He fell silent and lay back once more, his brow knitted in a puzzled frown.

"And the wyrm…?" Diana asked. "Are they one of the tainted

creatures? Raskyuil seemed to consider them more like highly intelligent beasts. Just how fine is the line between what's tainted and what's not?"

"Many of the beasts and mortal beings, even ones with long lifespans, can become tainted. It is a fundamental corruption that begins at their core. For those who are sentient, it is more difficult. There needs to be a seed of darkness within them. Once they are tainted, it eventually wipes away the blessings of the gods, and they are forced to feed upon souls to sustain themselves. It makes them stronger, and those who have glutted themselves no longer age. Some of the worst among them cannot be killed but must be trapped and put into slumber."

Diana shot up to a seated position and gaped at him. "Are you saying that people can become infected and turn into immortal monsters—like fucking vampires?"

"The analogy is perhaps accurate, although vampires themselves are not tainted—at least not to a degree that is problematic, as they consume blood and refrain from devouring souls. Though I don't particularly enjoy their company," he amended with a lopsided smile. "The wyrms are one of the most susceptible species due to the fact that they live deep within the earth. Some are favored among certain gods for their fierce protectiveness over places held dear to them, but that alone will not save them. Their nature as dwellers within the deepest caverns make them vulnerable, just as vampires have their thirst that makes them vulnerable, and mankind has qualities that make them vulnerable and turn them into terrible abominations."

She chewed her lip as she considered his words. Rarely had she heard of a person that she could consider truly evil. In human history, it had been the exception rather than the norm. Even during the height of the crisis, when the ravagers burst from the underworld and created havoc on Earth before they mysteriously disappeared, she knew that the ugliness was from the creatures.

Only later did humans learn that not all ravagers were terrible monsters. Rather, the worst of the destruction had been carried out by humans in the grip of madness. She couldn't wrap her mind around the fact that there was probably a divine purpose behind it, or that a god might have willingly set them loose on the world.

Such a deity wasn't one she cared to know.

All of that, however, compared to what was staring at her now… Soul-eating monsters that thrived on mass destruction, killing the living and devouring their souls to give their bodies life. This was far worse than the ravagers, and that was saying a lot, considering that the ravagers had been a plague. Terror slipped up her spine as she imagined entire towns filled with dead people, their flesh torn, and their souls ripped away and consumed.

"Your fear is climbing," Silvas observed calmly.

"For good reason. I'm fucking terrified. Now I wish you hadn't told me. It would be easier to face all of this without knowing just how terrible these things are. They will destroy what is left of us, won't they?"

"Perhaps," he acknowledged. "But we will not let them. Humanity is favored among the gods. If you believe nothing else, believe that. They love you dearly, more than any of their creations. Although they are limited in how they may act, they will not allow your kind to be wiped from the face of the Earth. Believe that. They preserved your species from the wulkwos, or ravagers as you call them. They will not allow the Tainted Ones to end your existence."

She swallowed the terror that beat at her. She had to have courage. For some reason, his words gave her a glimmer of hope, and she was able to find her inner strength. Just being near him seemed to help. But she had to know…

"The silvanus who was dead in the woods… did he look like

that because his soul was eaten? Is that how all the victims of the Tainted Ones appear?"

Silvas looked at her sadly and shook his head. "The silvanus appeared that way for the same reason a faun might, or one of the lesser spirits… Because while we are material substances, we are not technically flesh and bone the way mortal beings are, despite our similarities. The bones that remained were compression of his being at the moment his soul was destroyed."

"So a human would be…" She gagged on the bile that rose up her throat at the thought of encountering rotting human remains, horror frozen on their face from their final moments as their soul was torn out of them. Tears trickled down her cheeks, and her throat burned as her entire body began to tremble.

The sound of rustling fabric and soft jangle of metal didn't prepare her for the sudden presence of the lucomo. Dropping down at her side, his arms banded around her and pulled her against his chest. Although he held her stiffly, his words gave her some measure of comfort.

"We will destroy Cacus. I swear it. There is little I can do about the creatures outside of my domain, but I will make certain that this threat, at least, is neutralized. The Eternal Forest will not be a source of suffering and destruction."

She leaned against him, pressing her cheek against his chest, and she mutely nodded. It was no guarantee, but it was something—and she would take every fighting chance that came her way.

Slowly, his warmth penetrated her, forcing her body to relax.

"Sleep," he whispered down into her hair. "We have far to go. Another day of travel and then we will be entering the Hyperborean Mountains."

"I'm afraid a wyrm will return if I fall asleep," she whispered, hating her weakness.

She felt his hand touch her hair before stroking through it.

One stroke followed another until he was soothingly petting her in a way that had her relaxing even further into his embrace.

"It can't creep up on me. I will smell it. You can trust your safety to me while you slumber."

Diana looked up to meet his colorless eyes. His gray pupils appeared even larger in the dark. "You promise?"

"Yes," he murmured.

She believed him.

CHAPTER 17

The mountains were brutal. She thought that traveling through the forest had been rough, but it had nothing on the mountains. Miles of blinding white stone stretched ahead in an unwelcoming craggy landscape. Worse, as they climbed higher, the temperature gradually shifted to a bitter cold. She was certain that soon the rock would give way to snow and complete her misery.

It was bad enough that the cold wind seeped into her bones. Diana was besieged by tremors that shook her entire body in an attempt to keep warm. She cursed the mountain and wanted to curse the stubborn silvanus. She missed the warmth of Silvas's body now that she trailed behind him. After they left the foothills, they started the climb on foot once Silvas considered it too unsafe for her to remain clinging to his back. The distance between them grew as the hours of silence continued to lengthen, broken only by orders the lucomo issued in a clipped voice. He did not so much as look back at her even then.

She didn't understand why he was even bothering to drag her up the mountain in his wake. He should have just sent her with Raskyuil. The injured troll at least would have been better company. Silvas did not appear to need her assistance or desire her presence. She could have fallen off the mountain and he wouldn't have noticed since he didn't deign to glance her way.

As much as Diana hated to admit it, that hurt. It made her angry, and she cocooned her heart in those feelings to protect it from the dismissal. The more she struggled to follow him up the mountain, the more resentment began to burn in her belly.

Eventually, she noticed that she was lagging farther and farther behind. Silvas walked so far ahead of her that he often disappeared into the landscape, visible only by the strands of white hair blowing on the wind. Not only could she barely see him most of the time, but the strange awareness between them had vanished as well, leaving her feeling even more alone on the mountainside.

Something was different the day before. Yesterday, they traveled through the forests without saying more than two words together when they stopped for breaks. Each time, Silvas shapeshifted into an enormous white crocotta that put Keena and Keech to shame.

It was perhaps a good thing that he was so large since she ended up having to strap the bundle of his armor to the saddle harness that Dagani had worn. Diana hadn't seen him go to retrieve it, but when he produced it for her with instructions on how to put it on him and strap down his armor, she had felt a new rush of sympathy for him.

Not that she gave to voice to it or acted on it. The hard look in his eyes as he spoke made it clear that any softer sentiments would be unappreciated. His expression told her all that she needed to know about his expectations. He expected compliance and nothing more. He didn't want her sympathy or any comfort, despite what little he had offered to her when she was scared. At that moment, she understood just how much a stranger the ageless lucomo was.

This perception was reinforced every time he regained his true form. He hadn't been inclined to speak, and Diana was left to her own thoughts more often than not. Truth be told, she wasn't certain what she expected him to say to her. What did they even have to talk about? She snorted as she recalled Raskyuil's concerns that the lucomo would want to keep her.

Not fucking likely when he seemed to be happy to forget that she was even there.

The last words he had spoken to her were when he had allowed her a rest break just before they began their ascent. He had explained in as few words as possible that they would need to climb the mountain rather than fly up. He didn't know where the strix was nesting, and if he took the form of a griffin or roc to approach, she would be forewarned of their presence.

Diana didn't have a clue what a roc was, and since he had seemed to be in a hurry to convey information and depart, she held her tongue and fell into step behind him. The hope that she would find some kind of companionship with him—even if it were a peculiar brand, like what she had found with the troll—vanished.

With a disgusted click of the tongue, she kicked the loose stones in front of her. Why was she allowing this to affect her so much? So what if he was ignoring her presence? It was no different than how most of the guys in her town behaved toward her once she showed no interest in sacrificing her freedom for the promise of safety and comfort—as much of it as they could promise—that they offered.

Diana wasn't even sure when she began to look at her captor as any sort of companion. She had to be crazy to even consider it! She had to depend on Silvas to survive, nothing more. As long as he didn't let anything kill her, he could walk miles ahead for all she cared. It wasn't like she even noticed how far away he was when his pale form disappeared.

It was ridiculous to feel such unease with the distance between them. She was doing fine.

A snowflake dropped on the tip of her nose, and she cursed under her breath. Naturally, it would start snowing. Why not? It was bound to happen. Diana had just been waiting until they hit the higher elevations and encountered snows that not even late spring could completely remove from the peaks.

Squinting against the curtain of snowflakes, Diana realized that she couldn't see any sign of Silvas. There wasn't even the telltale flick of his tail, or the flutter of his hair in the wind. Her unease grew into a quaking panic, and something wrenched in her heart as if a void had sprung up inside her.

Silvas was gone.

As the first fingers of panic twisted within her gut, Diana's first instinct was to shout for him, but she clamped her mouth shut against the impulse. She didn't have a death wish. She didn't want the strix to find her first and discover her alone and helpless on the side of the mountain. Fear crawled through her as she imagined the monstrous sorceress landing in front of her on the snow, her wings swooping as they beat the air. Long, clawed fingers stretching for her…

Shivering, she pulled her cloak tighter and distracted herself by inventing new curses to send after the lucomo. Diana continued to climb, fully aware that snow slicked the stones, making every step treacherous. Her pace slowed even more as the falling snow become thicker, a northern wind churning it, whipping it around her like an impassible wall, making the world an indistinct mass of white. The white rock had been bad enough, but now she was snow blind. The wash of falling snow had turned the entire world white without even a break of blue sky visible now.

She slowed, feeling the ground with each tentative step before putting her weight on the deepening snow. Her muscles quivered with each step. She could feel the dull ache building around her joints and the pressure that felt like it was squeezing her skull, but there was little she could do about it. Fear was like a living entity crawling through her, beneath her skin like shards of ice sinking into her blood.

The strix was out there was somewhere, possibly even hunting her now…

Diana needed to find some sort of shelter where she could wait out the storm. The longer she walked on blindly, the more she risked falling off the mountain—or being found by something straight from her nightmares.

Diana sighed, but couldn't even see the faintest wisps of steam against the surrounding whiteout.

"Fucking ridiculous," she muttered to herself through chattering teeth.

She stumbled, landing on her hands and knees in the snow, ice rushing into her protective gloves and soaking her knees and her calves where it seeped in around her armor. A hiss of shock escaped her, and she pushed herself back to her feet. Straightening, she squinted. She could have sworn that she saw something—

A shadow broke through the snow, striding toward her, down the slope of rock and snow, wings stretching out and moving against the wind. Icy blue eyes were all she could see clearly as their glow pierced the storm. It loomed over her even at a distance, its eyes focused on her with a predatory stillness.

Diana stumbled back, her feet sliding in the snow. Her heart hammered against her ribs as she pulled out the sword at her side. Her bow would be rendered nearly useless by the weather. The slide of metal was drowned out by the howl of the wind, which seemed to rise as the creature came nearer.

Terror clogged her throat, but she raised her sword and swung it with all her strength in a less than graceful arc, praying she would get lucky again. Fencing club never covered sword fighting in a damn snowstorm.

A hand shot out, snatching her wrist and stopping the forward momentum of her arm. The hand that gripped her wrist was masculine, sinewy with muscle. It squeezed, and the sharp pinch made her cry out as the hilt dropped from her hand. Her assailant pushed forward, forcing her arm against her chest as a behemoth among males leaned in close to her.

Large blue eyes, rounder than a human's, stared down at her. They were set deep in a wide face with a beak-like nose and a long beard. She thought that Silvas was pale, with his pure alabaster coloring that made him almost radiant, like some sort of heraldic white stag. This man was somehow paler, so much so that his white face bore an icy blue undertone. It made a strange contrast against the rosy stain of his cheeks and the crimson hue of his downturned lips.

A long, dark cap of curling hair snapped around him. Nestled within his locks, a crystalline crown appeared, almost like ice erupting in jagged peaks from his brow. From the corner of her eye, she was aware of the dove-gray wings stretched out wide, the feathers rattling in the wind as they fanned the air.

Relief rushed through that she was not in the clutches of a monstrous strix.

It was short-lived, however. If not a strix, then what had her?

"The living are not permitted beyond my peaks," he rumbled, his deep voice carrying like the low moan of glacial ice. "Why do you trespass upon my domain?"

His domain? She searched her memory, trying to recall those inhabitants of the Hyperborean Mountains that Silvas had mentioned.

Silvas... *Damn him!*

The male shifted closer, his head tilting to the side. "A human," he muttered. "What would a human be doing here? It has been many ages since I've touched the warmth of a woman." The words were so reverent that it was almost distracting as he lifted his other hand as if to touch her.

Whoa!

Diana twisted away to escape his touch. Unlike the touch of Silvas, she didn't feel even a drop of the strange attraction that had simmered since the first time the silvanus touched her. Instead, her skin crawled.

"Aquilo, halt," Silvas's voice rumbled, forcing the male to drop his hand and turn to face the silvanus.

Silvas's dark antlers cut through the veil of snow as he stepped forward. Even as close as he was, Diana had trouble seeing him. It reassured her though that, aside from his antlers, the brilliant glow of his white eyes was at least visible. Just being in his presence was enough to calm her a little.

A grin split Aquilo's face, and his body shook with his deep laughter.

"Silvas, the great silvani lucomo of the Eternal Forest… To what do I owe this pleasure?"

"I have come to retrieve something of mine," Silvas replied coolly, his eyes locked on the male's offending hand still gripping her wrist.

"Did you lose this human, by any chance?" Aquilo asked, amusement still in his voice as he gave her arm a small shake as if to taunt him.

"As it happens, I did."

Silvas appeared as unconcerned as usual, but his eyes narrowed on the hand.

"The Hyperborean Mountains are not a good place to vacation with a lover, Silvas. At least have some respect for the domain of the northern winds," her captor protested jovially. His enormous barrel chest shook again with his deep laughter.

Had she thought his wings were like that of a dove? She was

wrong. As they folded in, she saw darker specks along the back of them like that of an owl. With his curved nose, pale wings, and large watchful eyes, he reminded her slightly of an owl. Her heart might have taken that opportunity to leap out of her chest if she hadn't heard him more or less refer to himself as the north winds.

The lucomo moved closer, his features coming into focus as his attention left her hand and shifted to Aquilo, to give him a bland look. Despite his expression, Diana felt a prickle of tension from him as the awareness that had been absent came flooding back. Although he gave nothing away, Silvas was sizing up a potential threat. Then it was gone again, leaving Diana confused and empty once more.

"I would not consider your mountains to be a place that I would care to visit in leisure," Silvas observed dryly "I seek the strix who recovered Nocis."

Aquilo's face wrinkled in a grimace. "I should have suspected as much when I heard that there was a silvanus roaming my mountain. Especially given the disturbances that I have heard rumors of." His lip curled in disgust. "The Tainted Ones. You will find what you seek easily enough. The strix, Mora, nests in the southeastern side of the next peak, in a small pocket of stone two-thirds the distance up the mountainside. I suspect you will smell the stench of death and magic long before you catch sight of her."

"I have no doubt. Many thanks, Aquilo. Now if you might call off your wind, we'll be certain to arrive at our destination quicker, and without incident."

Aquilo nodded and stepped back a pace. Though his hand was still fixed on her arm, he turned at an angle away from her. With his opposite hand, he lifted an enormous horn to his lips from the belt that held a sapphire blue tunic strapped over woolen pants. His massive chest expanded as he sounded the horn.

A deep echo crashed through the mountains that shattered the wall of snow around them. The wind died immediately, and the snowflakes disappeared from the air, leaving only powder in their wake.

Silvas inclined his head in gratitude as he spoke and placed his hand on her elbow, just above Aquilo's grip on her forearm. She watched as his eyes narrowed when the other male didn't immediately release her. Instead, the spirit's hand tightened, and Silvas's face pinched with displeasure.

Aquilo's frowned and glanced toward the next peak, his dark head shaking.

"Taking a human to a strix's cave is foolish."

"Nonetheless, I shall," Silvas replied.

"Leave her with me. I will care for her, and you will be unhampered over the mountain passes," Aquilo offered.

Silvas fell silent, his gaze fastened on her captor. Diana thought he would agree to be rid of her unwanted presence. To her surprise, however, he shook his head, the ornaments from his antlers rattling with the strength of his objection, nostrils flaring as he bristled. Out of nowhere, his hostility rolled through her, taking her breath away.

Diana squeezed her eyes shut as her stomach churned. The flashes of this strange shared awareness came and went in an instant, unsettling her to such a degree that her body was reacting to it physically.

"I considered it only because I do not wish to risk her against the strix, but no. Diana's destiny is wound with mine, and too much hinges on our success. It has been foreseen. She is mine, and I will not be separated from her."

"I would like to point out that I came across the female alone, without any protector," Aquilo retorted, smiling in amusement at the lucomo's refusal.

"A mistake, nothing more," Silvas ground out.

"Mistakes are dangerous in our world."

Silvas did not respond other than to peel his lip back from his sharp teeth in warning.

Aquilo released Diana's arm with a loud sigh. "How disappointing that you would take a fragile human to that monster's cave. However, I cannot argue against those that the gods touch with the oracular sight."

Thrusting his hand into a pouch hanging from his belt, he removed a small silver pennywhistle and offered it to Diana.

She glanced over at the silvanus uncertainly. Rather than appearing offended, he tilted his head toward her in encouragement. Swallowing, she managed a small smile at the towering spirit of the north wind and accepted the gift.

"If you require the winds, calls us with that." He positioned her fingers so that they covered all the openings. "Play D to summon the northern wind." He lifted two fingers. "Play F sharp to summon the eastern winds. Play B for the southern winds, and G for the western winds."

He showed her the placement of her fingers for each note and repeated it until she remembered them. Only then did he step back with a nod of his burly head. "May the great gods favor your efforts."

Pale wings flashed, and with a blast of frigid air he was gone.

"Come," Silvas growled as he stalked away, once again completely closed off to her.

Diana crossed her arms over her chest and glared at his back. "Mistake, my ass," she mumbled. She plodded through the snow after him, trying to ignore the disconcerting pull she felt toward him.

CHAPTER 18

Silvas clenched his jaw as he walked among the rocks. He was not deaf to the mutterings behind him, but tried to ignore their sting. Her opinion shouldn't have mattered to him. When had he ever concerned himself about what others thought of him? Yet it did matter, even more since her anger and disappointment pricked him like needles and tasted like ash on his tongue.

He knew the cause of it, although he had ignored all the signs. The strong pull to her, the sensitivity toward her that developed after they touched… it had been a portent to the bond. He had found his uxorem, his mate.

It was undeniable, and it, in turn, had triggered instinct—that which drove the species of the Eternal Forest to join with their mates. Not only was he aware of her existing within him, but he was also tormented by the fires in his blood, the ceaseless hunger that worsened as the days passed.

There was only one way to slake the need, and that was by finishing the bonding process and claiming her for his own. *His* uxorem.

The need to claim her tore through him, gnawing at him, and

he stepped faster to provide himself with some relief. Not too far this time—he couldn't risk losing her again. It had been among the most terrifying moments of his life when he turned around to pull her closer to him within the rising storm and discovered her missing.

At first, he had been unable to comprehend that she was gone. She had been right behind him! Her sorrow had eaten at him, and it had not become any better when that sorrow had shifted into confusion, then frustration, until finally anger and resentment joined the turmoil. The chaotic flavor of her emotions had overwhelmed him, sensitive as he was to them through their bond. He could not shut off the flow from her and so had suffered in silence. Yet it was nothing compared to the terror that sprung to life in him as he imagined horrific possibilities. Of a predator or the strix herself finding his female vulnerable and alone on the mountain.

Flying into a panic, he had followed her scent the best that he could in the storm as he shouted her name, his voice drowned out by the wind. Finding her with Aquilo had instinctively made him want to exert his claim and bind her to him.

But he couldn't do that.

To his shame, he had ignored her as much as possible, selfishly absorbed in his own discomfort and an undeniable fear of a vulnerability that he had never before experienced. Dagani was gone, but he had punished her for making him *feel* it even after he delivered the final peace to the crocotta by returning it to the forest.

He ran from it.

He ran so hard from everything he felt that, although he had known she was struggling, he hadn't so much as looked behind him to make sure she was keeping up.

He had to live with that guilt. Just as he had to live with the oath he had made in haste when he thought it a small thing to offer her to soothe her. Because she was human, he had considered her inconsequential despite the warning from the vegoia. Now, however, he had greater insight into what Dorinda meant. He had understood the moment he felt Diana's grief as if it were his own. As his uxorem, he would despair if separated from her. Even with her near, but their bond unsolidified, he felt like he was slowly fracturing.

He had been foolish, and because of that, Silvas was restrained by his promise, just as all spirits and gods were bound by their oaths.

He had not wanted her to suffer similarly, so he had blocked her out so she wouldn't feel swayed by the hunger consuming him. It wasn't flawless, and he felt the response in her rising to meet him every time he reconnected. Yet in the end, he had hurt her, and he didn't know how to correct the error.

What a mess.

Raskyuil was not wrong when he predicted that Silvas would suffer more than most other males. As the son of Turan, he was born to be more susceptible to the domain of his mother, just as he had once reveled in her lifegiving power.

His thoughts turned to the dove that had fluttered before his throne just days ago. He had been certain that it was a communication from Turan, and he been both right and wrong. There was no message for him except a warning of what was to come. He saw his mother's hands all over their predicament, and he didn't know whether to thank her for bringing him his uxorem or to curse her for upsetting his world at such a dangerous time.

In truth, at any other time, he might have greeted the bonding with joy, but now it terrified him. *Him!* He who feasted on fear and was sustained by it!

Now Diana erroneously believed that he desired to get away from her. If only she knew just how wrong she was. He wanted her more than he had ever wanted anything. He wanted to renew the life of the Eternal Woods with a celebration of their love.

Tail flicking, he glanced back at her, unable to deny the thirst to lay his eyes on her. Her arms were crossed over her chest, holding her cloak close to her as she glowered at the ground. He shook his head and bit back an annoyed grimace at the jangle of the ornaments knotted around and imbedded in his antlers. He wanted to tear off the shining gold ornaments draped over him by nymphs who had once sought his favor. They felt as artificial as their affections had been.

"Can you not glare at me?" Diana snapped. "I know you aren't happy having me here. I'm not exactly thrilled either."

She picked up her pace, and just as she tried to pass him, he stretched out a hand and caught her arm. She froze under his touch and glared up at him. His thumb caressed her elbow through her tunic. As he pulled her in, her eyes widened at him in surprise, her soft lips parting. He yearned to taste them, and it was only with great resolve that he did not follow through.

His eyelashes lowered as he gazed down at her, staring at eyes that were nearly blue with emotion. "You are wrong, you know."

"About what?"

"Everything." He sighed again, uncertain of how to explain. "You don't understand the nature of my kind and what I need and require. I tried to spare you from it, to give you freedom, but have only succeeded in making things worse. I don't wish there to be any separation between us."

She frowned up at him. "You don't?" she asked. "Because you sure could have fooled me."

"I do not." He lifted a hand and let it skate down her arm. "I am overwhelmed by feelings that are alien to me which I cannot control. You make me feel things that I never expected to feel. I always thought when I bonded, it would be to another immortal." The last he said softly, half to himself.

Diana shook her head. "I don't understand. What do you mean by bonded?"

Silvas squinted as he looked at the mountainside. "This isn't a good place to discuss it. Night will be falling soon. We'll need to find shelter, and then I'll endeavor to explain it to you."

Her lips pursed. "You promise?"

He smiled as he leaned down and brushed his lips against her forehead, feeling the alarmingly cold flesh against his mouth. "I promise," he whispered.

"All right. I suppose I can wait," she grumbled. "But let's hurry because, between you and me, my tits are about to freeze off."

Caught by surprise by her bold statement, he laughed, earning him a small smile in return.

"We can't have that," he said as he tucked her cape more snugly around her and added his own over it despite her objections. Although the air was cold, he knew that he didn't feel it as intensely as she did. "If you allow me, I can believe I can get us somewhere to rest soon if I am permitted to carry you."

She raised an eyebrow. "Now this is an interesting turn of events. You're actually asking to haul me around now?"

Leaning down further, he brushed his nose against her neck. "I won't entirely reform my ways… but I can concede this much to get your permission before I misbehave."

Soft hands patted his breastplate as she choked out a laugh. "Fair enough. Let's get to shelter and warm up."

He nodded and stretched out his arms. They would have the best chances of finding shelter if he risked exposure and sent one of his shadows out. The strix would sense it if it strayed too near her peak, but he was certain that he would find something nearby.

The feeling of his essence stretching and becoming thinner was as disconcerting as always. He knew from her gasp what she was seeing as she watched him become a shadow. In his mind, the entire world was rendered in shadows, but he knew that to her eyes he would be the unrecognizable one as his shadow form broke free, all darkness except for the burning light of his soul like a star within it. Silvas felt his light divide in a system of stars as all his possible forms watched him with glowing eyes, waiting to be selected.

The eagle. He needed the eagle for this task.

He heard the cry of the raptor in his ears and the violent tug as it separated from him and tore into the skies, allowing the world to condense around him once more as his form snapped back into place.

"Holy shit!" Diana laughed, her fingers gripping his arm.

He allowed himself to soak in her pleasure, and watched her face light up with happiness as she stared up at his eagle self. Through the eagle he looked down on her too, enjoying the sight of her upturned face even as he enjoyed the smooth perfection of her cheek from where he stood at her side.

"What is that?" she breathed in wonder. "Did that really come from inside of you?"

He cocked his head and regarded her with amusement. "He is me. A fragment of me."

"That's amazing!"

Silvas chuckled, a strange happiness shooting through him as he stooped low to swoop her up in his arms. Even cold, she smelled warm and inviting. He wanted nothing more than to bury his nose in the crook of her neck and breathe in that sweet scent. A shiver wracked her frame, and he wrestled against his desire with the iron control born of centuries of existence.

"Come then," he murmured as he adjusted her weight in his arms. "Let's get you warm. My shadow eagle will mark the way."

She curled against him, arms wrapping around him in delight as the dark bird soared over the mountain ahead of them. Through her, he was able to see just how magical it all was. It made him recall his youth, when his shadow forms were new to him. She made him feel that way again as he experienced the marvel of it all through her.

It was a precious gift to regain something that he had become so jaded to over the millennia, something he had thought he had long ago lost—his sense of wonder.

Carrying his female in his arms, he moved with greater speed than she would have managed on foot. He was soon glad that he was carrying her when a steep cliff dropped away, leaving only a narrow ledge that he was able to pick his way along with sure steps. Diana clung tighter to him, her face burrowed against his shoulder as she trusted him, despite the terror that he could feel beating at her. It beat at him too, but he opened himself and sent waves of warmth and security to her until it eased to a more manageable strength.

Her fear soothed, he followed the path laid out through the eyes of his fragment. As he crested the slope, he stopped, clutching Diana tighter to him. Ahead, he could see the second peak rise as a dark shadow against the sky. Even from where they stood, it seemed forbidding, a blemish on the heavens, but he did not worry about it now. There were more important things to attend to…

His uxorem.

He smiled to himself. Just below the rocks where he stood, his shadow eagle had found the entrance of a cave.

CHAPTER 19

There wasn't much that could be done to make a cave comfortable, but Diana had to hand it to Silvas—he certainly tried. After stripping off his armor and building a fire, he managed to coax bits of moss that had accumulated in one corner to grow until it made a bed for them to lie on if they didn't mind squeezing together in the small area. It would be a tight squeeze, at that.

Setting her own armor against the wall with his, Diana straightened and frowned down at the makeshift bed at the other side of the cave. As she watched Silvas drape his cloak over it to add extra comfort, she knew she couldn't complain about the accommodations. Despite his recent attitude, he was making an effort to see to her comfort. She could refuse it, but the alternative was to go without.

Although she was still pissed about the way he had been acting and the fact that he lost her, his sudden reversal in attitude had been surprising, to say the least. At first, she wasn't sure if she should trust it, not until that strange sixth sense of awareness came flooding back in and, once more, she could feel his mental touch.

Diana still didn't know exactly how she knew. There was a familiarity to it. When she focused on it, she could almost feel the weight of his hand on her skin and the faint scent—that sweet spiced smell—that she recognized as his own. More than that, the touch on her mind felt alien and ancient. Even as he watched, his colorless eyes fixed on her in a manner she would have called unnerving just days earlier, she could feel the intensity of emotion wash through her.

She felt his admiration for her, his pride, as well as the territorial nature that wanted to cocoon her in a safe place. And his fear. Among all that, she also felt the all-consuming fire of desire, an endless need that tortured him and made her own desires spring to life again. Diana pressed her legs together, her face reddening as her sex throbbed so strongly that she squirmed and panted for breath.

It was crazy how intensely she felt… everything.

She met his eyes and watched as the corners crinkled when he smiled knowingly.

"What is this between us?"

Silvas cocked his head at her, his golden draped antlers tilting at a regal angle. He observed her for what felt like an eternity before he spoke.

"It is the bond. It started the moment that we touched, and even now goes unfulfilled. In most beings, it manifests as a strong pull and necessity to be with each other… The pull itself is called 'Instinct' by many in the Eternal Forest."

"I definitely feel that," she muttered, and he grinned in response.

"With ancient beings, those of us who were once considered minor gods, such as myself, the attachment can be deeper. It is both a blessing and a curse."

"A curse?"

That took her by surprise.

Silvas gave her a wry look. "Immortals do not feel things the same way that mortal being do. I would say there are even fundamental differences between the way humans, trolls, orcs, and the various mortal races experience life and the spectrum of emotions. Because ageless ones, or even the long-lived races such as the aelves, have intense passions for those we are bonded to—an almost obsessive need and love for our uxorem, our mates—our long lives mean that many other emotions are filtered or experienced from a distance. To be exposed to human emotion… it is unsettling."

"And that's why you've been distant… because you're unsettled."

He inclined his head in agreement. "I did not realize that we had begun to bond until I felt the full force of your emotions… Your terror when you faced the wyrm struck me brutally, but less so than the full force of grief magnified by distant sorrows and regrets until they were a torrent within me. Distance gave me some relief, whether accomplished by shapeshifting or keeping physical space between us."

It made an odd sort of sense. He hadn't started acting weird. If it was all part of this "bonding" that he spoke of, then it was something of which he had little control over. Except for the manner of dealing with it.

He wasn't off the hook for that.

"And you lost me—on the mountain where literally anything could have happened," she reminded him.

She wasn't sure if she imagined that he winced, but she hoped that he had. She wanted him to see how thoughtless he had been.

"I did," he agreed solemnly. "I do not recall ever being as frightened as I was when I discovered that you were missing."

"You were an asshole," she stated.

He didn't say anything, although a flicker of remorse appeared his eyes and she felt it thrum through her before it was gone. She sighed. More things that immortals didn't feel strongly. She wondered if he would have felt a stronger emotion had she been injured, or worse.

When she said as much, he looked at her aghast, and the horror that struck her was so strong that she found it difficult to breathe.

"Never say such things lightly," he growled. "I would have destroyed the mountain and then grieved and raged until the gods descended to contain me. Possibly my mother would have left Cyprus and confined me herself out of her fondest affection for me, hopefully before I did too much damage."

Well…, that answered that question.

Diana cleared her throat. "Where do we go from here?"

Silvas gave her a speculative look and lifted one shoulder in a shrug. "There are no real options. The bond will continue to make its demands. You are human, so its effect will build unnoticeably at first, I suspect. No amount of distance will change that. It will become a pressing need that will eventually drain you and make it difficult to sleep."

"And there is no cure for it?"

He laughed, the deep sound rolling over her making her belly quiver as if tongues were licking her, and he shook his head. "The bonding is determined by the Fates and cannot be denied or ignored. For those races who dwell among the realms of our worlds, it is something that is looked forward to." His voice dropped to a soft rumble. "The timing is unfortunate, as I have longed for my uxorem for centuries. I have imagined every touch of worship I would give to her throughout the long eons of my existence. Every touch, every flavor, every sigh that would be mine—every shout of ecstasy."

Heat flushed through her body at the promise in his voice. Her imagination had no problem supplying suggestions for where he could get started. She shifted, her hard nipples scraping against the fabric covering them as a rush of heat flooded from between her thighs, dampening her crotch. She squeezed her legs even tighter, the scent of her arousal apparent even to her. She had no doubt that he could smell it.

She wasn't even sure if she liked it, and yet she couldn't deny that she longed for him in a primal way.

It was her choice. She decided. She didn't have to follow the insistence of her body, but she was pragmatic enough to know that she also didn't have any interest in fighting against her need every day.

The silvanus's nostrils flared, and he growled low in his throat. "You are needing," he murmured. "I can smell the perfume of your cunt from here."

A shiver ran up her spine at the crude words.

"I still haven't forgiven you," she stated baldly.

The corners of his lips turned up, a soft gleam brightening his eyes. "I know. It will be interesting to see if I can eventually change your mind and win your affections."

"If I fuck you to settle this bond between us, it means nothing. We may be bonded, mated, or whatever you call it, but it doesn't mean that what I want has changed."

He hesitated, giving her a curious glance. "You would still wish to return to the human world?"

"Yes. It is my home. My family is there. If I… bond with you, I want to make sure I can still go back home."

She had to. Who would tend to the graves of her parents and grandparents if she wasn't there to do it? Who would take care of her grandparents' house and weed the garden? She was all that was left of her family. Not going back would be like abandoning the memory of everyone she had lost. There was no question about it. Besides, she didn't belong in this strange world.

Silvas frowned, and she thought she saw a flicker of disappointment, but couldn't be sure because the link between them closed for a moment. Her heart sank at being shut out, however briefly. His expression was impossible to go by as he studied her. He turned his head away, staring toward the entrance of the cave.

"There will be no demands that you stay here. I can find you when the need becomes great enough to make it necessary to satisfy our discomfort." He glanced over at her, his lips twisting slightly. "This is not an unheard-of arrangement, especially among those mates who need time apart after several millennia."

"I think I can live with that," she finally said.

She could live with it, but she hated how cold he made it sound. Diana pressed her lips together as she acknowledged that no matter how much she disliked it, it was perhaps the most accurate description of what their relationship would be like.

His expression darkened, the lines of his face hardening with a certain deadliness. "I will not tolerate another male to sniff around you. I cannot. Knowing that another male is touching what is mine will drive me to madness. Understand this: I will claim the territory around your home as my own and terrorize any male who dares approach you."

Diana drew in a sharp breath, her pussy clenching. That shouldn't turn her on so much. What he promised to do was beyond the limits of reason. It should disgust her that he would have no problem carrying out his threat, but instead her arousal spiked. She wanted to crawl into his lap and rub against him.

As if he were reading her mind, Silvas seated himself on the mossy bed and opened his arms to her in an invitation. The outline of what appeared to be a massive, swollen cock pressed against the front of his pants. It was obvious even from where she stood.

Her uncertainty prickled at her. Should she trust his word? So far, he had followed through and been honest with her even when he delighted in scaring the crap out of her.

But that was also part of his honesty. He never pretended to be anything other than what he was.

She begrudgingly had to admit that she appreciated that quality. So many people in her town put on a brave face and pretended to feel things that they didn't. They hid their true wants and fears from themselves as much as from others. Silvas was unapologetically who he was, and he was offering of all that to her.

That had to count for something, even weighed against his recent behavior.

Diana took a step forward and then another. He didn't attempt to persuade her, nor did he tease. He just watched her, the intensity in his luminous eyes increasing with her every footstep.

Despite his stillness, she could feel the surge of need coming from him. Although he didn't so much as blink, she noted the way his ears tilted toward her and his muscles tensed with anticipation. But he didn't move. He didn't attempt to reach for her. He just patiently sat there with his arms open, waiting for her to come to him.

Once she stepped between his legs, she slowly lowered herself until she was kneeling on the soft moss bed. Her hands came to rest on his knees as she met his gaze. His pale gray diamond-shaped pupils expanded, rounding out as a rush of his desire swept over her.

It wasn't just lust. Lust could be solved with a quick fuck and then forgotten about. They were taking the final step to link themselves together, and although she had all assurances that she could go on with her life afterwards, she craved that closeness, to pretend even for a few hours that she was loved once more.

Anything could happen tomorrow, or the next day. Ever since the devastation, she hadn't dared to want much of anything for herself. She had made do with what fortune gave her. She wanted this.

Balancing her weight, Diana leaned forward into his arms.

She felt those powerful muscles move up around her as he lifted her tunic and tossed it to the side. Bared, she scooted forward and slid her hands up his chest until she was able to coil her arms around his powerful neck. Aligning herself over his cock so that they intimately pressed together, she leaned into him so that her chest pressed against his.

Diana could feel his lifeforce sing to her from where they touched. She was aware of the heat of his hands and the light caress of his pale fingertips skating over her skin as he drew his palms down her arms. The soft white fuzz that covered his skin felt like velvet, and Diana closed her eyes, delighting in his touch. When his hands reached her elbows, he leaned forward so that his arms could slip around her back and pull her tight against his chest.

He growled, the sound vibrating through her from where their chests met, his eyes brightening like two white-hot flames.

"Now you are mine, Uxorem."

CHAPTER 20

Diana felt his hot hands slide down her back to her hips. He squeezed and pulled her closer against him, dragging her sex across the hard length of his arousal. Although cloth separated them, her eyes rolled back as he moved her over the hard knobs of his cock, each one striking against her clit.

Her fingers dug into his shoulders, and a small hiss of air escaped her.

"Silvas…" she whimpered and squirmed against his grip.

To her chagrin, the lucomo ignored her silent demands as he dragged her back and forth at an excruciatingly slow glide against his thickening bulge. His head dropped down against her cheek, and she felt his tongue slick against her ear before trailing down her neck.

"Patience," he purred. "I have an eternity to worship you."

"Yeah, well, I'm human. We aren't the most patient… I'm more into instant gratification, personally," she panted. "At least in some things," she amended. "This definitely counts as one of those things."

He chuckled and, on the next slide, thrust up against her, the contact making her choke on a startled cry of pleasure. It immediately shifted into a soft groan as he continued to rock her back and forth in a hard grinding motion against his cock. A shiver ran over her skin, followed by sparks of pleasure racing through her that responded to the tightening in her belly. Her breath was coming in shorter gasps, each one sending a pulse down to her clit.

Her orgasm hovered just in front of her, and she reached for it eagerly only to have Silvas stop and press her firmly down, hindering her movement. Diana shrieked in frustration, her hips jumping against his grip as her building orgasm dissipated.

Drawing back her head, she glared at the silvanus.

"You fucking dick," she seethed as she slapped his chest.

He lifted an eyebrow in amusement and rolled his hip beneath her. The action surprised her so much that she had to cling to him to keep from being unseated. This was apparently the reaction he wanted because he turned in one swift move, tipping her to the side in the mossy cushion of their bed.

Leaning over her, still pressed in the cradle of her legs, Silvas ran his fingers over her collarbone before sloping down the swell of her breasts to linger on her nipples. Careful of his claws, he gently began to pluck at her nipples, making them harden, distend, and flush to a rosy red hue. As he toyed with the sensitive tips, his eyes lowered to half-mast in pleasure as he observed his play. Diana noticed the purr that resumed just before his head dipped to nuzzle the mound of flesh.

The slick, cold touch of metal dangling from his antlers against her skin made her jerk in surprise and hiss. His eyes lifted and fastened on her as dark tongue slipped out to stroke over her nipple. The alternating heat of his mouth and the cold, sensuous slide of the metal made her arch into his touch.

Raising one hand, she tangled her fingers within the bejeweled strands of gold that teased her. The move had been instinctive on her part; she hadn't even realized she had done it until

Silvas pulled away and pried her hand free. Kissing her palm, he set it against his chest as Diana leveled him with a hurt look.

She wasn't allowed to touch his jewels? That was some kind of irony.

Silvas groaned and shook his head, the gold clattering again. "Do not look at me like that. I cannot bear to have you touch them."

So that's how it is.

"I guess my hands aren't good enough to touch them?" she asked before she attempted to withdraw.

Silvas pulled himself higher over her body, blocking her beneath him, until he was able to look down into her face. She was left with little choice but to meet his angry eyes.

"*Never* say that of yourself," he hissed. "I would be pleased to have your hands touch me anywhere. But I hate for you to touch them, but not because I don't want your touch. I don't wish you to touch them because… I am ashamed of them," he snarled as he looked away.

Diana was so surprised by the outburst that she stared up at him. He didn't speak for several moments while he attempted to regain control of himself. When he looked at her once more, his expression was hard.

"I allowed this. My vanity allowed females to adorn me in jewels to win my favors. I will tell you truthfully that I displayed them like trophies. Ropes of jewels from numerous nymphs and denizens of my domain for them to honor me as their king. I was proud of them," he said, but his eyes were hard with shame. "Proud of how easily I won them. But now I wish for nothing more than the ability to remove them so that nothing remains of them. I wish no reminders of others when I'm only yours."

Diana blinked at him. She hadn't expected this, especially not after she insisted on going back home. His devotion and dismay over the gold falling in brilliant waterfalls of metal and gems from his antlers made her heart ache.

"They are imbedded into the antlers. I can't take them off," he rumbled, flawlessly predicting her question. "I would, though, if I could."

"I don't mind them," she whispered, and found it to be true. The reminders of former lovers sucked, but the shining glints against the white velvet fuzz covering his skin, and the pure ivory hue of his hair—she couldn't deny that they were beautiful. Her eyes trailed over them as she felt his fingers pet her again in what she guessed was a soothing stroke.

"You don't?" he asked.

She shook her head. "I don't. In fact, I think that you should let me touch them. I can claim them as mine—every single one."

His lips in a sweet smile as he lowered his head until his jewels caressed her cheek. With a gentle hand, she stroked several the chains that drifted over her skin.

The tension in him was noticeable, but soon he relaxed as she continued to touch the adornment. Silvas started nuzzling her again until he retraced his path, trailing gold down her chest in his wake as he returned to her breasts, where he had left off. His tongue slid out eagerly over her breast once more.

A sigh left her, and she arched up to meet the touch as he did it again. He played with it, lapping at one and then the other, pinching and plucking at them where his mouth was not engaged, before finally sucking a nipple fully into his mouth. She could feel his tongue swirling around her nipple in the wet heat. He left her nipples to lightly scrape his sharp teeth against the sides of her breasts before tackling her nipples again with eager licks and tugs until she was wiggling beneath him, unable to get enough to push her through to release.

When he was finally finished teasing her breasts, he licked and sucked his way down her body, paying attention to every inch of flesh he encountered, laving it with his tongue and pressing sucking kisses as he reached the lacings of her woven pants.

She didn't know what she expected when he encountered the barrier, but it wasn't to nuzzle the fabric or to grip the lacings with his teeth and tug them loose. The obstacle dealt with, Silvas buried his face once more against the front of her pants, nuzzling through the material until it fell away and his nose brushed against her panties. Diana jumped at the contact, and he drew back with a curious look. His eyes glinted with a playful light and his lips twitched mischievously.

"How many layers are you cocooned in, uxorem?" he teased.

"Consider it like unwrapping a birthday present," she said.

"I have never had a birthday present," he said, a deviant grin already starting as he looked up the length of her body from where his mouth was pressed against the top of her silk-covered mons. It should have made her wary. Instead, she felt a surge of excitement and wiggled against him. He plucked at the material as he leaned forward to whisper. "How does one usually go about opening them?"

His fingers dipped inside her pants to scrape against the silky material of her undergarments. There was something so provocative about the simple gesture that she could feel another hot wave of arousal slip from her sex, and she shivered when he ran his finger beneath the edge of her panties.

"Well," she said, trying to find any semblance of rational thought in her head again. "They're usually torn open, but don't do that… These are the only underwear I have."

She laughed when he immediately got a familiar look of interest in his eyes. He let out a long, beleaguered sigh, which made her stifle her laughter. He didn't seem to mind, however, because his eyes glittered down at her with genuine amusement.

She squealed at the feel of his teeth as they nipped her through the fabric.

"You tease your mate," he purred. The twin pearls of his eyes shimmered, his gray pupils so blown out that they reminded her of the gray bands in a moonstone.

He kept his eyes fixed on hers as he peeled her panties and pants off her at the same time.

Her sex and lower body bared, Diana felt herself turn red. She hadn't trimmed down there in months, and it had been even longer since she had a bikini wax. Although she still shaved every now and then with a razor, she knew her legs were hairy too given that she couldn't recall the last time she had bothered.

Silvas paused and gave her a curious look as he reluctantly dropped his hands away from her clothes. He drew back and frowned. "If you are changing your mind..."

She shook her head in the negative and cleared her throat. "I'm just a little... ungroomed. I'm hairy," she added with a bright flush.

"I was under the impression that is how your species was created," he responded wryly. "Believe me when I say it is not a deterrent."

With a snap of his wrists, he yanked her pants down all the way, exposing her lower body before his eyes. He petted her cunt with one hand as his eyes ran over her.

"As I expected," he purred. "Beautiful."

CHAPTER 21

As Silvas spread her thighs, Diana's belly tightened with anticipation. Her pussy was so wet that the cool air upon it sent a jolt through her, her hips canting up instinctively. A low growl filled the air, and then his mouth was there. His breath was warm against the flesh seconds before his tongue flattened on the mouth of her sex like a slick, hot brand as he lapped.

She moaned, her muscles clenching as she writhed against his mouth. His tongue was rougher, flatter, and hotter than a human's. The first swipe made her pussy clench and her thighs shiver. He made a sound of contentment, his fingers stroking her hips, as he teased her with his tongue, dragging it along the entire length of her sex, from the back of her cunt to her aching clit. He barely swiped against the bead of flesh before returning to his exploration.

Her frustration built. She needed relief—needed more.

She jerked hard against him, her hands coming down around his antlers, tangling in the mass of gold. He stiffened, his eyes darting up to meet her gaze and his mouth pausing against her sex.

"Mine," she whispered, acting on the possession that rose sharply within her.

His pale eyes gleamed, and she felt his mouth curve against flesh. She dropped one hand to tangle into his hair and tugged as she watched pleasure flare in his eyes. His lips parted on a snarl as he shifted his weight on top of her, his body coiling with tension as his attention dropped once again and locked on her exposed, intimate flesh. His mouth caressed her once in a soft kiss, his nose grazing her clit in a tantalizing promise that had her shifting her hand back toward his antler to tug his head more insistently. Diana watched as a visible tremor ran through him, his eyes half-closing in bliss.

With a loud moan, Silvas dove, his tongue driving into her, striking the sensitive spot inside her channel with such frenzy that it sent sparks flying through her. He wiggled his tongue, exploring the area as he tapped his tongue in quick succession against the cluster of nerves. Diana's body lit up and she clenched around the invading organ as she brought her legs against the sides of his head.

A dark chuckle escaped him as he pulled away only to graze his teeth along her clit before flicking it with this tip of his tongue. A hard gasp left her on a strangled note. His grip tightened, pinning her in place as he growled against her clit, the vibration sending pleasure shooting through her seconds before he sucked the nub into his hot mouth. He tugged on it hard before laving the entire area with his tongue once more. Diana twisted under his mouth as he fell upon her, feasting on her as if in a frenzy.

He burned for her. She could feel it as much as she could feel her own blood cry out for him. She surrendered happily to the invasion of his urgency and pleasure as he dragged every whimper and cry from her with his lips and tongue.

It was as if an inferno brushed through her. Lust roared

through their budding bond, his desire feeding hers and her need feeding his. But it was more than that. When she focused on the bond forming between them, she could feel his affection curl through her laying beneath the uncontrollable wave of his desire —the instinct that demanded to be satisfied.

At the caress of his hand against her side, affection and desire spun together into an unbreakable cord between them as their pleasure built. It pulled taut on her as his lips tugged again on her clit. Without warning, her climax exploded. A hot rush of energy exploded through her blood as her pussy flooded anew. She would have been embarrassed at the way she soaked his mouth, but it was difficult to feel anything but cherished when his delighted growls filled her ears as he lapped it up.

Diana attempted to squirm away, her breath coming out in whimpers as he tormented her, feasted on her until he lifted his head and met her eyes. He gently unwound her hands from his antlers and stood up.

Diana watched him as he stood over her. Despite her orgasm, her lust hadn't cooled at all. The heat that rippled through her made her feel like she was about ready to crawl out of her skin at any moment. She tried to imagine how much worse it could have been if she had continued to ignore the demands of the bond. Would it have been like this all throughout her waking hours? Already she had been feeling the unyielding pressure of desire that never seemed to let up. She panted and twisted uncomfortably against his cloak beneath her.

"Soon," he murmured soothingly.

His expression softened, but as his eyes roamed over her, they glittered down at her with unconcealed desire. Holding her gaze with his, he worked quickly as he unlaced and kicked off his boots before shucking his pants. The movement was shameless as he exposed himself to her scrutiny. She had no doubt that he enjoyed every lustful reaction he provoked from her. And he was provoking quite a number of them.

Not that they weren't well deserved.

He was truly beautiful. His inhuman appearance added to his appeal in her eyes. Her gaze ran over him, enjoying the way the soft white velvet fuzz covering his body almost seemed luminous in some areas where the firelight touched it, while the valleys of his muscles were shaded. The shadowy path of his abs led her gaze in an unerring path right down to his straining cock. Fully erect, the white length turned a deeper gray as it progressed along the swollen length to the tip.

Diana licked her lips as she pushed herself to her knees. She needed to taste him.

Silvas held his body perfectly still as she gripped his hips, his eyes fastened on her. She could feel the eagerness, adoration, and longing from him, and it fueled her own excitement. He seemed to be exercising great control to allow her to enjoy herself and explore his body. Yet the moment her tongue touched his cock, she saw that control fracture. The thick muscles of this thighs quivered, and he drew in a ragged breath, his eyes becoming more luminous as they followed her every movement.

She proceeded to tease him as he had teased her. She lapped the bumpy length, exploring the unique texture of his cock with her tongue. She paid special attention to the head, tracing the edge of the crown and flicking her tongue again the nub at the tip that secreted a honey-flavored essence. A low groan rattled out of him.

Pulling back a little, Diana licked her lips, fascinated with the way the flavor fizzled and popped on her tongue. "What is that?"

"My mating venom," he hissed with a raspy snarl as she rubbed her thumb against the nub, watching another tiny bead of substance rise out of it. Her thumb stilled at that word. "Venom?"

"It brings pleasure only," he assured her in a thick voice as he noticeable fought for control. "It is necessary for when we lock together in mating."

"But it won't hurt me?" she asked.

"It will not. You will feel only incredible pleasure when it is inside you."

That was good enough for her in her fevered state. Her mouth already had a pleasant tingle. Diana nodded and wrapped her lips around the head, sucking him into her mouth as she took as much as she could. She was overwhelmed by more of the fizzing flavor, but once he was in her mouth, no more than a few drops emerged as she began to move up and down the length.

Silvas's raspy moans and growls filled the cavern as she bobbed on his cock, sucking him deep and withdrawing enough to swirl her tongue around the head. He began to move his hips in small, shallow thrusts in time with the pace she set, and she became aware of a hand tangled in her hair, the claws very lightly scraping against her scalp as he held her to him. His tail wrapped around her ribcage, the soft tip flicking her left nipple. His cock twitched once in her mouth, and the taste of sweet wine from a trickle of precum hit her tongue before he jerked her head away with a low snarl.

"Not like this." He hissed. "I need to be inside you to end this torment."

He dropped to his knees in front of her and crowded close, his hands slipping around her calves to pull her legs forward out from beneath her ass. His lips claimed hers, his tongue sweeping into her mouth as she moaned. She reveled in the feel of it and his sweet flavor.

Diana dropped back onto the mossy bed as he prowled up her body to settle between her thighs, their mouths locked together as they drank from each other, their tongues twining together.

As they kissed, his hands slipped beneath her ass, the claws scraping in a light sting as he drew her bottom up closer to his pelvis. His cock slipped along her pussy, each bump striking her clit as he thrust against her. They both moaned, and he released her mouth to brush his lips along her jaw as Diana twined her arms around his neck, rocking against him. He slipped against her again before lining his cock up at her entrance.

It was large and intimidating, far more than she had ever taken, and just the feel of it against her took her breath away. She didn't have much experience, but enough to still know when she was in over her head. Instead of being worried, she felt need coil through her at the press of the wide head against her opening.

She arched against him as her legs locked around the back of his thighs, urging him to press into her. Silvas didn't need any more invitation than that. He caught her gaze with his, hands on her thighs as he held her against him. He lifted her bottom just enough so that she could feel his tail as it wrapped around her waist, anchoring her to him. He dropped his cheek fully against hers so that his lips rested right against her ear. She could feel the silken glide of them against the lobe as he spoke.

"You are mine," he hissed.

He surged into her at the fall of the last word from his lips, his cock breaching her in a long, hot glide. There was a slight burn from the stretch, drowned out by the resulting pleasure crashing through her as he fully seated himself. She was achingly full as her sex rippled around his cock. Moaning, she felt the sharp press of his claws as he tried not to move so that her body could adjust to his invasion. It was sweet, but her own need was boiling within her.

She didn't want slow; she needed to be taken hard and thoroughly.

Diana bucked against him, and she felt his tail tighten seconds before he drew his hips back and snapped them forward, spearing into her. His cock slammed forward with such force that it made her cunt cream, and her breath left her with a ragged gasp.

"Yes! Just like that!" she cried out.

He didn't respond except to run his tongue up her throat and nuzzle the sensitive flesh, his purr filling her ears as he thrust into her. Diana pressed her heels against the back of his thighs, her hands digging into his back. She rocked against him, rising to meet him until his rhythm increased to the point that she was unable to do more than hold on as he rutted into her with abandon.

Her moans broke into cries as his growls took on an eerie pitch that she had never heard before. Tones shifted and glided together in a beautiful, howling moan that rose from his chest. His thrusts became deeper and harder with a feverish desperation which echoed the mounting orgasm trying to claw its way out of her. When his cock hit just right, deep inside, a forceful orgasm ripped through her.

Diana dragged her fingernails down his back as she wailed. Silvas pounded into her, trembling as his eyes brightened to a white-hot glow. His lips pulled back from his teeth from the effort. With one final thrust, burying himself deep, she felt an odd pinch. She gasped but the pain was again swept away as another orgasm rocked her. She could feel the bulges on his cock swelling further, rubbing in such a way that it extended her climax into a continuous series of ripples.

Desperate to anchor herself, she sought something to focus on, and her eyes came to rest of the cradle of his clavicle. There, she watched in awe as what looked like a perfect pearl push out from beneath his skin just above his heart. It shimmered there, catching the light from the fire.

Another wave of pleasure swept her away, carrying her higher as he threw his head back and released a roar that shook the rocks around them. Deep within her, his cock jerked, massaging a sensitive spot as if it were attached with every splash of his hot seed. Heat surged through her veins, infusing her with such pleasure that she was only vaguely aware of Silvas looming over her.

She felt the press of his lips against her shoulder in a sweet kiss, but it was followed by a searing pain as two sharp fangs drove deep into the flesh. Something dropped against her clavicle, and pain lanced her there as it began to burrow into her. In desperation, certain that she was going to drown in the horrible sensation, Diana tried to twist out from beneath him only to find she couldn't move.

The tip of his tail brushed against her clit as another pulse of liquid heat rushed through her womb. Ecstasy rolled over her with such intensity that it swept away the agony, and she embraced it as darkness descended around her.

CHAPTER 22

Silvas lay beside his mate, his fingers trailing through her loose hair as he held her, waiting for her to recover. The bonds had snapped so tight with the final release of his mating venom that it almost rendered him unconscious. A contented purr rumbled through his chest.

He held his mate, his long-awaited uxorem. His joy was tempered with the dread of the difficulties still ahead of them and with the knowledge that, even should they escape those trials unscathed, his mate would return to the human world. It wasn't an impossible situation—many beings lived separate from their mates—but it was one that left a bitter taste in his mouth. Silvas brushed his lips across her forehead, vowing to treasure every moment in her company.

It did not escape him that, even in the heights of the Hyperborean Mountains, he could not find a private moment with his mate. It didn't bode well for a future where their intimate time would be stolen whenever he was able to sneak over the forest borders rather than enjoying the protective magics of his quarters.

A whisper of movement, a flutter and soft crunch of snow,

came from the mouth of the cave, and he gave it an impatient look.

"You might as well come out," he said gruffly.

Three mountain nymphs crept around the edge of the cave. Each swaying step was wide and silent, their lithe bodies bent in a partial crouch as they moved like shadows. Their dark gray skin blended in against the stone except where the strongest firelight illuminated their features. All three had tangled braids of dark hair that swung with every move. Three sets of golden eyes ranging from dark amber to pale citrine watched him, and blood red lips parted as they sniffed the air and drew close to the fire.

One of the oreads crept forward, parting from the others. With a long finger, she spun a small bead on the string of her bow as she considered the human in his arms. Silvas tightened his grip possessively, his eyes narrowing on the nymph. She inhaled deeply, a smile curling her crimson lips as her large amber eyes glowed with undisguised pleasure.

His lips thinned. "What do you want?" he snapped.

The nearest oread smiled, undeterred by his hostility.

"It has been ages since a god has taken a bride," she observed. "When we scented your joining, we had to come and witness for none other was nearby to do the honor."

"I required no witness," he said.

Her brows lifted in surprise. "A god should be so honored."

"I am a silvanus."

The nymph's grin widened. "Is that what you tell your bride—that you are just another silvanus of the woods? You who were the first, the divine son of Turan." At his answering silence, she laughed. "Then she doesn't know that the first line of silvani sprung from you when, in your youth, you had lain with mortal women within your holy wood."

Silvas bristled. "I haven't been that male in over six millennia. It is so far in the mists of the past that I barely remember more than brief glimpses of that age. I have no need for those memories. It is not who I am."

He didn't even remember the women who had mothered the first silvani, nor was he certain which few of the silvani had sprung from his loins. He left the propagation of the species to his sons. There had been only one other opportunity in recent centuries, and that was when he took Alseida as his consort. That the dryad hadn't born a new spirit of the wood, the forests in the mortal world already declining as they were, he considered a blessing.

"You cannot escape who you are."

"I am exactly who I am, and nothing more."

The oread snorted a derisive laugh. "You are only as much as you care to be. You were born to be so much more. Do you think that the rest of the immortals do not notice how the Eternal Forest languishes? It has been that way for centuries."

"For which you can thank Alseida," he retorted angrily.

The oread cut her hand through the air, demanding his silence with such authority that he felt a chill. Her stature seemed larger, her coloring shifting to a light golden hue. She stepped toward him, soft golden rays of light bursting from her as she took on her true form. Towering over the nymphs behind her, the appearance of the goddess was now difficult to mistake. She was no mere oread. Dark curls reformed into a tight knot bound at the back of her crown as luminous green eyes fixed on him. With each step as she approached, her bound and shortened chiton fluttered around her knees.

Silvas clutched Diana closer to him, his body hunching protectively over hers. The gods were unpredictable at best. If she lashed out against him, he would not be injured, but he worried about Diana being caught in the middle of it. Raising his eyes, he met the angry gaze of the goddess of the hunt. She made a disgusted sound of impatience as the nymphs behind her giggled.

"I have no interest in harming your bride, Selvans. It wouldn't serve my purposes. It is my hope that your bond to her will return you to *your* purpose. The forest requires life to thrive and flourish, to bring health to not only the divine realms but the woods of the human realm as well. This is your duty as the king of the Eternal Forest, Selvans," she snapped, her words vibrating through the cave. "You must resume your authority and full responsibilities."

He lowered his eyes, frustration stirring deep within him and an unsettling fear. He recalled what he had been when he had thrown aside his sword and abandoned his place among the gods. He had been so near a monster himself; he couldn't risk exposing his mate to that.

"I cannot be that male," he growled out, burying his nose in Diana's neck as he breathed in her comforting scent. "I will not risk harming her."

The goddess cocked her head and then crouched down at his side until they were nearly eye to eye. She reached forward and flicked one of the golden ornaments hanging from his antlers so that it swung.

"Look here at the god of the woods, wearing the jewels of a mere king granted by an admiring court," she scoffed.

His lips tightened at the observation.

"My uxorem has claimed them," he growled. "I feel no shame wearing them if they are hers."

The goddess snorted and glanced down at Diana, a soft smile on her lips. Lifting one hand, she skimmed it over his uxorem's hair.

"My namesake," she said, "she would have made a fine oread." Her eyes lifted and met his. "She is stronger than she appears, Selvans. She was designed by the Fates to be yours. Do you think that she, of all beings, wouldn't be able to handle the darkness within you? Lifetime after lifetime, she has waited for you, and you never sought her out, confining yourself in your misery in the palace that you turned into a fortress against the world, even as you protectively confine your sister beneath your palace floors."

A more urgent tone filled her voice. "Change comes, Selvans, and with it incredible danger. You need to hurry home and reclaim the Eternal Forest. Bring life back to it before it is lost to *his* hunger."

"You speak of Cacus."

She inclined her head silently.

He leaned forward, his brow furrowing. "If it is so important, why don't the gods become involved?"

"The gods *are* involved," she informed him coldly. "The Tainted Ones arise once more—you know this. Do not think that we are not all forced into the battle of the turning of the cosmos. The Fates have set Cacus as your responsibility. Secure your forest, Selvans, and bring life back to it." Her arrows rattled in her quiver as she stood again, looming over him. "Now I must return to my own hunt."

She glanced once more at Diana as his mate sighed, shifting against his chest with the first signs of waking. The goddess backed away, returning to the form of the lithe gray nymph as she stood once more beside the fire.

Diana stirred, her eyelids fluttering before her eyes, deepest green, looked up at him in confusion. She grimaced as she touched where he had bitten her, the wound already healed and the lingering marks fading.

"What the hell happened?" she asked, her voice hoarse from sleep.

"A natural reaction to the bonding," he assured her. He nodded toward the oreads to give warning that they were not alone. "We have company."

His mate turned in his arms, her eyes widening as she took

in the wild appearance of the oreads. Unlike other nymphs, oreads were clothed in animal skins, their long hair worn in coarse braids. Their half-nude bodies with their long limbs, gray coloring, and orange eyes made them look dangerous and predatory.

The goddess in the form of the oread inclined her head and smiled. “Greetings, bride of Selvans.”

He frowned but blanked his expression as Diana turned quizzical eyes on him. “Selvans?”

“An old name,” he explained. “I prefer Silvas in this age. Sometimes immortal ones feel the need to forget the past and reinvent ourselves.”

The goddess snorted. “Some more than others. Yet there comes a time where trivial things are set aside, and we need to remember and embrace who we really are.”

He ignored the barb and helped his mate sit up as he felt her need to greet their visitors properly. She was obviously still disoriented and recovering. Now was not the time for any significant revelations. The golden cord of bond was newly forged. No need to distress her so soon. Not when they still had the strix to deal with.

“Our visitors are oreads, nymphs of the mountains,” he said. “They concern themselves with the fecundity and balance of the wild mountains. Among all nymphs, they enjoy the hunt the most. You might occasionally see them in the mountain foothills of the Eternal Forest. Some mortals find them frightening,” he added, which made the nymphs grin. He didn’t want her to feel any shame if she found them unsettling.

To his surprise, instead of being fearful as he expected her to be, she smiled at them.

“Honestly, I’m more afraid of the green-haired woman in your palace who looks at me like she wants to squash me like a bug. Not that you aren’t truly impressive and worthy of awe,” she added. “I have no doubt you are perfectly capable of terrifying anyone you wish. I truly appreciate your kind greetings.”

The nymphs laughed, their grins widening at the acknowledgement, and they inclined their heads in a show of respect. Silvas’s eyebrows raised at the gesture. It was no small thing to be so honored by an oread, for they rarely bestowed any honor to one who was not among their own.

One by one, the oreads slipped out of the cave, their purpose complete, leaving only the disguised goddess with them in the cave. She toyed with the string on her bow, her lips curving in a teasing smile as she watched him out of the corner of her eye.

“I am pleased that I of all beings was here to greet first the bride of Selvans. It is only right that I be among those who bear witness to your rise, though I spied doves lingering when I approached with my retinue. A strange sight in the mountains,” she added with a teasing smile.

Silvas groaned, wondering just how much of the bonding his mother caught.

The goddess chuckled as she turned away toward the opening of the cave. Glancing over her shoulder, she couldn’t resist making one last parting shot. “Keep in mind, if you ever tire of the *silvanus*, you will be welcome among us.” Then she ducked out of the cave, returning to the mountainside.

Diana pursed her lips as she stared after the goddess, caressing the bond mark on her clavicle with a fingertip. “That was…interesting.” He reached forward and stilled her hand, not wanting the flesh around it to get irritated while it finished merging. She turned around in his arms and gestured to it. “So is this… What did you do to me?”

Silvas met her eyes, feeling along their bond. She wasn’t angry or scared. He exhaled slowly. He hadn’t wanted to admit how worried he had been that she would reject the changes that would come with their bond. This was the most visible change so far, and her acceptance of it was a big step that would pave the way for her acceptance of her new life.

"It is my *vinculum marcam*, my bond mark. When we finished our bond, a piece of my soul separated from me to join with you just as I took you into me." He caressed her shoulder where he could still see the pale imprint of his bite.

"You bit me." She raised her eyes until they met his—and hauled her arm back to punch him in the shoulder.

He caught her wrist in his hand and raised her fist to kiss her knuckles. "Why are you hitting me?"

"Because that hurt, asshole," she snapped.

He raised an eyebrow but smiled at the lack of heat in her voice. Her fingers relaxed as he continued to kiss them.

"The venom from my fangs and my cock would have made certain that the pain was fleeting and that you felt good," he said.

She grumbled her agreement. "Okay, that part was really great. Still, a little warning would have been nice."

He gave her a curious look as he took her hand in his, brushing the back of it with his thumb. "If something causes you to feel physical pain, do you prefer to watch it or look away and try to ignore it?"

Diana's brow furrowed. "I'm not sure where you're going with this. I guess the pain is a little easier to handle if I don't look at it, especially if I'm getting a shot or something. It's a bit easier if I'm caught unprepared… Oh. I guess I do know where you are going with your question."

Silvas nodded and pulled her into his arms. His heart was gladdened as she settled comfortably against him. "I worried that if you had been aware of it, you would have not been able to relax enough to be able to complete the bonding. That your body would have built up a defense to resist the venom. I didn't want you to experience more pain than what was necessary in our bonding."

"I suppose that makes sense," she said. "Still, from here on out… I prefer to for there not to be secrets between us. If something is going to affect me, I want to know about it. Especially if it's something big."

He inclined his head in agreement. "Very well. I suppose now is a bad time to tell you that you are no longer human."

She shoved back in surprise. "Say *what* now?"

CHAPTER 23

Diana scrabbled down the side of the mountain, her footing precarious. The gleaming white rocks were dry and stark as if the snow had never touched them, jutting up like jagged teeth from the ground. Silvas stood just ahead, watching her with a concerned expression. Even his long tail whipped behind him in agitation. He had been hovering ever since they left the cave.

It had only become worse when they encountered the broken path to the next peak.

He turned his head, staring at their destination before he turned back and fixed her with a thoughtful look. Even among their bond, there was a watchful, wary stillness. She could feel the tension in him. He was worried, and that realization surprised her. He always seemed unshakeable, and at times amused with everything.

Even when he told her she was no longer human, it had been delivered with a raised brow and a little smirk that had annoyed her. It didn't get much better when he set her on her feet and suggested that they move on as if the matter were inconsequential.

Anger churned hot in her belly. That she understood. The strange sense of gratitude took longer to fathom. It was because, despite his atrocious delivery, he had imparted important information she needed just as she asked. She had figured it out about the third hour into climbing down the fucking side of Mount Doom. At that point, she wouldn't have been surprised to see a pair of hobbits bypassing her at the snail's pace she was going.

Barely balancing on the sloped rock, she frowned, squinting. The blocky rock formations in the distance twisted and bulged in rolling motions. They cast grotesque shadows as they moved. The more she stared at them, the more she could make out the defined shapes of thick bodies that were supported with long, heavy limbs.

"You know," she called over to Silvas, who had stiffened at the first spike of her fear, his ears pricking toward her. She barely avoided toppling over as she leaped to the next stone, keeping the threatening figures visible at all times out of the corner of her eye. "For not being human anymore, I'm disappointed with the fact that I haven't gained any new abilities."

He turned to look at her. "Abilities?"

She glared as she slipped down the side of one massive boulder. "I'm supposedly not human anymore and yet here I am, practically falling off the side of the mountain."

"I did offer to carry you," he reminded her.

"Yeah, but I didn't want it to seem like now that things are… you know… bonded and all between us that I don't need to carry my own weight."

A shiver ran up her spine as she glanced toward the creatures. If she wasn't mistaken, the misshapen creatures were keeping pace with them.

. . .

Silvas's lips twisted slightly, though the smile didn't reach his eyes. If anything, he seemed hyper focused on her now, his expression tight. She felt his concern as he prodded along their bond. It was the only sign of just how unsettled he was.

"Is that issue of your concern that I am sensing?" he asked softly, his head canting to the side. "You are doing a remarkable job if your plan is to slip off the side of the mountain as you've nearly done thirty-five times, or, at the rate we are going, to camp out on the rocks tonight," he murmured.

"Ouch. No. My point is, shouldn't I be scaling down the side of the mountain looking sexy and perfectly at ease like you do?" she stated impatiently. "Or at least have good enough vision to figure out what the fuck those monstrous rock things are over there, because they are creeping me the fuck out," she nearly shouted. She gestured in their direction with a wave of her hand. She was definitely certain that they were staring at her now, if the reddish glowing pinpricks of light reflecting in their eyes was anything to go by.

As Silvas jerked his head around in their direction, the one at the front suddenly stretched up twisted arms raising to the sky, jagged, sharp ends hooked menacingly as it slashed through the air in her direction, a bellowing, blood-curdling howl raised in the air. What the actual fuck?

"Mountain trolls," Silvas snarled.

His lips curled back from his teeth as he hissed loudly in fury. Turning in place, Silvas took two bounding steps toward her as she watched the creatures tear large rocks from the ground. Strong arms ripped her up off her feet. She was flying through the air as he skidded off the side of the rock before spinning and leaping for another foothold as a giant boulder whistled by them. The impact of it crashing against the ground nearby vibrated through Diana as the rock burst into hundreds of pieces. She cried out as several stung and abraded her skin painfully.

"Trolls? What the fuck… They don't even remotely resemble Raskyuil!"

"Mountain trolls are different," he growled as he effortlessly leaped again, neatly evading another massive, plummeting rock. "They are large, aggressive, and possess limited intelligence."

"Can't you use your kingly influence to scare them away?" she demanded. She ducked her face against the protective shelter of his body as another rock exploded around them.

Silvas chuckled dryly as he sprung lightly from stone to stone. "What influence? Unlike the forest trolls, they don't form any sort of recognizable social organization. They won't acknowledge my authority. You see the larger one in the front and the two smaller in the back?" he asked as he gestured with his chin toward them.

Diana risked another glance in their direction and nodded weakly. Though they were too far away to see much in the way of clear details, their size difference was easy enough to make out.

"That is the only sort of social unit you will ever see mountain trolls in," he stated as he dodged behind a wall of rock. "The larger troll at the fore is the female, the two others are the males in her harem. I am guessing she is a younger troll, since on average an adult female will have anywhere from five to seven males in her harem. They protect her and any young that are born and follow her direction."

"So why the hell are they attacking us? We pose no threat to them. We aren't even anywhere fucking near them!"

He chuckled humorlessly, his arms briefly squeezing her tighter to him as he picked up speed. "Because, while they are usually scavengers, they won't hesitate to kill anything that looks like it may be easy prey. Apparently, your manner of descending the mountain attracted their attention," he informed her wryly. "The males will attempt to kill you from a distance with the hope

I will abandon your corpse so they can safely approach with their female to eat at their leisure. Normally they would turn to stone when touched by the sun, but it seems they are able to move under the cloud cover to hunt. But we are about to disappoint them."

With several more leaps, they were safely within the jutting rise of rocks that began to ascend to the second peak, the trolls left far behind them.

Silvas set her on a flatter stone with lanky pale green brush clinging to some loose soil crumbling around it. Fishing out some dried meat from their supplies, he pressed it into her hands and gave her the waterskin. Diana scarfed it down, grateful for the nourishment, her hands trembling despite their current safety.

"Will they follow us over here?" she whispered.

He shook his head, his eyes narrowing as they fixed on a point behind her. "No. The strix's nest will keep them away. Your nose isn't strong enough to pick up the smell now, but you will as we get closer. The smell of rot, death, and the bite of magic is not something that you will miss."

Diana turned her head so that she too looked up at the ascending slope of the peak. Her stomach bottomed out nervously. A thick gray mist clung to the stones as it appeared to roll down the slope of the mountain. The stones—what little she could see pushing out from the mist—appeared to be splashed with black in some places as if so many bodies bled out over them that it permanently stained the rock. As she stared, she watched the mist roll on itself. At times, with the shifting of a breeze, it seemed to coil back, exposing a portion of bare rock, but it never lasted. Within minutes it would roll back over the spot, and it never once dissipated.

With a particularly strong gust, she nearly gagged as a rank, sour smell filled her nose. It contained the sharp metallic scent of blood and of something unfamiliar, like the acidic bite of ozone after a storm.

"We are going there," she murmured.

"Yes," Silvas replied unhappily his eyes scanning over the mist, looking for any sign of weakness.

"Fuck."

He turned an understanding look upon her, his lips flattened as they pressed tightly together. She could feel the coil of tension and the rush of hostility and apprehension that filled him when he looked once more upon the shrouded stone.

"Indeed."

CHAPTER 24

Silvas hopped up on a narrow rocky ledge, his chest expanding as he scented the air. The pungent smell filled his nose unpleasantly, but he didn't detect any movement from the strix. That wasn't surprising. So long as they didn't attract her attention, she was unlikely to emerge from her cave before sunset.

Diana glanced up at him quizzically, but he waved her on to keep to the more stable path as his eyes narrowed at the distant figures of the mountain trolls. They'd given up the pursuit and were ambling back to whatever cavern they were holing up in. It was peculiar. Normally mountain trolls would never come anywhere near the territory of such a dangerous being as the strix. Not even a mature female with a large harem would risk her family so recklessly. His ears tipped as he listened to the female howl miserably, his mouth turning down in sympathy.

His mate stilled as another louder howl pierced the air. "You feel sorry for them? They wanted to eat me," she whispered furiously.

"I would never have allowed that. I would have killed them if I needed to. Truthfully, it probably would have been a kindness. I believe they are starving," he replied as he dropped down once more to her side, satisfied that the trolls were retreating.

"Starving?" she murmured, her brow furrowing as he felt a soft tug on their bond. Despite her words, Diana had a compassionate heart, a rarity in his world. He found himself instinctively reaching for her, wanting to hold her close and lose himself in their bond. Instead, he nodded, keeping his attention on their surroundings, searching for any sign of danger.

"That would explain why they are risking a hunt under cloud cover in the daylight. Not to mention in a strix's territory, of all places, where they could easily be killed in a territorial clash. As I said, normally they are scavengers, feeding on game brought down by predators, although they are known to eat copious amounts of fish in the lower mountain rivers."

"Like bears, then," she observed as if comparing them to a common predator made all the difference in the world.

Silvas found it charmingly naïve, but she wasn't wrong when it came down to their roles in the balance of nature in the different realms. Still, he understood the sentiment behind the correlation. Mountain trolls were unpleasant to tangle with and generally would be inclined to eat anyone they encountered if they could, but they were doing as they were designed to do. He didn't wish to harm them if he could avoid it.

"An apt enough comparison, although a mountain troll would eat a bear without hesitation if they felt they could overwhelm one," he observed with a humorous twist of his lips. He immediately sobered, his ears twisting to catch the slightest sounds around them. Things were worse in the mountains than he imagined even after their visit earlier that day. "If something is causing such huge disruptions in the ecosystem, enough to send Aquilo from his great house to scour his mountains, and oreads hunting, we do not want to be caught up here where we are at a disadvantage. I am not without defenses, but my strength lies mostly in the forest," he admitted as he reached down to assist her up the steep incline.

As they climbed higher, the weather steadily grew grayer and more oppressive with the electric weight of magic stirring in the air around them. As the hours passed and the sun began to drop in the sky, a strong gust picked up, drawing in black clouds around the peak. Silvas pulled the length of his hair back and quickly bound it with a cord. The stench of the strix's nest was getting stronger, and even Diana wore an expression of disgust as she made a noticeable effort to breathe solely through her mouth.

He could feel the pulse of power through the atmosphere like a crack of lightning. The strix was beginning to awaken. He gritted his teeth as he bowed his head against the wind. It dragged uncomfortably against his antlers, but he hoped that it cut the wind enough to provide some minimal relief for Diana who now, at his insistence, clung with one hand to his belt as she climbed.

As the wind increased in strength, he worried about his uxorem losing her grip on him and falling from the mountain. He was tempted to pull her up into his arms again and carry her the remaining short distance to the cave entrance, though it meant subjecting her to the full force of the wind. Silvas reached behind him, one hand clamping around her wrist to hold her securely to him as they increased their rate of climb. Just behind him Diana gagged and moaned.

"Fuck… That smell! I'm going to puke."

He turned slightly, releasing his grip on her wrist to frown with concern at his mate, his shoulders hunched to continue shielding her as much as possible. Her face did look unnaturally pale. His concern raised another notch as he reached forward and rubbed his palm against her cold cheek.

"I know," he murmured. "If you need to get sick, there is no shame in it. Tell me and we will stop."

She gagged again and took a deep shuddering breath. "No. I

think I'm alright. It's just awful. You weren't kidding about how bad it is."

He nodded his head in understanding as he faced forward. Firmly wrapping his hand once more around her wrist, he continued their upward progression as he squinted against the rapidly increasing gloom.

Up ahead he could see the dark crevice from which the terrible smell emitted. Even from their short distance away he could make out sun-bleached bones scattered outside. Mingled with them were those that were black with rotting flesh belonging to various species. Some were animals, but most were noticeably younglings. He couldn't tell offhand what the species was since outside of coloring patterns, most younglings of the different species looked similar structurally until adolescence. This was a sight he hated for his mate to see.

He considered waiting to full nightfall to spare her. But to keep their advantage, they needed to make it the rest of the distance before the strix fully awakened and was alerted to their presence. He was unable to shield the one person that he wanted nothing more than to protect. Gods above forgive him.

The daylight had waned considerably from the sky as he finally pulled himself level to the crevice. He had to break Diana's hold and transfer her grip to a secure handhold so that he could leap up to the flat rock that jutted out from the side of the cliff, no doubt worn down from centuries serving as a roost for the strix. Kicking the foul mess of bones out of the way as much as he could, Silvas leaned down and lifted her up.

The moment Diana's feet touched the stone, she glanced around, her face filling with horror as her eyes rested on a small skull. She grabbed a protruding rock and leaned over the side, her body spasming as she vomited. He closed the distance between them, gently drawing back her hair before stroking her back with one hand until she ceased heaving. Wiping her mouth with the back of her hand, she straightened, giving the entrance a dark glare.

Inside he could hear the low creaking sounds of the strix stirring as his ears turned toward it. Pulling his sword free, he reached back instinctively to grab ahold of his mate, anchoring her to his side. They couldn't fight that way, but as they entered, he felt better having her in his grasp for as long as possible.

The sound of brittle bone fragments was loud underfoot as they entered the cavern. Silvas immediately concentrated on the flow of power through his body and pulled at a thread of it, drawing it through him. His magic was typically limited to his influence on the forests, but summoning light was a skill that most immortal races possessed, and all gods could accomplish with minimal effort. While he didn't need light to see, he wouldn't leave Diana so impaired. He felt a crackle of warmth around the crown of his head as his antlers sparked, releasing a burst of light between their inner spikes. The glow didn't cast its illumination far, but it served their purpose.

The light cast its glow on tall pillars carved from the natural cave formations as detailed carvings and paintings graced smoothed walls gilded in many places in gold and adorned with precious stones. In the distance, he could see a giant tripod brazier. An angry sound drifted through the cavern—a muffled, shrill snarl.

Bones skittered loudly as something moved heavily in the depths of the winding cave system. A raspy flutter of huge wings echoed around them. His eyes slid to Diana, feeling her anxiety rippling through their bond. She kept pace at his side, her movements fluid despite her unease. An arrow was already nocked in her bow, the string pulled marginally back in preparation to fire. Reassured that she was prepared, he crept forward, taking care to make as little noise as possible.

The resonance of an unmistakable scrape of large claws dragging against stone was followed by the loud clatter of falling stones as the strix drew closer from within the heart of her nest. She was still too far away to see accurately, even with his superior eyesight, except for the brilliant yellow eyes that appeared like a pair of glowing sparks, flashing at them as a raspy chuckle filled the spaced.

"Strangers to whet my appetite?" she queried. He could hear the click of her teeth, and her wings appeared as looming inky shadows within the dark. "I think so," she hissed to herself, each vowel drawn out in her aged voice.

There was a rush of air and a loud thump that sent billows of dust and dirt toward them. Silvas gestured to Diana to hold her position as he warily stalked forward. His eyes narrowed. He was able to see much further beyond the glow of the illumination than Diana. A slim silhouette moved, and an ethereally beautiful woman emerged from the shadows. Her dark hair hung in a wave down her back and large golden eyes peered at him, a tiny smile tugging on red lips. A gray gown ghosted around her legs as she drew closer. She exhaled a strange perfume that rolled through the cave. It glittered briefly, thickening into a curtain that seemed to surround him, confusing his senses.

He blinked his eyes as everything blurred and tilted around him, godly power surging through the air. There was something almost familiar about it, but he couldn't quite grasp it. Where was he? What was he doing? His eyes refocusing, Silvas smiled in welcome. His mate smiled as she walked toward him, the fragrant flowering vines crawling up the walls slid against her skin as she brushed by him. His body hardened eagerly as he watched her draw nearer, her hips moving seductively with every step. His smile slipped a little in confusion. Since when did Diana walk that like? For that matter, how did he arrive there? Last he recalled he was searching for something… He strained to recall what, but shook his head as rosy perfume rose around him, seeping into his senses.

His smile returned. It didn't matter. All that mattered was that he was home with his uxorem. Diana's hair was loose around her shoulders and a gray dress clung to her body. Her fingers toyed with the lacing at the front and he watched as one side slipped down, baring her shoulder. He took a deep, shuddering breath, trying to capture her scent. To his frustration it eluded him. A low growl escaped him in his frustration as he stalked forward. He needed his mate, *now*. He needed her under his fingers and her cunt beneath his mouth.

She grinned in invitation and her eyes trailed over him as he stalked closer to her. The robe fell away, revealing her lush figure. He licked his lips, his lust surging through him in need to claim his mate. He reached down to loosen his pants and frowned as his hand encountered armor. Dropping his gaze, he glanced in confusion at the dark belt that protected his loins. Why would he return to his chambers in armor?

"My love," Diana's voice whispered huskily, drawing his attention with another fragrant cloud, there seemed almost to be a thread of impatience to her voice in that one word. "Don't make me wait. I *need* you."

"Yes," he murmured, his cock surging impatiently.

It didn't matter why he was wearing the armor. He would be divested of it quickly enough. He pulled away its lacings and let it drop loudly to the floor. She sighed happily, a rosy mist exiting from her mouth as she drew nearer, her hand stretching out toward him. Enticing him nearer. He was nearly close enough that if he sprung forward, he would be able to pull her up into his arms.

"Silvas?" a familiar voice called. It sounded strained with tension and he scowled. Who was interrupting his intimate time with his mate?

He growled low and menacingly as he turned away from his mate. He would deal with the intruder and then return to sink into Diana's sweet heat. He scowled as he was unable to focus on the stranger. Their figure blurred and warped every time he tried to focus on them. It had to be a threat. He didn't know of any being within the Eternal Forest who had such capability. He bristled with hostility as his eyes narrowed on the threat.

"It's a terrible monster, my love," Diana whispered behind his back in a soft breathy voice. "Show me your strength and dispatch it quickly and return to me. I will show you such pleasure. It has been ages since I've had a strong male in my bower."

He cocked his head at the strange turn of phrase, but he couldn't afford to be distracted now. His lips curled back from his teeth as he advanced on the stranger.

CHAPTER 25

Diana froze as she watched Silvas stalk toward her, his expression a picture of utter menace. Just moments before he had been talking to the shadows just beyond her line of sight. She thought she heard a voice emerge, but she had had difficulty catching the words. His agreement, though, had been clear. Her heart thumped painfully behind her ribs. For an instant, he paused. He cocked his head and he slowed slightly, but once more the air filled with the sickeningly sweet smell and his expression once again became aggressive, the gray bands in his eyes blown out more than she had ever seen before.

Fear pounding painfully in her chest, she raised her arrow in a warning. "Silvas? What's gotten into you?" A perplexed look crossed his face and she felt a shift of awareness along their bond as if he were fighting with himself, but it was fleeting as his brow drew down and his face hardened. Her stomach sank as she realized that he was staring at her without any recognition. Instead, he was advancing on her as if *she* were the enemy.

His posture radiated hostility. His head tilted forward, brandishing his dangerous antlers, and his long tail was slashing through the air behind him.

"Please," she choked out. "Please, stop. I don't want to hurt you."

His lips peeled back in a cruel snarl and he lengthened his stride.

He wasn't stopping!

She choked on a fearful cry at the way his face wrinkled in a terrible grimace. The angle of his head cast much of it in dark shadows, all except those glowing white eyes and the teeth flashing at her. She stumbled back, her arrow dropping free to the cavern floor at her sudden retreat. She noted its fall with dismay but didn't take the time to stop and retrieve it. She shied away, uncertain in the face of his fury, her mind desperately trying to grapple with the sudden change that had overcome him.

The male who faced her was a stranger to her. His hand tightened around his sword, his face a terrible mask of fury. This was not the same male whose hands and mouth had studied every inch of her body, or who held her close to his chest. In his eyes, she was a threat, and his reaction was terrifying. Her breath escaped her in a small cry as she noted that her attempts to evade him had successfully backed her into a corner of the cave with little opportunity to escape.

Desperately she cast her gaze behind him. She didn't know what she was looking for, but she immediately stilled as she saw a woman grinning triumphantly. Her crimson lips were stretched inhumanely wide, her large yellow eyes gleaming in the dark like a predator. Diana was out of time.

With a roar, Silvas leaped forward, his sword arcing through the air. A cry tearing from her lips, Diana tugged sharply on the bond between them as she raised her bow to block the downward swing of the blade. Power flooded her, and she pushed every bit of it through her as the weapons connected violently. The resulting crack of the strike from where the bow slapped the flat side of the sword was thunderous as power unleashed and rolled, bringing loose rocks falling to the cavern floor. Diana's eyebrows winged upward as the sword, knocked free from his grip, skidding loudly against the rocky ground some distance away.

Silvas's head turned, his gaze tracking the movement of the sword only briefly before he turned back toward her with a furious roar. Diana, possessing a good idea of the source of her sudden strength, whispered an apology as she yanked on their bond again, infusing herself once more with incredible strength. Without hesitation, she raised the tip of her bow, striking him full-strength against the cheek, providing the opening to dart out of the way with an unaccustomed burst of speed.

She teared up, knowing that she wouldn't get far. Already she could hear Silvas's snarl and the slide of his boots across the floor as he headed toward her, preparing to attack again. She was under no illusions. She would not be able to hold out in a long-term fight against him. She ran blindly, knowing that at any moment Silvas would catch up to her. It was humbling to know that if he hadn't finished bonding with her, she would already have been caught. She could hear his boots getting louder as he quickly closed the distance between them.

"Destroy the intruder!" the woman screamed, her voice rising into a terrible shriek. Another burst of mist shot from her mouth and thickened as it hit the air.

Diana felt something within her stutter, and then her perception sharpened as she focused on the woman. There seemed to be a shift in the air around the lithe figure that almost reminded Diana of a mirage. She was not what she seemed, and she was using Silvas. This had to be the sorcery of the strix. The woman's mouth parted impossibly wide, jagged teeth showing between the perfect lips in an enormous, devouring maw. Immediately she could envision the child-eating creature hiding behind the beautiful illusion.

“Eat this, bitch,” Diana bit out as she pulled a new arrow from her quiver.

Pressing her lips together, she raised her bow and pulled the string taut. Her breath stilled within her. Sighting down her arrow, she took aim, and released the arrow as she exhaled. The sharp snap of the string sounded overly loud to her as it sent the arrow soaring toward its target. She watched it fly free as a hard body slammed against hers. The rake of claws burned where they dug into her flesh, but she smiled as a pained cry filled the air.

The weight above her shifted and Silvas bellowed loudly as if in agony.

CHAPTER 26

Anguish filled Silvas as he watched the arrow slice through the air toward his mate. Her cry shattered through him as it hit true, burrowing into her chest. A burst of power followed so strongly that he crouched low, every part of him crying out to reach his mate and try to save her. He dug his claws deeper into his enemy, hatred filling him as he watched his mate stumble back. Power wavered around Diana and he frowned in confusion, a sharp pain piercing his head as the air rippled and blasted from around her.

In that blast, the world around him shattered. Bewildered, he watched as his private chambers fragmented and fell away, leaving only coarse gray stone. A sickness filled his stomach. If this had all been an illusion… He looked toward his mate. Where Diana had stood a monstrous female shrieked and pulled at the arrow lodged in her breast.

Silvas shook his head in denial. Where was his uxorem?

A feminine whimper of pain reached his ears and he looked down, his chest seizing painfully as he beheld his mate. Blood welled up around his claws, and though he hadn't yet dug them in terribly deep, he could clearly see the wounds left upon her delicate skin and the tracks of blood staining her flesh red.

His hand fell away briefly before he hauled her up firmly into his arms. Fear flooded her, and the rancorous scent filled his lungs. She obviously thought that he was still under the influence of the strix.

"Shh, I have returned to myself. All because of you," he whispered against her skin.

She held herself stiffly in his arms for but a moment longer before relief filled him as her weight sank against him. A low sob rushed from her, tearing into his heart. Silvas clutched her tightly to his chest. He didn't want to consider what could have happened if she hadn't broken the enchantment. He had been certain that he was fighting a threat and had been prepared to deal with it accordingly. It had seemed so real. He had no doubt that the magic was being fueled by the power of Nocis. No ordinary strix would have been able to deceive a god so easily.

If the problem didn't lie within himself.

That was an unsettling thought. Had he spent so much time refusing his proper place that he had become weakened as any other immortal? If that were the case it was no wonder the Eternal Forest was so vulnerable to attack.

Straightening, his eyes narrowed on the creature who had caught him in her illusion. He heard Diana scramble to her feet at his side. Never taking more than part of his attention off the strix, he shot his mate a warning look, cautioning her to stay back. In his peripheral vision he watched as she curled her lip in disgust and surmised that she wasn't going to listen to him. He comforted himself with the fact that, although she was a bloody mess, she wasn't nursing any gaping wounds. He cut her a disapproving look which she completely ignored.

Silvas grit his teeth, but after what had just happened, he didn't feel like he had any grounds to rebuke her, nor could he argue with the fact that she had most likely saved them both. Swallowing his objections, he slid his body between his uxorem and the strix with a clear warning growl rising in his throat as he faced off with the monstrous sorceress.

Her wings flapping angrily, letting loose pale gray feathers into the air with every burst. Even as he stepped forward, she stilled, her wings laying momentarily limp at her sides as she turned her head, following his advance.

As he stalked toward her, Silvas noticed that the centuries had not been kind to the strix. He suspected that the illusion of the beautiful dark-haired woman in the feathered cloak bore some semblance to what she had looked like when she had obtained the sword: fertile, ripe womanhood at the height of her beauty. It was clearly not a new ruse for her. She had attempted to use that illusion against him, but had switched tactics quickly when her power failed to take hold of him. It was only when she had adopted the guise of Diana that she had found a weakness to exploit.

Now, however, there was no hiding what she was, and how the magic of the sword had unnaturally twisted her. She was not made to wield such divine power. Her skin hung withered from her frame, and she suffered from large balding spots not only in the feathers on her body but also in the mane of hair that fell from her head. Only clumps of scraggly white hair remained. Rheumy yellow eyes focused on him shrewdly, yet there was something off in those depths. While Nocis had extended her life unnaturally it had not kept her young, healthy, or sane. Madness gleamed in her yellow eyes as she watched him, her wings jumping excitedly at his every step.

Wheezing as she held a withered arm over her wound, a wild cackle of laughter escaped her. Mora swung her head rhythmically but with no purpose, her dark gray lips pulling back from the jagged remains of her teeth. Though her limbs were thin, her torso was bloated. From her condition, he suspected that more was left to rot from her meals than what she had succeeded in bolting down. Few of her teeth were left, and her lethal claws were broken down to fragments. His stomach turned as he imagined the pain that her victims had suffered, slowly bleeding out from where the broken claws ripped and scoured them rather than the quick brutal death that the species was known for. Parts of her mouth were stained with rot, saliva slipping frequently from her gaping mouth. Mora was a terrible shadow of the lethal, regal nature of a strix.

He felt another unfamiliar twinge of guilt.

All of this because he had rejected his purpose and discarded Nocis.

Silvas met her eyes, the sword in his hand held out from his side, ready to strike. “Where is the sword Nocis?” he demanded, his voice rolling through the cave.

“You will not take mine,” she spat, dark fluid flying from her lips as the raspy words were barked in a shrill voice at him. “You will die. Your pain will be mine to feast upon, your sorrow as I kill your female the wine that I shall drink. And then I will tear your flesh and swallow you until you are nothing more than rot and filth to be scraped from the floor.”

“Looks like we are going to have to get it the hard way,” Diana commented in a hard voice.

His eyes cut to his mate and her lips thinned, her hand tightening around her bow. She gave a slow nod of her head. She would follow his lead.

Keeping the tip of his sword pointed toward the floor, he moved closer, circling. As he circled, his eyes strayed around the nest, looking for any sign of the sword. Wherever she had it, she kept it hidden well away. He could feel the pulse of its power, but his eyes could not locate it. A wave of power rocked the cavern as Mora raised her wings, snapping them with a burst of power. Energy arched through every blast, blue tendrils lighting up the air. The power contained the distinct bite of Nocis and it called to something in Silvas's blood.

He snarled as he braced himself against the current of power. Nearby, Diana wrapped her arms around a column to keep her steady on her feet, her bow clattering against the stonework as she maintained her grip on it.

Mora's voice broke into a series of sharp words, and a blast sent both Silvas and Diana flying back to a far wall, their bodies impacting loudly. His breath whooshed out of his lungs and his mate's cry was mostly drowned out by the percussions of power that continued to hit them.

Baring his teeth, Silvas felt his fangs and claws grow, energy pulsating from his antlers as he swept a clawed hand forward against another lash of energy. His magic burst from where his claws struck the ether. Each time he struck out with the aetheric claws, the blood red lines of power rolled through the air until they slashed into the strix. Mora shrieked, her body jerking.

An arrow whistled by his head. It startled him briefly, but a grin stretched wildly across his lips at the spark of aelven power that flowed from the forged tip. There was no way to guess how Diana's power would manifest, but the sparks of aelven light that sprayed in its wake stirred an excitement within him. It sunk deep and the strix writhed with a blood-curdling scream. Diana immediately loosed another, her aim true as Silvas darted forward to drive his sword into the soft belly of the strix and end her life.

The sword struck, releasing a thick flow of black ichor over his hands. Mora jerked away, dislodging the blade as she struck out, sending a wall of wind tearing into him with the tiny stones from the cavern floor. Disoriented, he swung his blade again, taking pleasure in the way it bit into her once more, but the strix bared her teeth. Even as she twisted in pain, she slapped him away with her wing. A piercing shriek filled his head with bolts of pain.

At his side, Diana cried out as she crumpled. He turned to make his way back to his mate, but she flashed him a savage snarl as she drew to her feet once more. Tears of pain streaming down her cheeks, she raised her bow and let loose another series of arrows. Half missed their target, but the satisfying sounds of the hits echoed through the cave.

The strix's shrill cry ended with a wet, choked sound as Mora gurgled, two arrows buried in her throat. Claws raked down the flesh in an attempt to dislodge them, blood spewing. Silvas sent another volley of aetheric claws that had Mora stumbling back, her feathers darkening as the blood seeped from her copious wounds. But still, she stood!

Circling around, he stepped close to his mate, his eyes scanning the strix. Between his sword, his aetheric claws, and the aelven arrows, the strix should have been brought down many times, even if drawing the power of Nocis from wherever it was hidden in her nest. Cursing, Diana tossed aside her bow, her quiver empty. Pulling out her sword, she gave it a slow practice swing to warm up her shoulder. She gave him a small, tight smile, her own blood streaking down her body, not only from the wounds he had inflicted in his madness but also from the strix's magic ripping into her.

"Silvas… I don't know how long…"

A soft smile curved his lips. Even wearied she was at his side. He couldn't ask for more in a mate. Perhaps his mother's meddling had worked in his favor after all. Reaching a hand for her, his thumb caressed her cheek. "Only for as long as you can manage," he murmured. "When you cannot, find a place to hide until it is finished. I will protect you, uxorem. You've done more than enough."

Her lips parted as she met his eyes, but after a considerable pause, she nodded in agreement.

Dropping his hand, he squinted around the room, his eyes skimming over the strix attempting to steady herself. “If only I knew where it was,” he muttered. Turning his gaze back toward Mora, he stiffened at the sight of the large strix charging toward them. Her claws reached outward, the broken remnants hooking as her mouth opened wide soundlessly. Without her enchanted voice, she was falling back on her most basic attack.

Silvas stepped away from Diana as they both raised their swords. When the strix leaped forward, they moved together as one, striking, driving their swords into the creature. Silvas reached up and dug the claws of his opposite hand into Mora’s wing. A papery tearing sound rang out as he wrenched the wing, tearing it viciously with the full force of his strength. Blood splashed as the strix gurgled pitifully, her yellow eyes shining with hate.

He followed the action by swiftly breaking her arm before she could attempt to gore him with her claws. Diana hadn’t managed to tear the other wing, but it was noticeably broken in a place where her sword had struck it, flapping uselessly. The arm that the strix had attempted to strike her with was ravaged with numerous cuts until it looked nearly butchered, just barely holding together with sinew and bone. It was gruesome, but effective, and Silvas felt an upwelling of pride.

The good feeling was interrupted as Mora attempted to snake down her head to bite him, but he reached up and grasped her jaw as he twisted his sword. With a downward yank, he heard the satisfying sound of bone breaking as her jaw shattered in his hand. Rotting ooze and saliva dripped all over his hand, and he sighed. He was definitely going to have to clean himself thoroughly before he touched his uxorem again. Pulling his sword free, he watched dispassionately as the strix dropped to the ground where it writhed pitifully. His lips peeling back in a snarl, he stabbed his sword into the body.

"Die already!" he hissed!

Mora gurgled, and he suspected it was with laughter. With the power of the sword, given time that which remained of her body would gradually knit together. Whether her wing would grow back or not was questionable. She wouldn't have any such opportunity. One way or another she would be dead when he left there even if he had to tear her apart bit by bit.

A soft gasp drew his attention to his side and Diana looked up at him, her eyes wide. "Silvas… what does this sword of yours look like?"

His brow puckered in confusion. "It is ebony black with a black diamond set in the pommel."

Diana's hand snaked out toward something dark glittering among the feathers just below the strix's breast. Her hand curling around the thick cluster of feathers, she ripped them away, revealing the glittering black jewel of Nocis.

Silvas's eyes widened. That was why Mora was impossibly stronger, much stronger than she should've been even as keeper of the sword, and why he couldn't get an imprint of where it was —she had merged it into her body. He could see the bulge where the sheath of the blade pressed outward from where she had magically fused it to herself.

"Stupid creature," he snarled, throwing a disgusted look toward the strix.

At his words, Mora thrashed to shake him off. Even in her deranged state, she was trying to protect the source of her power. Digging his claws into greasy flesh, he ripped it apart, separating muscle from her abdominal wall. The gurgling and wheezing became louder as he tore free handfuls of flesh, shredding through feathers until the sword wiggled loosely in its bed. Gripping the hilt, he yanked it as he stood.

The sword ripped free, dumping the black and putrid inner organs of the strix all over the cave floor as they spilled out. His lips curled as he felt the familiar tendril of power stroke over his senses from the sword. It attempted to drown out his bond with Diana, but the bond surged as his mate drew closer to his side, her eyes narrowed on Nocis.

CHAPTER 27

Diana was not sure if she liked Nocis. Although it hadn't felt sentient, the way it flooded over their bond had frightened her. She had no doubt in her mind that it was extremely dangerous. Watching the dark stone pulse from where it was embedded in the strix was enough to send queasiness through her belly. Silvas's eyes were trained on her, his brow puckering with worry as he strapped the sheathed sword to his back.

Its sheath alone was larger than the sheath for his other blade and, now that he had cleaned it with the cloth from his belt, she could see that it was almost as dark as the sword itself and studded with deep red stones. Garnets maybe?

The squelch as he pulled his other sword free from where he had twisted it into the strix made Diana grimace. The mess was truly disgusting, though at least the smell couldn't get any worse. A disappointed sigh rattled from him and she eyed the reason—the aelven-forged blade had broken off in Mora's corpse. Silvas dropped the sword with a shake of his head.

"I'm not surprised," he muttered. "Backed with the power of Nocis, her magic was potent enough that I fell victim to it. I am honestly amazed that it didn't work on you as well. That her final defenses shattered the aelven blade despite all the magic forged into it ought to have been expected."

Why had she been able to resist it? Her eyes trailed once again to Nocis. A shiver ran through her. As silly as it sounded, that sword made her twitchy.

"Don't worry," Silvas soothed in a calm timber. "Nocis had a terrible effect on the strix, but it won't harm you."

"I'm not so sure about that. I am not even certain I want to touch it," she admitted. It was unsettling enough feeling the energy of the sword touching upon their bond. She didn't want to get any closer than that.

"There won't be any need. Unlike my armor and weapons, the sword is made so that it becomes a part of me when I shift."

Diana balked. "Wait, isn't that dangerous? You saw what it did to Mora."

He shook his head and gave her a small smile as he steered toward the cave entrance. "This sword was crafted for me, and unlike the long-lived strix, I am an immortal being. She was vulnerable in a way that I'm not."

"Okay," she muttered doubtfully as she fell into step beside him.

As they stepped out onto the ledge, a cool wind swept by. Diana greedily sucked in a deep breath of the fresh air, relieved to no longer be within the confines of the strix's nest. Although the wind had died down, night had long since fallen. Wrapping her arms around herself, she shivered. Silvas's glowing eyes turned toward her.

"We won't go far. Even by flight, it is a long journey back to the Arx. I won't risk you falling in your exhaustion. I will carry us down to the upper foothills of the mountain. There we should find a small stretch of ground to comfortably take our rest before we continue on."

Nodding her agreement, Diana backed up just enough to give him room as Silvas changed into an enormous griffin. Yet he looked different than he had before. Instead of the white feathers he had possessed, the tips of his feathers were now inky, and his coat was speckled. She paused to stare. To her surprise, he didn't seem to notice the difference, he merely cocked his head at her curiously when she didn't immediately seat herself on his back. He rumbled at her questioningly, but she didn't voice her concerns. Even to her, it seemed like a silly thing to be hesitant over. Directing a tight, nervous smile at him, Diana hauled herself over his withers and seated herself comfortably.

Silvas turned his eagle-like head in her direction, a soft clicking purr coming from him as he stepped lightly, swaying his body briefly, making certain that her seat was steady on his back. His purr became louder with approval before he abruptly faced forward once more and leaped gracefully from the ledge, his wings spreading wide to catch the currents as they dropped.

Diana's heart dropped into her belly. This experience was far different than the rapid rise from the ground that she had experienced before. For a heartbeat, she knew terror as they dropped until Silvas angled his wings to catch a current and beat them a few times so that they dropped at a gentler decline. The world around them was silent except for those occasional beats of his wings as he adjusted their descent, and Diana clung to him, her own breath loud in her ears. Her eyes, however, were attentively trained on the landscape of stars in the heavens around them. Those tiny glowing lights were comforting in a world darkened by nightfall.

They soared for a time, but before long they touched down on a relatively flat stretch of ground, and Silvas saw to her comfort at once. Diana was grateful since she could barely see anything outside of the shadowy outline where the moonlight illuminated the edge of a rock here and there. She noticed that, while he wasn't inclined to bring back the illumination between his antlers, he was careful to see to her needs. He made quick work of cleaning her wound, but to her surprise it was already rapidly healing. Once he assured himself that Diana was settled comfortably, Silvas eased down behind her, drawing her against his warm, bare chest.

"No fire?" she mumbled.

He shook his head. "It is better not to call any other attention to our presence on this mountain. We will rest for a few hours."

She prodded at his bare chest, her finger stroking over the light fuzz of fur that covered his body. "Won't you be cold?"

His chuckle rumbled from his chest under her ear. "No. I wear clothes because I enjoy them, not for warmth. Rest, uxorem," he whispered.

Diana nodded and leaned back against him to leach some of his heat, and she drew the warmth and peace of their bond around herself. She still had some awareness, though she was fading fast into slumber, when she felt him also relax and drop down into the warm pulse of their bond along with her. She yawned and wondered if he would also sleep, or what immortals did to refresh themselves. As he settled more deeply against her, it certainly felt enough like sleep to her. She yawned again and dropped into the thick fog of slumber.

It hadn't felt like she slept long, and was in fact still dark, when she was awakened by a snuffling, growling sound at the edge of their camp. She knew that Silvas had also awakened from the coiled tension in the arms wrapped around her. A low vibration like a voiceless growl came off him, his glowing eyes stark white slashes in the dark.

Three large icy blue orbs—much larger than a typical eye—stared back, their position shifting as if each one belonged to a separate creature. Diana was aware of Silvas bristling, the growl starting to ripple from him as they drew nearer.

"What is it?" Diana whispered as she attempted to keep her eyes on all three.

"We have been hunted," Silvas replied bluntly, his voice just barely audible. "It seems that the mountain trolls are more desperate than I had believed for them to have tracked us for such a distance."

Although his body coiled tightly, and his vocal attempts to warn them off, there was no true worry coming from him. The territorial aggression, on the other hand, there was plenty of. Despite that, he was attempting to scare them off rather than outright attacking.

Normally she had found such control to be admirable—when three enormous trolls *weren't* eyeing her as if she were the last cookie in the jar. Swallowing, she stared up at the three eyes floating at a considerable height above her. An arctic chill ran through her blood.

Two split off and advanced with loud, lumbering steps. She wagered that those two were the males. Their snuffling grew louder as they sniffed the air, drawing in deep gulping breaths. A low growl, like two boulders being ground together, filled the air. Diana winced as the resonating sound pierced her skull, making it throb.

"Give," one brute demanded. "Give sweet morsel to us."

There was no mistake in Diana's mind just who he was talking to and who the sweet morsel was. She hated the whole damsel in distress shit, but she felt no shame as she dug her fingers into Silvas's bare thighs. She felt the movement of air as he shook his antlers in answer, the adornments rattling softly.

"No. No give. Mine," Silvas hissed back, replying in a way that she was certain that the creatures had to understand.

Their reaction was instantaneous.

Angry snarls greeted his refusal, and something large slammed against the ground. She wasn't sure if it was a rock or a club. Whatever it was, it was huge and made the ground vibrate beneath her. The one on the left suddenly moved forward in two rapid strides, a vicious growl rumbling up from its chest leaving no doubt as to its intention. Diana felt a scream of terror bubble up her throat, her fingers fumbling for her sword when, just that quick, Silvas deposited her on the ground and surged to his feet.

His sword hissed as it slid free from the scabbard, a pulse of violet light like that of a black light that kids had enjoyed when she was younger, appearing around the blade. The sword arced through the air, and the beast bellowed as something heavy hit the ground and a hot liquid splashed against her cheek. The metallic scent of blood filled her nose and Diana gagged. As her stomach roiled, the troll's screams of pain echoed through her head.

As she heard the troll stumble back, the other male charged, and the sword raised at a whistling speed. This time it did not make contact as the male skidded to a stop at what she assumed was a safe distance from where the glowing tip of the blade pointed in the air. She could hear the loud, furious gusts of his labored breath as he growled and snorted. The female, lurking a short distance away, let out a panicked cry as she drew back farther. Both males turned their heads toward her, their eyes disappearing from sight in the path of their movement. They rumbled uncertainly to each other, and Diana could feel the hot pulse of excitement that suddenly ran through Silvas. It was low level, insidiously creeping through him as his mind was focused with watchful stillness on the trolls.

Fear crawled through her as the darkness swelled, covering more and more of his bright presence in their bond. To her relief, the males strode away with angry growls, the one still intermittently crying out with pain as they followed the track of their mate. As their footsteps gradually dragged away, Diana let out the breath that she hadn't realized she was holding. Her lungs burned with relief as it expelled from her and she stood on shaky legs, making her way toward the pulsing violet light that outlined the sharp edge of Nocis. Her fingers trembling, she reached out and felt for his shoulder.

Silvas jerked in surprise at her touch and he swung around viciously, the violet hue coloring the edge of his eyes as they fixed on her. She felt his hand come up and grip the side of her cheek roughly.

"Mine," he growled, his eyes glinting dangerously —possessively.

There was no softness or softer emotion in his face. This was different than the magic that coerced him in the cave. Although the source was the same, the dark energy of the blade spinning its influence upon Silvas, in the cave, at least, he had looked upon the strix who had assumed Diana's form with a measure of affection.

There was nothing of that in the male who stared down at her.

It was as if he was consumed by the power, leaving nothing of him but the raw destructive strength that was at the heart of his nature. She had felt that steel core of him, but the power of the blade amplified it until nothing else was surfacing.

And that was only after one little skirmish.

What would happen to Silvas if he continued to use the blade? If he went after Cacus with it? How much would be left of him when she looked at him as she fought by his side?

Diana's eyes widened and a tremor of unease made her draw back against his grip. She was unable to break his hold, but he must have seen something in her eyes because he frowned in puzzlement, his face leaning forward as his nostrils flared. He scented her cheek and through her hair. She could barely feel him along their bond and had an idea that his sense of her was likewise obscured.

He jerked her forward, his thick erection pressing against her belly urgently as he caught her lips with his, his tongue sweeping dominantly into her mouth, stroking in an aggressive invasion. It frightened her, but just as his savagery excited her when they first met, she felt her belly heat with desire. She opened to him and accepted his darkness. Her hands caught in his hair and she tugged sharply at the length, drawing him closer.

Gradually his mouth softened, and Diana felt the darkness draw back from around their bond as he resurfaced, a golden presence in their bond once more. His mouth drew away, caressing her lips worshipfully until he pulled away, his pearly eyes staring down at her in wonder. And regret.

His hands caressed the sides of her face before he lowered his head to capture her lips again. He broke free long enough to rid himself of the sheath strapped around his chest before drawing her sharply against him once more. His hands made quick work divesting her of her armor and clothes as he sought to touch and taste every exposed inch of her. When he drew her to the ground, he lay upon their cloaks and tugged her over him, her legs parting around his hips. Her cunt rubbed against his cock as his dragged her down for another kiss, their bodies slipping against each other as he rocked his hips, inciting her need until she squirmed upon him, eager to be filled.

Gripping her hips, he surged up into her, drawing her sharply against him. A moan escaped her as the bumps on his cock stroked through her. The bite of his claws against her hips was erotic as they rocked together, her body pitching as he lifted her and slammed her down with every upward grind of his pelvis. Their coupling was violent as she surged against him, her own frenzy climbing. Digging her fingers into his pectorals, she drove down, her pussy gripping and squeezing around him with desperation.

Somewhere amid her upwelling of need, Diana became aware of his tail sliding around her waist. It tightened, holding her locked in place as the furred tip grazed her clit. The flexible tip beneath the fur tweaked the sensitive bud as he canted his hips and pounded in a ceaseless rut up against her. Diana ground back against him, but that was all the movement she could manage, and all she had the presence of mind to do as her orgasm ripped up from her core and splashed through her in a hot wave of ecstasy.

Silvas snarled, thrusting up into her repeatedly until a roar of completion burst out from deep in his chest as his hot cum splashed through her channel. She could feel it seeping from around them as he continued to grind against her, sending her into new waves of pleasure until they finally collapsed, locked together, on the hard ground.

As they lay there, Silvas tucked her head beneath his chin. As he held her, neither of them spoke. Her silence was partly because she was afraid to break their contentment with her concerns about the power of the blade—especially after he pointedly told her not to worry about it.

She did worry. She thought of little else until sleep finally claimed her.

CHAPTER 28

Although it was not efficient for situations where they may need to fight, Silvas enjoyed carrying his mate in his shifted form. As before, Diana's warm body clung to him as they descended from their camp in the upper foothills of the mountains and began their trek to the Eternal Forest. His mate's excited exclamations at the view of the mountains from the air over the sparkling expanse of white stone warmed his heart and gave him a new sense of joy in flight that he hadn't felt in centuries.

Though it would have been a pleasure to carry her over the breadth of the forest so that she could see it from above, her flesh was still easily damaged like a mortal and he didn't want to risk injuring her by having to drop through the canopy of the trees for one of the frequent stops that she would still require. It would take many years, perhaps centuries, before the last traces of her humanity faded away. Until then, he would have to be careful with her. As he flew over the final stretch of the lower foothills, he intentionally ignored the churn of discomfort that his sister did not guarantee that Diana wouldn't be a threat against him. His heart pinched with the uncomfortable knowledge that just because she was his mate, that didn't mean that they were guaranteed anything.

In fact, if Dorinda was to be believed, all that was guaranteed was that Diana's presence was going to change everything. The more time he spent with his mate, the more he hoped that she would not ultimately be a threat that he would be forced to dispatch—he doubted that he could survive such a fate. Many minor gods have gone to rest before in times of grief. Silvas was certain that would be his fate if he was forced to destroy his mate and earn the wrath of the Furiae for shedding the blood of one's bonded. He held to him a glimmer of hope that it would not come to pass, and with that hope burned another that maybe she would permit him to keep her.

Someday.

Even if he had to wait at the edge of her mortal forest for the span of a human lifetime to collect her.

Silvas grimaced to himself as he dropped before the thickening tree line, gracefully avoiding the larger trees that straggled out from the edge of the forest. Although a human lifespan was a brief flash of time, he didn't care for the idea of being separated from his female for that long. That was if she wasn't determined to languish, haunting the mortal world, refusing to leave. Although many spirits kept apart from their bonded mate for centuries at a time, he found the thought of it deeply unsettling. He was becoming so accustomed to her presence that the idea of separation left him with a feeling of deep panic that he couldn't quite place.

He wasn't getting attached. He refused to succumb to such foolishness. It was just natural due to the bond that he felt the need. That was all. Shaking away the unsettling thought, he folded his wings and crouched just enough that Diana was able to slip off his back.

Yawning, she stretched and glanced around. "I take it that we are breaking for a few minutes?" she asked as she dragged their supplies and his armor from where it was harnessed to him.

Freed from the bindings of the harness, Silvas gave a leisurely stretch of his wings and jerked his head in reply. Seizing hold of his true form, he felt it dissolve to reknit itself, every muscle and bone reshaping and popping into place as he solidified. A small, enchanting smile stretched her lips as she appreciatively looked him over.

"I'll never get tired of seeing you do that. And the eye-candy that comes after is quite a nice vision too," she murmured.

He grinned at her easily, his heart lightening quickly at her admiration. Only Diana was able to do that to him. "It is perhaps one of my more impressive gifts," he admitted, intentionally being vague about what gift he was referring to.

Diana's eyes widened as a husky laugh left her lips. "Nicely played."

Dipping his head fleetingly in acknowledgment, he raised his eyes to the trees, noting the way the limbs bent and swayed toward him in greeting. His lips curved as he breathed deep of the forest, relieved to have returned. His smile widened as he turned his attention to his mate.

"I suppose we are traveling by ground now," Diana mused as her eyes took in their surroundings. "Any chance we can walk a bit. I know that we are in a hurry and all, but it would be good to stretch my legs for a little while before I'm in the saddle again."

"We can walk for a short time, I think," he agreed. "But first, rest and see to your needs. We will have some rations for now, but when we settle for the night, I will see what I can hunt for our meal."

She gave him a grateful look as she sank down between a couple of thick tree roots, her back resting comfortably against a tree. To his surprise, the tree immediately lit up with the multitude of tiny motes of energy released as the hamadryad reacted to

Diana's touch. His mate made a soft sound of delight in her throat, her eyes watching the drifting lights for a long moment before falling once more on him.

"I don't recall the trees reacting to me this way when we were coming through."

He grinned and rested his hand on another tree, which after a couple of heartbeats began to light up in turn. "The hamadryads of the Eternal Forest differ from those that are constantly around the palace, it takes direct touch. Your tree is responding to you."

Diana's eyebrows shot up as her head whipped around to look at the tree behind her. "To me? How is that possible?"

He grinned at her innocent wonder. The first centuries were going to be ceaseless sources of fascination for his mate. He hoped to be present to witness her every new discovery.

"We are bonded. I told you before that you are no longer human. Although it will take time for your transition, as my uxorem the Eternal Forest will begin to recognize and respond to you."

"This is so fucking cool," she whispered as she trailed her hand along the surface of the tree. The sparks of light followed the direction of her touch, making her laugh with delight. "I wonder if the trees around my house would do this."

A heavy feeling sank in his stomach, but he forced a smile as he replied. "As you are now… they would recognize your touch and react. I suspect after a time any tree near your home would have the hamadryads in a state of ecstasy, like those that grow around Arx, for being near you over such a long period."

She raised an eyebrow in his direction. "I thought it was because of their relationship to the palace?"

He shrugged, a chuckle rolling through him. "There is not a great difference between me and my palace. Arx was a seed I planted. Much like the *vinculum marcam*, except not quite so profound, it is a part of me. I am connected to it even if Arx as it is was the result of an accident."

Drawing her hand away from the tree, she folded them in her lap and raised her eyebrows at him. "An accident? Oh, this should be good. Please go on," she laughed at his pained grimace.

"Mind you, it is a distant memory, so I am a little fuzzy on some of the details," he grumbled reluctantly as he dropped down beside her. "You must keep in mind that at that time I had just recently been given responsibility over the Eternal Forest. I was a very young and lusty silvanus, who was perhaps equally captivated by the various nymphs as I was with exploring my new domain." His lips twisted in a self-deprecating smile. "I hadn't yet understood the nymphs' lust for sexual desire and passion. Although they may mate or take a lover into their bodies, many of their interactions require no sexual consummation. As a young silvanus, it is not surprising that I fell into the more common category."

"That must have been frustrating," Diana chuckled.

Silvas rolled his eyes and shot her a glower. "Some sympathy, uxorem. Do you wish for me to continue this story or not?"

"Sorry," she said around a strangled chortle. "Please continue."

He huffed in irritation but smiled himself, delighting in her willingness to play with him. Although as a predator he had enjoyed the taste of her fear, this was what he needed from his mate. Her passion, her playfulness… and hopefully, eventually, her love. Clearing his throat of the emotion that unexpectedly swelled within him, he continued his story.

"It was not unusual for nymphs to work me up until I was pained with need and leave me to resolve my passions on my own effort. Dallying with nymphs makes a male quite intimate with his hand if they are not inclined to mate with you. On one occasion some of my seed ejaculated directly onto a flower bud as the nymph scurried away. The flower petals immediately dropped away to reveal a large pearly seed. Before I could even pluck it up and investigate a wind stirred it just enough that it fell into a crack in the earth. Almost instantly the ground surged with rock and vines burst up into a modest dwelling. It was unplanned and had some unfortunate consequences." He thought sadly of his sister trapped forever beneath the stones of Arx. He leaned his head back against the tree willing the thought away. "After that, it just grew over the centuries as it was needed and however it desired."

Turning his head, he met Diana's eyes and found her staring at him her lips parted in wonder. "That is both amazing and a bit disturbing," she admitted. "Are you saying that it's alive… as in, sentient?"

"To a degree," he admitted.

She shivered. "I'm going to try not to think of it as a living house when we get back or else I'll never be able sleep there again."

Silvas wrapped one arm around her genially. "No ghosts. I can't guarantee that Arx won't kill under any circumstances, but it is not evil and it does not contain the ghosts of the dead."

"Really splitting hairs here, Silvas," Diana said as she leaned against him.

He dropped his nose into her hair and smiled to himself.

They rested for there for a couple of hours, during which Diana entertained him with stories of her life in the human world before the wulkwos—or ravagers, as she called them—disrupted human civilization. When it was time for them to be on their way again, he stood to drape the harness of supplies over his shoulder and reached down to tug her gently to her feet.

As they stepped into the woods he glanced at his mate, affection filling him at the sight of her upturned cheek as she glanced up at the trees around them. A peace fell over him and he decided that he liked this. He liked it very much.

CHAPTER 29

The trek back to the palace went quickly, though Diana couldn't help noticing that the forest seemed quieter than it had been before—and it wasn't due to a giant white crocotta loping through. When they had ridden out with Raskyuil, there were the sounds of birds and insects in the air. Now it was nothing but unnerving stretches of silence. Although he didn't speak of it, she felt Silvas's concern through their bond.

When they made camp, he had been so tense that he paced the campsite, keeping guard as he warily watched over the camp. For three days, he didn't close his eyes, nor did he allow anything to distract him. It had been uncomfortable bedding down with his glowing eyes scanning the trees. Whenever they settled on her, need had sprung to life inside her. His nostrils twitched and flared but he had made no move toward her.

She understood the reason, and damn if the forest didn't freak her out even more now, but three days without his touch was maddening. Her desires plagued her. She needed to taste him on her tongue, to scent the height of his passion—admittedly a strange impulse for her—and take him deep within her body.

The need, although it died away after a couple of uncomfortable hours, to her horror never truly ceased, nor was she able to satisfy it manually by her own efforts. It always returned stronger than before, making her body quiver and squirm as if stroked by a hundred feathers. It was worse if it hit when she was in the saddle, her pussy teased through the fabric of her pants by the rocking lope of Silvas in the crocotta's form. It left her panting, sweat glistening on her skin as she flushed hotly. As the days passed the episodes were getting more frequent.

By the end of day two, Diana had come to the brutal realization that she wasn't sure how long she could go without his touch. She had been reduced to a crying, whimpering mess until Silvas had been so filled with concern and his own need that he stopped and roughly took her over a felled tree, rutting into her upright so that he could watch their surroundings. If she couldn't make it through two days without practically crawling out of her own skin, how would she survive any distance at all from him?

That was a sobering thought.

As much as she was afraid of the forest, she was almost more afraid of suffering days on end without comfort or release.

And the forest terrified her. It was as if something within the forest was watching and waiting while everything quietly died around it. It was not unlike what she had felt when she had come across the destroyed jeep, yet now the entire forest felt that way. The deeper they went, the darker and more oppressive it felt. Her skin prickled as she leaned lower against Silvas, relieved by his nearness.

Silvas rumbled comfortingly at her, his pace slowing so she could lay more easily against him. Diana looped her around his neck, her cheek nestled against the thick scruff of fur. She tried to ignore the gray light of the forest around her, focusing on the pulse of the power running through his body, and the hum of his presence through their bond. Dark, twisted branches reached toward her out of the gloom, and a peculiar haze seemed to cling to the forest. With the silence, it made the trees appear as deathly sentinels looming over a killing field. Diana scrunched her eyes closed, her heart pounding. She just needed to make it the short distance remaining until they arrived at the palace.

A loud crack broke through the silence, and Diana's eyes snapped open just in time to watch the mist suddenly whirl as if pushed by a large hand. Another crack sounded, and then another, the brush rippling and stirring as if being plowed through. Up ahead a tree wavered as if something heavy landed on it and the branches began to shake before going still. Her hands clutched nervously in Silvas's fur, her eyes were fixed on the tree as they neared, its one limb extending over the path ominously. Her fingers tightened as her head pounded the closer they got, the branch swaying slightly with the shift of wind.

Suddenly it shook and bowed sharply as the weight of a hideous, gaunt creature landed upon it. Marbled in hues of green and brown, the creature's muddy appearance made it all the more grotesque when paired with the elongated, narrow features of its face and the thin, claw-tipped fingers that gripped the branch as it leaned forward, balanced by a long, outstretched tail. Much of its body was covered in pieced together clothes, the most noticeable of which was a red conical cap out from which poked its long, tapered ears. Its dark, beady eyes peered down at them as a wide smile pulled at its lips, revealing a mouthful of needle-sharp teeth. Diana's breath stuttered at the terrible smile.

Diana jerked back, a scream welling in her throat as the thing pounced. Silvas growled, his pace faltering, but it did little to save her as the thing barreled into her body. A scream broke from her throat as the creature's weight sent her flying from the saddle. Silvas had slowed enough, however, that the impact was bruising at worst. The breath left her lungs in a strangled cry of pain. She could feel its claws digging into her as it scrabbled over her.

She attempted to knock it aside, its terrible teeth flashing far too close to her face as it crawled across her. She cried out, tears streaking down her face, certain that any minute its teeth would lay into her skin and peel away her flesh. A metallic sound of impact greeted her ears, followed by a familiar angry snarl. Her tears turned to sobs of relief as the creature was suddenly pulled away with a snap of strength. It squawked in surprise. Standing over her, Silvas, naked except for the sword strapped across his chest, held the creature high in the air with one hand, his face creased with anger as he gave it a shake.

"You frightened my uxorem, goblin," he snarled.

"Sorry, lucomo," it squeaked in a high, grating voice. "I was excited. I did not mean to scare her."

The words penetrated the terror fogging her brain, and Diana sat up and looked at it curiously. It was no longer smiling. Instead, the lines of its face were pulled into a frown as it hung from Silvas's grip on his long tail. Its beady eyes shifted over to her, and once more that terrible smile stretched over its face as it gave her a happy wave, its long ears turned toward her. Despite the savagery of its teeth and claws, it looked so ridiculous that Diana found herself smiling in return as she stood.

Silvas let out a disgusted sigh and dropped the goblin on a nearby stump. "Goblins can be vicious little things, but often more mischievous than harmful, and none of the goblins of the Eternal Forest will harm you, Diana," he assured her softly.

The goblin pulled the cap off its head showing an unruly spike of fur as it nodded rapidly in agreement. It had an unsettling appearance that was a little too ugly to have anything truly comforting in its appearance, but Diana felt herself relax despite her earlier terror. Its brows shifted up like the remorseful stare of her grandma's old hound that had trailed after her as a child.

Brushing off its hat, it gave her a small smile. "I hoped to be the first of my line to greet our new ati, our queen. I am Borbekel, son of Dirdankis and Entihela."

Diana froze at the greeting. She didn't know how to address the whole ati thing… She couldn't be a queen. Her eyes slid over to Silvas. He stared back, his expression ambiguous and watchful.

He was lucomo of the silvani… Crap. She hadn't even considered what that meant for her when they had mated. Glancing back down at the goblin, she watched as the tiny male grinned widely, displaying sharp rows of teeth once more.

"I trust that everyone knows of the bonding," Silvas said.

Borbekel trilled in amusement. "All of the Eternal Forest felt it when your bond snapped in place with your mate. It has been a light within the darkness that has descended as of late. At least for most of us, that is. Alseida's screams could be heard throughout the palace grounds. She is quite displeased," he chirped.

Silvas waved a hand. "Alseida's opinion matters not. She can learn to cope with the new situation. If she cannot, she would be wise to leave Arx and spare herself exile to the human world from the Eternal Forest. I am more interested in hearing of this darkness."

Borbekel hopped in agitation, his long ears flopping slightly. "It is quite unnatural. For days, not a beam of sunlight has penetrated the forest. The trees have begun to grow twisted among themselves, and an unnatural mist clings at all hours, such as you see. It has been thus since your protection left the forest."

Silvas's jaw tightened, and she felt his frustration and anger lick through their bond. His eyes scanned the woods as if searching fruitlessly for something. "My task has been successful. I am reunited with Nocis—spread the word so no one doubts or worries." His eyes fastened on her. "We must hasten back. Now that I have the sword, I must confer with the oracle so that I can ascertain where we might seek out our prey."

His muscles tightened as he stepped away before they loosened to take the form of the crocotta once more. Silvas's eyes within the animal pierced her, and Diana hurried to strap the harness and all their gear on him once more as the goblin darted away through the brush. Borbekel's departure was the only sound in the forest outside of the chinking of the armor as she fastened it once more to the saddle. Within minutes, they were racing through the final stretches of the forest.

It wasn't until she caught glimpses of the telltale glow of the hamadryads announcing their impending arrival at the palace that she relaxed. Although Arx looked as dark and foreboding as the forest itself, and the light of the surrounding hamadryads appeared weaker against the gloom, it promised some rest and respite while they figured out their next moves. Diana leaned over Silvas's shoulders, but a smile sprung to her lips as the crocotta pack sprung from a sheltered area hidden beyond the courtyard. She recognized Keena immediately, her heart swelling with pleasure as the massive female bore down on them with all her clan. Keech was close behind his mate as they barreled forward.

Silvas snapped his tail and yipped as he rounded into the courtyard. The entire crocotta pack fell to his sides, following him in a seamless movement, scattering nymphs, fauns, and even what she could swear was an elf as they came to a gradual halt.

Diana barely had time to remove herself from Silvas's back before they were set upon. Silvas stood naked among his court, his pale flanks visible among the crowd, no space to even dress himself in the clothing that was still packed with his armor. Although many of the throng acknowledged Diana's presence and bowed to her, soon she was forcibly edged out until she stood alone with the crocottas.

Annoyed, Diana turned away from the sight and found a comfortable place to sit with the pack while Silvas dealt with his court. She was furious and… dejected. He had taken her as his mate. Now that they returned to the palace, she felt like she was once again a nobody—an intruder, for all that his court cared, save one excitable goblin. She knew that there was much that would demand his attention with what happened while they were away, but she couldn't help but feel the bite of resentment toward those who forced her out so easily. She felt a small ripple of concern through their bond, but it was distracted at best.

A low whine met her ears, and she glanced over as Keena nudged her hand with her muzzle. A reluctant smile tugged her lips as she noticed that the giant crocotta was attempting to comfort her. Reaching forward, she rubbed her hands around Keena's ears, and the large beast sighed. Keena settled down beside her, the crocotta's large body angled to support Diana's back while the rest of the pack dropped down to sprawl over the courtyard stones.

Leaning into Keena, Diana was determined to make herself comfortable and get some rest when a shadow fell over her. Glancing up, she scowled to find a familiar dryad standing over her. The female's lips pinched together, a dark flush climbing her cheeks despite her attempts to look composed.

This had to be Alseida.

"The lucomo will be busy for the remainder of the day. I am to escort you to your chambers," she said waspishly as she eyed the crocotta with obvious distaste. "Come with me."

Shoved into a room. Of course.

Plastering a smile on her face, Diana stood, her fingers giving Keena one last pat before following the dryad into the dark, cool interior of the palace.

CHAPTER 30

Alseida led Diana through the labyrinth of halls within the palace. This time, fully aware of the nature of the place —of Arx, she reminded herself—Diana looked at her surroundings with interest. Every stone wall that dripped with moss and vines was an amazing part of the living structure and seemed to communicate to her in passing. The beauty of the corridors was almost enough to make up for the unpleasant company. She unfortunately couldn't miss the looks of loathing that the dryad shot in her direction, though she pretended ignorance of the female's bad temper.

The dryad practically growled as she opened a door that led into a familiar room. Diana recognized Silvas's opulent chambers immediately. The only thing that was missing was the narrow door that would have led to the room she had been kept in. The door was gone. If nothing else, the palace itself recognized her place, and the walls of the room were blooming with beautiful fragrant flowers hanging in lush clusters from the vines that knotted over the walls.

The troll who'd been waiting just outside the room when they arrived hurried in after them. His arms laden with food and drink, he set them out upon the table with a quiet smile before hurrying over to the large stone hearth. The fire was very welcome. Diana sank into a chair as the room lit up with a cheerful light, the warmth working to knock the chill from the room. The male flushed at her murmured thanks before darting from the room, hastened out by Alseida's glower.

Diana didn't blame him. She suspected that if the dryad oversaw any of the staff in the palace that she was probably a terror to work for. Diana wouldn't linger either. In fact, if she could escape the female herself, she would've jumped at the chance. Especially as Alseida suddenly loomed over her, her beautiful face twisted with anger, fangs gleaming. And she wasn't alone.

A cluster of nymphs stood behind the dryad, each one just as beautiful as the next, and each female with a hard, unwelcoming expression on her face. Several pairs of dark, fathomless eyes gleaming at her with interest and a hint of menace.

Where the fuck had they come from?

Swallowing back her fear, Diana raised an eyebrow at the dryad. Some part of her still wanted to shrink back in fear as she had done that first day, but things had changed since then. She had changed. She refused to be cowed by the vindictive bitch. "I think I am all set, you can go now," she said flatly. "And take the nymph sisterhood with you."

The dryad's nostrils flared, the golden yellow hue of her cheeks darkening. "You do not order me about. You do not belong here," she hissed. "This was *my* place and I will not allow some human interloper to usurp it."

Diana's other eyebrow raised to join the first. "It seems that Silvas doesn't share that opinion. If I'm not mistaken, *I'm* the one he mated. So regardless of who was here first, my human ass is here now. You are the one who doesn't belong in this room."

A hard smile curved the dryad's face as she ran a hand along the bed familiarly. "It is only a matter of time before he will yearn for me again. Did he tell you that we were lovers for centuries? He and I in this bed…" a low sound of pleasure escaped her lips. "And still he keeps me here close at hand. Do you not wonder why that is, little human?"

Silvas and that horrible female… *For centuries?* Nausea rocked Diana. The dryad's smile widened.

"He didn't tell you." Alseida laughed as several of nymphs behind her smirked and someone giggled. Diana didn't miss that there were a few pitying faces among them, and a couple looked distinctly uncomfortable. "Poor clueless human. But I'm hardly surprised." The last was addressed to a dark-haired nymph standing directly to the side. The nymph pouted at Diana before erupting into laughter.

Diana knew she would hate herself for asking, but she couldn't seem to help herself. "Why are you not surprised?" she whispered.

The dryad smirked as she reclined comfortably on the bed. "Do you imagine that you are the first human woman Silvas has taken to his bed? In the old days, he sired an entire race of males on human women whom he seduced in his forests. He never stays with them, though. True, he may have mated you for a hidden purpose of the gods that we do not know. But he will never stay with a human. He never has. He will always yearn for nymphs and the pleasure that we are capable of bringing."

He had sired children? How had that never come up in conversation? Diana clenched her fingers into a tight fist, hidden in her lap. She wouldn't betray how much this affected her, not until she spoke to Silvas first.

"Go home, human," Alseida hissed. "Take an escort back to your world and forget about Silvas and this place. This world is not for the likes of you. Leave him to us. Only we are worthy of tasting his desire."

Several nymphs broke away from the group, their bodies flowing as they circled the table at which Diana sat. Their eyes were fixed on her, their smiles cruel, their lips whispering of how much they enjoyed the taste of the lucomo, his need for them and the desire upon which they slaked their thirst and the pleasure they gave him. No human could provide him with what they could stir in the being of the lucomo. He was theirs. Alseida stood in front of all of them her lips curved ruthlessly.

Anger streaked through Diana at the dryad's taunt. "I will hear the details of his past from Silvas, not someone else," she said. "Regardless of any discussion that occurs between us, you will never chase me away, Alseida. And I shall never relinquish my claim on Silvas."

Alseida snarled and stalked forward, lifting a clawed hand. Diana braced, fists raised to defend herself, when some nymphs who had been lingering apart from the rest pushed themselves in front of Diana. They shielded her with their bodies as they faced off with the dryad.

"We do not approve of this," a female at the fore said. "This is not the way of our kind, to threaten harm on other females—and for what? To enjoy the pleasures of a king who has not desired our company for centuries? When is the last time he accepted any of us? Can you not see as plainly as we that she bears his *vinculum marcam*? You are a fool, Alseida, if you think that this confrontation will change anything, other than bringing about your eventual exile from the palace. Accept that your time at his side is over." Alseida glanced at other nymphs, who lingered in their places around the table. "I will lend my support to such ugliness no more."

The nymphs slipped out, abandoning Alseida, until only a scant few remained. The dryad practically vibrated with fury as she stared Diana down, anger and embarrassment clear on her face. Most of the nymphs had abandoned her, calling out her pettiness, and even her supporters looked at her with pity. Diana wasn't sure whether to feel sorry for the dryad, or to watch her back in case the female attempted to stick a knife in it. As Alseida advanced with a scream of anger, Diana sprung up from her chair, any sympathy she might have held vanishing instantly.

"Alseida, stop!" a deep voice growled as Raskyuil stomped into the room, his eyes flashing with menace on the nymphs. The lingering females squealed as they fled, all but the dryad, who even paled and quickly backed away from Diana. Despite her reaction, the dryad stiffened and glowered down her nose at the troll.

"What gives you authority to command me, guard?"

"Silvas asked me to check on his ati," Raskyuil replied, his arms crossing over his chest. "And for good cause, it seems. You are not welcome in this room, dryad. You were to escort the ati to her room and nothing more. Leave now, and be thankful that the nymphs alerted me to your tricks when I passed them in the hall, for if I had been a minute longer and you had harmed her, Silvas would have cast you to the sands of the great desert rather than anything as kind as exile into the human world."

The dryad sailed out the door, leaving Diana and Raskyuil staring after her.

The male beside her chuckled. "I've wanted to tell off that haughty nymph for years now. About time she had someone to burst her deluded little bubble the way she's sailed around here for years like the mistress of the palace."

"Glad to see that you arrived safely and mended quickly so that you could adequately perform as my rescuer," Diana replied as she took in his healed body. He had a few new scars but was whole. "I mean, damn, you healed really quick."

"Aelven healers," he said dismissively. "They are among the best in the forest." His gaze slid over her as a smug smile pulled at his lips. "So, the ati, our glorious mother queen, has arrived," he said thoughtfully. "I do believe I won our wager."

"Oh, shut up," she snorted, earning her more laughter from the troll. She kept her tone light. She didn't want to let on that it made her uncomfortable to hear him address her as ati. There had been no change in their long-term plans, nor was there any indication from Silvas that he intended to keep her. Not that she was even sure she wanted to remain in the Eternal Forest. Regardless, she wasn't going to let the dryad try to strongarm her out of the palace. "Mated to the lucomo or not, I haven't agreed to stay yet," she replied coolly.

"Oh, you will," he smirked, and Diana rolled her eyes in exasperation.

CHAPTER 31

Silvas made his way down the staircase into the lower cavern, his hand gripping Nocis at his side. Even there the mist was curling in thick wisps. It seemed that there was no escape from it, not even within the depths of Arx. He felt a sting of guilt that he had sent Diana to his rooms, and with Alseida of all beings, but the dryad had been attempting to ingratiate herself and he had lost patience with her behavior. Sending her to escort Diana somewhere that she would be safe and waiting for him upon his return seemed like the most expedient option.

At least he had promptly sent Raskyuil after them a short time later just to be certain that the female didn't torment his mate in any fashion. He had yearned to follow them, but the compulsion to speak with Dorinda had been strong. Silvas only made one stop, and that was to store his armor in the armory so that it didn't impede his movements on the narrow staircase.

A low growl escaped him as he descended deeper into the cavern. He had the feeling that he was going to have to do something about Alseida. So many of the nymphs looked to the dryad for guidance that he had hesitated far too long in removing her from the palace grounds. Her jealousy and possessiveness would not be tolerated any longer. Not when he had his uxorem at his side. He would have to keep a guard on his mate until he was certain that Alseida was far away and no longer a potential threat to Diana's safety.

Ahead of him, the mist churned around the rock of the fountain, and he drew up short when Dorinda climbed upon it, her tail sliding easily among the stones, whipping against the mist. Being foul of temper and unforgiving toward him, never had she come to greet him without his summons. Judging by the displeasure on her face, he suspected that she had been waiting. Slowly he drew close to the edge of her pool, his eyes never leaving the vegoia whose sharp gaze tracked his every step.

"Dorinda," he offered a cautious greeting.

Her lips stretched into a hard, wide smile. "So… you return, and with Nocis in hand I see. Finally, the scales are weighing out to where they should be. Just in time, it would seem," she observed archly.

Silvas frowned at the blunt statement. That she didn't seem especially surprised about the state of the Eternal Forest was concerning.

"Did you know that this would happen?"

Dorinda rolled a shoulder in a shrug as she let out a long hiss of frustration. "I suspected that Cacus would take advantage of your absence—you have undoubtedly seen evidence of his influence before you departed the forest—but never had I believed that the forest would succumb so quickly. Already it is dying. I can feel it here, even beyond the roots of your palace, below the deepest roots of the trees. I can feel it withering." She shuddered, and for the first time he saw, behind her mask of disdain, the very real fear in her eyes.

A prickle ran over his spine as he sent his senses out through his woods. She was right. How had he not noticed the decline of the forest as they traveled home? Had he truly been so distracted?

When they arrived, he had noted that the hamadryads had appeared weaker, but he had blamed it on the gloom. He should have known something wasn't right.

He gritted his teeth, a dark anger surging through him. He had allowed his infatuation with Diana to cloud him to his duty and to the heart of the forest. Perhaps she truly was a danger to him. Until he could determine how far the threat that she possessed extended, he would imprison her in his rooms where she would be watched at all times. He would post guards at the doors, and he would personally observe her during the night for any sign of betrayal when she was most vulnerable.

His heart wrenched, the pain lancing deep, but he pushed it away. He couldn't be foolish in this. He had recklessly trusted Alseida; he couldn't afford to ignore the signs and make the same mistake again when it came to Diana.

This time, there was even more at stake.

Setting his jaw against the pain, Silvas blocked Diana out, their bond dimming as he shut out her light. The agony that rose within him was like severing a limb from his body. Pushing through it, he straightened and pinned his sister with a firm look.

"Speak without riddles once more. Tell me, what do I need to do to save my forest?"

Dorinda stared back at him intently as the words flowed from her lips. "Go to the place in the depths of the woods, where the waters of the Pegaeae are touched by the full light of the moon. There you will wash the stain of the strix from Nocis and lay it out for the blessing of the queen of the night. Even this will not be enough to defeat Cacus. You must restore yourself and release the shroud with which you have been surrounded. Surrender yourself to the Pegaeae and be cleansed of the miasma that separates you from your true self. Rise again, Selvans, god of the Eternal Forest."

Instinctively, he sought his mate on their bond for her strength and gentle presence. He recoiled when he felt the block on their bond.

He had to do this alone.

"And what," he forced himself to say, "do you now foresee of Diana?"

The vegoia cocked her head and hesitated, her eyes seeing beyond him. "As the weave of fate changes with every action, the pattern that emerges shows the queen risen against the king and the world quakes with the impact of their blades. She will rise and you will be undone until…"

"Enough!" Silvas barked, his heart weighed down with a sense of great sickness.

So, it was true. He had no choice. His hand gripped the hilt of his sword, and a tremor swept through him, shaking him to the core. He could not allow her to rise as a threat to the forest. His heart bled and his body quaked with the suffering that swept through him.

The vegoia laughed from where she twined around her rock. He shot her an angry look, his lip curling back from his teeth with a loud snarl. It startled her enough that she went silent.

"Do not mock my pain," he bit out.

Her disdainful snort echoed through the cavern. "You will bring about your own pain, idiot king," she rebuked.

Her tail snapped against the rock as she flung herself into her pool. He stared after her, watching the ripples until they finally ceased. He'd insulted her—that much was obvious—but he couldn't bear to hear another word of the sad fate that awaited him. To have given him a mate destined to be his enemy… The gods must have wanted him to suffer. He could barely breathe through the agony biting into him.

"My apologies, sister," he whispered toward the pool before spinning around and stalking back to the staircase.

Ascending to the lowest floor of Arx, Silvas sealed the

entrance and turned to face the shadowed sentinel awaiting him. Raskyuil leaned against the wall, his eyes gleaming in the dark. He was the only one among Silvas's guard who knew the location of the descent to Dorinda's cave. The male cocked his head curiously.

"What is the word?" he asked in a low gruff voice.

"I am to make for the spring of the Pegaeae so that Nocis and I may be purified and restored," Silvas said as he swept by the troll. He heard the male peel himself from the wall and his footsteps following as expected.

"You seek to restore your godhood? About fucking time. I shall inform lady Diana to prepare then."

"No," Silvas snarled, startling his guard. He took a deep breath, fighting for balance as he gripped the hilt of his sword. No doubt Cacus was tracking her somehow and would seek to attack him when he was vulnerable in the water and his sword was away from his hand. "You will increase the guard on her chambers. She is not to go anywhere unaccompanied, and she isn't to leave the room at all at night. Keep her there until I return."

He sensed Raskyuil's frown behind him as they ascended through the halls leading toward the courtyard.

"Forgive me for asking, but wouldn't it be wiser to take her with you? You said that your fates were sealed together in this task… I would imagine a trip to the Pegaeae Springs would be especially important for her to accompany you."

"I was mistaken. She needs to be guarded and watched, far from Cacus. Keep her away," he growled, every word sinking as a shard into his heart.

"I see," the troll grumbled. "And what would you like to me to do with Alseida? She was threatening Diana earlier. Even had a group of naiads with her."

Silvas could barely control the impulse to hunt the nymph

down and eject her from his territory. Despite everything, he refused to let anyone harm her.

He would deal with his uxorem himself.

"See to her removal at once. She is to leave the halls and lands of Arx and never return," he said, struggling to keep the tremor out of his voice.

In his peripheral vision, he saw Raskyuil snap his head in acknowledgment. "Yes, lucomo. I will see to it immediately."

Stopping in the courtyard, Silvas turned and watched Raskyuil's shadow depart before quickly pulling off his clothing and casting it to the ground. Reaching out with his senses, he embraced the form of a roc, letting the giant eagle flood through his mind.

Never again would he take the form of a griffin nor crocotta. He would miss running with the clan, but he wouldn't torture himself with the memory of her legs clasped around him and the pleasure he found with her body close to his.

A frustrated cry left his throat as he flapped his wings and leaped into the air. Two beats of his wings and he broke through the trees, leaving the palace and his mate far behind him. It would take him half the night to travel to the spring, and he didn't want to delay his return even for a minute.

CHAPTER 32

At high moon, Silvas descended into the silver-lit grove. The leaves of the trees, though weak and half-withered, bore testament to the beauty of this sacred place. The fountain itself was almost crystalline as it reflected the gentle light.

Dropping beside it, he released the form of the roc, the feathers drifting away from him as he resumed his true form. He stood there upon the moss-covered rocks that lined the edges of the spring and waited, his body taut with tension. His tail flicked slowly, the only movement he allowed himself, as his eyes fixed on a silvery spring that fed into a natural rock basin.

The water rippled, and slowly a naiad, her silvery hair flowing around her shoulders, stepped out. She was radiant, the drops of water appearing as stars on her dark body as if born from the royal womb of the night, and her eyes the darkest blue of watery depths. Her gaze fell upon him as she waded into the shallower waters until all above her sex was exposed to the air. Her naked body was supple with muscle, her breasts high and round. She was undoubtedly the most beautiful of nymphs. Her hot gaze slid down his body, lingering on every sculpted muscle. Her tongue stroked over her lips, the scent of her desire perfuming the air.

"It has been a long time. It has been ages since I have enjoyed such a fine feast for my eyes. What brings the lucomo to my spring? Is it because you desire to lay within my arms and watch the ages pass us by?" she breathed in enticement. "Do you desire me above all things?"

Lust spiked briefly through him in reaction to the powerful nature of the naiad, his cock swelling in reaction. A low growl broke free from his chest. He traveled too far to play her games to test his will and the true desire of his heart. His lust was a superficial reaction to the nymph's beauty and it only served to make him ache for his mate, his entire being grieving in separation from his uxorem. His temper immediately flared to life.

"I did not come for you, Thera, pegaeae nymph. I came to seek your spring's divine blessing to restore us," he growled. Lifting Nocis high, he imbedded the sword in the soft ground between the rocks in emphasis as his words rang out.

The nymph's flirty demeanor dropped away to be replaced by a soft smile as she stood, the lapping silvery waters flowing over and around her. Her hand stretched forward beckoningly, her voice ringing out as she addressed him.

"Very well, Selvans," she intoned, her voice sounding hollow and roaring as flowing water. "Approach with Nocis and return to your glory."

Yanking Nocis free, Silvas stepped down into the fountain's pool, the forest quiet except for the fall of water and the gold chiming lightly from his antlers. The water was cold and biting, plunging through him as he waded deeper. With the sword outstretched, he handed to it the pegaeae. Her dark hands outstretched and took the sword.

Stepping back from him, Thera waded deeper into the water to approach the fountainhead. Rather than rough, weathered stone, it had been carved in some past age to resemble a lion's head, the water gushing from the opening beneath its mouth.

Raising the blade laying lengthwise across her palms, a hum vibrated from her as she lifted it to the view of the heavens where the moonlight shone down through a break in the branches. A sheen ran along the length of the sword as she plunged Nocis beneath the fountain's spray. Silver light burst from the edges of the sword where the water drops struck it.

The nymph lowered it until it was completely submerged. The water lit up as if the moon itself was contained within the round pool. The hum became louder, deeper, as the water rippled and bounced from the epicenter. The sword, beneath the water, appeared darker, negating all light that surrounded it. This was the nature of the sword. Tendrils of miasma were pulled away, burning all the darker like the empty blackness at the center of a flame.

When the pegaeae lifted the sword from the pool, the waters parted so fast that not even a drop remained as she turned to present it to him. She met his eye, her expression hard as she laid the sword on a cloth woven of white fleece beside the fountain. He'd not seen where it had been procured from but wasn't surprised that she would have such necessities for attending the cleansing.

"Nocis is restored. Beware, Selvans. Even when you are have returned to your full power, and the miasma separating you from your divinity is washed away, Nocis will be a terrible burden. It was not forged to be a companion, but to be a weapon to destroy that which threatens the cosmos. It is not evil, nor does it attempt to deceive, but by its very nature it cuts through the rational mind to lay bare the primal instincts of the one who holds it. You know this. The logic of your mind and the truth of your heart will suffer when you hold it without a counterweight. Even the darkest night is not without life as the celestial light of the multitudes of stars and the moon shines down from the vastness of the cosmos beyond."

He flinched as she reached and gripped his forearm in a hard grasp. She ran her fingers over the fur covering his arm, her regard intense as her eyes met his. "You are a primal being. You bring life and vitality by being a creature of death, thus you are born white, that which contains all the colors but is none. Death washes and cleanses all things, restoring all to their original state. You feed and sustain through decay, and it has kept the Eternal Forest thriving when the balance is not disturbed. That harmony has been torn away. *You* need to find *your* light so the life of the forest can thrive, but also so your nature doesn't consume you and destruction become absolute."

"Riddles, Thera? Do you see yourself a vegoia now?" he asked, his jaw clenching.

He was frustrated with his inability to understand what she spoke of. It was similar to what the goddess had spoken of to him in the mountains, which made his entire being go still. Something tickled his awareness, but when he tried to touch it, it slipped away from his grasp.

Silvas exhaled. "What light, and where do I find it?"

The nymph shrugged with an apologetic smile. "Despite your accusation, I am no seer. I only know the nature of the sword through my contact with it during purification. Just as I have a glimpse of yours because you stand in my pool. Insight is not foresight. These are two different matters. It seems prudent when dealing with Nocis to warn you that you require an anchor to the world of the living."

"Consider your advice heeded then, as much as I can," he said.

A source of light to anchor him? He thought of the lamp of the infernal gatekeeper, but he doubted that Charu would offer it, not when it was bound to his mate. He hissed low between his teeth. He could inquire of Dorinda, but he already felt like time was growing short with the forest withering all around him. Even in the pegaeae's grotto, he could see the touch of death everywhere.

She noticed the direction of his gaze and her expression turned sad. "Yes, even here in this holy place, you can see the devastation."

"I will right it," he vowed "On my oath, I will fell Cacus and restore the Eternal Forest. I can do no other. It is the purpose of my existence. If the Eternal Forest dies and takes with it all the forests of the living worlds… I don't know what would become of me without it."

"I know what you would become because I see it dwelling within you," she whispered, her body leaning toward him as if there were a secret to be shared.

He swallowed and inclined his head. He didn't want to know, but at the same time, he couldn't not know. He had to consider not only how his decisions impacted the forest, but how they might affect all of existence.

She drew closer, her breath touching the bottom of his ear. "Your destructive nature without purpose would be as a plague on all the worlds, Selvans. Everything you touch will wither and die, every place you set your feet will decay all around you. You need the Eternal Forest as much as it needs you. You know that you are inexplicably linked, and have known for ages, even if you have forgotten as mists of time clouded these memories."

He nodded as she drew away, her hand slipping down his arm to grip his hand in hers. Thera tugged him forward, leading to the fountainhead of the spring. She gazed up at him, a soft humming sound starting up in her throat. Standing so close to her, he could hear a second strain that had a beat to it like the song of frogs. The fall of water filled his vision as she stepped away, the silver streams inviting him to be embraced and renewed, to release that which had weighed him down for centuries.

The water called to him even as the song of the nymph lulled his mind into peace. As her fingers unwound from his arm, he stepped forward, his hands raising in supplication. He thought of his mother, her soft smile, the first face he saw when he came into existence. Silvas saw it again as he submerged.

It didn't feel like water. That was his first thought. It felt like a rush of light around him. It swept over him with such force that his back bowed. Ice pricked at his skin as the water drove into him until it pervaded every part of him, stripping away that which obscured him into the form of the lucomo who held court amid the woods, washing away his memories.

Images flashed by him, one after the other, picking up speed as power welled up within him. As the last vestiges pulled away, Selvans threw back his head and roared monstrously… and his pearl white eyes opened. The gold tumbled from his antlers, splashing into the water lapping at his hips. He stared at it blankly. There was something he should remember about that glimmer, a golden bond connecting to his soul, brighter and lovelier than any other. The thought made him wary, so he reinforced the block between him and that soul. There was a reason for it, even if he couldn't recall it.

The wind stirred, and he shivered.

He needed to return to Arx.

Rushing out of the pool, the water raised and parted before him as he charged to the shore. He bent midstride to pluck Nocis from its nest and slung it over his shoulder, its familiar weight remembered by his body. He took to the air on massive wings that sprouted at his will, no longer contained to mimicking the creatures of the forest like a silvanus.

He was Selvans, the first of silvani, god of the wood. May the gods have mercy on whomever threatened *his* forest.

CHAPTER 33

Diana stepped out onto the balcony overlooking the garden. The perfume of the flowers below filled the air, and she drew in a deep breath. If she wasn't mistaken, her sense of smell had improved. She could make out numerous notes from the strange flowers in the garden beds. In the moonlight, she could see the pale petals of the nightblooms.

It was peaceful there, but she hadn't been bothered by a soul since she heard the commotion of Alseida being dragged from the palace grounds. She was exiled, Diana had learned from a naiad who was tasked with bringing her meals.

She found herself unable to rouse any sympathy for Alseida. Her field of fucks was fallow.

The dryad hadn't taken her exile well. By some feat, she had broken free of her escort in a final attempt to get to Diana, unaware. The sound of her body slamming against the door had been startling enough, but that was only the beginning. Alseida had clawed and pounded at the door as she fought off the guards. Diana heard every disturbing sound through the door, but they stopped abruptly when, presumably, the dryad had been hauled away.

Diana assumed as much, judging by what she had witnessed from the balcony. The mussed nymph had been a sight as she raged and fought every step of the way, screaming as she was hauled into the trees. It had given her no pleasure, but she had felt relieved knowing that threat had been removed. That was a small gift in the face of the turmoil gnawing at her.

She caressed the balcony rail with one hand, gazing at the thick vines that made the railing. The garden was the only thing that preserved her sanity over the few days since she had last seen Silvas. Never had she questioned her grip on reality until she experienced the choking sensation that closed her bond to Silvas. At that moment, she could do nothing but scream. She had scraped her hands against the walls, begging for her mate in a mindless panic, begging to be released from the confines of the room that imprisoned her.

Arx had responded immediately. The wall beneath her hand had shaken, sending her reeling, the rocks grinding as they shifted and realigned themselves. The moment she stepped outside and breathed the fresh air, her appreciation for the unique nature of Arx struck her. The palace held her and offered her what comfort and stability it could, her emptiness still crushing her from within.

In the darkness, a spark had lit inside of her, and then another, twining through her heart. From out there in the forest, she felt a network of connections all around her, hundreds of thousands of souls touching her being. It had begun with sensing the heart of Arx itself, and then she could feel the hamadryads weeping and calling from nearby. Touch upon touch flooded through her until she felt like she was the center of the entire cosmos of life that made the Eternal Forest.

After the initial rush they had faded back into the recesses of her mind, but, unlike Silvas, they did not desert her. They were there, dwelling inside her, if she closed her eyes and sought for the connections. And above them all was Arx glowing within her, a part of Silvas even as she carried a part of him through his *vinculum marcam,* connecting them together. A slight smile tugged at her lips as a spiraling vine sprung up to cling to her hand with soft caresses.

How odd to feel such appreciation from a construct of stone, and yet she could feel it as if something deep within the foundations of the palace recognized her and loved her. It sounded crazy, but it sparked a warmth of returning affection within her. It entreated her, spoke to her in soft creaks, and the groans she hadn't heard before that were so low in pitch she was certain they were below the normal human range of hearing. The palace crooned to her, welcoming her home. Even the trees themselves bent toward her as if bowing their leafy heads, a soft thrum of adoration pulsating through her soul.

Diana frowned, her heart clenching painfully.

She had caught hints of feeling such adoration from Silvas, enough to shake her determination to return home, and instead explore further the bond between them. She wanted to sink into their bond and take him within her, and it hurt that he had cut her off. It was a gaping wound in her soul, bleeding out her life in a slow trickle of sorrow.

Glancing up at the moon, she shook her head. The hour was late, and it was just shy of a week since she'd last seen her mate. Where was Silvas?

Every time she had asked the burly males guarding her door, they had turned away with little response other than that they were ordered to keep her safely confined to the royal chambers. It didn't make any sense! Unfortunately, she hadn't fared any better with the naiads who tended to her.

Turning from the beauty of the garden, she paced back through the room until she arrived at the door. Placing her hand upon the handle, she pulled it open, the quiet creak announcing her presence. On the other side, the door was filled with the familiar sight of the backsides of two large males. One was plainly a troll but the other was a male she didn't recognize. Taller, with thicker features, his skin a deep moss green with prominent tusks pushing up from his mouth, and a fall of dark hair braided down his back. His lack of tail also made him distinct from the troll at his side. Both males turned simultaneously at the sound of the door opening, their scowling faces bending down toward her.

Smiling up at them, Diana knitted her fingers together in front of her as she returned their regard. "Hi boys, I was just going to slip out and see if I can find Silvas. It seems that, as usual, you've made yourself into a second barrier, though. If you could just scoot a bit so I can get out, I will be on my way and won't disturb you further."

The unfamiliar male scowled, his eyes narrowing on her as the troll gave her an apologetic look and shook his head.

"We can't allow that, ati," he muttered reluctantly. "We have our orders."

She raised an eyebrow. "Orders to keep me locked in this room day after day?"

The male shifted uncomfortably but nodded his head. "Yes, mistress."

"It's been days though!" she shouted. "I understand that Silvas is worried, but this is ridiculous."

The troll shrugged. "Be that as it may, we can't let you out. He said to keep you here, confined within the walls of this room. You're not to be allowed loose in the palace. We are not to allow you out nor anyone inside without express orders to do so. The command comes from the lucomo. He will see to you when he returns."

A blinding pain of betrayal struck her, locking her fingers tightly together with the tension that snapped through every muscle.

She couldn't believe it. He left, and was actually keeping her imprisoned within the room while he pursued Cacus without her. Her hand dropped from the door. So much for the bullshit about needing her. She had swallowed that and had not only allowed herself to be put in danger, but to lay with him… and she mated with him believing that they were destined for each other. How much of all of that was due to his influence? It had felt so right, but now everything had the distinct smell of bullshit. Her throat tightened as her stomach rebelled with a wave of sickness that seemed rush up from that void within her.

"Oh. I see," she murmured, ignoring the concern on the troll's face. Even the other male raised an eyebrow at her as if weighing her reaction. Pulling a stiff smile to her lips she stepped back. "Well, thank you," she said as she pulled the door shut.

Diana stared at the door for some time, her emotions running through her in a confusing riot. What reason would Silvas have for locking her in the room? She had no doubt that it had something to do with his absence from the bond. He blocked her out and locked her in, obviously quite intentionally. Any thought she had that his absence was unintentional, that perhaps he went somewhere in attending his duties that disrupted the flow between them, vaporized beneath the piercing light of truth. It just left more questions in her mind.

Why would he do this to her?

She paced through the room, her eyes straining toward the garden, hoping to hear anything at all from him as she walked from one side of the room to the other. Over and over she retraced her steps, her turmoil increasing with every pass.

Where exactly was Silvas and why had he so abruptly abandoned her without a word? They were supposed to be in this together!

The thoughts kept circling her mind as she paced until her legs became weary and her energy waned. Desolation was slowly creeping into her as the night trickled by and the moon crept farther through the sky, where it was visible in the narrow break in branches until it sank out of sight. With tears of angry frustration, Diana finally allowed herself to drop across the bed, wet streaks flowing from the corner of her eyes and over her cheekbones to get lost in the hair beyond her temple.

She didn't know how long she lay there staring at the lines of the ceiling, drawing out pictures from them in her mind. Her breath left her in an unhappy sigh, her eyes drifting shut. She would sleep and hope that the next day brought her something better.

Her eyes closed, darkness swam around her, cut off from the soft glow of the hearth. She allowed herself to settle deeper into the arms of Arx as she sought her rest. A quiet surrounded her, but only for a moment before it was broken. A low, pained groan that swept through the palace, jerking Diana from her sleep. Her skin crawled with the scurry of invisible insects bolting from crevices and hidden corners as Arx shuddered and groaned yet again. Bolting upright, she slipped from the bed, her body bracing as she cringed from the vibrations of pain that erupted from her. The roar of breaking stone and snapping vine filled her as Arx bellowed its fury, but it was not alone in the agony that threaded through her mind.

There was a ripple of anger and fear that rose from all around her as a silent alert surged through the palace. It crested, gathering strength, a tsunami of despair and terror. Rising above it all, glimmering through her mind, the hamadryads screamed their fury, their fingers reaching to rend, impale and ensnare. Diana could sense the gore that dripped over the limbs of the trees as they fought the encroaching darkness.

The darkness was as a slick smear of oil through her mind, cut through the forest, brutally destroying everything within its path. It roared viciously, breaking through her mind as it ripped its claws through the track it cut into the Eternal Forest, its sides heaving from thousands of wounds and broken limbs of trees that tore into it in an attempt to protect Arx.

Wounded and angry, its poisonous touch clawed into the trees, severing the lifeforce of the hamadryads. Diana's heart wept and bled as their cries of fury shifted to despair and pain, their lights pulsing before slowly blinking out, one by one. Whatever it was, it was tearing through the perimeter, leaving naught but devastation in its wake.

Spurred by forest dying all around her, Diana ran out onto the balcony, drawn up short as she gripped the railing and stared out into the forest. She could see the path of attack as the trees blackened before her eyes, the hamadryad soul lights brightening and blinking out as their noble trees fell in twisted, rotting remains. She squinted, trying to catch sight of the source, fear rising as a hard knot in her throat. She caught sight of inky hooves slashing and clawed hands tearing…

The door behind her burst open with such strength that it slammed against the stone wall. Diana spun around, her hand at her throat as her heart attempted to leap from the confines of her chest. A relieved breath released on a ragged gasp. Raskyuil stood there with the guard assigned to her door, his tail flicking behind him anxiously as his eyes ran through the room, searching for her. The moment they fell on the balcony where she stood, the male grunted and strode over to her side.

A heavy hand dropped down on her shoulder as he peered down at her. "Ati, are you okay?"

Licking her lips, she nodded weakly, the cries of the dying overwhelming her. She paled, shaking beneath his grip as he glanced down at her with concern. If she looked as fractured and torn apart as she felt, bits and pieces of her dying with the forest, she had no doubt that she looked deathly herself.

"All the death, I feel it screaming through me, and it just

won't stop. What's going on? Where is Silvas?" she croaked against the scream building in her throat. She couldn't stop the flow of agony from suffocating her.

Raskyuil's hand tightened on her as he looked sharply toward the males lingering by the door. "We need to get her out of here."

The green male shifted in place, his heavy brow lowering. "That is not our orders."

A loud growl sounded from Raskyuil as he pinned the male with a hard glare. "I'm the head of the guard and I say we are moving the ati out. I will answer to the lucomo. If I must do it without your cooperation, orc, then get out of my way."

The other troll edged forward, his face wrinkling with concern as Raskyuil shouldered some of her weight, helping her to remain upright as another torrent of agony swept through her.

"What is wrong with the ati?" he whispered hesitantly.

Raskyuil gave him an impatient look. "I don't know," he growled, nudging the other male aside as he hauled her out the door.

Diana stumbled forward, nearly stepping on the goblin who waited there, hopping from foot to foot. Borbekel's beady eyes peered at her expectantly, and she could feel their weight seeing through her. He let out a sound of exclamation and muttered to himself worriedly as he looked up and down the hall.

"Move, rodent," Raskyuil snarled as he swung his foot as to kick the goblin out of his path.

The smaller male, knee-high compared to the troll, shrieked and dodged, his small tail whipping as he let out a high-pitched hiss.

"You must hide her!" the goblin shrieked, his small arms waving through the air toward a long dark corridor.

"I'm not stupid, goblin. I am well aware of that," Raskyuil snarled as he hauled her up into his arms and strode quickly down the hallway.

Borbekel's head shook as he raced at their side. "You don't understand at all. You have to hide her someplace where she will be surrounded by magic and deep within the ground. Goblins know these things. We see what you do not. As fate designed, the life of the Eternal Forest and its inhabitants are bonded to her. The very part of her nature that would feed vitality into the Eternal Forest and fertility in beasts and plant-life that dwell within it, the death of the forest is tearing her apart. Cacus is killing her. We need to get her someplace safe where the bond will be muted."

Raskyuil snarled loudly and leveled the goblin with a hard glare. "Are you certain of this?" At the male's nod, he cursed and changed direction, moving quickly down another hall. "I know the place, then, that she'll be guaranteed safe. May the lucomo forgive me for violating his secrets."

CHAPTER 34

Diana panted through the pain swamping her, the halls blurring together as they turned down one and then another. Vines rose from the walls, guarding over their passage as they passed beneath them. The guards looked uneasily at the twisting plants, but Diana patted Raskyuil's shoulder soothingly.

"Don't worry, Arx guards us," she whispered hoarsely, her fingers digging into his shoulder weakly as she clung to his side. She gave a meaningful glance up to the plants.

She felt his hesitation, but he nodded over the top of her head. "Arx protects. Move," he snarled to the guards as they rushed down the hall.

The stones of the hall behind them pushed out like jagged teeth as the vines coiled everywhere, waiting for their prey. The palace shook again as if something were climbing through it rapidly, breaking down walls rather than treading down winding halls.

Cacus. She knew it was him. The taint of his presence was swamping through everywhere he stepped, every passage he carved out for himself, the sickness pervaded. She could feel it stealing into her bones even as it swamped through Arx.

"The hidden courtyard is just this way," he grunted, his eyes sliding down to her. "Not much further, ati."

Diana nodded, sweat pouring from her brow as a tremor swept through her. Just ahead, she could see the bend of the hall where it led to another corridor.

Just a little further. She had to hold on just a little longer. She had to believe that her sanctuary was close. She could feel something, a secret below in the greatest depths.

The orc bellowed as he jerked away, his weapons falling heavily on the stone flooring. Raskyuil half turned, shouting out to the male as Diana peered over his shoulder. The orc was pulled through the air by a blood-red, flexible appendage. From her vantage point, Diana studied it, and her stomach turned as she realized that a long tongue had wrapped around him and was drawing him back into the darkness. The orc fought, stabbing deep into the organ with a dagger in a frenzy as rivulets of inky ichor dripped from it. The creature never relaxed its hold, but drew him back until he disappeared into the shadows as Raskyuil put on another burst of speed. The orc's furious roar turned into pained howls, and Diana ducked her head against the troll's shoulder, sobs of horror shaking her as she desperately attempted to muffle the cries.

Her tears fell, wetting paths of wide rivers streaking down her cheeks as they made the bend and raced down a sloping passage. She could feel every vine that snapped loose from the walls, every tree shuddering to whip deadly limbs. Rocks burst from the walls, stabbing jagged ends into the flesh of the beast and falling to crush him with their weight. It did little more than slow him down, but Diana could hear the angry, pained sounds of Cacus in the near distance as Arx rose up against the monster.

"Iktan," Raskyuil bellowed to the other troll as they approached a sharper bend, ornate walls crumbling in on themselves, "secure the next corridor."

The unburdened male nodded and pulled out ahead of them at a quicker speed, making it to the passage. He drew to a halt and glanced down it before turning sharply to them again and waving his hand forward.

"Thank the gods," Raskyuil growled. "We're almost there, ati. Just a little farther. Hold on. Just around the corner is the hidden courtyard."

The goblin bounded beside them, glancing worriedly behind him with such frequency that Diana also watched the darkness behind, trembling with fear. This wasn't how it was supposed to go. She was supposed to be at Silvas's side as they destroyed the monster. He would have been a force which Cacus would not have been able to contend with. Wiping her tears with one hand, she turned forward just as Raskyuil stumbled, her fingers biting into his shoulder as his arms bound tighter around so as not to drop her.

A golden yellow woman, her body stained with inky veins running through her, her green hair laying limp around her face at broken, brittle lengths, stepped out of the shadows, unseen by Iktan. Her red lips parted in a wide grin as Raskyuil shouted a warning. The male turned, his eyes widening just as the dryad's hand morphed into a thick branch. It struck him through the neck with such force that he was pinned briefly to the wall, his body trembling and tail swishing wildly as he gurgled and attempted to draw in his last gasps of breath. She giggled and pulled her arm free, her hand reforming as she stepped forward.

"Alseida, you were banished from the palace… What…?" Raskyuil snarled.

She laughed and stepped over the body of the troll. "And you thought I would just take it lying down? You threw me out to wander the depths of the forest alone, and *he* found me. He showed me what delights he possessed and promised my place. I am the queen of the Eternal Forest. Me. *Me!*"

"You are not the ati," Borbekel hissed. "You are death, a plague on the forest. You always have been. Your greed has warped you. Your kind is meant to preserve the forest and yet for centuries you have been an infestation and rot that invades the trees of this woodland, dryad," he sneered.

The smile fell from Alseida's lips, her face darkening with rage. Her hair lifted around her, the locks twining and thickening like layered vines, the tips tapered and lethal as they snaked through the air, growing longer, reaching out for them.

Borbekel let out an ugly, hair-raising scream as he leaped forward, releasing from his pouch several bundles that flashed upon contact, their magic slicing over the dryad, burrowing in an attempt to dig deep within her with their colorful fiery tongues to infest her. Alseida shrieked angrily, her claws digging at her flesh, stripping chunks away as she attempted to root out the magic, more of the blackness from her skin flowing into the open wounds, burrowing into her with dark, surging tendrils that made her scream louder.

The goblin pounced again, but Alseida snarled and snatched him out of the air. Diana cried out as the other hand gripped into him and the dryad smiled grimly at her. She knew by that smile that the goblin was about to suffer because of her. Diana sobbed in denial, silently begging the dryad not to follow through.

Alseida's smile hitched wider and a cruel laugh left her at Diana's grief. Seconds later, Borbekel screamed as the long needle-like thorn claws dug in into his flesh, tearing through flesh, muscle, and bone. She laughed as he screamed, and even as he fainted when the pain became too great, she still laughed as his innards dripped from his body and splattered on the ground with one last rip, tearing the male nearly in half, held together only by his spine. She shook him in Diana's direction, his eyes staring out sightlessly, before throwing him to the floor. Long, curving thorns protruded from her body as she stepped closer.

"I will have my crown, but first I will destroy my rival," she snarled. "There will be no ati, only me as the consort of the dark lord of the wood. My power will be absolute, and death will fall as I will it."

"*Madness!*" Raskyuil shouted, shifting Diana's weight in his arms to safely draw his enormous ax and heft it before them.

Alseida eyed it and smirked. "Do you think I shiver at the sight of your iron, troll? No ax will fell me. Cacus has made me more powerful than you know."

Her arms raised, her lips widened once more to a grin as she turned her arms like a magician, showing one side and then the other. Before their eyes, the limbs lengthened and became as two great thorn-covered spikes that she held out threateningly from her sides. They bumped and scraped against the walls as she strode toward them. The inky veins slid over her like rapidly growing rivers, making her skin bulge as they crept up the rest of her body, streaming through her face until they finally hit her eyes. The two orbs blackened into dark pits.

The troll stiffened, raising his ax as he adjusted his stance. Diana leaned heavily against him in his arms, assailed continuously with the agony of the collapsing forest as her body spasmed intermittently. She stared at the dryad through half-closed eyes, a spirit of suffering stalking toward them. Alseida didn't merely want her dead. She wanted her to suffer and bleed. She wanted to see her beg.

Hopelessness rolled over her. Within that darkness she felt familiar sparks flowing toward them, rolling hungry, angry energy, tearing through the creatures that slid over Arx and fell into their path. The crocotta!

Diana's lips slowly parted, a grim smile tugging at them as she met the dryad's empty eyes. "Fuck you, Alseida," she croaked. "You won't have the forest. The forest will have you… It will consume you and feast upon your bones."

The dryad laughed. “And just how will you manage that, little human?”

“Not me,” Diana wheezed. “Them…”

A side tunnel ripped open through the walls from the outer courtyard as the massive bulk of the crocotta clan barreled through, their eyes glinting with a peculiar glow as Alseida met their gaze. Her body stiffened as she froze, unable to escape as they slammed into the dryad. They warbled and snarled as their teeth sank into her, tearing and goring as vines snapped out from the ground and walls.

The first vine speared her, leafy tendrils borrowing through her. Each tendril burst ragged open wounds from her body in dozens of places as the dryad shrieked and struggled. The crocotta backed away, their sides heaving as more vines sank into the nymph. They stabbed into her flesh, piercing through her body to hold her aloft before slamming her against the wall.

Vines slid down the wall, reaching for her as the remaining upraised vines wound around her, their thorns stabbing into her as they anchored her high against the wall, nestled into the hanging vines flowing all around her. Her cries were swallowed by the thick layers of Arx’s vines until all that remained uncovered was the head of the nymph that sagged forward, groaning with pain.

Raskyuil’s grip tightened around Diana as he stepped away from the gruesome sight. The solid sound of impact jerked his head around, staring down the dark hallway from which they’d come. Diana looked over his shoulder, her breath rattling in raspy pants as one heavy footfall was followed by another, the sound of hooves crunching over debris as their pursuer drew closer.

The crocotta whined and backed away as Raskyuil stumbled back. Diana’s mouth went dry as the beast stepped into the low light of the remaining glow pods that clung to the walls. Large, malformed hooves the size of dinner plates rang against the stone flooring as four giant legs met a torso resembling the shape of a horse.

Deep red in color, he appeared almost as an unnatural centaur warped with spikes. Curved horns erupted from the skin along his spine and flanks. His red cheeks bulged with tusks, licks of fire and smoke drifting from between his lips before a long, thick tongue swept out, tasting the air with small flicks before retracting into his gaping mouth.

His eyes turned toward Alseida, who strained against her bindings.

"Help me! Free me, my king, so we can destroy them—together as we are meant to," she whispered.

The crocotta danced further away as Raskyuil backed quietly from the dryad, taking pains not to draw attention to them. Cacus's heavy hoofs echoed as he took slow measured steps toward the nymph, his eyes narrowing on her thoughtfully.

"Poor little love," he crooned in a deep, echoing voice. Despite his words, there was an edge of mockery to his voice as he stepped closer. His tongue slipped out of his wide mouth, sliding over her face to trail down her neck. Withdrawing it, he chuckled malevolently, the sound crawling over Diana's skin as she silently counted each slow, sliding step that Raskyuil took, backing them toward the hidden courtyard.

Alseida's eyes widened. "Cacus, please. Free me. I'm your mate. We joined beneath the dark of the moonless night."

His head cocked as he studied the dryad. "Yes," he hissed slowly. "An unworthy mate, so easily ensnared. I will swallow your essence and make you one with me. Better to try again with a more deserving female," he growled. "You have served your purpose."

Even at their distance, Diana could see the dryad's empty eyes widen, her mouth gaping in terror as Cacus opened his mouth wide, his jaw dislocating like a python, and dropped his head down. He bit off Alseida's head with one snap of his massive teeth. Throwing his head back, it dropped further into his powerful jaws. The corridor was filled with the sound of crunching as he chewed her skull, pausing only to sweep his long tongue to gather the fragments of the nymph's residual being. A dark slime seeped from his mouth, and the dryad's remains began to collapse around her neck, showing the bones of a destroyed immortal.

Diana whimpered. She lay limply in Raskyuil's arms as he spun around, racing into the hidden courtyard, the sounds of the vine encasement cracking all around them. Each crack was accompanied by the meaty sound of immortal substance being torn away and consumed.

Clinging to the troll, her eyes trailed over the crocottas, lingering on Keena in the lead and the duskier Keech. With each breath she could feel the forest falling down around the palace as the pets of Cacus wreaked devastation, his very presence a blight seeping into the ground. Everything around her felt dark, a fog descending over her as she flopped in the troll's arms. She was barely aware of him clutching her tightly to his chest as he bent down to whisper in her ear.

"To the belly of the Earth with you through the hidden door of the unseen. May Silvas's secret stair deliver you to safety."

A groan of pain left her as Raskyuil draped her over the furred back of a crocotta. Diana barely had the strength to lift her eyelids as she slipped into the cool darkness below the halls of Arx. As the door swung shut and latched behind her, she heard the challenging roar of a troll greeting battle.

Her eyes drifted closed and she sagged, sliding precariously on the beast. By some miracle, she didn't fall from it onto the stairs. It was only when they reached level ground that, when the crocotta crouched, she dropped to the floor.

Chaos spun around her, and Diana's back arched with the pain that swamped her where she lay on the hard, stone ground. The thousands of connections twisted within her, demanding her, calling to her—pleading. A spark lit within her, a white flame that grew with every supplication until it was an inferno twisting through her in a raging firestorm, compressing with her every breath until it was a crackling orb of power held within her.

Diana's eyes flew open, her mouth gaping in a silent scream. Her body arched once more as the white fire erupted through the bonds tied to her soul, flooding them with strength and power. Arx rumbled overhead, and the pale silver light burst through her mind, accompanied by a piercing pain on her brow like two stakes driven deep. Her light flooded through the Eternal Forest. She was aware of it even as lost as she was in the darkness of the lower levels, her entire being crying out for her mate.

Spent, she lay in darkness, a warm body nestled next to her as Arx shook above and the sounds of battle faded, punctuated only with the pained roar of the monstrous Cacus before silence fell. Her eyelids fluttered, but at long last, she closed them and succumbed to the weariness that overwhelmed her. At least she no longer hurt… and she hoped that the brave guard found his peace as well.

Head lolling, Diana was lost to oblivion.

CHAPTER 35

The sound of dripping water echoed around Diana. Was she dead? If so, she was disappointed. She had assumed that if she were dead, her worries would be gone and the emptiness and pain running through her would have ceased. Instead, she hurt and felt out of sorts.

"No, you are not dead," a soft, sibilant voice answered with an amused chuckle.

Had she said that aloud?

Groaning, Diana cracked open her eyes, turning her head to face the stranger at her side. She gasped at the sight of the grinning female beside her. As colorless and pearly as Silvas, the female had startling blood red eyes, and instead of legs possessed a serpentine tail that coiled in a relaxed fashion on the rocks of the cave.

A low whine sounded behind her seconds before a dark snout shoved into her face, blocking the sight of the snake woman. Diana blinked up and smiled at the crocotta that stepped carefully over her to nuzzle her.

"Keena, you saved me," she whispered, her fingers digging

into the thick fur as she pushed herself to a seated position and hugged the wide head against her chest.

"Strictly speaking, the troll saved you… but I do suppose that the crocotta deserves some credit for getting you down the staircase to my lair without dropping you on your head," the female at her side observed in a wry voice.

Peering around Keena's bulk, Diana eyed her, her fingers clutching at the fur as she remembered Raskyuil shoving her into the darkness as that thing—Cacus—devoured Alseida. In the darkness, she had heard Raskyuil's roar of fury and pain.

Glancing toward the staircase illuminated by only a few strategically placed torches, she didn't see any sign of him. Diana couldn't hold back a hoarse sob. "Please tell me he's okay," she choked out.

The red eyes studied her. "He lives yet. I feel him digging himself out from the rubble of the wall that collapsed on him, though Cacus has fled."

"How do you know all this?" Diana whispered.

The female smiled. "I know because I am Dorinda, the vegoia trapped beneath Arx. I see and know many things, just as I know that you are the uxorem of my brother Selvans. You know him better as Silvas, the irritating god playacting as a king."

"God…? How can that be?" Diana asked as a shiver betrayed just how much she was unnerved.

Silvas couldn't be a god. Despite everything, even if she was deceived on the nature and depth of their relationship, she did carry his *vinculum marcam*. He was hers… wasn't he? How could a woman be married to a god?

Dorinda made a disgusted hiss as she rose and shifted away, moving toward a crevice in the wall of the cavern. "My brother is a fool, that's how. He wanted to escape from himself and hide away, living with the casual freedom of a simple spirit instead of the role for which he was born. We share one mother, he and I, but his destiny was far greater than what he made of it—and the pitiful condition of the Eternal Forest shows it. I recall the way the forest looked when it was young. Did you know that during the day the trees would part to allow the glorious light of Usil, the king of the sun, shine down and nourish us all? It wasn't this dark pit of despair. All manner of beings called this place home as they traveled between the worlds. I loved the monokerata most."

"What's a monokerata?"

Dorinda smiled, the expression making the female's face seem younger, erasing the lines of bitterness. "Amazing creatures. Large horses, white as snow except for their necks and heads, which are red. From their brow sprouts a single horn that is white, black in the middle and then red at the tip. The horn provides all manner of wellness, for which men once coveted the magical creature." Her smile slipped. "They were nearly wiped out from the Eternal Forest when my brother took Alseida to his bed. Her greed weakened the borders that hid the entrance from mortals."

She peered at Diana as her smile turned smug. "You wouldn't have found your way into our world without help. Mother brought you here even as Cacus hunted down and chased his victims into the woods where he could consume them at his leisure." She sighed and brought forth a jug and two cups. "But at that time, it was not the case. The monokerata were nearly hunted to extinction for their horns."

Diana gaped at her. "Are you talking about unicorns? They're real?"

"They are, but they stay hidden in the few parts of the forest that still see the sun. I miss seeing them, but that was before I was enclosed within the earth," Dorinda said, her face hardening.

"Boy does that sound familiar," Diana muttered. Shaking her head, she looked askance at the serpentine woman. "I don't understand. If Silvas… er, Selvans… is your brother, why has he locked you away all this time?"

Dorinda snorted as she set down the cups on a flat rock that almost seemed to be fashioned like a table. From the jug, she poured a rich red liquid.

At Diana's questioning look, she smiled. "Wine to settle our nerves is called for, I believe. As for your question… To his credit, he did not intend to trap me in here, but he did not correct the situation either. He decided that it was what fate had decreed, that my oracular waters required protecting. Between us, the protection doesn't bother me so much… but his arrogance gets irritating. He won't permit me any access to the surface, keeping the entrance to the cavern completely sealed. Even if the forest has gone to Aites, I would still like to see it before it dies," she murmured as she swallowed back a mouthful of red wine.

Lifting her own cup to her lips, Diana froze and glanced up. "Wait, what? What do you mean before the forest dies? What's wrong with the forest?"

"You tell me you can't feel it sickening, the decline? Granted, it is drowned out at the moment by the devastation Cacus caused in his attack." She tilted her head and considered Diana for a moment before sighing. "No, of course you wouldn't know. You have no point of reference for what the forest should feel like to know that what you feel is alarming. You are basing it on the seasons within your own world, which force the trees into slumber in so many places. Listen, human, the trees here do not sleep and do not decline unless they are withering and preparing to die. If that happens, there will be no more Eternal Forest and no more trees anywhere. Without the Eternal Forest, eventually everything dies," she said in a low voice.

Diana faced the vegoia. "Sil… Selvans left me here. I don't understand why you're telling me all of this if there's no way I can stop it."

The female's lips twisted as she poured more wine into their cups. Diana hadn't even noticed that she drank of all of hers until she watched more ruby liquid splash into her empty cup.

"As I said, my brother is a fool. He let that female Alseida warp his trust in any female that may have influence over him. He thinks that you are a detriment, or possibly even a threat against the forest because of your bond. It is something all beings of the forest suffer from, that all-consuming hunger in the early days of the bonding when instinct rules, but my idiot brother does not consider this. If he feels that you will be used as a weapon against the forest, he will do anything to protect it. He doesn't see just how much he *needs* you."

Dorinda tapped her temple. "*I* have seen, ati. He may be destruction, but you are both queen and mother of life for the Eternal Forest. Those two words encompass the full meaning of ati. He needs your light to balance him. If he would have stuck around long enough to hear my entire prophecy, he would have known that," she muttered.

Groaning stone echoed from above, and Dorinda looked up and smiled. "It seems that Arx survives even this. I wager it will take it longer to reconstruct all of its beautiful passages."

"Yes, I've felt its presence within me," Diana admitted.

The vegoia cocked an eyebrow. "Interesting. I would not have imagined that your bonds through the forest would have extended to include the palace."

"It's not through the forest. It's through Silvas—I mean, Selvans. This name change is really going to be an adjustment," Diana said. "I can't feel *him* anymore. There's just a gaping hole where he was in our bond, but it seems that because both Arx and I are bonded to him and carry a piece of him within us, I have this bond with the palace like it's also a part of me."

Dorinda set down her cup. "Now *that* I did not foresee. It means Arx will heed you, and why it tried to protect you without Selvans' instruction. You shall be the heart of the forest even as

Arx is the structure of the axis for our world. He will amplify you, I believe, once you are on the throne by my brother's side." Her lips curved. "Blessed changes," she said with a small chuckle. "It really is a period of change."

Another rumble sounded above them, followed by a loud scraping sound. Dorinda tensed before backing away toward a dark pool. "It seems that you have company. It is best that I make myself scarce. If Raskyuil is attending, I foresee Selvans following on his heels. Sometimes it is better if we are not in the same space together when it can be avoided. Just remember what I've told you. Selvans needs you, but the sword obscures everything except his need to destroy to protect the forest. Stay strong," she hissed as she slipped gracefully in the water with a flick of her pearly tail.

Diana stared after her, mulling over the vegoia's parting words as the door swung open with a groan. She didn't move from her place until a large hand gripped her shoulder and turned her roughly. Raskyuil stared down at her, relief on his face.

"Thank the gods you survived and are well."

"Indeed, the female is. Now I wonder why that is," a dark voice purred from the staircase.

Excitement surged in her chest, and Diana searched the shadows until she found her mate. That feeling withered, replaced by dread. The pearly eyes that glowed down at her in a menacing stare were that of a stranger.

He descended the steps, and she made out smaller secondary horns that curved out from his brow between the rack of his antlers, and little protrusions that pushed down from the corner of his jaw at either side. A long spike jutted out from each of his forearms. His tail whipped behind him as he walked, a cruel smile tugging on his lips.

"Silvas?" she whispered as she felt Raskyuil tense behind her, his hand gripping hard on her shoulder.

CHAPTER 36

Selvans stared at the female standing in front of him. She seemed so familiar. He could feel an awareness of her pulsing through him as desire licked through his body. The surge of lust he had felt toward the nymph paled in comparison to what he was experiencing now. It made his body tremble and filled his mind with desperate longing.

He knew her, but why didn't he remember her?

At first glance, the female was unremarkable. She possessed little of the refined beauty of the immortal ones. So why did he yearn for her like no other? It was disconcerting and suspicious. She was pale and bruised, dark circles beneath eyes that appeared a deep green sparked with flecks of gold. Her hair hung in a tangled mass over shoulder, and he watched as she pushed it back with one hand, her eyes imploring him.

Whoever she was, she recognized him and seemed just as perplexed that he did not know her. The common tongue name that he had taken refuge behind fell from her lips, the sound sweet as it twined through him. It thrummed along the edges of the bond that was sealed off from him. He was certain that his reaction had something to do with the purpose of the barrier in his mind, but knowing that did not comfort him. He had to have had a reason to have blocked her out. He could not trust her. Even less knowing that she should not have survived the appetite of Cacus.

His eyes narrowed on the small human as he weighed the matter before him. Arx was in shambles, great swathes of trees were destroyed, and corpses littered the palace grounds. He had seen the remains. The crystalline skeletons of nymphs suspended in agony as their beings were consumed, the remains of satyrs and fauns curled up on themselves. He had witnessed what was left of goblins killed by the masses as they attempted to flee, and a field of orc and troll corpses bleeding freely over the earth where they made their last stand, their bodies ravaged and withered from their souls being torn out.

Even the majority of his crocotta clan lay broken in the inner courtyard. Keech and a few of the older pups had survived. He was relieved to see that Keena had also made it. It was a small gift in light of the horror he had witnessed among the broken stones of Arx and the blackened and broken trees of the hamadryads. Everywhere he had looked as he landed within the courtyard was stained with death.

Through that destruction, this soft female had survived. The possibility of her being involved was not something he could risk being in error. He had to preserve the forest. If he could not trust her, what was he to do with her? He had no stomach for killing vulnerable humans. He inhaled, his brow furrowing.

She didn't smell like a human. He bristled as he backed away from her, his cock swelling with a painful, raging need. He couldn't identify what she smelled like, and that disturbed him, even more since his body surged eagerly, demanding that he pin her beneath him as her perfume danced over his scent receptors.

Selvans growled and shook his head to clear it. She had to be an unnatural creature masquerading as human. He couldn't detect the taint on her, but if she made herself convincingly human to his other senses, she may have had the ability to disguise that as well. His hand sought his sword, a rush of wariness flowing through him, igniting his aggression. She was seeking to manipulate him. He would not allow it!

"Lucomo," Raskyuil rasped. Unlike the female, his guard wore several deep gashes running over his body, among them four furrows bisecting the left side of his face just shy of damaging his eye. They were half-healed and ugly, but at least no longer bleeding. It was the obvious work of one of the healers rushing to tend to all those who were injured as a number of beings had converged on the palace to help the wounded from nearby villages.

Despite the male's obvious pain, his hand remained planted on the female's shoulder as he addressed Selvans. "We need to leave. Cacus has fled. He'll carve a path of destruction, leaving nothing but death in his wake. We must put an end to the threat at once."

Selvan's gaze focused on the offending hand, growling. "You're right," he said. "Step away from the female."

Raskyuil stiffened, his expression turning calculated. Damn troll was too observant. "Would you not prefer that I help your uxorem?"

Selvans stiffened. *Impossible.* This was not his uxorem. He would never have set a barrier between himself and his mate. She had to be a seductress, a beguiling weaver of enchantments and illusions. She must have tricked his guard by some magic designed to convince him. That had to be how she gained entry, and how Cacus had made it through the palace's defenses. Arx was a deadly fortress to any who forcibly enter.

"Move," he hissed. "She has clouded your mind. I will deal with the betrayer."

The female startled, her mouth gaping open, no doubt surprised that he caught onto her lies. Without waiting for a response from Raskyuil, Selvans strode forward, fury filling him.

He would tear the male's hand away and disable him if Raskyuil dared get in his way. Nothing would stop Selvans from terminating the creature who brought death to his forest. As an ally of Cacus, she was no better than an unholy consort of the Tainted One. She was the vilest of females in his eyes.

His upper lip pulled back from his fangs at his advance, his stride breaking at the sudden grief that flooded him. He stumbled, his body shaking with emotion until he wrestled it back under control. He was a god! He was not subject to such weaknesses.

"No!" Raskyuil shouted as he stepped in front of her and brought his ax up against Nocis.

The clang of metal striking shook the cavern as the troll-forged ax splintered at the head. Selvans glared at the male over their weapons, a menacing growl vibrating in his throat.

"You would dare raise your weapon against me?" he rasped.

The troll met his eyes, regret shining in his gaze as he inclined his head. "I'm sorry… I can't. I must protect the ati. You are not well, lucomo."

"I am myself again," Selvans snarled as he pulled his sword up once more, the darkness of the blade seeming to absorb the light around them. Good. Let his adversaries fear him. Once more, Nocis would be put to the use for which it was forged. "I am the god of this forest and all within it, and I will see to it that all threats to it are vanquished!"

Raskyuil raised his ax once more. The broken metal made one of the double blades lean at an angle, the gouge a blazing scar against the metal. Still, he did not submit, even with several wounds weeping from where they were reopened. He dared to raise his weapon, though his arm shook, the muscles strained from the last blow.

"Diana… is no threat… to you or this forest," the troll rasped.

Selvans shook his head. "It is a pity that I cannot risk believing that. I take no pleasure in what must be done." He grimaced. "Truthfully, it pains me inexplicably, and I see no reason why it should. I have no memory of this female." He ignored the pained gasp from his faux mate. "All I know is what I must do, even if it means going through you, my friend."

"So be it," Raskyuil mumbled as he swung his ax.

He still possessed enough strength that its edge whistled with the force of its swing, but Nocis intoned a song of death as Selvans brought it around and cut through the air. Their collision rained sparks as the troll forge's magic ax shattered beneath the godly might of Nocis. The blade cleaved through the heads of the weapon as it wrenched free from Raskyuil's hands. The other male roared at the impact that sent him flying back into the cavern wall.

Staring at his fallen friend with regret, Selvans stepped to the male's side and sighed. "You brought this upon yourself."

The troll winced, his eyes rolling up to return Selvan's regard. "You bring whatever sorrows come… upon yourself," he replied in a faint voice.

Selvan's lips twisted as he turned away, his eyes fastening on the female watching him with sadness shining in her now blue eyes.

He cocked his head. There was something so familiar about those eyes.

"I am sorry," he rumbled as he stepped toward her. They were not just empty words. His sorrow tore through him, clawing at him, and he felt a wetness on his cheek. Raising one hand, he wiped it away in surprise. Never before had he wept. He hardened his resolve. He had no patience for such sorcery.

Selvans surged forward with a roar. The female stumbled back, her hands searching for a weapon she did not possess. The energy of Nocis curled through him, and triumph surged over him. But as she slipped back over the rocks, a sleek, white body shot up from the waters just behind her. A hiss rattled through the air. Selvans responded with his own furious roar as he wheeled to face his sister.

Dorinda bared her teeth and drew something up from the waters as she coiled on the fountainhead rock of her spring. Her red eyes glowed as a pale silver blade cut through the water, and she pulled it up. He stiffened, preparing for attack, but as she swung her arm forward, she made no move toward him. Instead, she released the blade, sending it spinning through the air.

His eyes followed the path of the blade. A light of its own seemed to wink from the depths of it as it fell to sink, tip down, in the ground in front of his foe. This new betrayal cut deep. For countless centuries, he and Dorinda had an uneasy relationship, often bordering on hostile, but never would have he expected her to betray him like this.

Turning toward the female—Diana, he recalled Raskyuil calling her—he eyed his adversary. He watched as one slim hand reached out and grasped the hilt of the sword. She pulled it free effortlessly from the rock and soil that confined it. Raising its point until it was held out between them in a clear warning, she stared back at him. Her face fell with grief, though her sword arm remained steady as she held the blade out against him.

Reluctance coiled through his body as he met her eyes, and an uncomfortable awareness sparked within him. He wasn't going to be able to hold any kind of drawn-out fight, nor could he provide her any opening to attack. He needed to end this matter quickly before his bewitched instinct turned against him. Growling, he swung his sword, hoping that the strike would be clean and her death mercifully quick so that his sorrow would not know greater heights.

Her breath was loud within the cave, or perhaps it seemed so because despite his best intentions he was highly attuned to her. Every breath, every move… He longed to capture every moment of her existence for what remaining time he had before Nocis shattered her soul.

The silver blade glowed as Diana drew back and swung it. As she moved, a change seemed to come over her. Her eyes blazed with a sapphire light, and the blade flared as it met the void of Nocis. A brilliant flash erupted at the epicenter of contact as the combustion sent them both skidding back over the cavern floor. Half-crouched in an attempt to regain their balance, they regarded each other as the cave shook and numerous rocks broke and fell all around them, scattering over the ground. Selvans' eyes widened as he stared at her.

Never before had any weapon withstood the power of Nocis. No aelven creation, nor anything forged by troll or orcish hand. He would not have believed it if he hadn't seen it with his own eyes. The blade did not break, nor did it fly free from her hand. It had not even a scratch marring its length. For the first time since its creation, Nocis failed. Her blade pulsed with power even as an unearthly glow rose around Diana. She unwaveringly returned his regard. At her side, Keena, who had arrived too late to interfere, pushed her way forward. Her lips peeled back, baring long fangs. The crocotta stood stiffly, her fur bristling as she growled viciously in uncommon defense of the female that shook him.

Awareness skittered through him again, and he came close to lowering his blade. Tightening his hand, he frowned at her as he heard the scraping sound of Raskyuil hauling himself to his feet. He was not concerned with the troll. There was little that the male would be able to do against him. This female, however, possessed an unexpected power that tugged at him relentlessly. His instinct rebelled against his constraint as he faced her down and felt a tremor run up his arms.

"You will not succeed in your task, betrayer," Selvans hissed, keeping an ear tipped toward Raskyuil and one eye on the crocotta.

"*Betrayer?* What are you talking about. Silvas—shit, I mean Selvans? We mated! I'm yours and you're mine, no matter what lengths you went through and what lies you told in order to get what you wanted. And I can prove it!" she shouted at him, her body shaking with fury.

With one hand, Diana gripped her tunic and yanked it down, revealing the swell of her breasts. He was distracted by the sight, a sense of familiarity running through him. As if creeping through from some corner of his mind, he recalled the feel of them beneath his mouth, the smell of them, and the taste. Desperate to escape the fragmented memory, he jerked his eyes away, but froze when his gaze landed upon the pearly *vinculum marcam* embedded in her clavicle, pulsing subtly with power.

The truth of her words slammed through him, an agony piercing deep into his heart. It couldn't be—he couldn't have forgotten his uxorem! He fought against the fog obscuring his memories as he struggled to recall anything of her.

There was nothing there.

Squeezing his eyes shut, he stepped back on shaky legs and turned away, his eyes falling on Raskyuil. The male eyed him cautiously and Selvans shook his head.

"I yield. Remove this female from the Eternal Forest, Raskyuil. No further harm will be attempted on her from me."

The troll tipped his chin in acknowledgment before making his way over to Diana.

Without glancing back, Selvans strode back to the staircase. Raskyuil would do his duty. Meanwhile, he needed to begin his hunt for Cacus. His nostrils flared as he caught the lingering stench of the Tainted One. A soft voice, however, pulled at his heart as he left.

"Silvas, what happened to you?" Diana whispered.

Selvans wished that he knew.

CHAPTER 37

A sob broke free from Diana when at last Silvas was gone, and she leaned against Raskyuil. It wasn't fair. He was gone. He didn't even know her anymore and looked upon her as if she were his enemy. A thick arm wrapped around her as the troll hugged her close, comforting words murmured to her that did little to ease the ache in her heart.

Would the suffering of an unfulfilled bonding have hurt as much as this? At that moment, it didn't seem likely. Every part of her that had cried out for her mate in his absence, that had suffered without his presence in their bond, was grieving in an intense sense of loss. This time she had to suffer through watching him walk away from her, and hear with her own ears his damning words as he instructed Raskyuil to take her away.

Silvas… No, he wasn't her Silvas. He was Selvans, a stranger who she shared a fragmented bond with. She had to face a horrifically long life, alone, never seeing him again. Her body racked with pain, she turned in Raskyuil's arms and took the offered comfort.

"Selvans is a fool," Dorinda said with a snort, her tail tightening around her rock. "He blocked your bond before he saw the pegaeae."

Choking off another brittle sob, Diana blinked at the female as she attempted to focus past the emotions raging within her. "I don't understand."

The vegoia frowned toward the staircase. "I was blind to it when he came to me. I sensed a change in him, but I didn't understand it at the time. He's typically a moody bastard anyway." She sank lower into the water, a sigh leaving her lips. "Restoration from the spring isn't a bath or a simple washing. It violently strips away all the illusions you hold onto and all the miasma that separates you from your true self. With that much power repressed, it rippled during purification. Since he refused the bond, it literally removed your presence from him. It stripped away his memories of you. He suffers as you do, but he is confused and angry because of it. Nocis feeds that anger."

Swiping a hand over her face, Diana looked at Dorinda. "What do I need to do?"

The vegoia lifted an amused eyebrow. "Wait."

"Wait?" Diana deadpanned.

"He can't ignore the bond forever. It will draw him back to you." She craned her neck as she scanned the roof of the cavern, her eyelashes fluttering. "The forest will manage for a time," she intoned, her voice echoing through the cavern. "It will wait for you. It requires both of you for life to return once more. It will sleep and Selvans will hunt Cacus, but without you, his hunt will not bear fruit. When the mortal season turns, he will find you once more. Watch for him."

Diana stared, uncertainty warring within her. Did she want him to return for her? Although her heart and mind cried out for her mate, after he tried to kill her, part of her was more inclined to hide from him at this point.

"Very well," she said. "I will watch." Noticing the weight in her hand, Diana extended the sword out to Dorinda. "I think this is yours. Thank you for letting me use it."

The vegoia gave her a mysterious smile and drew away. "The sword Anola is not mine. It is yours, ati. It was always meant to be. I merely am the vehicle of bringing it to its rightful owner."

With a soft laugh, Dorinda dove back into the depths of her pool, leaving Diana alone with Raskyuil and the crocotta.

Turning away, she faced the troll, who was assigned as her escort out of the Eternal Forest. It was almost ironic that she was now to suffer the same exile that Alseida had only days earlier. It gave her only the tiniest bit of comfort that even in the grips of paranoia, Silvas had seen to her safety and ordered the nymph removed. Only this time she wasn't sure if it was for her safety or for the safety of the Eternal Forest. She suspected that not even Silvas knew.

Raskyuil glanced over at her, the fingers of one hand prodding his wounds. He regarded her quietly as he assured himself that he wasn't gushing blood. Eventually, his hand dropped away, and he cleared his throat.

"I suppose we ought to be leaving," he grumbled.

Diana nodded and attempted a smile. She doubted it was convincing since it felt strained to her, but at least she made the effort.

Raskyuil chuckled and patted her arm. "That's my ati, brave queen. Listen to the vegoia. Things will work out. I think it is about time we got you home. Do you recall anything of where you came into the forest?"

Diana thought back and described everything she remembered of what the forest looked like where she had emerged, right down to the faun she met. Raskyuil seemed familiar with the male because he nodded.

"The portal is not far," he said. "We will go on foot and allow Keena to reunite with her mate, if he still lives, and see to what remains of her clan. It won't take us more than a day of travel. That particular faun has his territory closer to the palace than most," he stated as he slowly walked forward. "This place may sleep for a time, but it is not going to be the same for me. Not after all of that."

Glancing sideways, Diana peered up at him. "What will you do?"

Grumbling, Raskyuil kicked away the broken remains of his ax and shrugged. "I'm thinking it is a time for a change. Seek what destiny the Fates have in store for me in your world." He gave her a crooked smile as he strode away, his heavy steps echoing in the cavern. "If nothing else, it should be an adventure."

"Yes, I suppose it would be," she agreed as they ascended the staircase.

The troll stopped at the top of the staircase and cast her a worried glance. "Prepare yourself. This isn't going to be pretty."

Diana gave him an arched look, but then the door opened to a world of absolute devastation. Raskyuil's face shut down, no doubt hardening himself to the sight he had expected to see. Diana, however, felt like she had been punched in the gut as he hustled her through the hidden courtyard. She didn't know with any certainty what he didn't want her to see but had a strong suspicion when she heard Keena's mournful cries rise before they were joined by far too few voices of the clan. Of what she did see, there was almost nothing familiar of the grandeur that was Arx, and the beautiful groves where the hamadryads had dwelled were nothing more than a blackened ruin. Even the gardens, when they finally came upon them, were withered and ground into the mud, a swarm of pixies forlornly attempting to prop up the crushed plants.

She didn't cry, however, until she saw the bodies of the dead. Diana sobbed in silence as they picked their way by the remains. Everywhere she looked, she saw dozens of the dead, their souls torn from them, bodies discarded where they fell in agony. Raskyuil said nothing as they walked. They were like wraiths among fields of death. The shadows gradually became longer until they finally left them and the palace behind as they entered the forest.

They fell into a rhythm over the hours, Raskyuil leading the way and Diana following silently behind. A chill crawled over her skin when they passed a dirty jeep tipped on its side. She glanced at it in passing, drawing the troll's curious gaze. Tightening her lips, she said nothing, and so they plodded on. It seemed like ages ago that Silvas had cornered her there. The reminder hurt even though the horror of the wreckage had faded over the weeks she had been in the Eternal Forest.

She didn't even notice when they passed through the barrier, but she thought she heard the sad coo of a dove when they suddenly broke through the trees into a familiar clearing. A makeshift altar jutted up, with its offering vessels. Her eyebrows winged up at the sight and she drew in a sharp breath of surprise. Breaking into a run, Diana raced through the woods, Raskyuil's startled shout following her. She didn't stop running until she broke through the trees.

Slowing to a halt, she looked down the hillside at a sight she had been uncertain if she would ever see again. Her grandmother's darkened cabin sat quietly beside the lake, a blush of growth surrounding it as late spring flowers bloomed throughout the garden. Tears filled her eyes and she spent a long moment just staring down at it as Raskyuil pushed his way through the brush to her side.

Looking over her shoulder at him, Diana watched the large male wrinkle his nose in an uncertain distaste. His nostrils flared, scenting the air as he squinted and took in the landscape.

"So, this is the human world. It looks less… impressive than I thought it would be. Where are your human wonders?"

Diana laughed and shook her head. “I’m afraid you’re looking at the wrong area for any kind of wonders. This is all farmland and small towns. Even before the ravaging, it was pretty quiet. I doubt that even in the remnants of the city you will find much that is truly impressive, though once there was.”

He grunted and followed her down the hill, his eyes scanning the distance as they made their way toward her home. Within minutes they passed through the garden gates and Diana dug her spare key from a flowerpot beside the door. Raskyuil trailed her the entire way, peering curiously over her shoulder as she unlocked it and pushed it open. His steps sounded impossibly loud on the wooden floorboards as he followed her into the cabin.

Craning his neck, the troll looked with interest at her simple furnishings and decor, things that her grandmother had collected throughout her lifetime.

“This is your home?” he asked.

She nodded as she shut the door firmly behind her. “This was my grandparents’ home, but it has been mine for a while now. I guess I still kind of see it as belonging to them even after all this time.”

He grunted again without comment as he continued his exploration. Diana busied herself building up a fire. She considered flicking on the electricity to give him a surprise, but she hated to waste the power from the generator unnecessarily. The fire, however, seemed to relax him, and at her invitation he lowered himself into a chair to rest.

“Do you think you’ll stay long?” Diana asked an hour later as they sat down to a simple dinner. The meat and bread had spoiled in her absence, but she’d found a few staples to put something filling together until she had the opportunity to hunt.

He shook his head as he took a bite of food. He grimaced at the fare but offered no complaint. “A day or two perhaps,” he grumbled. “It is best if I don’t stay too long. I suspect that if anyone notices my presence it won't go well for you. I need to figure my own way from here."

Diana's lips pressed into a flat line, but she couldn't disagree. No one in town would understand a troll among them, not after the horrors of the ravagers. They would immediately lump him together with them.

So it happened that, on the third day, Diana stood at her doorway in the wee hours of morning as Raskyuil, armed with what provisions she could find for him in town, threw the pack over his shoulder with a grim smile.

Sighing, she drew him down and gripped him close in a tight hug until his arms folded around her and returned the embrace. Pulling back, she blinked her eyes rapidly and smiled up at him.

"You'll be okay, won't you?"

His smile widened into a cocky grin. "Never doubt it, little ati."

"I am not your ati," she said, rolling her eyes. After everything that happened between her and Silvas, she felt uncomfortable with the title.

His smile fell. Leaning forward, his forehead nearly met hers as he peered into her eyes. "You will *always* be my ati. Even if I did initially offer to feed you to the strix. No matter where I am in this world, you have my loyalty."

"Thank you, Raskyuil," she whispered.

He gave her a slow nod, a friendly smile pulling at his lips as he straightened once more. She stood there in the doorway and watched as he walked away, passing through the garden gate. He stopped just at the other side and lifted his hand in farewell. She returned the gesture, her eyes stinging as he swung around and ambled away at a ground-eating pace. She didn't move from her spot until he disappeared.

Her heart heavy, feeling lonelier than ever, Diana sighed and turned to go back in. A brush of a cool breeze made her pause, and her eyes searched the horizon. Was Silvas out there somewhere, or was he still hunting within the Eternal Forest?

Shaking her head, she let out her breath and stepped back inside. It was time to try to get on with her life. Her long, long, lonely life. Grimacing, she drew the door shut behind her, wishing she could just close the door to that entire time and forget.

CHAPTER 38

Months later

Selvans growled as he crouched down close to the damp ground, his nostrils flaring to catch any scent of taint. *Nothing.* His claws dug into the earth with frustration. For months, he had been tracking Cacus in the human world, following the telltale scent of foulness. He had been getting closer, but now it was as if the creature had disappeared altogether.

Sitting back on his heels, he squinted at the light sprinkle of trees growing amid the grassy stretches. Just a few feet away a beautiful stone fountain stood silently with a single drop of water falling from it. The entire town had long been abandoned, the stench of death still clinging to it from when the wulkwos broke through from the underworld and tore through every human city and settlement. Already many places were being taken over by beings of the other world. So far most kept to themselves, away from the humans, but he knew that wouldn't last long. It was the nature of things.

This town was one that had yet to be resettled by any beings, nor did any take temporary shelter in its abandoned homes. Despair and forgotten memories echoed from every corner as the town lay silent, nature slowly overtaking the land once more. He could disguise himself to appear human enough when scouting around occupied towns or in any places where traces of humans still lingered, but he preferred to stay away from them as much as possible.

The flow of despair and forgotten memories was not an unfamiliar state for him, and he found lingering there to fit his current state of existence while he tried to work out what to do. The last of the autumn flowers were blooming in old overgrown flowerbeds, and the last flush of wildflowers tangled amid the yellowing grass. It was a late-season splash of color before they died like all things in this world. Soon they too would be gone. It made him long for the Eternal Forest and its consistent flush of beauty—consistent until it started to die, that was.

Experiencing seasons was unsettling for him. All around him, the trees were changing colors, preparing to sleep through the winter. The quiet of the hamadryads prickled through him uncomfortably, and he yearned to return to his kingdom. But he couldn't… Not yet. Cacus was too much of a danger, and lurked in the forests to feed, easily crossing the borders between worlds.

Dorinda was no help either. Upon discovering that Cacus had slipped into the human world, he had attempted to confer with his sister and gain the insight and wisdom of the oracle of the vegoia. She had been angry with him ever since he concealed the entrance to her cave, but never had she refused her assistance, even if he had to suffer with teasing. Now it was different. She refused to emerge from her spring and ignored every entreaty from him. Only once had she deigned to speak, a voice echoing from the spray of her water. "Seek your light." Nothing more, no matter how he entreated her, until finally he left and returned to the human world to pick up the fading trail of his prey.

Anger stirred in his breast anew. *Unreasonable female.*

The flutter of wings cut through the silence as a dove landed on the fountain. It cooed as it strutted, its head bobbing as it made its way along the edge of the fountain, pecking at the space in between the stones where seed had been blown and become caught. Another dove joined it, and then another, their wings beating the air. Selvans watched them, his skin prickling at their unexpected presence.

Sometimes a bird was just a bird… but sometimes…

The dry fountain gurgled, and his ears pricked toward it. He stiffened and then slowly stood, drawing himself up to his full height as water trickled and then splashed into the empty basin. The sweet scent of roses, myrrh, and ambrosia filled the air, and he saw a flash of gold moving behind the fountain seconds before a beautiful woman stepped around it. A playful smile danced on her lips, her amber eyes glowing with affection from her sun-bronzed face as dark ringlets of hair fell over her forehead and tumbled down her shoulders from the elaborate headdress she wore, studded with gems and flowers.

"Mother," he greeted her quietly.

Her smile widened, and she brushed her hands along the drape of her dress as she approached, a tinkle of gold from her numerous divine ornaments ringing in the air. "My Selvans, my dearest son."

He sighed wearily as her arms warmly enfolded around him. Her hand smoothed through his hair, and for a moment it was as if he were young again and he was at her knee as she showed him the beauty that dwelt within the heart of nature. Unconsciously, he leaned into her fragrant embrace, drawing her maternal warmth into him. He had felt so cold for so very long.

There was another memory of warmth, but every time he attempted to grasp it, it eluded him. He had nothing but a continuous freezing ache in the gaping wound within his soul. Torn deep, it had no origin that he could remember, but all he knew every day was suffering.

"I do believe that Eru would disagree," he snorted mirthlessly against her velvet sleeve. Drawing out of her embrace, he offered her a small smile. "All the world knows that winged spawn of the god of war is high in your favor."

Her warm laughter filled the air. "Perhaps he is the best known, but as you know, all of my children are favorite," she said with a wink. Brushing a stray lock of hair behind her shoulder, she looked over him critically. "And that brings me to why I am here."

He didn't bother holding back his groan. "I don't want to know," he muttered.

"Pssh, don't be that way. You always were the most stubborn of my brood. I'm not here to annoy you. I am here to help," she said cheerfully as if such news should please him.

He winced and attempted to deflect her sudden interest in him.

"Don't you have other children you can 'help?'" he asked.

At his demand, Turan frowned and set her fists on her ample hips, an ornate, folded fan clasped tight in her hand. Her golden cheeks reddened, and she looked for all the world as if she had received the worse of offenses by his question.

"Hush," she snapped in exasperation. "You are my current project, and you should be glad. You have royally screwed up everything! I practically handed the other half of your being to you, but you—you are too suspicious! You couldn't just gracefully just accept it! Not only that, but you rejected your uxorem! When did you cease to trust your heart, Selvans? This was not among the lessons I reared you with." Her tirade died down, and the last was said so sadly that his heart ached.

"Since trusting my heart nearly destroyed me and the Eternal Forest," he muttered. "I can't blindly trust any female to be as she shows herself to be. Certainly not a stranger who bears my *vinculum marcam* that I have no memory of. And yet now I am to find out that you had a hand in all of this, and I cannot thank you for it! You set a female in my nest hoping to seduce me into mating, and you clearly succeeded. For what purpose? To amuse yourself with some challenge for me that will rouse me into action in the direction of your choosing? What do you want of me?"

Turan squinted at him in disapproval. "You do not truly believe that Diana was at fault for what happened to Arx and the Eternal Forest, do you?"

He sighed and shook his head. He had too much time to think of it lately with Cacus frustrating his efforts to find him. Although there was a great deal of evidence against her, he recalled how she had looked when he burst in. She had been tired and pale as if she were just barely hanging on. As if she couldn't stand without being blown over by the smallest effort. She hadn't been glutted with power, feeding on the deaths of those around her. She hadn't tried to attack him; her strength had only come to her in a moment of self-defense. Regret rode him hard for how quickly he had attacked her.

He was glad that she was returned home safely by the one male he could trust to do it. A male who had defended her.

His mother continued to peer at him, her lips thinning into a tight line. "As I thought. As for the rest of your spewed nonsense, I have always wanted nothing less than the best for you. I had no choice but to hasten things along. The cycle is turning, and you've been alone too long, far longer than you should have been. I blame myself for not getting involved sooner, but I am remedying this oversight. Order is required for life to continue. You of all beings should know this and yet you are blind to it! Everything requires balance, my son. Even you. I want you to be whole."

"And who says that this female is truly the soul that is destined to be bonded to mine. You took my freedom away from me. You meddled where it was not wanted, and now my forest rests on the edge of oblivion because of that female. I don't have time for any ideas you may have conjured in your mind about her out of some desperate maternal hope. I will find my true uxorem when it is time and the Fates have willed it, not because you have orchestrated it," he returned tightly.

The thin fan folded in Turan's hand snapped on his head with such strength that it made his ears ring. His mother was not as frail and helpless as myth made her out to be. She didn't even hesitate to strike him solidly right between his antlers as she gave him an irate scowl. "Don't be cheeky. You know as well as I that you already have an uxorem. Just because I hurried things along, doesn't mean it isn't true. You felt the rise of instinct, you initiated the bond. I couldn't force anything other than set the right circumstances before you."

He snorted in disbelief, his brow drawing down into an impatient glower. "One that I don't recognize nor remember, and one who somehow survived Cacus's attack."

"You are still thinking of her in terms of what a human can survive based on her appearance. She may have entered the world as a human, but bonding with you changed her to who she was destined to be. You saw for yourself her power. Do you think that it wouldn't rise to protect her in an emergency? Or that those in the villages near your palace would have survived if her instinctive defenses hadn't destroyed that creature's tainted pets that he set loose upon your people?"

"I don't know," he growled. Turan threw her arms up in the air.

"Stubborn," she snarled, the elegant lines of her face contorting into a fearsome form, revealing the terrible strength beneath the beauty of the goddess. An angry growl rolled through her, but just as quickly it disappeared, and she peered over at him evenly though her posture was rigid with disapproval. "Even your warrish brother who enraged men into battles for their adoration had to bond to the female who was his soul. Despite your snarking about Eru, *he too* required my intervention. That did not make his bonds any less true. Why, if I had never set the obstacles before his bride, he likely would not have united with her and would have circled around her helplessly as she cycled through numerous lifetimes more."

"I am sure that they recall it the same way," he said dryly.

She waved a hand and made a small, irate noise. "Children are never grateful for the best efforts of their parents. But yes, they know the purpose for my interference and that there's reason to my methods."

"Of course, you would claim such after all was said and done, regardless of what suffering she had to endure to ensure their bond," he said sourly.

"I give up!" she huffed with an expressive wave of her hands. "Fine, chase your tail while what is left of your forest slowly withers away without you. I did my best to point you in the right direction, but even I know that sometimes children must work it out for themselves. A word of advice: follow your heart, and your instinct. They will guide you, and ultimately bring you home."

His jaw hardened as he looked away. Females, bonding, and sentimental platitudes did not help his situation. He snorted. Use his instinct… It wasn't as if he were not utilizing his instinct. It aided him in his hunt as much as it could, and it wasn't being particularly useful. As for his heart? He rolled his eyes. Leave it to his mother to be concerned about sentimentalities and bonding over very real concerns like the fate of the cosmos. Although his earlier memories were still shady from the expanse of time, he knew very well that she'd been pestering him for ages about finding his uxorem, even before the war with the Tainted Ones.

A low sigh drifted to him as he felt her come up beside him, her presence warm like the sun. "Despite your suspicious, stubborn nature, I do love you. Please heed my words. You will not succeed otherwise."

A waft of her scent surrounded him as lips lightly brushed his cheek. He turned his head, but a warm breeze whipped by him and Turan was gone, leaving him alone once again. The fountain at his side was silent and the water was absent without even a drop glistening from its basin. Even the doves had vanished in the breath of a moment. Desolated silence was once more his only companion.

Taking one last look around what had once been a city park, Selvans debated whether or not he should continue his hunt through the city. His mother's concern was touching, but the hunt drove him. He had hoped that he would find some clue here. There were many places that prey could hide within the human underground systems. His nostrils flared as he scented the air, turning his face toward a sudden breeze.

Nothing.

No. It was time to move on.

CHAPTER 39

ecember

Light snow fell outside the tavern, and Diana watched it wistfully. Their part of the country never got much snow, so the sight of it always seemed a bit more magical, especially as the winter holidays neared. The trees stood as silent sentinels against the winter sky, their boughs laden with snow. Though the sight was beautiful, she missed the soft murmur of the hamadryads that, as Silvas had once promised, had roused near her cabin. All throughout the summer, they had been one link to her life in the Eternal Forest.

A few times, she was tempted to use the flute Aquilo gave her to see if she could coax Zephyr, the warm wind of spring, to arrive earlier, but it seemed wrong to change the season just to suit her needs.

Sadly, summer passed too quickly for her liking. Although she had spent much of her days outside gardening and occasionally hunting, it just hadn't been enough time. She had watched as her new friends had become increasingly sluggish until finally, one day, they slept. Now she was alone. She didn't dare to spend too much time with anyone. During the summer she had discouraged visitors to protect the hamadryads from the foolish actions of frightened people. Now, however, there was another reason to avoid human contact. Someone was bound to notice a very significant difference in her. And not just the fact that her deep summer tan had failed to lighten with the wane of summer or that she had a barely perceptible fuzz covering her in a soft suede that seemed to be getting darker as the weeks passed.

She had a tail.

She kept it discretely tucked into her pants to the best of her ability, but she was afraid that someone would notice if she moved or bent wrong. It was not that she expected that someone was always ogling her ass, but one never knew. Her tail was hard to miss and had grown in overnight while she'd been enjoying the most wonderfully erotic dream in which she was still in that cave on the mountain with her mate. It had been a surprise, and her screaming and snapping it around caused quite a bit of damage before she got control of it. It had taken days to learn how to hold her tail and when to tuck her tail in against her leg, but she quickly gained an appreciation for it.

For one, unlike a lion's tail, which it resembled, it was prehensile. She was able to grip with it. After a few trial and error disasters, she appreciated having an extra "hand" to help her out. It was long and sinuous, tipped with the softest fluff that was longer than the length of her hand from wrist to fingertips. It was even longer and more luxurious than Silvas's tail, and that privately sparked an odd sort of pride within her. She almost wished that he were around so she could show it off. Paired with the fact that her ears were developing long pointed tips at the ends, she simply no longer looked normal. She had all fall to get used to her new features, but with the onset of winter and the more apt people were to get cozy with each other and crowd in closer indoors, it made her all the warier in town or socializing.

Aside from wearing long, bulky coats to disguise any peculiar bulges in her pants, she kept her ears covered the best she could with hats or hoods on the rare occasions, such as today, when she ventured into town. It was uncomfortable, but a necessity. She had long become accustomed to the odd looks from other patrons of the market and tavern. She didn't care what they thought of her so long as she got enough in trade with her barter to acquire the basic goods that she required. Even if she hadn't lost her position at the tavern, she would have had to quit by now… No great hardship though, aside from the rations of food that she no longer had access to.

She frowned down at her bowl of stew. She hadn't gotten anywhere near the trade credits she had hoped for the preserves and hides she brought to town. With supplies getting tighter, the value was reduced by half in trade credit. Soon she was going to have to kiss some of her luxuries like salt and sugar goodbye. She wondered if she could find a book on beekeeping at the open library.

"I'm telling you that I'm going to half to replant some fruit trees come spring. A blight took a good portion of my orchard this fall," a rough voice groused behind her. Diana's newly flexible ears turned beneath her hood toward the speaker with interest. "I've never seen anything like it. The fruit withered before we even had a chance to pick it. Nearly a quarter of the crop gone."

His companion grunted, the silverware clinking as they ate.

"Must be the same shit that's killing the trees in the woods near my place," the other man said. "They just up and lost all their leaves one day, trees rotting until all that's left are husks. We went and cleared out a bunch of them hoping to preserve the woods. Not sure if it helped. It certainly hasn't done us any favor for catching game. Hunting has been poor all autumn, and there's nothing to be found living in my neck of the woods. I've been finding carcasses rotting out in the sun like they just keeled over where they stood. Got to face the fact that the entire forest appears to be dying."

The spoon slipped out of Diana's hand, clanking against the side of the bowl, stew splashing on the table. Her breath caught in her lungs as she stilled, listening in on the conversation. The fur on her body prickled as if an electric current ran through it. It was starting already. She had been warned, but she had naively believed that she would have more time before they started seeing the effects of it in the human world.

"Might be a good thing considering the way it expanded with the mists. Maybe it's just nature correcting itself."

"Maybe, but damned if it isn't the eeriest of things. Everywhere I go in the woods just reeks of death. Come spring I may just work on developing some of the nearby land for crops. If the forest does die away, I can't risk my family going hungry. We're managing with our small number of livestock and the chickens. I think this is just it for the forest."

"Good riddance. That place is evil since the mists took it. Grow the crops, just stay clear of planting orchards would be my advice. We'll all be better off when that evil place dies."

Diana forced herself to her feet, her body trembling uncontrollably. She was seized with the need to see to the trees around her home. She hadn't checked them closely since the onset of autumn when the hamadryads had settled down for their slumber. She needed to take another look and make certain that the sickness hadn't reached her corner of the forest yet. She had to get out of there.

"Are you okay, Di?" the waitress asked, glancing up from the men she was serving.

Diana nodded in her head in a jerky fashion and stumbled back away from the table, her fingers wrapping around her sack.

"Yeah, I'm fine Stace—just not feeling well today. Perhaps best to head home and get some rest."

Stacy pursed her lips. "I don't blame you. Winter has been rough on all of us since the ravaging, perhaps more so this year than before. You get plenty of rest and I'll catch up with you when you're next in town." She hesitated. "It's been a while. Everyone is worried about you."

"Sure," Diana mumbled as she buttoned up her heavy winter coat and pulled on her thick wool gloves. She had no intention of getting cozy with her childhood friend or anyone else. Not after the majority of the people in town had applauded when a troll had been beheaded when he stopped in to trade for supplies the month prior. In retrospect, she was thankful that Raskyuil had slipped away when he did.

Throwing her sack of goods over her shoulder, she hustled out of the warm building into the snow. Although she was well bundled up like everyone else, the cold barely affected her even though she could see her breath fogging the air. Standing there at the entrance of the tavern, she scanned the street and grimaced as she saw Devlin, her latest and most persistent "suitor." There was hardly a week that went by without him visiting at least once. She didn't want to risk him seeing her.

Dropping her head, Diana adopted the forward momentum of the winter shuffle, her body drawn into itself as she slogged through the snow in a far less graceful manner than how she had walked when she arrived earlier that afternoon. As anticipated, he looked right past her as he hustled to the tavern, whether to catch a warm meal or because he had caught word that she was there and was hoping to intercept her, she didn't know.

Muttering a thanks to the gods under her breath, she quickened her pace, her strides becoming longer and lighter as she left the town behind her. Not for the first time she dwelled on just how much easier her life would be if she had brought Keena with her. Not that the townspeople would have allowed the crocotta to live among them. Diana predicted that in a few years, they weren't going to have much of choice as the beings of the other worlds flooded in to share this plane of existence. She had no doubt that she would be around to see that day.

Diana squinted against the falling snow and sighed to herself. She was already making peace with the fact that she wouldn't be able to stay forever. Not if she wanted to have any peace. Her world was nothing like the Eternal Forest. No one would accept that she wouldn't age, and while she had serious doubts that they would be able to kill her, she knew that it didn't mean that they couldn't make life uncomfortable or even painful for her. She would stay for as long as it was safe, then she would pay her final respects to her family and move on.

She debated perhaps just departing into the forest. It hadn't taken her long to figure out that the resident spirits didn't challenge her presence. The first time she'd seen the silvanus that guarded her wood they had both been surprised. Fear had raced through her, facing the male who had stepped out unexpectedly from behind a tree, and for a moment had regretted the fact that Anola remained stored in a trunk in the cabin rather than carried strapped to her.

Thankfully, Anola hadn't been needed. The silvanus had bowed low, his twisted horns scraping the earth as he solemnly addressed her as ati. It had been an embarrassing moment, but he not only gave her wide berth when she entered his forest, he often ventured to her home to leave wild game at her steps when the days were particularly brutal.

She wondered if she would have the same reception everywhere she traveled.

As she passed a small copse of trees a movement in the snow caught her attention, breaking her from her ruminations. A shadow slipped from behind the trees. Familiar dark antlers branched regally, and the two arcs of his new horns that had sprouted recently betrayed his identity. His body was just as tall and beautifully formed as it had ever been, a long fur cape wrapped around him, his hair stirring in the light wind. Ears tipped toward her, his glowing eyes haunting as he watched her, his lips parting with confusion.

Instinctively she reached for their bond and encountered the same emptiness that she had discovered every time she sought him over the months. Nothing had changed. Her heart lurched painfully, and she turned away, pretending that she didn't see him. He still didn't remember her. He was just as surprised to encounter her as she was to see him.

She shook her head. What was Silvas doing here?

Her heart, which rarely stirred with any sort of excitement or stress anymore, picked up its beat, pulsing through her as she rushed forward through the snow at a rapid clip. She did not run. It was stupid to run from a natural-born predator, even a divine one like the lucomo silvani. Even though she didn't hear his steps or even the exhalation of his breath, she knew that he was trailing after her at a distance.

That he wasn't running up to her gave her a small measure of reassurance. He wasn't attacking. He was watching and following her like just like one of her pesky want-to-be boyfriends. Couching his pursuit in those terms helped relaxed her more. It was nothing she couldn't handle. If she ignored him long enough, he would just go away.

A confident smile pulling at her lips, she settled in an easier lope as she crossed the wide, open grounds between town and her home. She felt his eyes on her, but she was no longer concerned. No doubt he would follow her all the way to her home. Well, she would just continue to pretend that she didn't notice him until he got bored and went on with his hunt.

A short time later, she was safely nestled in her cabin, sipping the last portion she had of hot cocoa that she had meticulously managed to stretch since the ravaging. It felt like a night that called for cocoa. Outside, she could hear the whistle of the wind picking up as she settled deeper into her crocheted blanket with a worn book in hand. She only got up to stir the coals back to life before settling comfortably into her chair again.

If she glanced out of the window by chance a time or two, she hadn't noticed anything out of place or unusual. If it weren't for the fact that she felt watched, she would have believed that he had left. It was only late into the night that she felt his absence. Strangely, it made her heart ache.

CHAPTER 40

Selvans watched the female picking her way through the snow around her house tending to her regular routine. After weeks driven nearly to madness by the pull of his instinct, he had been surprised to scent someone familiar.

Diana.

He had scarcely believed it and had followed his nose until he came across a bundled figure moving as lightly as a silvanus through the snow. He thought to stalk after her and follow her unseen for a time, but to his surprise she had stiffened and turned, glowing blue-green eyes piercing the distance. If there had been any doubt that she was no longer human, that alert, luminous stare had confirmed it.

Initially, he had debated on turning away and leaving, but he had been unable to. Instead, he had found himself following her to her dwelling where he shadowed it until he found an appropriate spot to make his nest in a large tree overlooking her home. Settled there, he was able to observe the activity in his newly claimed territory comfortably at his leisure.

At first, it bewildered him that she ignored his presence, but as the days passed, it turned to frustration and then anger. How dare she ignore *him*! She was the unasked-for presence in his life, and she pretended like she didn't even notice the lack of him when the only time he felt any measure of peace was now that he was by her side. It was infuriating, and it was oddly amusing and admirable watching the female move about her daily life as if their threads in the weave of fate had never touched.

Sometimes, though, he was certain that her eyes strayed to his nest when he wasn't intentionally concealing himself from her awareness—she was still a young immortal after all. He would catch her gaze turn toward him, and slowly it would light up as if she were reluctant to allow her true nature to shine through. After nearly two weeks of trailing her in her daily work, in her hunt through the woods and her ventures to town, he fell upon the reason. She was pretending to be human.

He couldn't fathom any reason that she would carry out such a charade. Although she kept herself well covered when she was out of her home, he caught a glimpse of her transformation as she passed a window. She had been uncovered, without even her blanket draping around her, hiding her away.

At first, he couldn't help but stare. He had found Diana beautiful as a human. Seeing her with long, elegant tail and a dark velvet of fur over her body took a bit of getting used to. But beneath it all, he saw the same female who haunted him. Yet she hid herself away, her tail bound to her body, like a butterfly newly emerged from its cocoon, still afraid to spread its new wings to fly. Human in appearance or not, he found he wanted to crawl over her and clutch her to him in rut. It was highly inappropriate to feel toward someone who was a virtual stranger, but his instinct dogged him.

The gods must have cursed him. Even now, his mother's last words to him haunted him with their taunting lilt. To feel such need for a female whose presence brought death to the Eternal Forest was a jest of the highest gods made at his expense. He didn't know what lesson they sought to impress upon him… Humility, perhaps. If so, it was terrible.

His tail lashed behind him impatiently as his eyes tracked her movement, eager for her to finish and return indoors where he could selfishly watch over her, but his ears pricked at the sound of crunching snow as an unfamiliar scent of sweat and spice filled his nose. Grimacing, Selvans turned, his body tensing with a predatory stillness as he caught sight of the human male approaching the house. A low growl rumbled in his throat and Selvans dropped from his nest as he cast an illusion over himself.

Though he still appeared much the same, his antlers and tail would not be seen, and his ears would seem more correct to the human norm. Striding through the snow with a snarl on his lips, he headed toward the hapless male.

Diana paused from where she was clearing snow from the walk around her home, her eyes trained on the male. She noticeably tugged her fur-lined hood closer around her face with her gloved hands in the pretense of being chilled as she strained.

"Diana! Good morning!" the male called cheerfully, his eyes glancing over her longingly as a waft of pheromones hit Selvans in the face.

He bristled, his teeth baring with menace. The only thing saving the foolish human's life at that moment was that Diana did not return his smile. Her fingers tightened around her shovel as her eyes narrowed warily.

"Devlin, what are you doing here?" she inquired politely.

Selvans gnashed his teeth. *He* wouldn't have been that polite. He wasn't going to be that polite once he got his hands on the male. A low growl stirred the air, making the perhaps-not-quite-idiotic male pause before masking his unease with a confident smile as he turned his full attention on her. A wide smile pulled at the human's cold-reddened lips, revealing a flash of white flat teeth in his bearded face.

"I just came to see how you were doing and if there was anything you need," he returned with pitifully transparent joviality.

Selvans wanted to rip the male's vocal cords and hand them to him so that he could keep his false speech to himself. Selvans had staked out this territory as his own. Even if he was uncertain whether he wanted to pursue the female or not, she was bound to him and he wasn't going to allow another male to interlope on his territory.

"No," Diana replied flatly. "There is nothing, thank you. I went to town and picked up a few supplies yesterday. My hunt has also been successful."

The human stared at her in surprise. "That is truly impressive. No one in town has been having any luck in the parts of the forest we typically hunt. If we had known that you were that skilled, we would have invited you with us a long time ago."

"Thank you, but I do better by myself."

The male flushed in discomfort and embarrassment. "Yes, I suppose so," he muttered. His hands clenched as he seemed to struggle to find another reason to linger. Selvan's tail whipped behind him, silently bidding the human to leave before something unfortunate happened to him.

"Perhaps something that needs doing around the house. We can make a day of it. I can give my useful skills in trade for a lovely meal by my hostess, and you won't have to muss yourself in unpleasant chores," he offered.

Bristling, Selvans strode forward. He had heard enough. He knew the moment that the male caught sight of him striding through the snow because the human became rigid with hostility, the sharp scent of masculine challenge in the air. Selvans bared his teeth in an unpleasant smile as he eyed his rival. Diana chose that moment to turn, her greenish eyes falling on him and widening.

"Silvas," she whispered. "What are you doing?"

"Only seeing what our visitor required," he cut in smoothly, his eyes running over the male disdainfully. "Welcome to our home," he purred dangerously. "It is fortunate that my bride was out here to greet you. If she had been indoors with me, we might have never taken heed of your arrival. In fact, you might have stayed outside for an uncomfortably long time," he bit out.

"Bride?" The human, Devlin, turned accusing eyes upon Diana. Selvans had to forcibly stop himself from plucking them from his head. "Since when did you marry?"

"It was recent," Selvans cut in smoothly as he circled the male before coming to rest at Diana's side. His female stiffened warily at his presence, which he didn't particularly enjoy, but his attention was focused on the male, whom he would take great pleasure in terrorizing. Oh, how sweet his terror would taste.

He nudged her back as he grinned at his rival. The human shifted warily, his eyes sliding over him. Selvans knew what he saw: the large but peculiarly pale human that he presented himself as. He whipped his tail out and struck the male with it across his knees. Delvin yelped from the sharp contact and stumbled back. He looked around wildly, searching for the source of the attack before his eyes flickered back to them.

He swallowed. "Did you see anything?"

Selvans raised his eyebrows and made a show of looking around with confusion. "No. All is quite as usual around here. I'm afraid that nothing exciting happens around here." As he turned to pretend to examine the snow-covered flowerbeds nearby, he whacked the male again, this time across the back.

"Shit!" Devlin snapped as he quickly backed away and spun around, searching the area nervously. "I swear to God, I felt something attack me. I'm not making this shit up."

"No, I'm sure you aren't," Diana soothed as she stepped forward and shot Selvans a disgusted look.

He shrugged shamelessly. He had no obligations toward the interloper. He was not a subject within his kingdom that would at least require some consideration. As far as Selvans was concerned, he was free to act as he must to protect his territory. Frightening away the male was far kinder than the alternative, but he suspected that his kind-hearted female didn't give that any thought. There was much within his imagination that he could do to the male to terminate his presence from her life… if Selvans enjoyed such torture. He did not enjoy the flavor of pain or suffering.

"Perhaps you should return to your home. You could have over tired yourself today," he suggested. He hissed through his teeth, using his power to rouse a nearby dryad to bend her branches enough that they rattled over the human ominously. Devlin's head jerked up, his mouth gaping open. Seeing the perfect opening, Selvans pulled his tail back again, his malicious gaze focused on Delvin. It was time to give him a sendoff he would never forget.

As he snapped it forward, Diana's hand shot out behind her to grasp his tail tightly. Her hard tug sent a pleasant jerking sensation straight down to his cock that made his toes curl in his boots. The tip of his tail immediately wrapped around her hand, a low purr rumbling from his chest. She immediately dropped it as if it were a hot iron, and he felt a twist of regret in his gut. To all evidence she was his uxorem. Regardless of any betrayal she may have committed, she should feel the same pressing need to touch that he was currently feeling. The same possession.

"Yes," Devlin stuttered. "You're right. I think I should head home."

"If you must," Diana murmured, but her comment appeared to be lost to the male as he stumbled rapidly back, tripping over his own feet in his hurry to get away.

Selvans snorted with amusement as the human tipped backward and fell into the snow. Diana made a sound of sympathy as she began to move forward. His hand whipped out, grasping her arm, a warning growl in his throat. She turned startled eyes on him but stilled as Devlin picked himself up from the ground and hastily made his escape.

Diana waited until the human was a distance away from the cabin before jerking her arm to shake his hand away.

"You and I need to talk. Now."

"But of course," he purred as he followed her inside.

CHAPTER 41

Diana stormed into her kitchen, Silvas's heavy steps falling behind her as he followed her inside. Selvans. *Whatever!* She was fuming. Of all the high-handed, arrogant males! He didn't want her, he attacked her and cast her back to the human world like unwanted garbage, and now he *dared* to interfere with *her* life!

"You are angry," he observed quietly.

"You think?" she snapped as she yanked out a chair from the table and pointed to it. "Sit."

A rattling sound echoed from his chest. "I am not a dog for you to command."

She spun around with a bark of laughter. "I don't give a fuck who you are. You're in my house, interfering in my life without my welcome or permission," she replied angrily. "You did not want me, spoke vile lies about…attacked me," she choked out around an ugly sob. "You threw me away. You have no rights here, Silvas or Selvans, or whoever the fuck you are!"

He cocked his head at her, his brow furrowing in confusion. There was a glimmer of pain in his eyes. Good! She hoped that the bastard hurt as much as she had the last several months. Her lips twisting with pain, she set two cups of wine from her meager stock on the table between them. His eyebrows raised at the cup, but he ignored it as he leveled her with a hard look.

"I did not remember," he rasped. "I still don't. All I know was that I returned home to see Arx nearly obliviated, hamadryads I have known for centuries destroyed, and those under my care killed where they stood. And then there was you—in a place where no other has ever set foot, a lone individual who survived virtually unscathed. What was I to think?"

"Probably should have thought to ask your sister, since she's the only one who seems to know anything of what is going on in the forest," she shot back. "For whatever reason, you blocked me out your mind and set a barrier in place without even talking to me. You left me alone in that room and then went to get cleansed with that barrier in place. It blocked every memory of me, you prick. How could you! How dare you! You convinced me to give in to the need of the bond, made me your mate, and then cast me aside. You didn't even have the balls to bring me home yourself like you promised. You had Raskyuil do it!"

His jaw hardened, and he shook his head. "I can't fathom what you have experienced because I don't know. I look at you and I see a stranger, one whom I need with every ounce of my being, who only came into my world because of my interfering mother, so I recently discovered. I don't know why I rejected you, nor the circumstances of our time together. I don't even know what draws me to you now. I only know that you are mine, and even though I am not sure if I want you, I will not allow another within my territory."

Meeting her eyes, he picked up the cup and took a long drink, his tongue swiping along the edge of the cup to finish the last drop.

"Unbelievable," she muttered. "Of all the egotistical stupidity. You should have just stayed away and left me alone with my grief instead of coming here and destroying me all over again. Thanks to you my life has been changed forever. I have changed. I'm no longer human, and the one place I wanted to peacefully live out the rest of my life so that I could someday be buried with my family, I'll have to leave so no one comes waving pitchforks at my door. I've seen what kind of ugly mob the townspeople can turn into. My entire life has been upended, and for nothing. After what you did, the least you could have done was give me the courtesy of leaving me alone!"

"You don't understand. You think I want to feel the way I do. To yearn and need endlessly with a pain that never dulls with the passage of days. I don't!" He sighed. "I don't wish to hurt you. I don't know what I want. I just know that I have been broken and empty the entire time I have wandered your world… and now Cacus has gone to ground." He drew his hand up behind his horns and swept his hand through his hair. "The only clues I have are that I need to follow my instinct and I need my light. My instinct fails me, and I cannot see whatever light I'm to seek." He paused, his brow furrowing in confusion. "What is my special light that I need?" he muttered.

"How the fuck should I know," she snapped as she shoved back her chair. Standing, she leaned forward and slammed her hand on the table between them, small claws shooting out from her fingertips, scoring the wood. "As far as I'm concerned, there is no light. Everything is one big, dreary shit hole. I feel broken and empty, and you left me like this. You tore out my heart and abandoned me and all you can think of is your duty. I mean, I get it. Everything is dying because of that asshole—but fuck you!"

His head snapped back, his pale eyes watching her in surprise. She didn't care—he was about to hear all about himself. Tears stung her eyes and she was helpless to stop her fury as it swamped over her. Her eyes narrowed on him; her lips twisted with grief.

"Never have I despised anyone the way I've despised you these last few months. I cursed you every night for what you did to me. Don't come to me thinking that I will feel sorry for you or pat you on the back and tell you it will be okay," she choked, a sob rising to her throat. "*You* don't fucking get to play the victim! I was beginning to fall in love with your surly ass—and let me tell you, despite how the nymphs have inflated your ego, you are no prize in the relationship department," she said with a curl of her lip, her grief swamping over her. She slapped her hand on the table again.

He was rigid, sorrow painted clearly on his face. His ears drooped and his head bent forward so that his antlers bowed slightly toward her. Fastening her eyes upon him, she whispered harshly in a broken voice. She barely managed to speak above a whisper, her voice breaking with horrible ugly sobs.

"What you did is detestable. I don't care if you are tasked to chase Cacus to hell and back for the rest of eternity, there is nothing that will change the way I feel about how little care you demonstrated toward our relationship. I trusted you with everything when you trusted me with nothing. To block me without any explanation or discussing it with me was the absolute worst thing you could do to me. You took away any chance for me to defend myself or prove myself innocent against whatever paranoid delusion you had fallen into because of that fucking sword."

She took a deep, shuddering breath. "What is worse—I had no idea at all that anything was wrong! Everything was so right just moments before, but as soon as we got back to the palace you pushed me away and were willing to believe the worst. Of course, you just disappeared. Why wouldn't you then? You abandoned our bond and me when I was alone and waiting in your room, in the company of no one except that dryad taking pleasure in tormenting me. How could you have done that to me! I had put my trust in you, and I leaned on you when I didn't dare do that with any other. It tore out my heart when you suddenly disappeared from within me. *You broke me!* By blocking our bond, you took every good thing that I allowed to grow between us and cruelly destroyed it with one move." She closed her eyes, a tremor shaking her body as her tears broke free.

Huge ugly sobs wracked her and she slammed her hand repeatedly until he swept it up and caught it against his chest. She hauled back her other hand and slapped him for all it was worth and kept struggling and striking at him until he folded her tightly in his arms, his tail sliding snugly around her waist as he let out a pained sound issuing from deep within him. Holding her in place, he let her rage flow freely over him. She struggled, her claws biting into him as she struck at him repeatedly until, finally, she collapsed against him and wept.

Exhausted, she lay within his arms, half dangling in his grip. At some point he had drawn her close to him, his purr surrounding her as if to comfort her even though his own shoulders shook with sorrow. She felt the hot splash of his tears against her neck.

All the fight drained out of her as she slowly disentangled herself to pull away and stare at him hopelessly. She was hurt with a wound that refused to heal. It ate at her and bled at the slightest provocation. There were no words that would magically fix things, and his words, while honest and true to what she knew of the situation from Dorinda, were not, unsurprisingly, any kind of balm for her heart. Even the sobs that wracked him as he held her did little to ease the burn of the wounds in her heart.

She wanted more than anything to continue to rage at him, to beat at him with her fists and wail her rage as she'd done the first month after she returned home. Every day she had suffered alone, screaming out her pain and anger. She wanted to take them out on him. But she discovered she had only just those last tears to shed. Now… now she was just tired.

"I am exhausted Silv… Selvans," she corrected wearily.

"Silvas," he replied. "I know it is not my correct name, but though I hate to admit it, it makes me feel a warmth within me when you say it. Like it is something special between us. It makes a part of me that worries inclined to forbid the name to ever be spoken again to drive that unknown feeling away, but I cannot. I don't know why that is—it just is." He raised his eyes and met her gaze.

"Know this, Diana, I am determined not to walk away again until I solve this mystery between us," he muttered with a stricken frown.

"There is no mystery here. You left," she muttered bitterly.

He swallowed and nodded. "I know what you say is true even if I don't remember it. It has to be. I hurt as well, far more than is natural, and it breaks my heart, shattering into numerous fragments that I can't heal. I swear, though, I shall never leave you again. In the end, if I still can't remember, then I will watch and see what made me bond with you. It bothers me more than I like that I can't remember you. Only after I am informed will I come to you, and we will make a decision between the two of us."

"And if my decision is no?" she asked in a hard voice.

He raised his eyes to her, the pearly depths streaking with hints of color from his grief. "Then it will be my duty and privilege to show what kind of mate I can be and change your mind. If the gods—and you—allow," he whispered hoarsely.

Pushing up from the table, he stalked toward the door as Diana followed behind, her expression set in a hard, unforgiving scowl. She leaned forward and grabbed the door handle, pulling open the door. The white landscape greeted him on the other side. She tilted her head toward it, and he inclined his head in understanding. He was not welcome there. Not yet. Walking forward, he glanced at her over his shoulder in passing, his voice low as he spoke.

"For what it's worth, I know what happened wasn't your fault," he said.

She stiffened, her lips parting, but she said nothing as he swept out the door.

CHAPTER 42

Diana didn't know what to make of Silvas. Despite her anger, the words he spoke were so earnest that for a moment it had been like she was there again upon the mountain and he was promising never to let her go. It weakened her, and she had reacted with fear, wanting to demand that he go away and leave her alone. She couldn't make herself so vulnerable to him again.

Even knowing that Cacus was hiding somewhere beneath the ground, the days slipped by pleasantly with their quiet daily routines. Diana knew the peace was a fleeting interlude. She could feel in the air that their stolen time together was trickling away. Cacus wouldn't remain hidden forever, and when spring returned, she felt a consuming fear that the taint would spread further through the forest. They were on borrowed time. If the monster only slept for the winter, she would have to make the most of it.

In the meantime, she took a reluctant pleasure in Silvas shadowing her throughout the day. From the time the sun rose every morning, he was there, crouched in the tree in her yard, patiently waiting for her to wake up.

She didn't lie to herself. It annoyed her at first, seeing him lurking in her tree the moment she opened her door to see to her daily responsibilities. The moment she stepped outside, he eased himself along the limbs like a panther before easily hopping the distance to the ground. Even with her most angry glower, he followed after her whenever she made her way outdoors. Whether she was tending to the chickens that cost many trade credits that summer or heading into the forest to hunt small game, he shadowed her at a distance. When she went back inside, he bounded into the tree and settled to watch over her cabin. Such was the way their days passed.

Yet most evenings while she sat alone in her cabin with nothing but her thoughts for company, she would hear his voice singing a lulling song of ancient times, when humanity was young and the expanses of the wild were great. It was a song of ancient trees and falling water and the quiet of eternity. It spoke to her soul, and she would pause whatever she was doing to listen to him sing. Most nights, she went to sleep with his song in her ears, soothing the nightmares she suffered from the terrible things she had seen that plagued her when everything was too silent and the comfort of their bond absent.

Before she knew it a week passed, and then another, until finally, as she stopped at her front door, her arms laden with firewood, she truly looked at him. He stared down at her patiently, his tail lightly lashing from where he crouched in the tree, his expression flat and unconcerned, and yet his eyes glowing with a familiar longing that she had thought she would never see in those pearly depths again. She cleared her throat, frowned, and gestured to the door.

"Why don't you come inside for a while. There are plenty of hours left in the day." She flushed a bit at how awkward she felt as he stared silently back. "I can make dinner and…"

He smiled and hopped down. "You do not need to talk me into

it, Diana. I am pleased to come inside and spend some time with you."

"Just until sundown," she added, and his smile widened.

"Of course, until then," he agreed.

They ate and spent a quiet evening together. They found a shared enjoyment of playing dice, and she taught him a few card games and amusing things she had learned over the years. In turn, he taught her simple games he claimed to see shepherds play when they wandered too near his forests in his youth. His presence broke the unending silence of her days, and every evening he slipped outside again to keep watch over her during the night from his tree.

After that day, every morning her walk was cleared of snow and her hens fed before she rose. All accomplished just after sunrise. It made her sick knowing how little rest he required, and that fact only amused him when she admitted it. It was only a small comfort finding out that, as time went on and her body adjusted to its new state, she would require less sleep. She began to hate how quickly the night came, but was almost grateful for that sleep for speeding past the hours until she could open the door and see him again.

The morning that she woke to find herself actually smiling and humming to herself as she got ready for the day, her tail lashing with excitement, she froze in shock. It felt so alien after feeling like she was barely existing for so long. Even in the Eternal Forest, with all the insanity that seemed to dog them, she never felt like she had a chance to stop and be happy.

Unbidden, fear raised so suddenly in her that she had to grip the edge of the counter to keep herself steady. What if he abandoned her again? The last time she had thought things were well and she had a new possible future stretching out before her, he had pushed her out and abandoned her. Her stomach twisted and her hands shook hard enough that she dropped her hairbrush in the sink. Blinking her tears back, she stared at her reflection in the mirror.

How would she survive it if it happened again?

Dropping her head, she panted, tears welling up in her eyes to drip into the sink. She was terrified of losing that happiness. That he would change his mind and take it all away again. It would break her. Round and round doubt whispered through her, reminding her of how much it hurt when she was cast out alone after finding something to which she could possibly belong. Even though she had made no decisions and had felt an obligation to return home, it had felt good to be needed and wanted… To matter to someone, and to feel the first kernels of the blooming of something more. And he had thrown her away—not wanted her—discarded her—left her. Her breath heaved in and out of her lungs as she screwed her eyes tightly against the wave of terror.

The loud screech of claws biting into porcelain startled her out of the cycling terror. Staring down at the black claws tipping her fingers, she paused, her breath releasing in a long sigh. Slowly, excruciatingly slow, her heart rate dropped back down to normal as she stared at those claws. They reminded her that she was not helpless. That she would go on. She let out a small chuckle. If he tried to toy with her again and abandon her, she was now in a position where she could make him feel the consequences of his actions. She was no longer a human to be toyed with and set aside, and he wouldn't forget it.

Turning her eyes back to the mirror, she truly looked at herself. Not a quick peek at a body that no longer seemed hers. This was her, and it spoke of the powerful being she had become. Her fur was growing darker, white dots appearing like stars in a darkening sky. Her tail was already fully black in color. A hand stroked through her long locks of hair, allowing the fading length to fall through her fingertips. Brushing her fingers back from her ears, she touched the soft, fur tufted, feline ears that now jutted out through her hair. Her ear twitched beneath her finger, the sensation tickling both her ear and hand as she smothered her laughter. Her eyes shifted from blue to green, sometimes caught between the colors, as she stared at herself, reveling in the happiness that bloomed within.

She hurried through her morning routine, her smile widening. Today they were going hunting. A thrill skated through her with barely restrained excitement. Hunting was quickly growing to be their special time together. Although they were silent as they strode through the forest, they hunted side by side, their shared excitement for the hunt rushing through them.

Grabbing her bow, she ran outside, a wide smile spread over her face.

"Good morning," she greeted him cheerfully as she plucked her bowstring.

She knew that he didn't rely on such things. She watched him leap onto prey and bring it down quickly, bleeding it out on the snow. Perhaps someday she would get to the point of being confident in her claws, been until then she liked the distance and comfort of the bow in her hand.

"Blessed morning, beautiful one," he returned as he grinned down at her, his eyes sparkling in the early light of the morning.

Silvas dropped from the tree with a happy purr. He seemed to purr quite often these days, and she loved it. She didn't examine the thought too carefully as they struck out through the snow. Lifting her tail in a delicate arc so that it didn't drag, she paced easily, her breath puffing in the air as he loped at her side.

She glanced over at him, noticing the way his eyes continuously took in everything. Aside from watching out for any possible threat and signs of game, she figured he probably never ceased in plotting how best to defend the territory from intruders. He seemed to do that a lot.

Just last night she had caught him studying a map that marked where the rivers ran through her forest and near her cabin, muttering to himself about what the boundaries of his territory were for him to defend. It was something he did very well and got an obvious pleasure from carrying out. Protection, he had said to her many times, was part of his purpose. She didn't wonder that he got a thrill from it. Last she heard, he had chased off not only some more guys from town, but also scared the shit out of people who attempted to enter into her wood to take game.

Silvas took exception to that. Since she took little and made her sacrifice clean and respectful, the animals still lingered in her part of the woods where those that survived the sickness all but disappeared from others. They openly submitted and offered themselves to her. As far as he was concerned, those humans who hunted in their territory were stealing from what he had deemed as her sacred wood, and thus were offending him.

Diana drew in a deep breath of air. Spring would be coming soon. Already the sun felt a bit warmer as the lengthening days were making headway into melting the snow, and there was a distinctive smell of wet earth and water permeating the air. A loud crack from the trees up ahead sent a flash of anxiety through her, and immediately she stilled. Barely had a startled breath escaped her lips when Silvas stepped in front of her. He noticeably bristled, his tail lashing angrily through the air away from his body.

"Show yourself," he demanded, a low growl echoing through his words.

The threat in his voice was thinly veiled, and his glowing eyes were fixed on the direction from which the sound came, yet he was surprisingly calm without a trace of true hostility. That he was wary but unconcerned had an immediate effect on her. The tension fled from her body, though she still watched this space warily as she felt a familiar presence move toward them.

"Larce," she called out in surprise, noticing the way Silvas's head snapped toward her, a frown pulling at his lips, likely due to the familiar way that she uttered the male's name. But how could she not be? Once she had met the silvanus, she recognized him as the presence that had lurked around the woods near the cabin. "It is not nice to sneak up on people, you about gave me a heart attack," she admonished.

A deep male chuckle followed as the silvanus she had seen before stepped out from the trees. His twisted horns had an ancient appearance, and he was distinctive with his peculiar tail that separated into three narrow tips halfway down its length. His eyes darted to her warmly, but it was upon Silvas that his gaze locked. Larce tracked the lucomo's movements as he approached. He raised his hands in supplication, an amused smile curving his hard lips.

"Peace, apa. I intend no harm toward your uxorem."

The male laughed as if such a concept were absurd. Her lips quirked because she couldn't imagine either the male actually doing harm. Fuck with her if she didn't observe the proper rules when in the woods, sure… but not harm.

Still… apa?

Diana stared between the males, trying to discern their relationship. Although Silvas seemed tense, there was no hostility between them. The silvanus's lips tipped upward as Silvas lashed his tail irritably.

Silvas shook his head in confusion. "Larce? I thought I recognized your scent, but this doesn't make any sense. What are you doing in such a new forest? I would have assumed that you would be lurking in your ancient haunts with your uxorem."

The male shrugged. "Cassia consented to come here for a time as a special favor to Turan. You know that the goddess has a way of garnering what she desires. She deemed it important that someone look out for the soul meant to be yours. It is not the first time we have relocated to watch over your uxorem. Whenever we are made known of her soul once more walking upon the earth, we followed, dwelling near her and watching over her during the course of her lifetime. I watched as she grew up, and when the forest expanded, I increased my territory holdings so no other spirit would interfere. You are welcome," he said loftily, his smile playful.

Silvas grunted in reply, but he relaxed, and his lips curved in amusement. They stared at each other for a moment before both males moved in and embraced. They chuckled and pounded each other on the back in a show of affection. Silvas reached his hands up to frame the other male's face and drew him down to kiss his cheeks and forehead.

Diana's eyebrows went up and she stared openly at them.

"I'm sorry, but I'm totally lost here," she interrupted. "You seem to know each other… What's an apa?"

Silvas's smile suddenly became strained and his ears tipped back. He cleared his throat and fixed her with a grave look. "Diana, as you know, I am very old… I have probably lifetimes worth of events, to be honest…"

"Apa means father," Larce interrupted, his eyes sparkling with mirth. "Ah, you didn't tell her that you had bred offspring." He chuckled at the disgusted look Silvas bent on him.

"I had meant to broach the subject… eventually… in a tactful way," he said.

Diana relaxed and laughed. "Oh, is that it? I already knew about that, though it was something I meant to ask about." She tapped a finger on her chin. "What was it that the horrible dryad said? Oh yes, I was told that you fucked and discarded humans after you had bred sons on them."

Silvas gaped at her. "I certainly did not! I was a lusty youth and may have dallied with human women as well as denizens of my woods. I certainly didn't intend to 'breed young' on them. It was a surprise when the first of them, Larce's mother, abandoned him in my woods, and he was brought to me to rear."

Diana raised an eyebrow. "And how often did this happen? From what I've heard, there are quite a few silvani out there."

"Only a few! I have four sons that I brought forth."

"Cassia and I have bred three thousand, two hundred and eighty sons," Larce announced proudly. As Diana turned a horrified look upon him, he grinned. "It has been a great number of centuries. There was no need from the Eternal Forest and the cosmos for us to have offspring that frequently… but time has a way of adding up," he said, laughing. "Unlike some, I check in with my young from time to time."

Silvas gave him a disgusted look. "Do not act like I do not check in on you and your brothers. I have spent much time over the centuries wandering between your territories and visiting with your families. I have held more infant silvani than I ever expected to."

Diana held back a sound of mirth as the males snorted at each other.

"Well, excellent then. You will come visit my domus and bring your uxorem to meet Cassia."

Silvas gave her a pinched look and she knew what he was thinking even without the bond. He didn't want to admit to his son that he didn't remember his mate or the events that occurred between them. Unfortunately, neither of them knew if he would ever gain his memories. They just needed to take one day at a time and see what the future had in store.

Setting a calming hand on Silvas's bicep, she smiled over at Larce. "That is lovely, thank you."

Beaming, Larce led them through the winding trees, past the altar, into a thick copse that opened into another portal that opened into a small pocket in a hidden grove. They stepped through it, and a familiar energy surged through her. They were back. Although it was a very small pocket of space, surrounded thickly by trees, they were back in the Eternal Forest.

CHAPTER 43

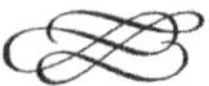

Diana was shocked when she entered the beautiful domus. Though simple on the outside, the inside was lush with beautiful fabrics, collections of antiques, and carefully polished antiquities displayed everywhere as one would beloved knickknacks. They were so casually displayed, a wealth of human history in one room, that it was awe inspiring, but also made her afraid to get too close to anything out of fear of breaking something. What surprised her the most, however, was the human woman who greeted them with a pleased expression. She kissed Silvas on both cheeks before she enthusiastically welcome Diana.

"It is such a pleasure to finally meet you!" Cassia exclaimed as she elbowed Larce out of the way. Her mate growled playfully as he moved aside, his mouth brushing a brief kiss at the top of her head as he made his way into the house.

Diana, however, had barely been able to form a polite greeting in return as she rudely stared at the woman. Though Cassia looked as young and beautiful as she likely was since the day that she and Larce bonded, her appearance was entirely human, from the sun-bronzed olive skin to the fall of dark curly hair and large, brown, expressive eyes. Her simple violet dress hung gracefully from her curves as she led them into the small sitting room.

"Please come in and make yourselves comfortable. It is so nice to have company. I was just speaking to Larce some days ago that we never have company anymore. There used to be silvani and fauns in and out of our domus daily."

"My love, you are thinking of how things were hundreds of years ago," he chuckled. "Besides, things have become far busier with the human world opened up."

She snorted and rolled her eyes. "I know, I know. Every being thinking they are going to make some name and reputation for themselves in the human world like the days of long ago. You and I both remember what *that* was like. Idiot men trying to kidnap you from the *monster*, sacrificed virgins—the human world has always been a mess, and it isn't going to get any better any time soon," she rebuked with a snap of her fingers. Switching gears, Cassia gestured to a comfortable chair. "Please do sit."

It was only after everyone was seated that Cassia, with the satisfied look of a woman completely in her element, went about attending to her hostess duties. Refreshments were brought and set out, along with nuts, olives, cheeses, and small sweets of honey drizzled dates in pastry. Diana's eyes widened at the food set lavishly in front of her. Although she had some of the hard cheeses that the local farmers traded for, it had been years since she had tasted nuts or had an olive. She had never had the sweet before, but she sighed with pleasure as it hit her tongue.

"Good, isn't it?" Cassia asked. "There are cultivated groves all throughout the Eternal Forest attended by the various beings who call this place their home. Many parts of the forest are dark and frightening, but when I see the crops like this… it reminds me of the potential it has for life," she murmured as she popped an almond into her mouth.

Diana raised an eyebrow. What little she had seen of the forest beyond the palace grounds had been creepy as fuck. Cassia took note of her expression and laughed.

"I recognize that look. I have eyes and know exactly what you see when you look at the Eternal Forest. It is sad, because I remember what it used to be like before its decline." She sighed and sat back on the thick cushion on the couch. "It was absolutely magical. It is no wonder that the monokerata no longer flourish here. But I wish you could have seen it the way I saw it then."

Cassia began to describe the Eternal Forest in ages past and Diana listened with awe. She couldn't even imagine this forest that the other woman spoke of. It sounded magical. Yet, even with such tales to entertain her imagination, practically the entire time, when she was not looking around awestruck at the beauty of the room, she was staring at their hostess. Cassia didn't seem to even notice since, after a while, she had begun to spend just as much time attempting to wrangle answers from Diana and Silvas about how they met and their time together—most of which Diana fielded.

Diana hadn't missed the flash of despair on Silvas's face, however, when bonding stories were exchanged. Instinctively, she reached forward and took his hand in hers. He froze, but then on the next breath, his fingers wrapped tightly around hers and she felt something within her respond to him on a primal level. It was an answering to whatever call he had initiated. She couldn't imagine hearing of a powerful, life-changing experience, knowing that he had participated in it, and yet to him it was like it never happened. He didn't speak. He just listened. But as the minutes slipped by, his grief for what he couldn't remember grew and became so palpable, even with their bond blocked, that Diana couldn't ignore it. She quickly changed the subject.

It was just as well. Her curiosity was killing her.

Leaning forward, she pinned Cassia with a curious look. "I'm sorry, this is terribly rude, but it's been eating at me and I just have to know. Why do you still look human?" For emphasis she allowed her tail to lightly slap the couch.

Cassia blinked at her in surprise. Diana almost thought that perhaps she had overstepped with the question when the woman threw her head back and laughed. Diana stared at her in bewilderment as she waved her hand and worked to control her laughter.

"I don't mean to laugh. Of course, you wouldn't know. I mean, I *am* surprised Silvas didn't discuss this with you, but I'm sure there is a reason. Larce told me before he bonded me, but I can imagine that the situation would be different between you and Silvas, since he's a god and not a silvanus spirit. Our experiences are thus different. As a bride of a silvanus, I am still human, but my life is bound to his. The bond extends my life naturally, but it doesn't change me. Brides of gods, who share a very particular, special bond, become elevated. You are taking a form that compliments his because your power is attached to his and balances his by nature."

A small frown appeared on Silvas's face. "Balances," he murmured to himself.

Diana would have given anything to know what he was thinking. It remained in the back of her mind throughout the rest of their visit. Their open affection was so sweet and yet it pierced her heart. She didn't dare glance toward Silvas lest he see just how much she wished to have that closeness. They were close… She wanted the words and the shows of affection. She just didn't know how to get there with him.

When they finally parted for the evening, Larce hugged her as if she were long-lost family and Cassia extracted a promise from them that they would visit again soon. Although their hunt had not been profitable in game, when they returned to her home, Diana felt a new lightness in her step.

CHAPTER 44

As weeks bled together and the winter passed, Selvans was true to his word. He left Nocis in a hidden place and set aside his fruitless hunt to openly explore the visceral pull he felt toward Diana. It was so intense that he had observed, with some amusement, that he was practically stalking her in his attempt to stay close to her. He hated every moment of separation when night finally came and he was sent out, because he viscerally knew that it hadn't been that way before. He was certain that he had held her close to him throughout the night. Unlike his brief affairs since he cast Alseida aside, the thought of having a female to hold close didn't feel him with dread or make his muscles tighten with wariness.

Perhaps because it was never clearer that she made no pretenses to entice or manipulate him. She didn't pretend to be anything other than who she wholly was. In that he found Diana to be crudely playful and possessing a stubbornness that rivaled his own. His lips twisted as he recalled their standoffs. Even when he was at his worst, she did not quake or break before him. She didn't hesitate to stand up to him even if it led to an uncomfortable impasse. That direct honesty sparked adoration within him, so it was natural that he instinctively sought to cleave to her.

Logically he knew that it was building on foundations started, locked away in the depths of his memory. If he ever wanted to enjoy that again or perhaps find his memories of her, he would need to relearn everything that his lack of wisdom had caused him to forget.

He desperately wanted to remember. It pained him that when he allowed himself to slumber, he was haunted by her, and fragments of what he suspected were memories faded before he woke. Whatever the visions were, he woke hard and aching, his heart breaking from the void within his soul where his bonded mate would have glowed within him. He finally understood what Dorinda had been speaking of when it came to light, and what the Gatekeeper's mate had been to him—Diana's presence was the only thing that brought light within him. She was his light… Without her, he was filled with a dark emptiness, eternally alone. He needed her, and not to destroy Cacus. He needed her to be whole.

He just didn't know how to bridge the distance between them that his mistakes had carved. Sometimes she looked at him and he got the vaguest impression of what it might have once been. To be able to freely touch, her affection raining down on him. Without that, his life felt colorless, though he strived to recapture his bond through every experience he enjoyed with his uxorem, every doubt that tormented his mind vanquished.

Selvans knew that many of his doubts were rooted in his poor experience with Alseida. It didn't take him long through casually watching her and spending time with her to realize that she was far from sharing any similarity with the dryad. Alseida never enjoyed his company unless they were fucking, and she could enjoy the flavor of his passion. She had used him to get what she wanted.

He was not innocent in it, either. He had used her as well by taking her as his consort for some semblance of comfort when he knew that she was not his bonded. He had chosen to ignore her jealous nature when he took her to his bed. Because of that, he was partly responsible for her fate. She had returned to the palace rather than moving on and had died for her effort. She never would have accepted Diana as ati. Her behavior proved what he had known and ignored of her nature. She would have done anything to destroy her rival.

He glanced up at where Diana sat in her chair. "Alseida let Cacus into the palace, didn't she?" he asked, disgust lacing his voice.

Diana jerked in surprise. Her lips pressed together, but she gave him an uncertain smile as she set down her book. The sadness and relief in her eyes made his heart lurch. He knew that she was remembering the terrible words he'd spoken when he had suspected her. How could he not have seen this then? How had he been so blind to the truth? He had been cruel and short-sighted. No wonder she had been hurt so badly and had been so angry with him.

"Yes, it was Alseida," she said, a long sigh parting from her lips as she sank back into her chair, her eyes staring off, looking back into her memories. "She tried to kill us in the corridors of Arx as we fled to the inner sanctuary. I was weakening, suffering as I felt every bond I had developed with the forest in your absence suffering and dying. I could barely stand when Raskyuil had come for me. He removed me from our chambers and attempted to flee with me, but when it became apparent that Cacus was within the castle he chose to head to the hidden courtyard. We did not make it there before we lost the other guards, and not before we were found by Alseida."

Her voice shook and a choked cry roughened her speech. "She killed Borbekel with her own hands. She would have killed us too if Arx hadn't saved us, but not even her alliance with Cacus saved her from his appetite when she failed him. While he was distracted with consuming her, Raskyuil hid me beneath the ground," she choked out.

Easing himself onto his knees, he wrapped his arms around her and drew her close to his chest. To his relief, she didn't fight his touch, but sank against him, tears pouring from her eyes with hard, ragged sobs. Only after she silenced did he drop slowly back to the floor again, his gaze trained, carefully observing her emotional state as his nostrils flared to provide more information. Once more he hated himself for blocking the bond. He would have felt her emotions and would have had some clues on how to soothe her if he hadn't been so stupid.

"I still don't understand how you escaped," he murmured. "That very thing that had initially incited me toward action, still confused me even when I knew that there was no way it could have been you."

She shook her head. "I don't even know, really. My mind was muddled, and I was consumed with pain and fear. I remember hearing Raskyuil cry out, and there was a flash of white light. I passed out at that point, but it was for the best because it stopped all that terrible pain."

Regret consumed him. She had suffered while he, with Nocis in his hand, had wanted nothing more at that time than to destroy her. He had thought so many horrible things and had thrown his suspicions at her.

Selvans groaned and rubbed a hand over his face. He really was a huge, arrogant idiot as his sister liked to claim. Gradually he let it drop and regarded her soberly. "I can never say enough how sorry I am. If I had known… No, it is no excuse. There is nothing that can forgive that."

"Nothing may be able to excuse it, but I can forgive you," she said softly. "I think I started to forgive you the day that you informed me that you knew that I didn't do it. This, though… This means a lot."

He grimaced. "I should have apologized sooner. I miscalculated how much you might have needed words of regret and apology. It very well may take me a few centuries to make it up to you… if you allow it."

A small smile played at the corners of her mouth. "I'm sure we can find a way of offering amends that will be satisfactory for both of us," she replied serenely before a wicked smile broke over her face. "I mean, groveling is fun and all, and you are free to do that for a little while, but I bet I can come up with something better."

Just that easily, she brought a smile to his face. His cock tightened with interest. He would be happy to make amends in any way that brought her pleasure and happiness. Not only because of what he had done to her, but because he took a personal delight in her happiness. That she considered accepting pleasures from him in atonement was a step in the right direction, even if it was mostly jest.

Truthfully, her outlook on their changing relationship was a never-ending surprise to him. Just when he was worried that he pushed her too far and pressed his presence too much into her life, she did not react with hostility as he thought she might. Their initial reunion had not boded well for any sort of peace between them, much less any hope for their bond, but somehow things changed. Granted, sometimes she was frustrated and yelled at him, and he did his share of growling and snarling as well. She even threw a shoe a time or two, which was a surprisingly painful projectile. But she also frequently reacted with mirth and kindness, and sometimes just plain mischievousness. Her lips pulled in a small smirk as she went back to reading, betraying her teasing mood.

A purr rattled from his chest from where he stretched out on the floor, his own lips curling with pleasure as he enjoyed their companionable silence. Although he wanted her writhing beneath him, he treasured this too. If only his cock would stop aching. It was pressed uncomfortably against the floor, betraying his heightened need. It was getting more insistent, and his skin was beginning to crawl with their demands. He was surprised that either of them had held out as well as they had during this entire period, probably because they were already bonded and it was just the stress of their systems needing to reconnect.

He winced as a thought occurred to him. He owed his mother an apology. He had vehemently denied his bond with Diana to Turan, obviously not knowing what the hell he was talking about and confused by Nocis's power. He would have to go before her to admit that she was right. Diana was the perfect half of him. Not only did she make him feel more whole, but she filled his days with warmth and laughter to such a degree that it was only in his moments alone that he found his mind turning to Cacus.

To his relief, he seldom thought about the creature during the day, his being filled with her presence. Whereas that might have concerned him before, he realized since his lengthy separation from the sword that his worry and aggression in searching for the creature was no longer immediately suffocating him with his failure to find his prey. He hadn't realized just how close he had danced to the edge of madness.

Such reasons were why he had abandoned the sword before. He hated that he would need it to defeat the creature. Once all was said and done, it would be locked away in his armory where it would sleep. Instead, he could enjoy the small measure of quiet that he had at this moment while Cacus slept and steal time away from the world with his female.

He couldn't get enough of her.

Even without yet joining his body with hers, he craved all her flavors. He desired her with an impatient, roaring need. He wanted more of her words, her touches and the clutch of her sex. He both wanted and needed her! No other being tasted as she did to him. Even the taste of her softer emotions was sweet on his tongue. It surprisingly satisfied him more than the tang of fear that he normally craved. In truth, her presence made him yearn to be closer to her more than any other ever had. Not only bodily, but within his mind and heart. They answered to the goodness within her that he had seen shine out when she met Larce and Cassia. She accepted his family and showed that she accepted him too, despite his darkness.

She was truly the light that Dorinda bade him to search for.

He felt a tear gather at the corner of his eye and blinked it away.

Sighing, he glanced toward the window where the day was rapidly fading away. Soon she would walk him to the door, and he would be forced to ignore the pain of separation washing through him to leave. He couldn't complain—it was their agreement. It didn't mean that he liked it, though. But still, he could give her this small thing. He would go and keep himself company in his tree. His lips quirked. It wasn't like he had much of a choice. He discovered that no amount of sweet words could convince her to change her mind once it was made up. Every evening he was shoved out the door shortly following their shared meal.

He wrinkled his nose at the window. He was not looking forward to it. The air had warmed up enough to rain. Although he was not susceptible to temperature fluctuations like a mortal, it was going to be a soggy, miserable night regardless. He was not looking forward to it. At least she seemed not to be in a great hurry to escort him out this evening. She sat with coffee in hand and her blanket tucked around her. Her dark tail flicked lazily as she rocked in her chair. He smiled at the sight and leaned forward, his fingers wrapping lightly around the fuzz so that it tickled his palm as it slipped free.

Diana's chair stopped rocking and she peered down at him where he was sprawled comfortably on the woven rug on the floor. One eyebrow raised at him as she flicked the back of his hand with her tail. He chuckled and attempted to snag it, but she snapped it away quickly, a snort of amusement leaving her.

Growling playfully, he lunged again, his smile widening at her squeal. As she attempted to evade his hand, she slipped out of the seat of the rocking chair just enough that, with a firm hand wrapped around her calf, he yanked on her leg and brought her sprawling over him.

The warm, rich scent of summer flowers and musk surrounded him as she fell into his arms. Taking advantage of the situation, he rubbed his cheek against hers. Chortling mirthfully, Diana pushed herself up just enough to peer down at him through her softly glowing eyes. He gazed up at her, his heart so full that the words slipped through his lips.

"I love you, Diana."

Her laughter died and she drew back further to peer down at him in surprise. "You love me, or do you just want everything to fall into place easier with Cacus?"

He shook his head. "Cacus is nothing. I have barely thought of him while I'm with you. I love *you*, Diana. Fate, Eternal Forest, Cacus… None of that matters to me as much as you do. You make my heart and soul whole. *You* are my one and only light."

Diana melted against him, her arms looping around his neck as they continued to lay sprawled together. He felt her fingers sifting through his hair to caress his ears and trail down the sides of his face to his jaw.

"I feel like I have waited forever to hear those words from you. I tried to tell myself what we have is good and that as long as we are both happy, that is what matters most. I didn't realize how much I needed to hear the words," she chuckled weepily. "I love you too, Silvas."

His heart leaped in his chest and he drew her against him, his mouth capturing hers with a growl. His tongue swept in her mouth and she rose up to meet him with a sound of contentment. As they kissed, their tongues twining together, power raced between them. He felt it, white-hot light shooting from within her into him. It ran through their bond, fracturing the block with a hundred points of light in his mind's eye before shattering it, flooding his mind.

Releasing her mouth, his head tipped back, and he cried out as memories came rushing back. He remembered the fear in her eyes when they met, her stubborn resilience when he challenged her in the palace, her strength as they traveled through the mountains. Every smile, tear and pained cry came back to him. Even the tears that fell when she reached her limit. They battered at him, overwhelmed every sense.

His heart broke, and he curled in to hold her close, savoring her brightness and the warmth of her attention, even the flicker of her surprise along their bond.

"I remember," he whispered into her hair.

"Thank the fucking gods," she replied seconds before she pulled back and punched him square on the chin.

Yelping, he brought his hands up. "Okay, I deserved that," he mumbled.

Diana laughed and yanked him up to claim his lips once again.

CHAPTER 45

Curling her fingers into his tunic, she worked it up over his body, taking care not to tear it with her claws. Unlike her, he didn't wear any extra clothing. He refreshed the same pair with a bit of magic that made her envious. They broke their lip-lock long enough for her to whip it off him, exposing the hard muscles of his abs and pectorals that rippled as he shifted his body to help her. Carelessly, with one hand, she tossed it across the room.

The flickering light of the fire played off his velvety skin and she leaned down to press a kiss against it. Making love on the floor in front of a roaring fire seemed a bit Hallmark special cliché, but she couldn't care less. She moaned as his hands aggressively swept over her. Even as her fingers were eagerly fighting to remove the clothing from him as quickly as possible, Silvas's claws tore at her clothes, shredding them from her body. She arched against him as his claws lightly scored her skin, his tail wrapping tightly around hers after he divested her of what was left of her pants.

Naked, their bodies rubbed against each other, their tails tightening and stroking together. Teeth nipped and Silvas pitched sideways, taking Diana beneath him, his cock sliding against the puffy folds of her sex as he stretched her out on the floor. She strained against him, her breasts rubbing his chest as an eager, breathy sigh slipped from her lips.

It was how she remembered it, how she dreamed of it—and yet it was better as his mouth claimed her body with heated kisses of adoration. She squirmed against him with every brush of his cock as he rocked against her, teasing her body with his until she writhed. The sting of his teeth was light, but the nips were strategically placed as he moved down her body.

Diana gasped out a moan as he attacked her breasts and her belly, nipping and sucking on her skin until she whimpered and pled as he worked his way down, warm floods of arousal wetting her thighs. The heat of his breath fanning her sex as his tongue stroked over her folds, laving, nipping and sucking at her slick cunt, sent her hips twisting into the air.

Arching against his questing mouth, she wrapped her fingers around his antlers. The bone beneath her fingers was oddly bare without all the jewels he used to have gilding and hanging from his antlers. She almost missed the way that it dropped in a cold shower against her hot body, but it didn't matter. She tugged on his antlers, feeling the press of the new shorter horns against her knuckles where they swept back from his brow. Her orgasm burst through her hard and fast. Silvas moaned as he lapped her clean before licking and kissing his way back up her body. Her hands broke free from his antlers as he loomed over her, his glowing eyes, brightened with passion, staring down at her as he pressed his pelvis against hers.

Grabbing her wrists, he anchored them to the floor on either side of her head as his large body rubbed against hers. Held by Silvas, she felt like she was dangling from a lifeline. Wave after wave of electric heat swamped over her, sparking at her nipples and her clit where his cock teased her with every brush of his body rubbing against hers, need pulsed through her demanding to be satisfied. Having her wrists pinned to the floor on either side of her by his large hands made it boil deep within her belly. Through the bond, she could feel the same desperation in Silvas as he waged his sensual attack upon every inch of her. With one last hard suck at her clit, she went over, her orgasm bursting behind her eyes as her thighs clenched from the force of it.

With a tilt of his hips, he speared deep in one firm thrust.

Her pussy rapidly stretched around his thick phallus, Diana jerked against him, sending him deeper into her. Silvas growled in response, his tail twisting and tightening around hers to hold her against him as he pulled back and drove deep again. She choked and drew in a ragged gasp, wrapping her legs around him to give her leverage as she rocked against him, wanting more of him within her.

A growl rumbled from her mate, his tongue slicking along her neck as his hips picked up a rolling rhythm that sent her jolting with every deep thrust. Her next orgasm powered through her after just a handful of thrusts, her pussy squeezing him, making Silvas snarl as heat bathed her insides from a release of precum. The sensation against her still sensitive flesh as she came down from her orgasm had Diana hissing as she canted her hips. The position forced him to drive harder into her, their breath coming out together and mingling in rapid bursts.

Diana strained against him, needing more. Silvas's dominant growl echoed in her ears in response. She felt a pleasant chill zap up her spine, and she writhed as he transferred both wrists to be pinned beneath one hand. His free hand stroked down her body as he stroked into her before curling his fingers tightly around her thigh.

Lifting her leg, he adjusted his angle, his hips snapping aggressively against her. His cock tapped within her, every bump stimulating the walls of her sex with each thrust. His breath panted in her ear as she felt his cock swell, the friction increasing to send her into another quick orgasm. As her body quaked, she felt the pinch of his cock sealing against her that sent him immediately grinding deeper into her. She shivered under the rough pummel of his hips as his breath panted against her skin, each exhalation a possessive growl.

The roar that broke from him echoed through the living room as his seed burst through her, spraying hot jets within her. Diana arched against him, and another orgasm lit through her as he held himself deep within her.

His arms quivered, and very gently he lay her down on the rug, his body still joined to hers. Curled together, they snuggled, their cheeks brushing, his lips trailing against hers and along her face and neck. She snuggled comfortably into his embrace, her body relaxed and her heart full. When his cock finally slipped out, Silvas sighed and snuggled closer against her, the dying fire warming their sides as they dozed in each other's arms.

A content feeling swept through Diana as she nuzzled Silvas sleepily. Although the future loomed over them like a twisted shadow, for right now they had this. They had each other, and that was going to make all the difference.

CHAPTER 46

Selvans kept a firm grip on his mate as they descended through the corridors of Arx. It hadn't taken much convincing to get Diana to return to the palace. Part of him had been worried that she would never wish to return to the place, considering the horrors that she had witnessed there and their own painful history in the cavern of the vegoia. Instead of being reluctant, Diana had readily agreed. At least the halls and grounds had been cleaned of all remains, and even Arx appeared to be rapidly recovering from its damage. There were still several broken areas that were leveled, or half rebuilt, but it looked far less of a sad case than it had months prior.

If he were truthful with himself, he hadn't wanted to bring her back to Arx until the palace had been rebuilt and the grounds repaired. Yet, they had both agreed that they would have a better chance of finding and defeating Cacus if they caught him while he was still aground. Diana had pointed out that the method had served them well with the strix, and he hadn't been able to argue with her logic.

The fact that he didn't want his uxorem anywhere near Cacus was another matter. He had spent considerable time the night before trying to work out a way to keep her out of it. He thought of leaving her with Larce and Cassia, but when he suggested it to Diana, she refused to hear it. She had taken a little too much pleasure in throwing back at him that Dorinda had emphasized that they were both needed, and reminding him of the fact that his sister was refusing to so much as speak to him without Diana.

He was less than thrilled with the situation and didn't bother to hide his feelings on the matter. He hadn't cracked a smile since they entered the palace grounds, though he had nodded respectfully to everyone who had greeted them. The one bright moment was when the crocotta clan came rushing around the ruin of the gardens to greet them.

"Silvas, I had a thought," Diana murmured at his side as they drew close to the exposed hidden courtyard.

Although it always had open-air access, it had been well concealed, but the outer walls had fallen, leaving the staircase visible to anyone who happened by. He was surprised that Arx had not yet started rebuilding there. He frowned at the crumbled stone and grunted as his uxorem's elbow jabbed him.

Selvans raised an eyebrow in silent inquiry.

Now that she had his attention, Diana fidgeted and gave him a warm smile. "I know that you and Dorinda have a strained and difficult history together, but what if you did *not* rebuild the hidden courtyard. The garden could be expanded in place of walls. We could even tap into her pool and raise a fountain to the courtyard where she can choose to spend time outside of her cavern. It's just that… well… she really misses contact with the outside world and, despite your intention to protect her, feels imprisoned down there."

"She told you this?" he asked.

"She did," Diana said, her free hand stroking the back of his. "She hates that she is missing everything, and the world passes her by without her seeing it anymore. It is not fair. And I think it would go a long way to mend your relationship if you tried to meet her halfway."

"You are suggesting complete surrender to her," he grumbled.

"She's not your enemy," Diana laughed. "And I'm thinking more of a compromise. You keep the staircase going down to the cave, and we can partially block it in with garden hedges to give her some privacy. Should there be any danger she can drop back down into her cave easily from the fountain."

"I suppose this compromise can work," he said sourly. "I still dislike that she gets exactly what she wants when she has been nothing but a thorn in my side."

"Technically, what she wants is for part of Arx to be moved, so you can rest assured that she's not getting exactly what she wants." Diana's eyes sparkled with laughter as she hugged his arm against her, her tail coiling comfortably with his. "Consider it a peace offering. Wouldn't it be better to have the vegoia on your side rather than tormenting you at every given opportunity?"

"I could just hang her by the tail until she decides to behave," he suggested. He was only half-joking. Perhaps less than half.

Her refusal to speak to him and her endless grudges didn't exactly make him inclined toward acts of goodwill. However, he had to admit that his uxorem had a point. If the changes could improve her disposition, he would follow Diana's lead.

Their footsteps sounded loudly on the stairs as they descended. The only other sound was the whining of the crocottas from the top of the staircase. They wouldn't come down. Dorinda didn't allow animals into her domain and had an unknown way of encouraging them to remain out of her cavern. In all the time he had known his sister, he had never known her to make an exception to that rule until Keena hauled Diana to safety.

As they walked toward the pool and the spraying fount of the spring, Selvans looked for any sign of the vegoia. As usual, Dorinda was characteristically absent. He frowned, wondering if his sister would once again ignore his summons. She had done a fine job of ignoring him so far, so he didn't really expect it to change.

He scowled at the water and opened his mouth to demand her presence when a soft chuckle filled the air.

"Finally, you stubborn ass. I'm pleased to see that you finally listened." With a twist of the waters, she slipped out of the deep fissure in which she had been hidden. Her crimson eyes settled on him as a smile pulled at her lips. "Or did you figure out the meaning of your own personal prophecy?" She touched a finger to her lips, amusement bright in her red eyes as she tilted her head to the side. "No, I am pretty sure that mother tracked you down."

"All of the above," he growled impatiently.

Her eyebrows raised, impressed. "I confess that I didn't expect that. In fact, I had a private wager going that Cacus would waken long before you returned with your uxorem." She turned a smile on Diana. "I am so pleased to see you again, quite healthy and furry. I highly approve of the tail, everyone should have one," she said cheerfully as she lifted the tip of her own tail out of the water.

The change in his sister's attitude with Diana's presence was nothing short of astounding. She was cooperative and pleasant.

"Why aren't you being your usual foul-tempered self?" he demanded.

His sister pinned him with an impatient look. "Because Diana is kind and considerate toward me. Something you are not," she said.

He tossed a bewildered look to his mate. "For this you want me to compromise with her? She is impossible! A scheming, manipulative…"

Diana rolled her eyes and folded her arms over her chest as she turned her attention to Dorinda. "We are going to provide you with access above ground and reduce the protective barrier so that you can enjoy some measure of freedom while still being able to get safely within the ground if you are threatened."

The vegoia blinked at her. "I did not foresee this happening," she mused. She turned to him, eyes narrowing. "Is it because you are just telling your mate what she wants to hear to gain my cooperation? I recall that you are a tricky one when it suits your mood."

He gave her a disgusted look but grunted. "No, it is the truth, as much as it pains me after all the trouble you have caused over the years. But you are my sister, and you did help my uxorem. Diana said that she believed it would be for the best, and I find that I agree with her logic even if I don't necessarily agree with the sentiment behind it. Still, it is logical to give you some measure of freedom and put our relationship to some semblance of rest and cooperation for once," he said grudgingly.

Dorinda raised an eyebrow. "That was perhaps the least gracious offer that has ever been extended to another being… ever… but coming from you that means it is a genuine one and is borderline sweet." She smirked and adjust her seat on her rock. "I am guessing that you are not here just because you miss me. You want to know about Cacus."

"If it wouldn't be too much trouble," he muttered.

Diana slapped his hip with her tail and smiled kindly at the vegoia. "Yes, we need to know where to find him before he comes up again from beneath the ground. Your help will determine whether or not we succeed."

"Not that you cared to oblige earlier," he added, and scooted out of the way before his mate could lash him again.

"Stop that," his uxorem hissed.

Dorinda snorted. "Pay him no mind. I don't. And you, brother, had I given you the information you sought earlier without your queen tied heart and soul to you, you would have succumbed to

Nocis and ultimately failed. I foresaw it and therefore refused your entreaties to spare you that fate. You're welcome."

"As you see, now I have my uxorem by my side… and my memories restored. Please," he bit back the wince at having to politely ask for a favor from his sister, "instruct us in what you foresee. Where might we find him?"

The vegoia smiled and tipped her head back, tail slipping through the water as she inhaled. A mist rose up as the water around her rippled and foamed. A light tremor swept through her body and then she jerked, her back bowing as her mouth gaped open.

Selvans moved forward in concern, ready to pull her out of her trance, when she snapped her crimson eyes open, appearing almost to bleed from their shimmering glow. Her voice hissed, each word drawn out.

"Cacus sleeps in a city of flesh… where vampires have been whispered to haunt, and the dead sleep above ground. He sleeps in a stone building of the dead… where he rests after glutting himself on thousands of souls… The bones of the living decorate his bower. He sleeps deep, but not for long."

Selvans frowned, frustrated with his lack of knowledge when it came to the human world. The place described sounded distinctive enough that he couldn't imagine why humans would ever wish to have inhabited the location at all. And they called his kind and the places they lurked monstrous!

He glanced at Diana and found her to be grinning.

"I know that place," she said with a laugh. "And my mother always said reading all the vampire filth as a kid was going to rot my brain, but thank you, Anne Rice! I even went on the vampire tour when I visited for Mardi Gras, the feast of the flesh, when I was twenty-one and legally able to drink. The story of Jacques St. Germain always fascinated me in particular. The place has some big-time vampire lore and above-ground cemeteries since the town is below sea level. He's sleeping in a mausoleum from the sound of it."

"We will need to find a portal to this New Orleans, then," he said.

Diana rubbed her neck and gave him a hopeful look. "Do you have a map?"

CHAPTER 47

New Orleans had fallen, and nature was creeping in to reclaim it. That didn't surprise Diana. After the ravaging, anyone who may have survived the madness from the wulkwos that had nested in the big cities had long since fled. There was no one to maintain the upkeep following the hurricane seasons. Shattered glass, colorful plastic, and broken boards littered the streets, scattered among other remnants of human life that had been abandoned. With the toe of her boot, she kicked away a tangled knot of plastic bead necklaces left by some tourist during the ravaging, no doubt. Plastic truly did last forever.

Ironically, while the modern houses were falling apart, the buildings of the Quarter that had stood for hundreds of years remained as gloomy gray sentinels. More than one building had tattered fabric clinging to the windows of what had been apartments and short-term rented rooms. It fluttered with the occasional breeze. Poppets stared out from behind the windows of various voodoo shops catering to tourists, their empty eyes mocking the living who dared to intrude in the city of death.

Ghosts and vampires. That was pretty much the legacy of the

city. That and New Orleans-style voodoo and hoodoo, though she didn't know much about those subjects.

At her side, Silvas twitched his tail tensely, his long stride steady as his eyes tracked anything and everything that moved. His nostrils twitched at the stench of rotting and decay that seemed to be clinging to the streets. Over the last four years, the streets had obviously been flooded numerous times and they were covered with a residue of decaying matter that had washed over them. It was putrid.

"What a horrible place to build a city," Silvas observed, his nose wrinkling.

She laughed as she kept pace at his side. "It was an important port because it's at the mouth of the Mississippi River. Many of the buildings in this part of the city are very old and stand as a testament to the prominence of the city even when it was young. It continued to draw visitors every year until the ravaging. The storms did quite a bit of damage each year, but it wasn't a terrible place, though maybe a little inconvenient and troublesome in some respects."

He didn't look convinced. He actually appeared rather put out about the whole trek through the city. They had already visited several cemeteries, breaking into tombs that seemed of adequate size to shelter Cacus. To no avail. Still, he kept watch, his massive rack moving from side to side as he scanned the gloomy shadows of the decaying city.

"Where to next?" he grumbled as he strode out ahead of her. His ears were twisting and his nostrils flaring. It was obvious that he was tracking something, but after so many false leads she was no longer getting excited when he did that.

Diana peered down at her map and jabbed at a spot. "We can try this one. It seemed a bit convenient if he were sleeping there since it was one of the best-known cemeteries in the city, but we have checked most of the others. We are running out of options here. So…"

A fleeting movement out of the corner of her eye brought her head up in a quick jerk, her nostrils flaring as she attempted to home in on the source of the shadow that darted among the buildings. Swallowing, she leaned forward slightly, squinting.

"Were you serious when you said that there were vampires?" she asked casually.

At least she tried to sound casual. She didn't want to admit that she still had a very human reaction to the idea of being hunted by a vampire. Her tail tucked against the back of her legs, betraying her nerves. Silvas, noting her hesitation and anxiety through their bond, frowned as he turned to pace back to her. His large frame loomed over hers, a warning growl rumbling in his throat.

"There are," he rumbled, his pale eyes narrowing in the distance.

Silvas's tail slipped around her waist, drawing her against him as he spread his arms in a defensive posture.

"Come out. We know you are there," Silvas called out into the shadows.

A pair of glowing red eyes flashed in the darkest corner like light catching off the eyes of a predator. There was a rustle of fabric, and she heard the soft click of footsteps on the street as a tall, lean man stepped out. His long hair fluttered around him, shaved closed on one side, as his form-fitting clothes, while a bit on the shabby side with no tailors around, were of a black and burgundy scheme and looked like they cost more than what she had made in a year when she had worked at the tavern.

"We don't want any more of your kind around here," the vampire said coolly, his accent muddled like one who spent a long lifetime traveling. "I suggest that you leave before I alert my nest to your presence. The humans here are under *our* safekeeping."

Diana's eyebrows winged up at the statement. "You have humans here?" She glanced around, seeing nothing but ruins. "Where? And why? I thought your kind killed people."

The vampire made a disgusted click but peered at her curiously. "We have a symbiotic relationship with the humans under our protection. We only require small amounts of blood from them in our diet, supplemented with animal blood and other nutritious foods for our kind…"

"He speaks of consuming internal organs," Silvas clarified for her, and she gagged. "Vampires need less than a tablespoon of human blood every week to keep them healthy. They otherwise raise livestock which they eat raw, everything from the blood and flesh to every internal organ and the brain."

"Very 'waste not, want not,' but still gross," Diana said with a shudder.

"Your speech would suggest you are a human, that accent from Virginia perhaps… but your scent and appearance say that you are one of the monsters that come from the forests," the vampire hummed with curiosity.

She gaped at him in offense. "I'm not a monster! I was human until I bonded to him." She hooked her thumb over at Silvas.

"We are not interested in hurting anyone, and are in fact surprised to hear anyone is living here," Silvas interrupted as he eyed the other male. "We are hunting a Tainted One—a true monster that may have killed and consumed many when he entered your territory. Cacus wouldn't have discriminated between your people and the humans when it comes to his prey. Have you seen it?"

"He looks like a misshapen centaur, breathes fire, and can dislocate his jaw like a snake to help him bite off heads," Diana added.

The vampire hesitated and drew forward slowly. "Yes. It has lurked around our city since early autumn. It was worse than the infernal wolves when it struck our city. We barely held on and protected the few humans that we could save when the gates between this world and the underworld sprung open. Since they were pulled out of this world, the human population here in New Orleans has been limping along. Then that creature—Cacus you call him—arrived and carved a path between the human population and vampire population both. It was a relief when it finally retreated to the tombs. We have been watching and waiting for any movement from it. We even tried to send a small group of our elite warriors to kill it. Their screams still haunt me."

Diana folded the map so that the cemetery she was looking at faced outward. She tapped on it with one finger. "Is this the place? Saint Louis Cemetery?"

He nodded solemnly. "If you are going there, I will alert the king."

Silvas raised a hand and shook his head. "Tell him, but keep the vampires out of the crypt until we have handled it. Cacus is our responsibility. We do not wish for further injuries among your people."

The vampire snorted. "And who are you that you think have a better chance alone, with no one but your mate for assistance, to accomplish what a number of our best could not?"

Diana bristled, her tail lashing behind her as she imagined rearranging his face. Silvas chuckled, his hand stroking down her back in a soothing action.

"Do not worry about us, vampire. This creature will not survive our encounter."

The vampire gave him a skeptical look and shrugged. "All right—it's your funeral. You will find it resting in a large crypt topped with a pious soul holding aloft the crucifix. The creature broke down one wall and burrowed itself within the soft earth. It is unfortunate that we didn't have a massive flood there recently. Maybe it would have drowned, or left New Orleans for a more comfortable resting place. Good luck. If by chance you are not just blowing smoke up my ass, you can find my nest here. I will carry a report of your success to the king's nest" He nodded up at the curved face of the two-story brownstone building at the intersection.

Diana raised her eyebrows and smirked. "So tell me, did you go and pick out Jacques St. Germain's rooms personally?"

The vampire grinned. "Always a pleasure to meet a fan," he said with a flourished bow. "I fear I am a creature of habit. Whenever I return to my old haunts, I'm always drawn to home." He inhaled with pleasure as he glanced up at the building. "I suppose it was fortuitous that I was caught here when the gates opened. If I had to suffer without modern conveniences, it might as well be in one of my favorite cities. I sincerely hope that you are successful so that we may meet again," he murmured, ignoring Silvas's possessive snarl as he stepped back into the shadows.

Diana pressed her lips together, uncertain if she should be squealing like a fangirl or be worried that a vampire was obviously flirting with her. "Well, at least we found out one very important piece of information. We were heading to the right place. We can take Canal Street up to Basin and follow it down to the cemetery."

Silvas nodded, shadowy wings extending from his body before they solidified into black-tipped white wings. Tugging her into his arms, he shifted his grip with his tail to plaster her body more snugly against his. The hard muscles of his legs bunched as he crouched down. Diana wrapped her arms tightly around his neck, her own tail looping tightly around him just before he leapt upward into the sky with a hard flap of his wings.

When they landed minutes later within the cemetery, the marble tombs brought a sense of nostalgia to her as they walked among them. She didn't have the same developed sense of smell to be able to recognize the scent of a Tainted One like Silvas could, so she stuck close behind him as he went up and down the aisles, his nostrils flaring as he scented the air to make certain the creature hadn't risen. In the distance, they could see the crypt jutting up high above the other tombs, and shivers scurried down her spine.

Vampire tours, voodoo tours, swamp tours in gator filled swamps, even local ghost tours in the quarter she had no problem with. The giant above-ground cemeteries gave her the heebie-jeebies, though. As they wound their way from the southern wall where they landed, her eyes widened at the familiar sight of Marie Laveau's marked tomb rising in front of them. Silvas strode right past it without giving any notice, but Diana slowed at its side and stopped, her eyes trailing on the dozens of marks of wishes made.

Placing her finger on the wall, her claw scratched out an X as she whispered to the voodoo queen who was no doubt working from beyond to keep her city safe. Few humans were capable of surviving the madness that set upon them by the ravagers. That there was a pocket of humanity in New Orleans doing just that was more than a little remarkable.

"Marie Laveau, if ever you loved your city and worked for its benefit from your revered place, honored as voodoo queen even as your bones rest, be with us. Protect your city and your people from the danger that hunts them."

Silvas's shadow fell over her. "You pray to a human soul?" he asked, his voice curious as he cocked his head.

Diana shrugged. "Why not? She was powerful in life. Why wouldn't she continue to protect her city even from her place of rest? Heroes have a special place of honor in the next world, I think. I can imagine she would be counted among that by many. I think she would have a hand in things going on around here."

His eyebrows raised as he considered, and after a moment, he inclined his head. "I shall remember that. Even human spirits can be powerful allies."

Bowing respectfully toward the tomb, he turned away, his tail flicking. He moved away only a few steps before stopping to look over his shoulder, patiently waiting for her to catch up. From Marie's tomb, they departed, following the line of moonlight leading to the crypt where the monster slept. Sliding fingers to her side, she gripped the hilt of Anola where it was strapped to her side.

CHAPTER 48

The broken wall of the crypt split open before them like a gaping wound, a terrible stench wafting up from it. Taint. Cacus lingered within there, just as they had been told. Selvans tensed as he stepped forward. The crypt was large, but not so big that Cacus's girth wouldn't fill most of the available space. They would have very limited room for mobility, and that worried him. By taking Diana in there, he would be risking her safety far more than he had even in facing the strix. He lifted his eyes and met his mate's gaze. She gave him an encouraging smile and tipped her head toward the entrance. Apprehension skated through their bond, but she faced the danger head-on, her mind focused and steady.

Still, he hesitated. Dropping his voice, he spoke softly to his bonded. "If you would rather wait out here, I will not think less of you."

Her brows drew down together. "You're not leaving me out here, asshole."

"Uxorem, this situation worries me. Though above ground, the crypt is small. If Cacus got ahold of you…" Fear for his mate surged through him, making his heart ache.

"So, what—I get left out here to worry about you instead? No. Remember what Dorinda said? We both need to be there. That doesn't mean you're in there where it's dangerous while I wait in safety out here. It means us both, fighting as one, against him."

He squinted into the gloom of the interior that was dark even to his eyes in the dim moonlit night. He expelled a slow breath and nodded. She was right. He would just take care the best he could.

"Stay behind me, at all cost. Do not leave my side for any reason."

"Let's get in there and end this shit," she murmured.

She stuck close behind him as he stepped inside. She was close enough that he could just barely feel the brush of her hot breath against the back of his neck. It reassured him as they crept forward.

A rumbling, quaking sound rocked the walls of the crypt and a lick of fire illuminated the room briefly as it fanned from the mouth of the sleeping creature. It slept on its side, its huge upper body curled in a relaxed pose, its head pillowed on its arm. The four legs were partially drawn up under it from where it had eased itself on its side. Selvans' eyes trailed over the Tainted One, looking for the best place to strike that would guarantee a quick death for him. The monstrous tail whipped, sending the rubble it came into contact with flying.

Selvans leaped back as another burst of flames seared the air, coming close to grazing his right antler. His eyes darted to Diana, pleased to see that she was tucked behind him, staring around at Cacus, her brow drawn down. He felt their bond quake as she faced the creature who had tracked her through the corridors of Arx. A small gasp left her at the sight of the monster curled on himself, her body rigid with tension.

"How do we kill him?" she whispered.

His lips tightened. "I don't know."

Diana's head whipped around, her mouth gaping. "*You don't know?*"

"It is not like there are instructions on how to kill Cacus. If you recall Hercules, a heroic son of one of the highest of gods, hadn't managed to do more than choke him until he fell unconscious. Myth likes to tell that he strangled the creature to death, but not even he could kill Cacus. I am a bit at a loss as to exactly how we should proceed. Most of the Tainted Ones I have slain had been minor creatures that existed before Cacus first rose from the belly of the earth."

"Right," Diana whispered back. "So we know it has something to do with Nocis, and presumably Anola since it was made as a companion to your sword. Should we try just stabbing him?"

Although he didn't like her getting quite that close in the tight spaces around Cacus, he couldn't think of a better suggestion.

"Take his flank while I go for the front. When you drive in your blade, be sure to put your full strength behind it so that the blade sinks deep. We will only have one chance at catching him unaware."

Diana nodded and crept toward Cacus's flank while Selvans walked around the front. His eyes fell on the creature's chest as it rose and fell. Raising Nocis, he looked over at his mate to make sure she was in position. She stood right at Cacus's side, her own blade's hilt gripped between both hands, lifted above her head with the sharp end of the blade pointed down toward the side of his monstrous belly.

Selvans' eyes returned to Cacus, drifting over him before fastening upon the thickly muscled neck. Most of the male's body was covered in dense muscle, but the throat seemed to be his best bet. It had weakened bands pressure cut into the skin, making the entire area vulnerable. Without shifting his eyes away from the Tainted One, he dropped his chin in an inclination of his head, signaling Diana.

Baring his fangs, he drove down with his blade. Nocis flashed with a dark, ultraviolet light. As if that light summoned him from the depths of his slumber, Cacus's murderous eyes sprung open as he wrenched his giant body away at the last minute. The blade succeeded only in nicking the flesh of his neck, a thin slash spraying out dark blood. The creature roared in pain and a white light filled the room at the exact moment that Anola sank deep into his side.

Cacus bellowed, its massive body rolling on its side. Its tail whipped, knocking Diana against a wall as another billow of fire blew from its mouth and it turned its head. Selvans streaked to the side, ducking out of the way, but his heart stalled as he heard his uxorem's frightened shriek and felt her fear snap through their bond.

Squinting against the smoke filling the crypt, Selvans could just barely make her out as she struggled to her feet. The breath he had been holding left his body in relief as he noted that she was unwounded. Her tail coiling around her, she leaped gracefully out of the way to avoid the Tainted One's thrashing.

Surging to his feet, Cacus leaped forward, his hooves clopping heavily against the floor for just a moment before his haunches bunched and he flung himself through the gap in the broken wall, Anola's hilt sticking out from where it was buried in his side. More stones broke away and fell from the entrance with a loud crash.

"Shit, shit, shit!" Diana cursed as she stumbled to his side. Her eyes were wild as she looked up at him. "What the fuck happened there?"

Selvans shook his head as he hurried out of the crypt, he sheathed his sword with one fluid movement as the fingers of his opposite hand curled around Diana's wrist, pulling her after him. "He reacted to the movement of the sword when Nocis moved in front of his face, and it woke up."

"Fuck. We're going to have to chase him down before someone else runs into him first."

Selvans nodded and summoned his wings as he gathered Diana close to his chest. With several strong beats, he was airborne, following the path of destruction carved out by the creature. They were gaining on him; Selvans could see the creature in the distance, barreling down Canal Street.

The street was filled with abandoned vehicles, so Cacus raced along a strip of road that Selvans could see the clear line of a track running down. A boxy red vehicle was knocked from its track as Cacus bellowed in rage. From the air, Selvans could see the sparks jumping up from the skidding where the metal siding of the box slid against the metal track.

All the obstacles were useful for one thing: allowing Selvans to catch up to the Tainted One. Soon they were soaring directly over the rampaging male as he kicked offending objects in his path and blew out fire in bouts of rage at a few of the buildings. It wasn't until Cacus set upon a large building that Selvans felt a chill fill him as human screams erupted into the night.

Everywhere people ran in a panic as they flooded out of the building. With a roar, Cacus set upon them, leering as he scooped up a human in each hand. A cruel laugh echoed up from the male's chest as the humans struggled in his grip.

Diana pinched his forearm to get his attention and she shouted in his ear. "Drop me on his back. I need to get Anola!"

He wasn't going to just toss his mate onto the back of a Tainted One! Diana pinched his arm again, harder, and glared at him.

"Are we in this together or not? I need my sword, and we need to distract him before he eats them. Drop me… now."

Gritting his teeth against the commanding tone in her voice—obviously, they would have to settle the issue of dominance between them later—he reluctantly did as she bid. Swooping low, he released Diana. With a beat of his wings, he circled again as he watched Diana land on Cacus's huge back.

The male jerked and kicked out his hind legs in surprise. To Selvan's relief, Diana managed to hold on. The creature's hands loosened in surprise, and the humans dropped the short distance to the ground. Assuring himself that Diana was fine as she scrambled for her sword, Selvans dipped his wings, preparing to haul them to safety until the blurring speed of the first wave of vampires arriving darted beneath him. Two split off from the group to carry the scampering humans to safety while the others converged on Cacus. Jacques stopped, peeling away from the group, and grinned up at him.

"Impressive wingspan there," the male shouted just before he dodged a vehicle similar to the one abandoned in his forest as it was lobbed through the air. It crashed against a wall, buckling the structure of the building as one side tipped beneath the crumbling wall. Jacques whistled at the sight and broke into a full run to join those attacking Cacus.

No longer needing to worry about the humans, Selvans circled in the air and winged his way back toward Cacus. The Tainted One bellowed as he shook the vampires off, Diana slipping nearly off his back in the process. He needed to get his mate off that creature!

Dropping to the ground, Selvans dismissed his wings and strode forward, the energy bursting off him in waves. He was not in the forest, but the plants were thick and lush where they had already begun to gather in tangles throughout the city. Calling upon them, he felt the threads of life weave through him.

Roots of trees burst up, spearing through the legs of the Tainted One, making the male writhe and scream with pain. Diana let out a shout and tugged at the same moment he dropped to the ground, her blade pulling free. She immediately braced her foot against his belly and sprang away, the dark drops of ichor falling from the blade that lit up once more like white fire.

As Diana fell free of the large body, vines snapped up, tangling around Cacus. The creature roared and vines snapped, but it was futile. The plants obeyed Selvans' holy power. Around his body a ripple pulsed, dark and consuming, a light shining around its edges. He snapped another tangle of vines, remembering the brittle remains of Alseida when he'd found her in the corridor of the palace, lifelessly wrapped in vines. Cacus's fate wasn't going to be any kinder than it had been for his blooded mate.

Cacus bellowed and wrenched his body. The roots broke off in his legs, blood gushing, and the vines pulled free of the ground. The vampires leaped off him as a burst of fire ripped from his throat. Cacus slapped his tail, the lethal end flaying a vampire as he attempted to get clear while the monster's massive jaws opened wide, his long tongue snaking out to wrap around another vampire before the male could get away. With a single jerk of the tongue, Cacus's prey was pulled into his mouth with a loud snap and wet crunch of masticated flesh.

Selvans clenched his jaw, his fury coiling through him.

The vampires stumbled, their eyes staring in horror as Cacus devoured those who fell nearest to him. Jacques, his arm held against his body at an odd angle, turned a weak smile on Selvans.

"There is another wave coming, and they are bringing an ally with them. We weren't prepared for this battle, but we didn't want to be defenseless, either."

"An ally?" Diana asked, breathless as she hauled up to Selvans' side. Her blood-streaked sword was held away from her body, clenched tightly in her fist. Her tail drooped in a clear sign of exhaustion already setting in after wresting her sword free from the brute.

Jacques nodded and then grinned, his head turning in the

direction of a side street from which Selvans noticed the clop of numerous boots hitting the road. "It looks like they have arrived."

Selvans craned his head and his eyes widened as he saw the number of armed vampires storming down the street. Their fangs were bared, their weapons drawn, but that was not what drew his attention. There was one distinctive male who topped them all in height, his green skin rolling with muscles, a long tail lashing behind him as a dark braid swayed along his back. A large, rough-hewn ax that appeared to have forged from scrap metal sat over his shoulder as he puffed a thick smoking tube clenched between his teeth.

Raskyuil's eyes fell upon them and his expression tightened, but he smiled around his smoking tube when his gaze fell on Diana. His head dropped in a respectful nod to her as he hefted his ax. Turning in place, he bellowed out to the vampires surrounding him. The small horde suddenly surged forward as Cacus snapped his teeth, crushed foes in his large hands, shredding them with his massive claws. His tail whipped around him, but the vampires had caught on to that and avoided it as much as they did his mouth. Raskyuil let out a roar as he leaped forward, swinging his ax in a mighty blow.

Selvans drew on the plants once again, sending them to wind around the monster once more. They kept getting torn up, and Selvans continued to add new layers to frustrate the male and distract him while their allies attacked.

"We need to do something…!" Diana hissed.

Drawing his sword once more from its sheath, he met his mate's eyes and nodded his head. There was no need for words. They did not know exactly how this was supposed to work, and even Dorinda hadn't been helpful about how their joint power would be utilized, but Selvans knew that if Nocis struck deep enough, it would destroy the source of Cacus's lifeforce.

His lips twisted cruelly as he eyed the male. Deep within, he reveled in the way that Nocis pulsed with dark power. Pulling away from Diana's side, his power continued to rise as he connected to the power of Nocis. He was distantly aware of Diana shouting after him, but he was consumed in what needed to be done. Raskyuil roared, his ax striking home against the Tainted One's huge legs, already damaged by the torn roots. Out of the corner of his eye, he saw Diana run by him, her bright sword flashing in her hand as she slashed at Cacus.

Selvans smirked. His mate had the right idea.

He had tried to do things the clean way, to use plants to choke out the male around his vulnerable upper throat where the bands of Hercules's arms could still be seen imprinted, damaging the muscle and tissue. Diana growled as she sank her blade in repeatedly, the dark blood splashing on her as if he were watching a primal war goddess. Her glowing eyes, now greenish, turned toward him and she nodded. Selvans breathed, drawing in the warmth of her scent.

As he got closer, he watched as vampires sank claws and fangs into Cacus, ripping out chunks of flesh, but none of them got deep enough to wound him. His thick, armored flesh protected him. Cacus reared up, his arms spreading wide, and Selvans stilled. There, just below the creature's sternum, was a mark—a vulnerable point. It pulsed like a heart beating.

Selvans spun out of the way as a hoof came crashing toward him, his sword drawing up in an arc to slash at the joint at the back of the knee. Cacus bellowed, but didn't go down. He hadn't expected him to.

A clawed hand struck out, but this time Selvans didn't move quite fast enough. Cacus lifted him off the ground and brought him up high, dangling him in front of his face.

"You won't win against me, little god," Cacus snarled as he gave him a shake. "I am just as eternal as you. I am a child of the mighty Earth, powerful beyond your imagining." His gaze slid to

Diana, who fell back, her white blade held in front of her defensively. “Your mate. I scented her upon you. So sweet and delicious. I think after I eat you, I shall consume her bit by bit. I shall relish hearing her scream.”

Fury vibrated through Selvans. He dragged his sword down over the hand of Cacus, severing several fingers, freeing himself. Blood sprayed, and the vampires roared in excitement.

“Don’t drink the blood!” Selvans shouted. “It is tainted. It will be your destruction if you consume it.”

The vampires wisely drew away from it, though there were a few who still cast the dark fountain longing glances. Instead, they marshaled for a renewed attack behind Raskyuil’s arm. As the attack converged again, Selvans harnessed the full power of Nocis. He felt the darkness ripple through, doubling back and growing strong. Death roared through his veins as he raced forward, darting effortlessly between swinging hooves and reaching claws. With one swing of Nocis, he severed the black tongue that snapped out and attempted to wrap around him.

His smile widened as he drew up to the breast. Out of the corner of his eye, he saw Diana turn, her eyes widening with the fear pulsing through the bond. He could barely feel as the darkness rolled powerfully through him. She didn’t have to worry. He would keep her safe.

“Silvas!” her voice shrieked out, barely surfacing over the roar in his ears.

Drawing back his arm, he thrust his arm forward as he felt the power uncoil, spreading down the sword in a thick wave as the tip of the blade pierced the vulnerable flesh. The darkness surged within him, consuming him as he angled his sword, seeking the massive heart beating within the protective cage of the ribs.

Cacus shouted out in pain, his entire body collapsing forward. Selvans’ smile slipped, his mouth gaping open as he felt the destructive force swamp through him, drawing out his energy, repurposing it into death. His entire being was being consumed by Nocis, the forest lord slipping away. Greenery wilted and blackened, falling from where it was climbing nearby buildings. Even trees dropped and withered into husks. He saw it, but was powerless to stop.

He now understood the danger. Cacus stumbled violently, taking Selvans back several steps with him as he twisted in pain, but unvanquished. Agony rushed through Selvans, a light flickering within him. He desperately clawed through his mind toward it. He needed it. The entire world around was nothing but darkness, and at the center of him was Nocis flaring with its dark light. He felt the hard impact of a body colliding with his. He couldn't see who it was, but a familiar scent wafted up to him. His uxorem! She ducked beneath his arms, sandwiched herself there between him and Cacus, the hilt of the sword in his grasp imprinted on her hip.

"Together, you idiot," she whispered in his ear. Her lips captured his, her light flaring through his darkness as their bond brightened within him. Her mouth fell away, and he almost cried in despair, but that brightness didn't go away. In the shadows of his mind, he saw her turn in his arms, her sword glowing brightly. Anola thrust deep, running through the gaping wound beside Nocis. The two lights fused, sending a burst of energy pulsating in harmonizing waves. Cacus bellowed, fractures of light rippling over his body.

Just behind Cacus, in the glow, he swore he saw a woman step forward, her eyes narrowed at the creature in fury. She pulled her shawl tighter around herself and lifted her hand. The fingertip touched and a spark shot through, shattering Cacus from within. Selvans stilled in awareness as he stared at the human spirit. Slowly she turned and met his gaze, a smile curving her mouth as one eye closed in a wink. Her lips moved as she spoke silently, the air moaning loudly around them, as another spark shot through Cacus. Selvans' mouth moved as he whispered his thanks. At the same moment, Raskyuil bellowed as he charged forward, swinging his axe.

Unlike other attempts, this time the axe struck true, embedding deep, ichor flooding out in huge gushes. The vampires hissed and set upon Cacus, tearing him apart with their weapons. Selvans knew he was roaring and could hear his mate's scream from the strength of their harmonized power. It surged through the joined blades, and beneath the blows, Cacus's flesh sluiced from him, exposing muscle and sinew that likewise fell away until all that was left were skeletal remains, still rattling with eons of condensed power. Another swing of Raskyuil's ax, and the creature blew apart into dust.

Weakened, Selvans wrapped his arms and tail around his mate before he sank with her to the ground, curling around her to protect her from their fall. Her breath fanned his skin, and love vibrated through their bond as her tail wrapped around his in turn. Selvans smiled before he slipped away with his uxorem secure in his arms.

They had triumphed; now they could rest. He was certain that he heard Raskyuil say as much before the comforting darkness swept over him.

CHAPTER 49

Diana brushed her pale hair behind her shoulder as she kneeled at the small headstones of her family. Carefully, she plucked away the weeds that had overgrown in front of the stones before placing a fresh bouquet of flowers at each one. The early morning light was still weak, but it assured their privacy since no one else would be out to catch sight of them. Her tail swiped against the newly exposed spring grass pushing up from the damp earth. Silvas stood behind her, his head tipped respectfully. Raskyuil, who had decided to accompany them back from New Orleans during the late hour, stood off to the side.

Swallowing, she smiled down at the headstones.

"Hi Momma, Daddy, Papa, and Nana. I haven't been here for a long while, and I'm sorry. I swore that I would take care of you, that you wouldn't be forgotten. I don't know who's going to keep the weeds from taking over your resting place, or leave flowers, but I guess things can't always stay the same. It's time for me move on. Nana, you always said that you expected me to leave and do bigger and better things with my life. I lost a lot of hope after you died and then the ravaging came. But you were right."

She glanced back and smiled at her mate. "I met a wonderful person who I love very much. I'm going to be going with him, so I won't be around much anymore, but I'll be keeping you in my heart and taking you along with me even if I can't be right here watching over your rest. I love you all so much, and hope to make you proud someday. I have a lot of time to work on it, after all," she said with a dry chuckle.

Standing up, she brushed off her knees and stepped back to Silvas's side. He pressed a kiss against the side of her head.

"Are you sure, my love?" he whispered. "We can stay a little longer. Dorinda did say that the forest would sleep for a while if we couldn't return immediately. If we want to spend a little time here, we can."

Diana leaned into his touch and shook her head, a smile on her lips. "No. I think I'm ready. I've been living here for a long time, never really happy and just going through the motions. It's well past time for me to realize that this isn't home for me anymore. You're my home, and we need to be with Arx and in our forest. It needs us. I realize all the connections I made with the forest and those living in it have become my family too. Time to go home to them."

"You are wise, uxorem."

"You're a good ati, just as I said you would be," Raskyuil interrupted as he lumbered forward.

He placed an unlit cigar between his teeth, his long green tail tucking around him. Diana looked pointedly at it and his smile widened around it.

"Since when did you start smoking cigars?" she teased.

"A couple months ago on the road, I was offered one in trade and discovered that I like them," he said with a chuckle. "Proves that the human world does have some decent things worth keeping."

Diana laughed. "Well, if a cigar does it for you, then whatever it takes." Her smile died as she considered him seriously. "Are you sure you won't come home with us?"

Raskyuil glanced at Silvas for a length of time before shaking his head. "Nah. My time is done in the Eternal Forest. I think I'm going to keep exploring this world, maybe starting a family or a clan of my own like they did in the ancient days."

Stepping forward, Diana wrapped her arms around him. "I hate that we are just brought back together and I'm not going to see you again. I owe you so much. I don't even know how it is that you managed to show up in New Orleans when we did."

"I was there for a few months, just after it went to ground. I knew you were looking for Cacus but I wasn't sure what it was. With my previous experience I stuck around and tried to help the vampires shore up defenses and get into a training drill. I figured Selvans here would show up sooner or later. You surprised me, though. I never expected to see you showing up for war when you had your slice of peace and quiet."

"I guess I am a little harder to get rid of, and quiet just doesn't seem to work out for me. Probably a good thing too, considering all the craziness that everything seems to get up to in the Eternal Forest."

His grin widened as he lit his cigar and nodded thoughtfully. "I'm glad to hear that you are going back. Maybe someday our paths will cross again." His eyes slid back over to Silvas and he inclined his head with respect. "Take care of your mate—and don't lose her again."

"Never," Silvas swore, his arm looping around her protectively.

Raskyuil nodded, lit his cigar, puffed on it a few times, and ambled away, leaving Diana alone with Silvas in front of the headstones. Diana stared after him, her lips drawn into a thin line.

"Do you think he'll be okay?"

Silvas didn't answer immediately, but his breath brushed over her in a sigh. "I think he will be eventually. He has a lot of anger to work through, much of it my fault, though he has struggled with his own demons for a long time. The Eternal Forest has been a hard place for many generations, and it has been especially unkind to the recent generations among the mortals who never knew the beauty of it before. I hope he finds the happiness and peace he needs here." He placed a kiss on her head. "I found it, after all. I have to have hope that those who mean the most to me will as well."

Diana nodded and leaned into him as they walked away. They followed the edge of the forest. She recognized every step of this path. She had walked this path for years that led between the cemetery and her cabin. Tipping her head back, her eyes trailed over the trees studded with tiny green leaves. As she expected, over half of the trees were dead. She knew that the only way of restoring the forest was to bring the Eternal Forest back to life.

"Do you think there's a chance of the forest getting better again?" she asked. "Cacus did so much damage. And that was with your forest already in decline. What if there's no way to bring it back to life?"

He pressed a kiss to the back of her hand. "I wouldn't worry about that. We will definitely be able to restore the forest."

"How?" she asked, her brow drawing down in confusion.

"Like this," he whispered.

Drawing her into a small cluster of trees, he spread his cloak over the ground and slowly, reverently took her off her clothes. His hands stroked and explored, sliding beneath the base of her tail and making her shiver. Her new form had erogenous zones that she had never imagined—around her tail and along her ears. Silvas zeroed in on them and used them against her until she was squirming beneath him.

"What does this have to do with the forest?" she gasped, as

another shiver raced through her while he ran his textured tongue against her ear.

"You will see," he murmured.

Stretching her out on the cloak, he covered her, his mouth and hands caressing her until she was so primed that he slipped into her with ease. Their bodies twisted together, tails slipping and knotting together as they met with eager thrusts. When he flipped her onto her hands and knees, she moaned at the loss of his cock. He didn't leave her wanting for long. He pulled her tail to the side and wrapped it around his arm, encouraging her to grip his forearm tightly as he thrust, his pace gradually increasing until they were outright rutting.

Diana's claws dug into the cloak, tearing holes into it as his claws clung to her sides, his hips slapping against hers until they surged to completion. Her scream of pleasure rose in accompaniment with his loud roar. The trees above them rattled like applause as they sank to the ground together in a sweaty heap.

Rolling over, she laughed and cuddled into Silvas's arms. "That was wonderful, as usual. I am still not sure what that has to do with trees, though."

"Don't you?" he grinned mysteriously and tipped his head to the sky. "Look up."

Diana turned her head to stare at the trees above them. Tears pricked at her eyes as she looked up at them. Trees that had been black and withered moments before leaned down toward them, flush with life, tiny green buds along the branches.

"We bring life," he whispered. "That is the balance that you bring to me, uxorem. Together, we sustain the forest."

At a loss for anything to say worthy of the moment, she clung to her mate, burrowing into his arms. They lay there for a time until his head tilted down, his lips trailing against her cheek. "Are you ready to go home?"

A smile pulled at her lips, and she blinked back tears of happiness. *Home.* "Yes. Home sounds perfect right about now."

EPILOGUE

Turan stepped through the small courtyard of the palace, a smile on her face as she watched her beloved son sit on a cushioned couch with his mate. Arx had fully recovered after the first two years, its form reshaping to leave the hidden courtyard where they currently sat open. It was their sanctuary, their escape when they needed a quiet moment away.

Turan chuckled. Selvans and his uxorem were much beloved in their forest. It was no wonder that they needed to escape to their private place so often. Within the first five years, their love went far to restore the health and vitality of the Eternal Forest. For that alone, they were honored. Her son did not take it personally that his mate received the greatest share of honor. All adored their ati, the queen and mother of their woods. They sought her blessings in all things, and when she brought forth a new being, a silvanae, the first daughter born in thousands of years among a species dominated by males, the entire forest celebrated.

She lingered at the edge of the garden, watching as the small silvanae, Aeliana, crouched to track a butterfly that fluttered from flower to flower. She chased it over to the fountain, the water catching the sunlight that the trees allowed in with their parted limbs. A serpentine tail coiled in the basin as Dorinda, her dearest daughter, reclined in the water, her eyes trailing after the little one.

Turan's heart warmed at the familial vision. They were so happy together, even with the merciless way Dorinda and Selvans regularly teased one another. The lucomo was currently ignoring the way his sister splashed water in his direction as he dragged his nose against his mate's cheek, his body close to hers. He never seemed to stop touching his uxorem, which was exactly how it should be, in her opinion. She silently congratulated herself.

True, she had a few small foul-ups—and really, it should have happened centuries ago—but she had been around in the cosmos long enough to know that everything always happened for a reason when it did. Even her choice to get involved when she did was part of the Fates' great weave. Not even the gods saw all of their plan, nor could they truly control it. Selvans and his Diana were yet another pair whose lives were woven together as a force within the coming changes.

Although chaos tipped the scales throughout the world, it still made her happy to know that she had a helping hand in the work of fate. She had assisted with Charu and his bride, and now Selvans had his own mate. Idly, she entertained herself imagining what gods might fall next. Her smile widened mischievously. Even the gods were powerless against the influence of the goddess of love.

Aeliana stood, her small tail rising in the air behind her with curiosity as her soft ears tipped toward the forest. Raising her hand, she squealed with laughter.

"Mommy, Daddy, look!"

Diana chuckled and pushed her mate's greedy hands away as she stood. Walking over to her daughter, she crouched low. "What do you see, sweetie?"

"Over there, in the trees… Look!"

Diana squinted into the trees, but then her eyes widened with a gasp.

"Dorinda, Silvas… Look! I can't believe it. It is a family of monokerata. A stallion, a mare, and two foals!"

Selvans stepped behind his mate, his hands slipping around her to hold her close as they watched the monokeratas, the unicorns, step among the trees. Turan touched her chest, her own heart brimming with awe at the sight. They had not only restored the forest but had begun to restore the monokerata once again.

Dorinda blinked back her tears. "Our world thrives and is once again full of spirits. The Eternal Forest lives"

In the human world…

Raskyuil clenched his cigar in his teeth as he squinted across the landscape. In the distance, there appeared to be a piecemeal settlement. He would stop in for a few hours. He needed to refuel his motorcycle and pick up some more supplies. In recent years, more and more settlements welcomed a mixture of beings. He appreciated not standing out so much in a homogenous crowd, but he was often bigger than most males and intimidated the larger share of females. He shrugged and lit his cigar.

He had plenty to barter for trade credits. Enough for supplies, and perhaps a bit of company if he could find someone sturdy who could take a rough ride. Fragile females were definitely off the table. A grin split his face as he kicked back his kickstand once more, turning toward the ramshackle town.

The local residents had best prepare themselves. He was no typical male… He was a dangerous monster.

** Spinoff series *Dangerous Monsters* will be coming February 2021, starting with Raskyuil's story. **

Aelves: an older spelling of the word "elves."

Ati: an Etruscan word that means "mother" but was applied to refer to queens. Notably used as a title of the goddesses Uni and Turan.

Aquilo: Roman name for the Greek Boreas, the god of the north wind. He dwells on the Hyperborean Mountains, the northernmost on Earth in Greco-Roman myth, beyond which existed the garden of Apollon, Hyperborea.

Cacus: also called Cacu among the Etruscans. In Roman myth, he was a monstrous being who was said to breathe fire and ate human flesh, who was defeated by cattle. By the time of *Dante's Inferno*, he was depicted as a centaur with serpents on his back and a fire-breathing dragon on his shoulder who guarded thieves. There is a classical sculpture with Cacus in the form of a centaur that I took as most direct inspiration for this book.

Crocotta: a mythic beast that was described by Roman explorers who entered Asia. Said to have been inspired by hyenas.

Domus: Roman term applying to a small, single-family home.

Dryads: spirits of the woods.

Eru: the Etruscan name for Eros, or Cupid.

Faun: a goat-legged and horned spirit of the woods and fields.

Freyr: the god who rules the realm of the elves in Nordic and Germanic lore.

Furiae: Roman name for the Erinyes, or Furies. Spirits of punishment for those who violate oaths or create crimes against nature (i.e., slaying of blood kin and spouses).

Goblins: small fey creatures that inhabit wild places who tend to be mischievous that show up in various parts of European lore.

Hamadryad: the spirit or soul of a tree.

Ichor: a fluid that flows like blood, usually a word ascribed to the "blood" of immortal beings and gods.

Lucomo: a Romanized word from the Etruscan word for king, *luchume*.

Monokerata: or *hippos monokereta,* as it was called, is the Roman origin of the medieval unicorn. Described as large horses or giant asses, they were another mythical fauna that was said to occupy India. They were entirely white except for the head, and had a tricolor horn of white, black at the center, and a red tip. Their horns when made into cups that gave prevention against health issues such as epilepsy, convulsions, and even poison.

Nymph: a collective term for a spirit (all female in myth) associated with natural bodies of fresh and salt water, trees, and mountains. They are typically benevolent but can be jealous and selfish, not above using trickery. They are often highly sexual spirits who were known for seducing herders and travelers, and lovers of gods. I built on this to give them a lust for the sexual energy they inspire but largely harmless in their nature.

Naiad: a nymph of freshwater. They are protectors of fresh water supplies, guardians of the young, and protectors providing clean water.

Oreads: Roman form of the Greek Oreads. Nymphs of the mountain. Oreads made a significant part of the hunting party of goddess Artemis.

Pegaeae: a type of naiad that is associated with natural springs. They are typically associated with restoring people to health and sometimes with prophetic powers. For the purposes of this book, I have extended it to purification, but this is not uncommon in the ancient world as several sacred springs were associated with purification, notably at Delphi.

Silvanus: the god of the woods. Silvani in plural.

Turan: Etruscan goddess of love, beauty, and passage of souls to the next world. Comparable generally to Aphrodite and Venus.

Twergs: a more ancient spelling for dwarves.

Usil: (Sol roman) Etruscan name for the god of the sun.

Uxorem: An Etruscan word that means "wife," it is used here interchangeably with mate.

Vinculum marcam: literally Latin for "bond mark." It is the fragment of the soul through bonding to one's mate that can be visibly seen on the flesh like a small upraised stone.

Wyrm: a draconic creature that resembles a giant serpent, sometimes depicted with wings.

ABOUT THE AUTHOR

S.J. Sanders is a writer of Science Fiction and Fantasy Romance. With a love of all things alien and monster she is fascinated with concepts of far off worlds, as well as the lore and legends of various cultures. When not writing, she loves reading, sculpting, painting and travel (especially to exotic destinations). Although born and raised in Alaska, she currently as a resident of Florida with her family, her maine coon, Bella, and pet bearded dragon, Lex.

Readers can follow her on Facebook:
https://www.facebook.com/authorsjsanders

Or join her Facebook group S.J. Sanders Unusual Playhouse:
https://www.facebook.com/groups/361374411254067/

Newsletter:
https://mailchi.mp/7144ec4ca0e4/sjsandersromance

Website:
https://sjsandersromance.wordpress.com/

Other Works by S.J. Sanders

<u>The Mate Index</u>

First Contact

The VaDorok

Hearts of Indesh (Valentine Novella)

The Edoka's Destiny

The Vori's Mate

Eliza's Miracle (Novella)

A Kiss on Kaidava

The Vori's Secret

A Mate for Oigr (Halloween Novella)

Heart of the Agraak

A Gift for Medif

The Arobi's Queen

<u>Monsterly Yours</u>

The Orc Wife

The Troll Bride

The Accidental Werewolf's Mate

<u>Sci-Fi Fairytales</u>

Red: A Dystopian World Alien Romance

<u>Ragoru Beginnings Romance</u>

White: Emala's Story

Huntress

<u>Dark Spirits</u>

Havoc of Souls

The Mirror (also part of Mischief Matchmakers)

Forest of Spirits

<u>Shadowed Dreams Erotica</u>

The Lantern

Serpent of the Abyss

<u>Argurma Salvager</u>

Broken Earth

Made in the USA
Monee, IL
28 November 2023

47533498R00225